As a Lovely Song

Donevy Westphal

Cover by Diane Turpin—. DianeTurpinDesigns.com

As a Lovely Song

Published by Westerness Enterprises LTD Box 52 Casey, Iowa 50048

As a Lovely Song / Donevy L. Westphal

ISBN 978-1-7349256-1-6

ISBN 978-1-7349256-3-0 (eBook)

Printed in the United States of America

BOOKS BY DONEVY WESTPHAL

EBENEZER: MY STONE OF HELP SERIES

If I Should Die
As A Lovely Song
All of My Tomorrows*

EBENEZER PREQUEL

Songs in the Night†

OTHER BOOKS

Gene's Story†

*COMING SPRING 2022
†Coming Soon

Then Samuel took a stone, and set it between Mizpeh and Shen, and called the name of it Ebenezer, saying, Hitherto hath the LORD helped us. (1 Samuel 7:12 KJV)

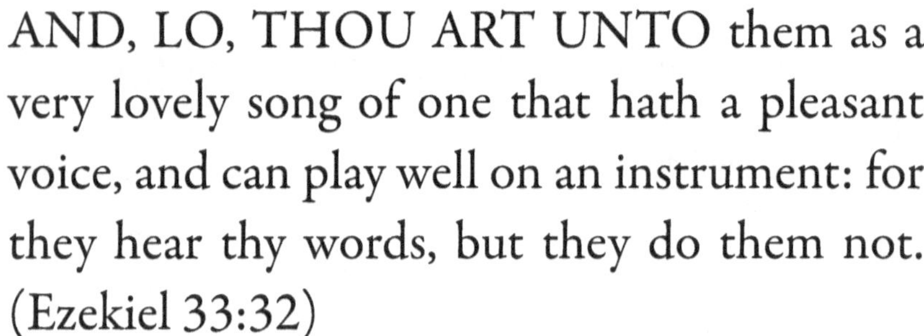

AND, LO, THOU ART UNTO them as a very lovely song of one that hath a pleasant voice, and can play well on an instrument: for they hear thy words, but they do them not. (Ezekiel 33:32)

Dedication

Dedication is what a writer needs to go beyond the first words on a page. Many elements go into building that dedication. At this point in the manuscript, the hard work of the task is done. Because of the tireless encouragement of the chosen few who have not flagged in their reinforcement for the project we have accomplished this goal. From long-time personal friends, family members, and newly added recent friends and readers this book is dedicated to that inspiration to continue to finish this step in our journey. Thank you, all of you, may you all read and enjoy this installment in the series.

Acknowledgments

Many belong here on the acknowledgment page. Those who have poked, prodded and commiserated with me as I struggled with writing, not just the first book, but the next books in this series—Those who have read the first book and encouraged me to not give up on the second novel. And there are those much closer to home: my son Benjamin, who was my first listener as I read the first draft out loud; My son, Levi, with his encouragement and his technical work without which this could not have happened; Kudos to my husband, Chris, who suffered silently through untold editors and their crazy edits and my mutterings about such editors and edits. I learned much through ACFW and their courses, and Jennifer and Jane my critique partners. And foremost I praise God who prepared me through life and much more through His wisdom to write this story. May this story be a blessing to all who read it.

~Prologue~

Police Chief Dave Mallory turned, sprinting toward the sound of gunshots. He slowed as he drew near the corner of the airport terminal and stopped to peer around the side of the building. A scan of the scenery from which the sounds had come revealed two bodies lying on the concrete, but no continued threat appeared. He whipped around the corner, dodging behind pillars as he approached the scene with caution. In the distance, he heard the shrill wail from the backup and ambulance he had radioed for.

Oh, God, no! Don't let it end this way! The pain ripped through his chest as he looked down at the body on the pavement. He bent down and felt for a heartbeat. *"Our Father which art in heaven, hallowed be thy name..."* There was still a pulse but his fellow law enforcement agent, Julius Armstrong, was losing consciousness. Dave knew the sickening smell of blood from his time as a medic on the battlefield. Julius needed help now.

He stood as the ambulance screeched to a halt. "Get that gurney over here! Now! Hurry! He's losing blood fast." *"Yea, though I walk through the valley of the shadow of death, I will fear no evil: for thou art with me; thy rod and thy staff they comfort me."*

"What happened?" the paramedic raced toward him with the stretcher.

"Don't know. Heard gunshots, came around here..."

"What about the other guy?"

Mallory turned to his backup. "How's he doin'?"

"This guy's gone. No pulse."

"Offer unto God thanksgiving; and pay thy vows unto the most High: And call upon me in the day of trouble: I will deliver thee, and thou shalt glorify me. But unto the wicked God saith..."

"Hello, Jack? Dave here. There's been a shooting. Can you round up Julius' people...Yeah, it's serious."

"...thou hast been my help; leave me not, neither forsake me, O God of my salvation. When my father and my mother forsake me, then the LORD will take me up."

CHAPTER—1—

"This has been a day and a half. It began so quiet and slow." Seth MacDonald and his father Lewis waited in the shadows between the hospital emergency room doors guarding Seth's brother, Joshua, undercover name Julius Armstrong, who occupied the wheelchair. As the inner ER door slid open, Seth looked over at his neighbor Jack O'Brien.

"Nurse Peterson sent his release papers from the desk." Jack stopped beside the three men and handed the papers to Lewis Senior. He studied the parking lot through narrowed eyes. "Any activity out there? Is it a go?" He pulled his farmer cap down low on his forehead.

"Sergeant Mallory has the Laundry Service van waiting for us." Seth twitched his head toward the van closest to the door.

"The man that shot Joshua wasn't playin' games. Maybe he's a lone wolf—The parking lot looks clear," Jack said in a low voice after he looked it over one more time.

His eyes constantly monitored any activity in the area. Pushing the ER door open he walked to the van and hopped into the driver's seat. Pulling the van around, blocking the passenger side from view, he parked in front of the door.

"Let's get this guy home," Seth said as he wheeled Joshua up to the van, and his father slid the big van door open. "Careful."

Seth and his father lifted Joshua, wheelchair and all, up to Jack, who waited in the van. Jack reclined the chair's back to a comfortable position and locked the wheels.

"We'll see ya at home, son." Mr. MacDonald tucked a blanket around Joshua then stepped back and slid the door shut.

Seth climbed into the passenger's seat. "Later." He waved at his father.

Jack idled the van from the ER parking lot into the street. "Well, partner," he said over his shoulder to Joshua. "You got your release. I never saw anyone so determined in my life." He shook his head. "The rest of your family will have to find their own way home."

Joshua turned with a groan and Jack glanced in the rearview mirror. "I suppose the adrenaline has run its course." Jack looked in the side mirrors as he maneuvered through the backstreets, then he glanced at Joshua again. "You had us goin' for a while. I never saw Nurse Peterson so excited in her life."

"It's good for folks to get excited once in a while." Joshua sighed then gritted his teeth.

"Stop moving. Don't open those wounds up—You've worn yourself out," Jack said soberly.

"Not completely, but just about. I can't abide hospitals. People telling me what to do, where to go, and hospitals smell like...hospitals." Joshua made a sour face.

There was quiet as the patient settled down and the medication helped him relax.

"Is he asleep?" Jack looked at Seth.

"He's resting at least," Seth said. "Joshua has a history with hospitals. He had a football injury back in the day—almost wiped out half the clinic before we could get him out. Part of the problem is the stuff they use in the operation. It brings out the Samson in him... What a way to end a career. Do you think there are more assassins out there, or will this be the end?"

"That's above my pay grade. So far I'm taking precautions until I know. Other than that, I'm sure the government people Joshua works for will take care of it." Jack pulled onto the highway heading to Beetle River.

"How did you get sucked into this?" Seth said.

"Our neighbor, Ralph Meecham, had ties to the big crime boss in Chicago. Evidence showed the increase in crime in Hermon merged with Joshua's case." Jack shrugged. "But Ralph and Dad—back in the day they both wanted the same girl, and Ralph never forgot nor forgave. They had problems for years. Diana and I had been married before I got out of the service, and of course, I brought Diana home with me."

"How'd that work?" Seth said.

"Not well. O'Brien and anyone friendly with us had a special place in Ralph's heart. Ralph and the Meechams took after Diana and me like fresh bait. Ralph and his crime syndicate were a separate problem and continued growing into a large problem until it affected the whole community. Sergeant Mallory and the Hermon PD were called in."

"That how you knew Sergeant Mallory?"

"I've known Dave—a long time. We were in the same class and on the football team together," Jack said.

"Friends then?"

"Yeah. High school together, both enlisted right after we graduated, came back about the same time as well," Jack said.

"I'm sorry about Diana. They should get that wrapped up soon as well, right?" Seth asked.

"Yes, and I'm glad for it. We all had that Meecham kid pegged wrong. I don't feel better finding out how she died, but to blame the wrong guy all these years." Jack pursed his lips. "Maybe I owe Philip Meecham an apology."

"I don't know that I could ever go that far as much devilment as he did." Seth scowled.

"Diana and I spent too long in our foolish pride. I lived with Dad after Diana and I had our argument as long as I did with Diana during our marriage. Dad advised several times that I should man up and apologize, but the words 'I'm sorry' and 'I was a fool' wouldn't come out of my mouth." Jack grimaced. "When young Meecham began stalking Ruth, Dad lit into me. I've never seen him so angry. I'd never heard my Dad use that kind of language before, and it shocked me... It made 'I'm sorry' and 'I was a fool' sound like a compliment." Jack drew a breath and exhaled. "I did go to Diana and say 'I'm sorry' and 'I was a fool.' I've learned we shouldn't take life for granted. All of the Meecham gang seemed rotten, but I was wrong to blame an innocent man all these years for Diana's death. I believe I could at least say I was wrong to Philip Meecham."

"Life has those moments. When Michael had his accident a couple of weeks ago Jo and I saw a side of Phil Meecham that shocked us both. For you to say that to him might mean more to him than any of us know." Seth thought quietly about Jack's words and about the little he knew of young Phil Meecham.

"Here we are," Jack said as he turned and drove up to Juan and Laura's house. "The last leg of our journey." He parked across the breezeway entrance.

Seth jumped out and opened the van door. "Jo, we're home." He gently touched Joshua's arm.

"If you will just help me into the living room..." Joshua began to stir.

"Jo, just calm down. Let us get you out, bro..." Seth looked up as Lewis Jr., his oldest brother, joined him. "We've had a time with Samson, here," Seth whispered.

"Before you begin to fight us," Lewis grasped the chair bottom, "I'm your older brother, and I'm telling you, relax, we've got it covered."

"Man, it's a good thing that fellow wasn't a better shot." Jack helped ease the chair to the pavement. "About an inch one way or the other, and this guy would've been beside the other guy in the morgue. Easy now."

"I don't know which of my nine lives I'm on. I think it's number eleven." Joshua groaned as he was escorted through his sister's large, spacious house into the living room.

"I've got your meds," Jack said. He pulled a bottle from his pocket. "You might as well take your next dose now—while you're sitting up. Then we'll slide you onto the couch."

"This couch is one of the most comfortable surfaces short of your bed," Lewis said. "I thought of pulling the hide-a-bed out but this smaller area should be easier to navigate. Here's some water." He handed Joshua a glass of water and arranged a couple of hospital Chux in place as Joshua swallowed his pain meds.

"Good to have plenty Chux in place in case these wounds start bleeding again." Joshua rested a moment, exhausted. "I don't want Laura's couch bloodstained when she gets home next week."

"Is that how long your folks are house-sitting?" Jack asked.

"Yes," Seth said. "Laura and her family get back at the end of next week and we have a surprise for them. They don't know Joshua and I are back."

"Well, let's get this done." Seth raised the wheelchair footrests and took Joshua's legs while Lewis supported Joshua's torso. Like clockwork, Jack took the wheelchair and the two brothers slid the patient onto the couch.

"I wasn't sure we were going to get you out of that hospital." Jack rearranged the pillows to make Joshua more comfortable.

"When that doctor saw the mess you, Dad, and Nurse Peterson made..." Joshua snorted. "I've never seen anyone look so funny!"

"The mess we made?" Jack's voice held a note of disbelief. "You knocked over the tray and sent the bed flying. It's a good thing you were indisposed," Jack said, "I thought the part when the doctor said, 'Nurse Peterson, Mr. Juarez is ready to be released. Are the papers ready?' and his eyes crossed and his ears wiggled was..."

"Nurse Peterson was calling you Dr. Johnson and him Mr. O'Brien by the time we left," Joshua said.

"Getting Lois—Nurse Peterson—flustered was one of our pranks in school." Jack laughed.

"Michael and I offered our help in the recovery room, but it was refused." Seth shook his head sadly.

"I'm sure they needed your help. That would have been a real circus, buddy." Lewis frowned. "Why did the doctor call Joshua Mr. Juarez?"

"Couldn't use his undercover name, Julius, or his real name, Joshua, for security reasons. I'll miss Julius Caesar Armstrong, but from here on out he doesn't exist," Jack said.

"I kept my cover until that assassin took potshots. Did you know before, or—" Joshua said.

"Mallory couldn't let on, and your cover as a journalist worked well. Thank God you came. We were at our wit's end."

"Television glamorizes undercover work, but it's a lot of grunt work and danger. This was Julius C. Armstrong's last case and it's a change I'm glad to make."

"You've earned a rest, Caesar. I left your water here on the coffee table, and here's the rest of the medication." Jack handed the bottle to Lewis. "And do not—I repeat—do not let it lapse, fella." He stopped to write the time down on a notepad. "I'm going to get that van back where it belongs."

"Later," Joshua mumbled, drifting into sleep as Jack left the room.

Seth and Lewis followed Jack out to the porch. "Thanks for your help." Seth dropped into the lounge chair. "These last few weeks have been real twists."

"This had to be the craziest three weeks of my life as well." Jack ran a shaky hand through his dark auburn hair. "I've been fighting this battle so long I can't believe it's over. I lost my mother and my wife, but I still have Ruth and Reuben. Keep an eye on your brother there. He's lost a lot of blood and isn't out of danger yet."

JOSHUA SLEPT, AND DREAMS like slivers of fog wafted through his world. Unintelligible voices floated around him, and camels walked in the desert led by people wrapped in robes with dark brown faces in a marketplace, in an ocean mingled with the fog. There was a whispering in the soft, warm breeze blowing around him.

A desert wind? His eyes were closed and he listened, straining to hear any sound. The whispering came again, but as he became more awake, quiet reigned.

Where am I? Who am I? He moved slightly, and a searing pain pierced his body. *Don't panic.* With caution, he opened one eye to a slit. *This isn't the desert or the jungle. There has to be a reasonable explanation. At least I'm in a room...Is it early morning or early evening?* He relaxed his mind and body. Nothing would focus; nothing made sense. A movement? Both eyes flew open.

"Mai, is that you, baby?" he whispered. *Mai? Why would Mai be here?* He closed his eyes again. Memory, like circulation coming back into an appendage that has fallen asleep, returned in gradual stages. From Mr. O'Brien, the car ride, the hospital, the airport, the agent with the tawny eyes, and the shooting. *How stupid of me. Careless, just plain sloppy. Unless I've passed on into...Is this a place of torment?*

He lay with his eyes closed listening. The whispering came again, but again it ceased and there was nothing but quiet. His mind drifted back into a haze. *Mom was going to be unhappy. Someone had not closed the door, and there were flies in the house,* he thought as something tickled his face. He attempted to brush it away.

As he raised his right hand again to brush the fly away, Joshua's eyes opened. "Junko? How?"

Junko ran her finger over his cheek; she was his fly.

"When and how did you get here?" he asked. Slivers of fog still wafted in his mind.

Ruth knelt beside Junko and Mai, his little child. "I'm afraid we were not able to communicate well enough to introduce ourselves," she said.

Joshua took a shaky breath. Speaking in Japanese he said, "Junko, this is Ruth O'Brien—a friend of the family." Speaking in English he continued, "Ruth—this is my wife Junko and my daughter Mai." Joshua laid his head back and rested. He looked up as Michael and Seth walked in from the living room. "These are my baby brothers, Michael, and Seth," he continued in Japanese as the two leaned on the back of the couch. "This is Junko and Mai." Again he rested. "Just where did you find my two favorite girls?"

"We didn't. They found us. You'll have to talk to Police Chief Mallory," Seth said. "We missed our chance to get the recovery room episode on film, but Dad thinks you've had enough excitement ...and probably enough exercise. We're going to pray over you this evening."

"Where are Mom and Dad?" Joshua asked.

"We're bringing up the rear." Mr. MacDonald walked in quietly with his wife. "We left the hospital at the same time Jack and Seth took off with you. Mom and I caught a taxi to Tweedle Dum's restaurant and Michael and Ruth took Jack's car and met us there."

"And someone found your lost family," Mrs. MacDonald said.

"Yes ..." Joshua stopped with a groan as he attempted to move.

"Take it easy, son. After that tussle we had to get you dressed it's a wonder you didn't open something up. It was bad enough when you were a little fellow. I'm much too old for wrestling now." Mr. Mac-Donald frowned.

"Sorry, sir," Joshua mumbled.

"Ruth? What are you laughing at?" Mrs. MacDonald turned and asked.

"I can see our dignified Mr. MacDonald wiping his face with that small towel, Dad with that sheet wrapped around his foot, and this fellow sitting in a wheelchair saying, Ready for inspection, sir!"

"You know," Mr. MacDonald reached into his back pocket, "I hadn't even realized it wasn't a handkerchief." He held up the towel.

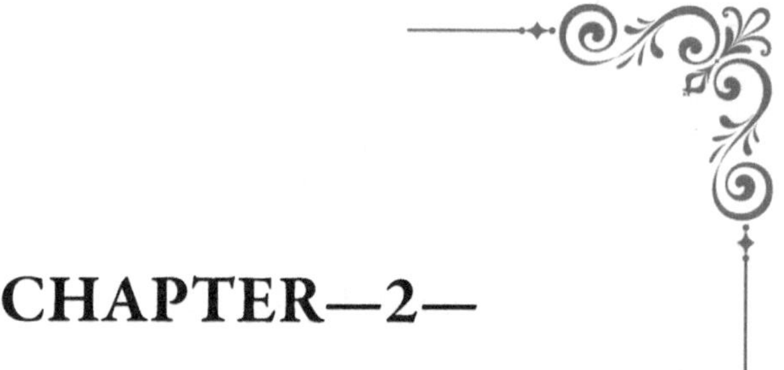

CHAPTER—2—

Joshua woke slowly cocooned on the comfortable couch. Junko and Mai slept on an air bed covered in pillows and blankets on the living room floor nearby. He'd had a good night's sleep. His pain meds carried him through the night, and now he watched the sky start to display its colors. The landscape around the house prevented an unfettered view of the horizon, but the brilliant colors he could see lifted his spirits. *The upstairs room over the garage would be like a bird's eye view this morning.*

Joshua threw the covers off so he could sit up. He slumped back, sensible of the searing pain in his thigh and left bicep. *That's alright; I don't feel like a bird this morning anyway.* He sat up with cautious, painstaking movement and with slow motion placed his feet on the floor, then slid to the edge of the couch.

Alrighty then—coffee. Sounds of someone rattling dishes, moving skillets, and sliding baking pans emanated from the kitchen. His stomach growled from the breakfast aromas that permeated the air. The tempting smell of sausage sizzling, and the scent of coffee rose with other delicious fragrances. Junko rolled over as Joshua stood.

Her eyes popped open, and she scrambled up. "Matte, matte!" she hissed. "I will help you. Always so impatient are you," she scolded in her language. Her face puckered up and scowled at him. "Let me cover the baby, first." She covered Mai and then turned back. "Okay, now." Joshua's tall figure dwarfed Junko's petite form as she supported him. They made their way to the kitchen step by slow step, leaving Mai snuggled in the warm covers asleep.

"Up so early?" Ruth turned. "Ready for coffee?"

"Are Dad and Seth outside already?" Joshua asked as Ruth brought a more comfortable chair for him.

"Michael and Dad are outside, Seth is still in the boy's room sleeping." Mrs. MacDonald poured him a cup of coffee.

"Ah, ha," he said. "Thank you." Joshua pulled his cup closer. After a moment of contemplation, he asked, "Where is everyone when I need them?"

"What?—and who do you need?" Ruth said arranging biscuits on pans.

"Brothers—even sisters..."

"Partners in crime." Mrs. MacDonald smiled.

"Yes, that's what I need," Joshua said.

"What kind of partner in crime are you needing?" Lewis Jr. came through the laundry room door.

"Well, ask and ye shall receive." Joshua raised an eyebrow. "Seth, asleep upstairs..."

"Oh... in the boy's room, Mom?" Lewis asked as he slipped out of his boots.

"Yes, he is." Mrs. MacDonald frowned at him puzzled.

Lewis's stockinged feet made very little noise on the stairs. There was a quiet whispering and rustling of papers, a short pause, then after a few tinkling notes from the piano, the opening notes of Beethoven's Fifth Symphony came thundering down the stairs. The sound from the hall above was loud enough—apparently to wake the dead—for something hit the floor very hard, and very suddenly. Only a wall separated Seth's bed from the piano.

"Oh, my!" Mrs. MacDonald said.

"Seth and—Lewis?" Mr. MacDonald walked in from the laundry room and stepped to the foot of the stairs as the pounding footsteps and the piano stopped.

Silence reigned. Then voices replied in unison, "Yes, sir?"

"No bloodshed in your sister's house."

Silence again for a short time, then the same voices replied, "Yes, sir."

"Wow," Ruth said to no one in particular, "Remind me to never get between those two. I imagine living in this family through their childhood was very interesting."

Joshua whispered to Junko and she began to giggle. Soon everyone else began to laugh. Seth and Lewis came downstairs, their fracas of a few moments before forgotten.

"Would you like to go outside to limp around?" Seth asked Joshua.

"I was going to put you to work," Joshua said. "but I've had better ideas, and we're too late. Michael's coming in and breakfast is ready."

"'MAKE ME TO HEAR JOY and gladness, That the bones which thou hast broken may rejoice... Create in me a clean heart, O God; And renew a right spirit within me... Restore unto me the joy of thy salvation; And uphold me with a willing spirit.'" Mr. MacDonald led a short Bible reading and finished with a prayer.

AS MRS. MACDONALD SCANNED the group, joy filled her heart. *What a blessing! Last week objects appeared like a fuzzy blur—now my eyesight improves every day. I'm so glad Mac's home.* She squinted in Seth's direction. *He's still the easy-going person he's always been. His face is still handsome, but there is tiredness around the*

eyes. A sorrow of the heart—a hard story to be told there—hopefully he and his wife, Gwen, can work out their problems.

She smiled watching the baby, Mai, and her mother, Junko. Both were small and delicate. *They remind me of a set of miniature dolls with silky black hair and gentle shy brown eyes.* Because Mai is so tiny she looks younger than a three-year-old. Wide-eyed she sat on Junko's lap, clinging like a little burr. Mrs. MacDonald could read her face as Mai clutched half a biscuit and stared at these strangers, talking in a strange language and laughing. Junko would take a bite of biscuit and sausage then give Mai a bite.

Mrs. MacDonald's mind switched gears and she frowned as Ruth leaned over and smiled at Mai. Everyone loved Ruth. She had become like another daughter after the murder of her mother, Diana, almost four years ago. Michael and Ruth should begin planning for their future now that the threat had been removed. Her mind wandered back to when Mac had asked her daddy for her hand in marriage. Her father didn't want them moving back to the mountains where he was sure she would die in childbirth...*but we have no objections toward Ruth. Nor do the O'Brien's have a problem with Michael.*

"Don't frown, Mrs. M.," Ruth leaned over and whispered. "It will give you bad wrinkles."

"YEAH, I GOT AHOLD OF Ronnie early this morning. He said the rent had come in the mail like usual yesterday, but there was a note giving him notice. So it's paid for one last month. Ronnie said he hasn't seen anyone around the apartment. Hasn't talked to Gwen, but I don't think he's being on the up and up. He kind of hedged about telling me anything." Seth's face darkened and pinched up into a scowl.

"Well, son—" Mr. MacDonald and Seth sat in the shade of the maple tree. "Ronnie would know something's up. He doesn't talk much, but he sure does listen." Mr. MacDonald took a drink of his iced tea and swirled the ice cubes while he thought. "I've got some phone numbers, but don't know if they'll help. Where'd you say she worked? If she hasn't given up the apartment yet—"

"She cooks, and she waitresses at Grandpa's Kitchen through the week in the evenings. And at Filer's Office two mornings—Tuesdays and Thursdays—each week."

"Hmm, hang on a minute." Mr. MacDonald turned toward the sunporch. "Amanda, I need a paper and pencil."

"Ruth's got it." The backdoor whooshed open.

"Thanks, Ruth." He turned back to Seth. "Okay, here you go," he wrote down numbers and names. "You need to return to Forrest City...

Seth looked down at his hands. "I'm not sure I can do that."

"Why would that be?" Mr. MacDonald said with a puzzled look at Seth. "You can't win her back over the phone, son."

"I—I'm..."

"Listen," the older man ran a hand through his hair. "There hasn't been a day in the last fourteen years that your mother and I haven't prayed for you. We didn't leave you. Everyone had a chance to come with us...but, this is your family—you do remember family?"

It was not his glass of tea that Seth saw as he stared into its icy depths. Scenes from his past— he and his siblings laughing, playing in the creek, riding ponies, playing tricks on one another— sifted through his memory. The years spent together working, sweating, living, and in some cases dying. His dad's family, Seth's aunts Meg and Laura, uncles John and Amos—even Grandpa MacDonald, always so close to each other.

"Yes, I remember." He smiled at the memory. "Mom didn't have a lot of family, did she?"

"No, she didn't. Why do you ask?"

"I don't have much memory of Grandpa and Grandma Stewart, but I sure remember Great-grandma Carrol. Didn't she have a sister?" Seth chuckled.

"Yes, she had one sister named Dora. They were quite a pair," Mac added with a laugh.

"I've never seen anyone who could ride as Great-grandma did. And I loved watching them speak. That English accent fascinated me," Seth said.

"When Aunt Dora and Great-grandma Jenny came for a visit the whole community came alive. It was always like that. The first time Grandma Jenny came to our neighborhood was when your grandparents, the Stewarts, took over General Stewart's manor house. Mr. Stewart had inherited the house and land from his uncle, 'the General' as we locals called him. It wasn't until Mr. Stewart fell on hard times that he moved his family to the hills of North Carolina. The manor house had fallen into disrepair, and the Stewarts had a lot of major adjusting to do. To top it off Mrs. Stewart's mother came for a visit shortly thereafter. She set the community in a tizzy."

"How's that, Dad?" Seth asked.

"Back when your momma was five years old, some of us were out berry picking when a big old rattlesnake must have woke up and stuck his head out of the bushes. We all froze in place. Great gramma Carrol rode up on her white gelding and before we knew what happened, she shot the head right off of that snake. Never have seen better shooting. Not unless it was at our chivaree when your mom shot a hole in the ceiling..."

"What?" Seth choked on his tea.

"Lewis MacDonald..." Amanda called out through the sunporch window.

"Story for another time," Mac said with a wink and a grin.

"After lunch, I have to do an estimate for Mr. O'Brien for siding and roofing. Are you free?"

"Yeah, I'm free," Mr. MacDonald said.

CHAPTER—3—

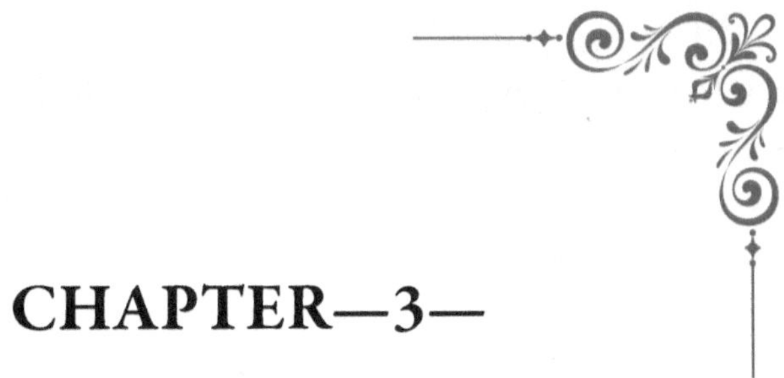

"You take." Joshua's wife, Junko, handed him a glass of water and his pain medicine. "Rest now."

"Slave driver," he teased Junko. *Slow down, and take it easy* were words that didn't register in Joshua's world. "Thanks, Ruth," he said as Ruth brought a box of toys from the attic. He smiled at Junko and Mai's eyes lit up.

"Ooh!" Mai squealed and clapped her hands.

He squeezed Junko's hand and lay back on the couch. *This is what makes life worth living.* Joshua allowed himself to sleep—resting more than he wanted. He slept for a while then woke; slept then woke again—several times. Each time he woke to the quiet sound of Mai playing. She looked quite fetching in the big pink hat with a feather that waved proudly. The next time he woke she had added a pink feather boa to the hat. He woke again— she had shed the hat and the boa and donned a long pink lacy dress and pink slippers. The thought slipped into his mind that *Someone likes pink in this family.*

"Do you like unicorns?" Mrs. MacDonald spoke softly to Mai. "You're likely to find just about anything in this toy box." She smiled as she knelt beside Mai. When she saw Joshua watching she came closer. "So, you're awake, Joshua." She helped him sit up. "It's wonderful to be able to see again after almost a year of being blind. Even if I'm not back one hundred percent. Just look at our little munchkin."

The pink feather boa draped around Mai's shoulders brought out the color in her cheeks. Unaware that she had an audience, she stopped and picked up a doll. "Der, der." She patted and clucked in a comforting manner. Bending over she put the dolly back into the cradle, as the big hat slipped down over her face. This happened with each doll, but she pushed the hat back and rocked the dollies.

"Her momma thought perhaps she should come out to the backyard and play in the sunshine and fresh air," his mother told him.

"Good idea, and I need to get up and around too," Joshua said.

"HELLO, GIRLS," MRS. MacDonald called to Ruth and Junko. She held the back door open for Mai. "How's the work progressing?" she asked.

"We are doing fine. Where did you find that sweet little girl?" Ruth asked.

"I found her in the toy box," Mrs. MacDonald said. "Junko, would you like a tour when you two have a moment? Joshua thinks you would like Laura's flowers and herbs."

A GENTLE BREEZE COOLED Joshua's face. He closed his eyes and relaxed outside in the shade listening to the laughter and chatter of the women wandering around the flowers and herbs. There was the gentle creak from the swing set until Mai scooched out of the swing and her tap, tap, tap when she climbed the slide. In comparison, the home he had left as a young man did not remotely resemble this place. Whoever had written, "You can never go home again," was right in this case. Not only the boy was different, but even the orchard was different. What was it that this family had that was timeless and enduring?

No matter what, there were two things he never doubted in his life. He never doubted his parents' love for God and their love for each other. In looking back, he should also never have doubted their love for their children.

"What are you doing, son?" His father settled into a chair beside him.

"Just thinking... and waiting," Joshua said with a thoughtful, sad smile.

"Anything you care to share?" Mr. MacDonald swirled the ice in his glass of tea.

"I wondered how can things be different and the same all at once. You left the hills out east to come to this flat, dry land. Your homes and lives are as different as the hills are different from this flat land. Yet your life is still the same—somehow."

"There are important things and unimportant things. I would pray that our lives are the same in the important things. Because of Hebrews thirteen verse eight." His father handed his open Bible to Joshua to read:

"Jesus Christ, the same yesterday, and today, yea and forever." Joshua looked up as the women came up the path toward them. "Ah," Joshua said, "and this is who I am waiting for—Thanks, Dad." He stood slowly.

"For what?" Mr. MacDonald asked.

"You and Mom have given us all a sturdy foundation to build on—without Jesus many things would have been different." Joshua turned. "Junko, I need you to help me."

"Yes?" she said.

"Yes. I need to get out of this person and back into myself. Mai doesn't know me like this. I always come back as myself. Someone did say there is a tub upstairs? And, Mom, do you still have those wonderful herbs for poultices?" Joshua said.

"Ruth," Mrs. MacDonald said, "you help them get the bathwater started and towels laid out. I'll get the herbs. Mac, you can help me for a bit."

They scurried around then left Junko to clean and patch Joshua's wounds while Mrs. MacDonald and Ruth worked on supper.

MR. MACDONALD MADE his getaway to sit in the shade and do some reading and studying. Besides the four seasons of spring, summer, fall, and winter there was also the season of the wind, and the season of the doldrums. When all signs failed the breeze would stop and the heat became unbearable. So far July had been tolerable.

Ten years ago when they threw the dart at the map and it landed in the Midwest, Mac remembered thinking, "I know God doesn't make mistakes, but...." Now as He listened to Ruth and Amanda practice a new song, he laughed. No, God doesn't make mistakes. God had made a place for them here. He sighed listening to the murmur of conversation coming from the room with the tub, and the tap of footsteps coming down the stairs. The sunlight shimmered across the pasture, but here the house and backyard were in the shade of the trees. Like a tiny shadow Mai appeared at the sunroom door. She stood unable to open the door.

Noticing the difficulty of her situation, Mac went to aid his damsel in distress. "Hello, Mai. Are you coming out to play?" he asked.

"I BELIEVE I'M GOOD to go." Joshua waited while Junko finished replacing his last bandage and helped him button his shirt. "Where is Mai?" Joshua asked as he turned to scan the backyard. "I don't see her." He frowned. "I do see Dad sitting at the table there."

Junko peered out the window. "Mai is sitting on his lap. I can see her jabbering at him."

"Ah, yes." Mr. MacDonald shifted in his chair and Joshua could see the bundle on his lap. She chattered away then looked up and smiled innocently. It was like watching a show with no sound.

"They seem to be getting along well, but it must be time for supper. Let's go rescue Dad," he said.

Joshua leaned on Junko as he hobbled down the steps and they made their way outside to the pair under the tree.

"I didn't know you understood Japanese, Dad," Joshua said as Mai, in a little bird voice, chirped away at her grandfather.

"I must admit I neither understand Japanese, nor do I have the gift of tongues, but I do know child language." Mr. MacDonald smiled.

"You have friends?" Junko tried her English.

"Indeed, I have a new friend." Mr. MacDonald smoothed the silky black hair out of Mai's face. She rewarded his efforts with a smile.

"Have you been talking to your grandfather, Mai?" Joshua asked.

"Yes, I have." She spoke in English.

"What have you been talking about?"

"'Bout my doggy and a flying pig."

"And what did grandfather say?" Joshua asked.

"I see. Dat's berry nice," she repeated imitating her grandfather's words.

During the laughter that followed Mr. MacDonald confirmed her words. "That's just what I said. I see she has your talent for mimicking, son." He looked intently at Joshua as they both smiled at the shared recollection of several incidents which had not been so humorous at the time of their happening.

"That's why I call her Little Parrot—and she chatters a lot sometimes. Mai understands and speaks English well for her age. Junko understands English but is shy about speaking it. She's afraid she'll get it wrong."

"Don't worry, even we don't always get it right," Mr. MacDonald said.

The sun porch door whooshed open and Mrs. MacDonald came out and plopped down. "How is my very most favorite Mai today?" She went nose to nose with her granddaughter.

"I am berry nice." Mai's face was prim and proper.

"You most certainly are." She planted a quick kiss on the little rosy cheek. "Time to eat, my loverlies."

"Let's do it then." Mr. MacDonald placed Mai on the path and stood. He looked at his son and winked. Holding out his hand to Mai, he said, "Come on, kiddo."

"Cm'on, keedo," she mimicked. Placing her tiny hand in his large one she smiled at him.

They filed onto the sun porch as Michael brought in the pitcher of iced tea. Seth chinked the ice into the glasses helping Ruth put the last of the meal on the table.

"We're all..." Ruth halted in mid-sentence. "You're right—That was some disguise." She stared at Joshua. "You fit right in now."

Mr. and Mrs. MacDonald looked sheepishly at each other and as if it had been rehearsed pointed at each other and declared in unison, "It must be his...her fault." They laughed.

"I see you're both in denial then?" Ruth said.

"I think it's a good time for our Bible reading and prayer...and supper," Mr. MacDonald said.

Michael opened his Bible. "I'm beginning here in Philippians the fourth chapter verses one through thirteen." He cleared his throat to read.

What a blessing. Mr. MacDonald sat back watching and listening to the conversation as the food passed around and the laughter of those gathered around the table. *What music to my ears.* As the meal wound down he observed the different characters—*Seth's slow manner made him seem lackadaisical and careless but he was neither. Michael had changed in some way. He was still funny, but with a purpose—Ruth appeared more beautiful—if that were possible. And Amanda*—Mac smiled across the table at her as the table was being cleared of food and tableware—*after all these years is still the light of my life.*

"There are some good points in that reading." Joshua finished his dinner roll.

"You are looking better this evening. How are you feeling?" Mr. MacDonald asked.

"I'm feeling much better, and this chicken Parmesan is very good." Joshua sat back from the table. "I don't think I need another bite."

"Joshua," Mac asked. "do you feel up to homemade ice cream at your brother's tonight?"

"Ah, dessert...well, the bath, Mom's herbs, and two days' worth of rest have gone a long way towards healing. Homemade ice cream may be just what I need." Joshua watched as the table was wiped clean.

"Good." Mr. MacDonald nodded. "Amanda, is everyone ready?"

"We are." She gave the counter one last swipe. "Let's go."

"HELLO, HELLO. EVERYONE find a chair," Lewis Jr. directed as the group came up onto the deck. "The ice cream is cured. All we need are willing victims to eat it."

Joshua limped over to the lounge and gingerly settled down with the help of his brothers as Junko and his mom tried to get several pillows in place. "Something's not quite right here," he said.

"Here, let me help." Donna, Lewis's wife, finished what the other two had attempted.

"Thanks," Joshua said. "Do you know how many centuries it has been since I've had homemade ice cream?" He took the bowl of ice cream and the spoon passed to him. "Seth, I had forgotten how much fudge sauce it takes for you, buddy!" Joshua chuckled as he watched his brother smother his ice cream.

"I don't want naked ice cream, dude." Seth frowned. "And chocolate's good for you."

"Did you get the estimate done for Pat and Jack today?" Joshua asked Seth.

"Yes, Dad and I went over and got the numbers. I need to get into town now and put some figures together for siding. They're also thinking about a new roof," Seth said.

"Kids, stack your bowls on this tray. David, take your cousin Mai with you when you go play," Donna said to the giggling children.

"Want to swing?" David asked Mai. "Or slide?"

Mai smiled at him. She took his outstretched hand they ran toward the playset.

"A lot seems to have happened since I've been away. Joshua—Seth, how did you come here?" Mr. MacDonald asked.

"I came as part of my last undercover job. Hermon PD called for help with a surge in crime—that tied in with an international ring that my group had been tracking." Joshua sipped his tea. "Lewis's appearance at the café the first day stunned me. And when I hurried down a garden path, at what I thought was the local Bed and Breakfast to help an older woman up, and I find my mother sitting on the ground looking for her...um...," he cleared his throat, 'dignity'."

Ruth looked at Mrs. MacDonald and pursed her lips. "My dear person," she raised her eyebrows and sat up straighter, "somehow that part of your story got left out."

"My dear person," replied the older woman, "you always get so excited—you know when I'm sitting in the wrong places. Like on the ground?" She smiled, an innocent look on her face.

"That complicated matters," Joshua said. "What a dilemma."

"Exodus eight and nineteen—Then the magicians said unto Pharaoh, this is the finger of God. We have prayed all these years, but what a tremendous surprise that was." Lewis Jr. shook his head.

"I can't even tell you how it made me feel." Joshua took a deep breath.

Lewis turned to Seth. "How did you come to be here?"

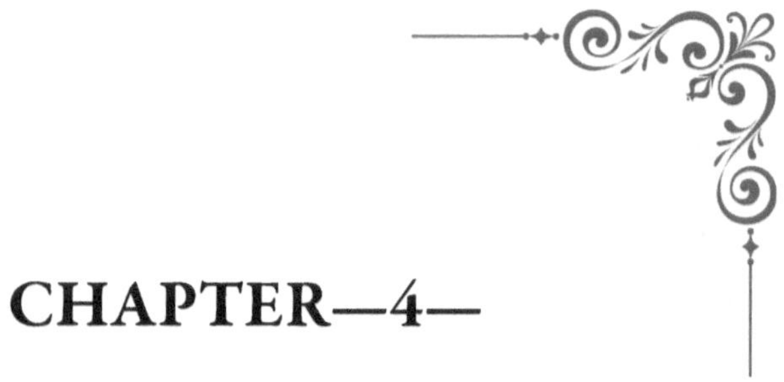

CHAPTER—4—

Seth had chosen to sit on the outskirts of the family ring, and during Joshua's portion of the story, the shadows had grown long. Lewis's question caught him off guard.

"Would anyone care for more iced tea?" Donna asked.

"Thank you, yes." Seth held out his glass, remembering when he was young and she joined their family. She treated him like the kid brother she had lost as a child, not as a brother-in-law.

Donna brought the pitcher. "There you go." She smiled encouragingly at him. Still pretty even now at age forty. She was quiet, although not shy. The twinkle in her dark brown eyes denoted humor lurking under the surface, much like that of his oldest brother. They were well suited for one another.

"Thank you, ma'am." He returned her smile as she filled his glass, before turning his attention to his part of the tale. "The night brother James died—Lily kept screaming, and screaming until they sedated her. That's what I felt like inside, but I didn't get sedated. James's death was unreal. Sara had married Bob and Peter and Judith had married and they were gone. Joshua was gone and..." Seth shrugged. "Our family had dwindled considerably. When you eight left—" He gestured at his dad and mom. "—Rachel and I had chosen to stay in Forrest City. However, we were like lost sheep, our feet smack against the line, living like we didn't know any better." His eyes and face darkened. Seth slowly took a drink of tea.

"But, Rachel met a young fellow from church—they've been married ten years and have four children." Seth smiled at his parents. "I kept floundering. On one of my trips back to church I met and married a beautiful young woman—Gwen. I stuck with the church for close to a year. Then I slipped back and forth and for eight years I've tried to get my feet under me, but... I just made us both miserable. Gwen left me a note. She said she loved me too much, and she'd had enough watching me try to kill myself. After that, I don't remember what happened. My memory picks up when I sit down under the maple tree over in the back of Laura's house... I didn't know it was Laura's house. I hurt bad and shook all over like coming out of an operation with no anesthetic. Add to that Joshua whom I haven't seen in over fourteen years, starts talking to me from somewhere. It's so dark I can't see anything. Right there I decided I must have died. And I'd ended up in the place of torment. Thankfully, for the last two weeks, I've been getting back on my feet and helping Jo." Seth sat quietly.

Joshua chuckled. "So we finished the case and even with the shooting, I can lose my undercover identity. The person from the shooting and the hospital is untraceable."

"That seems providential." Lewis looked at Joshua. "When you first showed up Joshua, I couldn't for the life of me understand why Mom had taken in a stranger. We were suffering persecution from several sides. All Mom would say was Matthew 25:35 'I was a stranger and ye took me in'...and to her, it seemed the right thing for her to do."

From the edge of the light, half in the shadow where Mr. MacDonald sat, he nodded. "I'm glad you two are back. Now the question is what are your plans?"

"I plan to look around here and take a bit of time to spend with Junko and Mai. Look for some land, maybe an acreage around here, and settle down. I've spent too many years like the song says in vanity and pride. I'm tired—real tired." The shadows played across Joshua's face.

Mr. MacDonald turned to Seth. "How about you, son?"

Seth pursed his lips. "Right offhand, I'm at a turning point. I've got the prospect of work since Jack and Pat are considering new siding and a new roof, and I want to get out of the rut I've been in far too long. Having said that, I need some fervent prayers that I make the right decisions and for Gwen's heart to be opened—softened to the idea of reconciliation."

"I suggest then we spend some time in that fervent prayer. Let's pray..." Mr. MacDonald bowed his head and paused to begin the prayer.

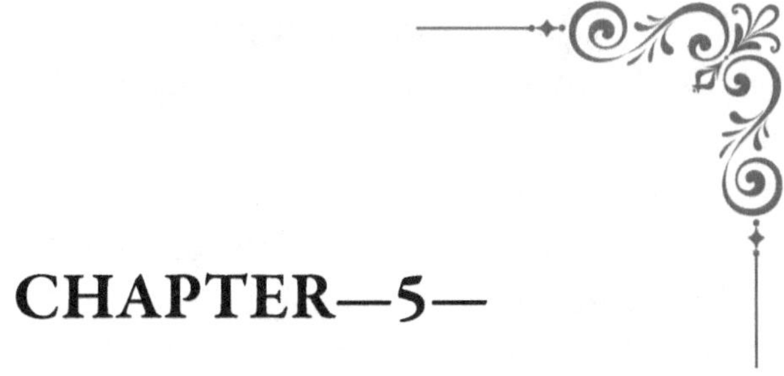

CHAPTER—5—

"Whoa, doggie! That do smell good." Seth inhaled the aroma of frying pancakes and bacon as he entered the kitchen the next morning.

Mr. MacDonald scanned the newspaper and sipped his coffee.

Mai had learned a new phrase and she spoke very seriously as her uncle walked by. "Good morning, keedo."

"Howdy, pardner," Seth drawled with a sort of wave of the hand.

She screwed up her baby face into a comical expression and repeated this new phrase, "Howdy, pardner." And back to the business, she went, placing her dolly carefully into the cradle.

Seth sat down across from his dad, and a cup of coffee materialized in front of him. "Thanks, Mom." He looked up with a nod.

"Sure." She patted his hand.

"Howdy, pardner." His dad looked over and grinned.

It struck Seth like an arrow in the heart...very few things happened that these two did not notice. How many times in the past had he thought they were dumber-n-dirt, just ignorant old people? Now they were wiser, and...younger.

"Morning, sir." He grinned back.

"How's it going?" his father asked.

"Not too bad, but I just got up," he answered as a plate of hot pancakes and several strips of bacon were plunked down on the table in front of him. There was lots of butter and hot homemade syrup. "Thanks," he said.

"Sure," Ruth said without the pat.

He offered a private prayer and began shoveling food into his mouth.

"Hey, you'd think those were good or something." Joshua limped in at the same time Seth finished the last bite of bacon.

"It's a hard job, but somebody has to do it," Seth responded, lackadaisically chewing and swallowing his last bite. "Je'et?" he asked.

"No, we're just coming in," Joshua said as Michael followed him through the door.

Mr. MacDonald stood and grabbed his coffee cup. "Come on. Let's move on out under the tree and let these hard workers have their turn at table."

"Yes, sir," Seth responded. "Thanks, Mom," he said, as she gave him a refill.

"Amanda—" the older man smiled as she filled his cup. "I'm 'bliged."

"You two skedaddle." She smiled at her husband.

As the door whooshed shut behind them, Mr. MacDonald wiped the dampness off his chair and handed a paper towel to Seth. "Here—"

"Thanks." Seth wiped off his seat and sat.

The two men sipped their coffee in comfortable silence listening to the morning sounds around them. The clouds drifting away revealed the blue sky filling with sparkling sunshine as the old black rooster at the barn split the air with a blast from his horn. The birds fed their young with an occasional skirmish and squawk.

"The seasons change so fast. Every year moves more quickly," Seth said.

"The older you get the more you want to grab life and dig your heels in to hold back the rush," Mr. MacDonald said.

"Yeah, I feel like that, and I'm only thirty-one. Sometimes I wish I could replay parts of my life...you know, redo it until I get it right."

"As a young man, how many times did you hear Ecclesiastes chapter ten quoted?" Mr. MacDonald opened his pocket Bible and read, "Rejoice, oh young man, in thy youth, and walk in the ways of thy heart, and in the sight of thine eyes; but know thou, that for all these things God will bring thee into judgment. Therefore remove sorrow from thy heart and put away evil from thy flesh; for youth and the dawn of life are vanity."

"I don't know how many times." Seth frowned and pulled at his upper lip. "But my heart never really heard it."

"And now what will you do with it?"

"That's the question—now that I have my life back, what am I going to do with it?" Seth spread his hands out in appeal. "It will be difficult without Gwen. I just don't know how I'll make it without her," Seth shook his head, the tears shining in his eyes.

"Seth, your trust needs to be in Jesus first. No matter how good a person is they will let you down sometimes, but God and Jesus... won't let you down. I wonder..." Mr. MacDonald rubbed his chin thoughtfully. "We've talked about this. If Gwen's stayed with you for almost nine years I'd say don't give up without a fight. Go back, tie up your loose ends, perhaps Gwen would be willing to leave Forrest City and move out here. Start a new life. We have room...if you are willing to submit to the will of God."

"Grandpa, come play?" Mai called as she and Joshua came out of the sun porch door.

Mr. MacDonald stood up, his face screwed into a frown. "You think an old man like me can go down the slide with you?" he asked in mock amazement.

Mai giggled. She ran to the swing and then waited for her grandpa to come help her.

"So, that's your game." He laughed as he sat her in the swing and gave it a gentle push.

"What do you think?" Seth asked as Joshua sat down. "Dad says I need to go back and tie things up. See if Gwen won't come back here with me."

"He's right," Joshua said.

"Sounds easy enough." Seth frowned and tapped on his coffee cup. "Only one or two small problems—money and time."

"I've got both right now," Joshua said.

"But you're still recuperating, Jo..."

"You're still a MacDonald, right? Surely you haven't forgotten the 'all for one, and one for all' have you?" Joshua scowled and raised an eyebrow. "I've got a car rented for me and the girls. We'll leave tonight and drive a few hours. If I get tired we'll stop, if not we'll spell each other driving. Take a week, go back and do some sightseeing while you tie things up, and get back here about the same time that Sis and her family get back."

"It always sounded so trite before." Seth wiped his nose on his napkin.

"What's that?" Joshua asked.

"Oh, Lord Jesus—I've missed you and all of this crazy family. I can't even begin to express the wonder of being back." Emotions wrestled across Seth's face. "I didn't know how lost I would be when Dad and Mom left. We went from being a large family to just Rachel and me. Something else died with James—and Sara had married and was gone. Peter and Judith went to Georgia. Her family is... 'well situated', you know." Seth curled his pinky finger and stuck his nose a little higher.

"No, I didn't know what happened to Sara or Peter. No one ever speaks of the past. Until last night I didn't have a clue as to what had become of them. And that was sketchy," Joshua said. "When I left, I felt abandoned—which was stupid. I was the one who stomped off. When I came back, somehow even though I introduced myself as Julius C. Armstrong ... I figured my mother ought to know me. Then

I discovered she had lost her sight. I felt even worse when I found out that even blind she had known ...from the beginning."

Junko brought a load of clothes outside to be hung on the clothesline. "Mai, do not tire grandfather."

Mai slowed her swing and with a worried look peered up at her grandfather. He in turn smiled at her in reassurance.

Ruth walked out the breezeway door at that moment. "Come, Mai. Would you like to come help me feed Wibble and Waddle?" She held up a small bucket.

"Oo has nuffing for feed, Woof," with a puzzled expression, the little girl peered into the empty bucket.

"Can she come with me?" asked Ruth.

"Go with Miss Ruth, honey. Mommy and I'll be along in a few minutes," Joshua said.

Ruth held out her hand to Mai. "Come along, sweetie." She smiled as they walked down the path hand in hand.

"What a picture those two make," Seth said. "Ruth will make a fine wife for someone. Is she Michael's girl?"

"Should be, but I can't say." Joshua frowned. "They're good friends, but I have never observed anything else."

"Well, he won't find a better young woman, or a prettier one either." Seth squinted at his brother. " He better be snapping her up quick or he'll lose her to some other dude,"

Joshua grinned at his brother. "Maybe now there'll be more opportunity, but both parties need to be agreeable. We MacDonalds don't steal our women anymore. We're civilized now, you know. Besides, heaven help the fella that tries to steal that woman against her will."

"What woman is that?" asked Michael as he joined his brothers. "And who is stealing women?"

"We were just commenting on what a likely lass Ruth is, and look how she gets along with children." Seth raised an eyebrow.

"She has a heart for children," Michael said.

"As your brothers, we were just wondering about, uh, about perhaps... someone in your life?" Seth was not so subtle.

Michael spoke seriously. "If I ever marry, I pray it will be someone like Ruth. She is the godliest young woman I know. She isn't...silly after young men."

"So?" Seth said.

"So—what?" Michael asked innocently.

"So, is there someone in your future?" Seth exploded.

"I'm praying there is," Michael said.

"Let's go see how Mai is getting along with the ducks and chickens," Joshua called to Junko as she finished hanging the clothes on the line. "I can see, Michael, you are just as hard-headed as the rest of us."

From the confused look on Michael's face, all the hinting seemed to be lost on him.

"WHAT AN INFERNAL RUCKUS!" Seth exclaimed as they came closer to the barnyard.

"You see," Joshua leaned on the fence rail, "if we leave tonight..." and he explained the plans to Junko.

As they watched, Ruth scattered the feed in various patterns while the ducks and the rooster with his flock of hens scrambled after the grain. Mai stood beside Ruth trying to grab one of the birds.

Michael joined them then opened the gate, and knelt beside Mai. "Whoa, here." He carefully put his arm around the little girl so as not to frighten her. "Be still, little peach blossom." He motioned and they waited...unmoving. "Watch here." He pointed to a greedy hen that was gobbling grain. He reached down and smoothly scooped her up and placed her on his knee. Mai looked into his kind face as she reached out her hand to stroke the smooth feathers. "Here."

Michael showed her how to hold her hand flat. "Now, let her eat some grain."

"Ooh!" Mai squealed with wonder.

"Okay," Michael said after a few moments, "We'll let the 'old girl' get back to business—" and they set her down.

"Here, baby," Ruth spoke kindly and offered the last of the grain for Mai to scatter on the ground.

Joshua winked at Seth, and smiled at Junko, as they watched the two young people and the child.

Seth sighed. *Oh to be young and in love. How many years had washed under his bridge?* He thought with a pang of regret.

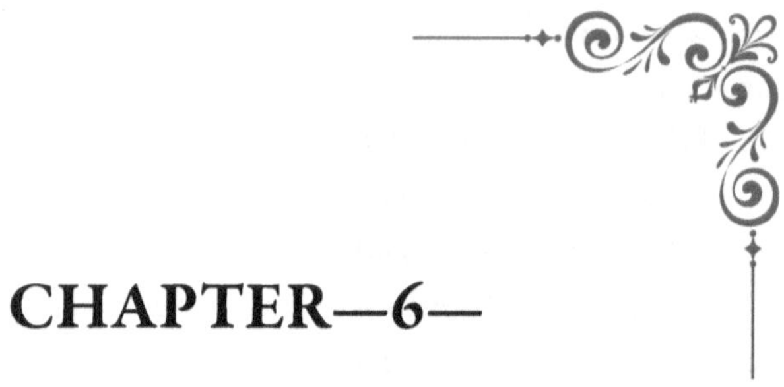

CHAPTER—6—

"We are thinking of leaving this evening after mid-week Bible study," Joshua told everyone when they got back to the house. "It will be easier for Mai to travel at night."

"There is no sense to lollygag around, I guess," Mr. MacDonald agreed. "If you are going to do a thing... get it done. Will you be up to the trip, Joshua?" He frowned.

"With the two of us driving, I should be able to rest enough, Dad," Joshua said. "Besides, you know we MacDonalds are not known only for our excellent disposition, but for our stubborn, hard-headedness, bull-strength, and ..."

"Ah, well, you could use most all of those adjectives, however, I know several folks, that might put in a disclaimer on that first one." Mr. MacDonald raised an eyebrow and smiled.

"Y'all get your things packed and ready to go. Ruth and I'll try to get some snacks and stuff ready for you to take along, kiddos," Mrs. MacDonald said.

SETH LOOKED AT THE lesson on forgiveness of self in his work-book. As Brother Wilson spoke on the love of God and forgiveness, he nodded in agreement. *How basic, yet how often it was misunderstood or ignored,* he mused as they stood and sang the beautiful hymn, "The Love of God." *That also is often misunderstood.*

After the few announcements, Brother Wilson took a piece of paper out of his Bible. "I pray that you'll bear with me." His hand shook slightly. "I have something to read. It isn't very long, but..." He cleared his throat and read, "Many years ago I left both my physical and spiritual family. Although I have not lived perfectly, because perfection belongs to God, I have not lived shamefully. Many people in the world would even say I lived honorably. However, there are some things wrong in my life. It is my purpose to begin to correct these faults. The first thing I want to do is repent, asking my physical family to forgive the pain and suffering our separation has caused all of us. I also want to renew my commitment to my God, my physical family, and my spiritual family. Signed—Joshua T. MacDonald."

The preacher cleared his throat again as he grasped the piece of paper. In the silence of the building, not a breath stirred as the congregation waited.

Brother Wilson removed his glasses, wiping tears. "I know prayers have been answered as Joshua and Seth have returned to their family. I cannot imagine the pain of losing someone you love, a child or..." his words came slowly as tears slipped down his face. He stopped to wipe at his eyes with his handkerchief then he blew his nose. "God, and our friends, the MacDonald family, have received their two sons, as it were, back from the dead. What a blessing and a joy. Praise the Lord. Let us have a special prayer of thanksgiving then the final song. Brother Cole, will you do the honors for us?" It was more than the powerful singing that made this congregation outstanding.

"IT'S TOO BAD YOU CAN'T come too," Seth told Michael later as he and Joshua's family were about to leave on their journey. "With all this stuff we have in here..." he said.

"That's all right. I'm busy here. We're spread too thin with Laura and Juan gone anyway," Michael added after a pause.

"Do you have everything?" Mrs. MacDonald looked at her list then showed it to Joshua and Seth.

"I think we do. Sandwiches, snack crackers, cut-up fruits, and veggies. We'll stop and get some horrible things like chips and cupcakes, and we have water, coffee, and some soda. We'll be more than fine, Mom," Joshua said.

"Well, then get out of here." His dad laughed and shooed them into the car.

"Goodbye, and blessings go with you." Mrs. MacDonald waved.

"Goodbye," chorused from the group as they backed around and drove off on their excursion, and those staying behind waved and called their goodbyes.

THAT EVENING RUTH SPREAD her new piano music on the rack and began practicing the scale. *What was that with Michael's sigh of relief as the group left the driveway? And the pause, and the evasive way in which he had declined to accompany them? And there was his promise of a few days ago. Well, we are busy here, and with Juan and Laura gone we're spread very thin, and Michael promised me some answers a few days ago. Maybe tomorrow...*

Ruth reflected on the people who surrounded her. Grandfather O'Brien had always been a stabilizing element in her life. He was an old man now, but he could still be just as surprising in the present as he was in the stories of him and Charlie Anderson. Mr. and Mrs. MacDonald had never been mysterious or unusual. She certainly had some praying to do there. People were like gems. Even those who appeared to be ordinary had many surfaces. She hit the first note on her new song.

"YESTERDAY WE HAD EIGHT people and the unseen guest for breakfast. Today there are only four of us. It was a good thing we got all of the laundry done," Ruth said as she and Mrs. MacDonald finished the dishes after lunch.

"I can't say that I'm sorry to have a bit of normalcy. We've had too much stress—more than usual the last few weeks. And you didn't get all of the laundry done."

"What?" Ruth stopped short and looked at her friend.

"I found a little striped sock, a size very small t-shirt, a little pink slipper, and a dolly this morning in the living room," Mrs. MacDonald said with a smile. "Our life was on the fast track. It makes everything so quiet now."

"It sure was," Ruth agreed. "What time is your doctor's appointment this afternoon?"

"It's at two-thirty. We'll have to be hopping along. Did you want to come?" asked Mrs. MacDonald

"No, I feel called to pray and just be quiet for a time. Later—when you get back—I would like some time to talk though."

"We can talk right now if you need." The older woman stopped and looked into Ruth's troubled eyes. She gently took Ruth's slender hand in hers.

"Oh... No, don't change your plans for me. My questions will wait, and I feel a need for prayer."

Ruth waved as they left then took her Bible and wandered down the path to seek solace in prayer in the special quiet niche under the cherry tree.

TWO HOURS LATER MICHAEL found the house empty and quiet. *Did Ruth go with Dad and Mom? I'm sure she said she was staying home...* Standing in the kitchen he looked out the window. *Hmm, could that smudge of color be her?* His feet made no noise as he approached on the orchard path. Was she asleep? He wondered as he came closer. That wouldn't be a comfortable sleeping position...she was on her knees, her Bible on the bench, and her head resting on her Bible.

She slowly raised her head. "Hello, Michael."

"You look like you've been wrestling with the Angel." Michael noticed her loose hair hanging in a long auburn braid with fine wisps around her forehead. Tears accented the slight flush on her cheeks against her unusually pale face. "What is it, Ruth? What torments you so?" he asked pained at her distress.

"I guess it must be almost supper-time, and it isn't even started yet." She avoided the subject while she accepted his assistance and slowly stood up.

"That won't work this time, Ruth." Michael still held her hand, looking steadily into her eyes. "You and I both know all the hot fudge sundaes in the world won't cure this ailment. Won't you share your burden?"

"The heart knoweth its own bitterness," she quoted, then picked up her Bible, intending to go back to the house.

"There's no hurry," Michael said. "We're going over to Lewis' for supper."

Ruth sat on the bench. "What was it, Michael, that bothered you about going back to your old home?" She gazed at him as he stood beside the bench.

Michael remembered thinking how absolutely stunning she was the first time Ruth and her mother had come to church. But she had taught him to value her friendship and look beyond her outward appearance to her inner beauty.

The breeze softly stirring the wispy loose fronds of hair framing her face and ruffling the delicate lace on the collar of her dress made an attractive picture that lazy afternoon. A cow called to her stray calf, a bird called to his mate, and Seth's words came back to

Michael—*we were just commenting on what a likely looking lass Ruth is and look how she gets along with children. Is there someone in your future?*— and his reply. *If I ever marry, I pray it will be someone like Ruth. I'm praying there is. Someone like Ruth, one of the kindest, purest, most godly young women I know.*

"Michael?" Ruth brought him gently back to the present.

"I was thirteen when we left Forrest City." He spoke slowly as they sat on the bench. "There are many unpleasant memories. All that I remember from that time is sorrow, and it's very painful even to think of it. I have no desire to rekindle those memories. When Seth spoke of James's death and his wife, Lily screaming? I remember the same feeling on both levels. Of course, I love Joshua and Seth. They are double my brothers. I have prayed for their return just as the rest of my family has. But I feel so much sadness because of their wasted years, the sorrow they have caused, especially to Mom and Dad. The picture of my father and mother holding each other and crying over the loss of their children is forever etched on my memory."

Ruth reached out to comfort him. "The past is something that helps shape us into who and what we are, but we have to move on in our lives," Ruth said.

"I feel so young and so old at the same time." Michael heaved a sigh. "I was so little when James and Lily were married I don't remember when the tensions and problems began that their marriage caused. Dad and Mom tried to isolate the problem to those involved...but when one of us hurt we all did. James and his wife hurt all of us. From the age of five till I was thirteen I witnessed the destruction of the people I loved the most. When James was killed, it devastated all of us."

"When your mom and I cried together, I only cried for one. I didn't know..." Tears rolled down Ruth's cheeks. "Often words aren't enough. We still ask why, knowing what's true with our mind, but the heart doesn't understand."

"Which," Michael said, "brings me back to you. I'm struggling since the end of Joshua's case trying to wrap my head around the fact that the threat is over. What is your burden?" *I never believed we would get to this point. Will there be a time when Ruth can be more than a sister?* "As the threat dangled over us with the persecution demanding ever vigilance I never saw the end. But now that threat is gone. What is left?"

"You are my dearest friend," Ruth said. "I appreciate your offer—"

"But," Michael's eyes narrowed, "you can't share? If at some time you feel you can trust me ..."

"It isn't trust." She sighed wearily. "I just can't share."

"You know I'll be here when you need me," he said with a heavy heart.

"YOU CAN'T IMAGINE HOW good it is to see again, even if it is still fuzzy." Amanda and Mac strolled up the path.

"No, I can't quite grasp the situation of being blind. If I were to put a blindfold on for a time, it would be *this is what it is like* not *this is what it is*. I could still take the blindfold off at some point," he said.

"Being blind for a season had its piece of good fortune," she said.

"In what way?!"

"It has sharpened my other senses—I see deeper than sight. I appreciate the blessing of seeing with my eyes...those are the major ones... I realize more fully how important it is to trust in God, His power, and His grace."

"That gives a person..." They were so engrossed in their conversation, that they had almost reached the two young people seated on the bench before they saw them.

"I pray we aren't intruding?" Mr. MacDonald stopped suddenly.

"No, no, we were just about to come back to the house. Would you like a seat, Mom?" Michael stood.

Michael had been ruffling his hair, a sure sign of mental distraction. Tears were still evident on Ruth's face, and Michael's handkerchief was being fretted over in her hands.

"You know jumping to conclusions is never a good exercise. Is there something we can help you two with?" Mr. MacDonald asked.

"No," Ruth replied too quickly. "We are...were... just wrestling against the spiritual host of wickedness," she said more slowly.

"Well, then," Mr. MacDonald said, "let's take up the 'all prayer and supplication' part of the spiritual armor." He removed his hat and bowed his head. Michael followed his father's example, and they prayed together...

"THIRTY JARS OF SOUR dills." The next day Mrs. MacDonald counted the number of jars of pickles cooling on the counter from the late afternoon. "It's kind of warm in the house. Let's go outside and sit in the shade, Ruth. Supper's finished and the kitchen's cleaned up for the evening." The two ladies grabbed their glasses of tea and walked past Mac and Michael, playing a quiet game of chess under the maple tree.

"We're going for a walk—you two finish your game," Amanda said as Mac began to get to his feet. Continuing around the house, and following the meandering path the companions came to the flowering alcove protecting the gazebo in the front yard. "We never did get to that conversation." Mrs. MacDonald broached the subject as they sat sipping their tea and enjoying the peaceful moment. "What is it you want to discuss?"

"I'm confused." Ruth pursed her lips. "I've been thinking on this conversation for some time, and...I knew of course, that when you moved here you moved away from something. But I was so young when we first became acquainted, and for other reasons I suppose, I didn't wonder much why there were no...pictures...no past. Your lives began here. Now I feel a longing to know more about the before."

Ruth waited patiently. There was no breeze, but the little day creatures were whispering their young to sleep for the night. The sweet perfume from the profusion of flowers in this section of the yard scented the evening air. There was the fragrance of growing corn, mown hay, and the sound of frogs at the pool were serenading anyone and everyone, and lightning bugs were beginning to flash their tiny lamps. A breath of peace settled about the pair even in the midst of pain.

"And know you shall, Ruth." Mrs. MacDonald broke her silence. "We have not tried to be secretive. Most of our past is part of the public record. You have heard how we came to be here from the other evening, but of course, there is more. The memories are bittersweet for Mac and me. As a young married couple we believed if we did our best before the Lord that He would bless those efforts, even if we weren't perfect," she said. "The way He blessed those efforts was not exactly the way we had in mind. Satan still has power in this world. When folks are bent on following their way instead of God's way, it's like trying to hold back the tide. But, I digress." She sighed. She took Ruth's hand in hers and studied the beautiful fingers slowly and carefully. There was a tiny gold ring with a pearl surrounded by diamonds on her right hand. "When Laura returns and life settles down I'm sure she will consent to give you a tour of the MacDonald family skeletons. I was so hurt and bitter. My first impulse at the time was to throw the pictures all away, but sanity prevailed and we still have them. They aren't just mine. They belong to all of us."

"God is the only perfect father," Ruth said.

"Why... yes, He is, Ruth." Mrs. MacDonald's eyes widened, startled by the turn in the conversation.

"Adam and Eve still rebelled against Him. And...many still rebel yet to this day." Ruth squeezed Mrs. MacDonald's hand.

"You blessed comfort. I don't know what we would have done without you." Mrs. MacDonald placed Ruth's hand against her cheek.

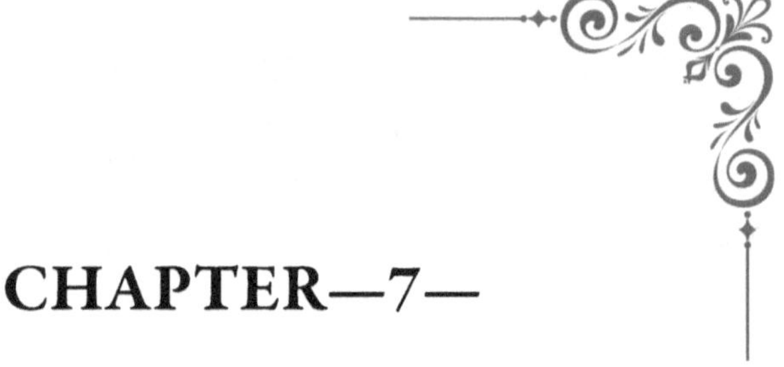

CHAPTER—7—

Seth waited for his brother at the café. On the face of the matter, it appeared as if his wife, Gwen, had just vanished. He had been everywhere, checked everywhere. Nothing. At the office and the restaurant where she had worked, either her co-workers did not know or were not confiding in him. He left a phone number in both places just in case anyone changed their mind, or she came back. Nothing. Seth had packed their few belongings from their small apartment and now waited for Joshua on this Monday morning for breakfast.

"Hey, how's it going?" Seth asked as Joshua slid into the booth.

"From the look on your face, I would guess you haven't found anything, huh?" Joshua said. "Have you checked with her family?"

"She doesn't have any family that I know of."

"No one?"

"No. In the past nine years, I don't remember anyone coming around. When we were married it was just Rachel, Lance—Rachel's husband—Gwen and I," Seth said.

"What was Gwen's maiden name?"

"Winters. Gwendolyn Aurora Winters," Seth replied.

"Winters? Sounds familiar somehow...How did she come to be here?" Joshua asked.

"Her parents were killed in a car accident when she was young. The proverbial 'maiden aunt' took her in and raised her. She and her aunt had a very close relationship, but when her aunt died, Gwen decided to do some traveling before settling on what she was going to do. The rest is history. We met and married during one of my good times, and then I made her miserable for nine years." Seth looked down at his coffee.

"No children?"

"We lost a baby boy a few weeks after he was born. He died in our arms as we were waiting in the emergency room." His face twisted in pain as the words hung in the air.

"Oh, my..." A look of horror settled on Joshua's face. "I can't imagine...I wouldn't even want to imagine." Joshua's face paled and he shuddered.

"It was worse than hard, but we pulled together for a while. Then I went down again. Gwen would like to have children, but with all of my ups and downs, she's afraid." His voice sounded hollow as he sat playing with a napkin. "I've just got to make it this time, Jo," he said. "I've just got to." He looked at his brother, desperation on his face.

"This may sound odd, but during our Bible reading last night we were reading Matthew chapter nineteen. Remember the camel's eye and the disciples asking Jesus who then can be saved?" Joshua asked.

"Yeah, sure." Seth rubbed his hands through his hair.

"Well, Seth, Jesus said, With men this is impossible, but with God all things are possible. That's your answer. With God all things are possible. We'll do our part. Let's pray now and then we will see where our day takes us."

"You're right, Jo." Seth took off his hat and bowed his head. "We thank You, oh God, and praise Your holy name. We humbly ask for Your blessing and guidance in finding Gwen. Please open her heart to give me another chance. And please, God, help me trust in You and continue to overcome Satan daily. In Jesus Name, Amen."

"Forrest City hasn't changed a whole lot since I've been gone." Joshua watched some of the people in the street. "Of course, you haven't been gone over a few weeks so you'd be used to it as it is. Are you ready to head out? I'll pay for these coffees then we can go." He handed the waitress the money and they walked to the car. "My girls are sleeping in this morning. At least I'm hoping they are," Joshua added as they drove to the motel. "Mai can get into things you wouldn't believe." He looked at Seth and grinned. "Well—maybe you would believe. I can't imagine how anyone survived all of us!"

"There are the girls," Seth said as they pulled up to the motel.

"It looks like they're heading up for breakfast. I guess we can go sit while they eat. Always room for another cup of coffee, right?"

"You go join the girls...I'm going to go talk to Ben over there." Seth pointed. "You remember Ben Coleman, don't you?"

"Not really...must have been one of the little kids," Joshua said. "Well, when you get done..."

"I NEED TO KEEP MOVING, Ben. My brother's back for a short visit and he's just visiting the sights and I'm along for the ride. It was good to see you. I hope all goes well with your new job." Seth turned to leave.

"Oh, I'm sure it will. Say," the man added as an afterthought, "it's too bad about Gwen. How's she doin'?"

"What do you mean?" Seth swung back around.

"That car accident she was in last week," the man said. "I'm sorry, didn't you know?"

"I've been away for a couple of weeks helping my brother. No wonder I couldn't get ahold of her on the phone. Since we came back I haven't been able to find Gwen," Seth said. "Was it a bad accident?"

"It didn't look good for the car, but all the report gave was that they had taken her to the hospital with multiple injuries," Seth's acquaintance said.

"You know I've looked everywhere...except at the hospital. Thanks again, man. See ya' later," Seth replied as hope mingled with fear.

"NO, GWEN MACDONALD isn't here." The woman frowned. "It has been fourteen days since the accident. She stayed overnight, but the injuries were only minor...except for a broken leg. Even that was a hairline break. Otherwise, it was bumps and bruises." Her eyes narrowed in appraisal as Seth and Joshua stood at the desk.

"Were you here when she went home? Who picked her up?" Seth grabbed at straws for any information.

"No, it was my day off," she said. "I was gone when she went home." The woman turned and called to someone in the copy room. "Helen, were you here the other day when Mizz MacDonald was discharged?"

"No," came a muffled reply, "but I believe Sylvia was."

"Sylvia was here," the first woman answered looking at Seth. "Hang on a moment, here she comes."

They watched as a stout older woman shuffled toward them.

"Here's a young man lookin' for his wife," the woman at the desk informed Sylvia. "Can you tell him anything about Mizz MacDonald?"

Sylvia took her time assessing Seth carefully. "So, what is it you want to know?" she asked as her eyes narrowed.

Seth was exasperated. After all, he was her husband. *No sense in losing my temper.* Taking a deep breath he began. "I've been gone for a few weeks helping my brother." He repeated his story. "I've been trying to get in touch with her but no success. We came back to get her, but I haven't been able to find her. We just learned of the accident and I hurried over."

"But the accident was fourteen days ago. You haven't been in contact with your wife for fourteen days?" Judging by her frown and squinting eyes she was weighing him in the balance, and he was found lacking.

There was a draft of fresh air as Junko and Mai opened the front door and came in. Mai ran to Joshua who stood beside Seth. Bending over he scooped her up and smiled tenderly at her as she ran her delicate little fingers through his hair. Standing it on end, she giggled and began patting his face.

The hard lines of the woman's face softened, and as a flower opening, she watched the pair. "What's your name, honey?" she asked, smiling.

Suddenly shy, Mai hid her face against Joshua's shoulder. Then the muffled answer, "Mai."

"Can she have a piece of candy?" the woman asked Joshua.

"Sure," he answered. "You want a piece of candy, sweetie?" He tickled Mai.

Mai took the offered candy, and she smiled shyly at the woman.

"What do you say, child?" Her father prompted.

"Arigato?" she replied.

"English, baby," he chided.

"Tank oo," she said with a smile.

Sylvia's attention turned back to Seth. "Well, young man, she called someone, and a young blonde woman came and picked her up. I don't know any more than that. She said she was going to stay with this gal for a while. There was some other creepy guy who came in asking for her not long after she left. It was the day after, I believe," she added with disgust. "Greasy black hair, beady eyes. I didn't tell him nothin'. He gave me the creeps." She shook her head, "Didn't tell him nothin'." She continued as she walked away.

"We're not much further than we were." Seth's face was miserable. "I've talked to all the girls Gwen might have gone home with already."

"And you've already talked to the preacher?" Joshua asked as they passed the church parking lot. He pulled to a stop at the park while Junko took Mai to play on the slide.

"Yes, I have so, what do we do now?" Seth opened his door and sat half out of the car, playing with a stick he had picked up from the grass. "Perhaps Gwen needs me and I can't even find her." He broke the stick into pieces and threw down a piece at a time angrily.

"We will have to leave for home no later than tomorrow noon. A message in the paper or on the message board is out of the question."

"I'm out of ideas." Seth threw the rest of the stick down.

"It's about noon," Joshua mused looking at his watch. "Let's catch something to eat at the Diner. " Joshua waved and motioned to Junko.

"I can put a message on the board at the Diner. It's a longshot, but better than nothing." He put his leg in the car and slammed the door shut.

"This afternoon I want to drive by the old farm place before we leave for home. You coming with us or do you have something else you want to do?" Joshua pulled back on the street heading toward the Diner.

"I'll come with you. I'd like to see the old house, and I don't have any new ideas. Everything is packed and ready to go."

Joshua parked in front of Grandpa's Kitchen restaurant. Walking to the door he held it open for Junko and Mai. Once inside, Joshua stopped to chat with a couple of old friends. "Well, how are you doing, Mary Beth? I'd like you to meet my wife and daughter..."

Seth nodded at several people before stopping to look at the pictures that covered the walls and pinning his message to the board. Grandpa's Kitchen was a landmark here from way beyond his remembrance. This town had been their hometown. "Hey, Jo, remember this?" He pointed to a high school football team photo as his brother approached.

"That is sure a trot down memory lane," Joshua said with a snort. "We used to play some football when I was in the Marines, but it's been years now. That's that game we played against Croftersville."

An older man stood up and put his hand on Joshua's shoulder. "And you, young man, intercepted the pass that the Croftersville quarterback threw at the second and goal at the two-yard line. You ran it ninety-eight yards back to win the game. I'll never forget that play. Everyone in the stands was on their feet screaming 'go, go, go!' What a night. We were hoarse when that was over. You weren't the biggest, bulkiest player we ever had, but I can't think of anyone better or faster."

"Coach Williams, what a surprise!" Joshua gripped his old coach's hand. "So good to see you."

The coach continued to point to several pictures and share his memories. "MacDonalds always had a good name around here. Seth did well in football, but, Seth, you were better here." The man stopped and pointed at the track pictures. "Seth was a long-distance runner second to none."

"Coach, what happened? I thought you planned to move to Florida?" Joshua asked.

"I did move to the Sunshine state, but I gotta come home to get my fix on occasion." He grinned. "You know family won't leave where they were raised, so I have to come back a few times a year."

"Good to see you. Tell your wife howdy for us," Joshua said.

"I'll do that. She'll be glad to know I saw you boys. She's waitin' in the car, so you have a good day, now."

Seth picked a booth toward the back and slid in. "Thanks, Marcia," he said as the waitress handed him a menu. "My brother and his wife will be sitting down too. Better bring another menu."

Joshua slid into the booth. "They still have good batter-fried chicken and home fries? I think Junko would like that. I'm looking at some barbequed beef. I think I'll get spicy. That's the way I like it."

"Marcia," Seth nodded at their waitress. "We're ready—Say, Marcia, you know where Gwen is? I heard she's been in an accident while I was away, and I..."

"Seth, I think she's moved. I don't know where. With that broken leg, she's not been around since the accident. Can't help you. You ready to order?"

"Moved? What..."

"Car—slid off the road. Kinda busy, fella. You want to talk I get off in two hours..."

"That's all right. Yeah, we'll take one order of three-piece home-style breaded chicken, three orders of home fries..." Seth waited until the waitress returned to the order window. "I don't know, Jo, this is getting over the top frustrating."

"Boy howdy. You can say that again." Joshua took a sip of his soft drink. He scarcely noticed as a lanky policeman entered the busy restaurant and looked over the crowd. The man approached their table, pulled up a chair from a nearby, and straddled it.

Joshua looked into chocolate brown eyes, inspected the black hair, slightly tanned face then did a double-take. "Chuckie! Chuckie Malone! What in the world!" Joshua became animated. "Man, it's been centuries! You don't look too bad, buddy, for a man our age!" They vigorously shook hands. "What are you doing in that uniform?"

"Joshua MacDonald, what y'all doin' back here, you old coyote?" Chuckie grinned.

"Just back for a few days to see the sights and show my wife the old farm. Say, meet my wife, Junko, and this is our little girl, Mai." He nodded and they swapped smiles. "So, what's up, buddy? You know—I'm in shock—you in that uniform." Joshua looked amused as well as shrewd. "I distinctly remember your love for that uniform back in the good ole' days—and how you expressed yourself when I enlisted."

"Times they do change," Chuckie said rubbing the side of his jaw self-consciously. "Ya know I think bein' young once gives me an edge," the officer nudged his pal. "I can anticipate things before they happen, ya know."

"I can see how that might work." Joshua raised an eyebrow and laughed. "You know Seth, of course. We've been looking for his wife. You don't have any ideas do you?"

Officer Malone frowned at Seth. "Yeah—I know Seth. How ya' doin', buddy?" He closely inspected the younger brother through wizened eyes.

Seth stirred his coke with his straw and looked down at the table. "Better—I'm doin' better." He cleared his throat and looked up. "I've been gone a few weeks, ya' know."

"I've noticed. No calls of loitering, or..." Chuckie paused, "or other things. No, since the accident I haven't seen nuthin' of Gwen, but she's prob'ly still laid up."

"Accident—well, we just found out about the accident. I've been working with Jo here for a couple weeks and couldn't get ahold of her, and now...You don't know where she's laid up, do you?" There was a ray of hope on Seth's face.

"Nope. I try not to meddle where I ought not to be." Chuckie Malone spoke abruptly.

"So, did you ever marry that little gal..." Joshua paused trying to remember a name.

"Arabella," Chuckie supplied. "No. No, she married Avery. Some of us have lonely lives by choice—some by chance." He gave Seth a reproachful look.

Seth swallowed his pride. "Joshua's been away, Malone. He doesn't know anything—no details anyway. You and I know the downside of things—and I have a lot to thank you for. I haven't always cared for the uniform you're wearing either. I know if I hadn't been a MacDonald, and you hadn't been my brother's friend things would've gone a lot worse for me. Gwen deserves better'n what I've given her, but if she'll give me the chance I am going to give her the better things she deserves."

"I certainly hope so, buddy..." Chuck Malone's brown eyes drilled into Seth's. "I certainly hope so. Well, Joshua, I gotta be goin'. Come see me sometime when I'm off duty and we can swap stories," he said as he got to his feet. "You goin' to be around for a time?"

"No, we're heading out tomorrow." Joshua was shocked and subdued by the exchange. "We need to get back. You remember Laura? She and her husband are flying back from overseas at the end of this week. I'm anxious to see her."

"Remember Laura?" Officer Malone exploded. "How could I ever forget Laura? She was the prettiest gal. I had my first crush on Laura Eliz'beth. Bet you never figured out why I was such a good friend." He winked at Joshua. "Now that's someone you kin remember me to, give her my love, and a big ole' squeeze fer me, buddy." He turned to Seth and sobered. Speaking more kindly than before, he said, "I don't know where Gwen is, fella', but if I see her, I'll put in a word for ya. Take care, y'all." He was gone as quickly as he had come.

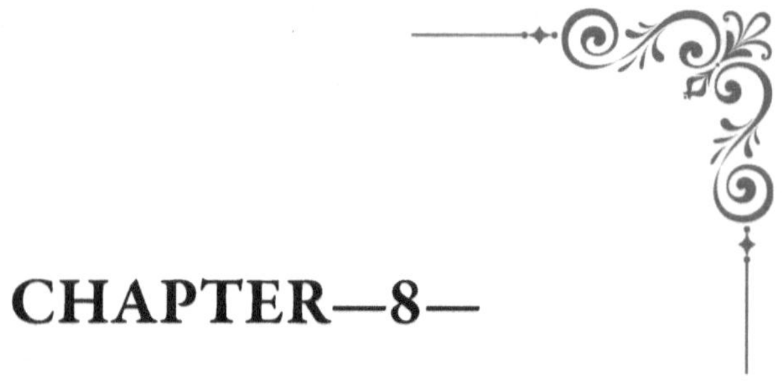

CHAPTER—8—

The road wound and curved from the valley up into the mountains, switching back and forth. The beautiful menagerie of native trees made the drive to their old family farm peaceful and relaxing.

The sunshine played through the leaves on the trees as Seth opened his eyes. "Odd, how things change and stay the same, isn't it, Jo? It's quite beautiful out here, and not near as far from town as I remember."

"There's a few more neighbors out here than there used to be." Joshua slowed along some of the back roads, checking the names on the mailboxes. "And some of the same families are still in the same old places. Wish we had time to visit more of the family." He turned and drove at a snail's pace down the gravel road. "There it is." Joshua stopped the car beside the driveway.

"The barn could use a coat of paint, but it's not in bad shape. The old shed must have leaned too far—it looks gone now," Seth said. "It looks like the house has been empty for a while." Seth pointed out.

"So many memories here." Joshua grieved. "Too bad it's empty. Houses go downhill so fast when they're not lived in." Joshua pulled into the drive and drove slowly up the long driveway to the farmstead and parked. "I guess you haven't been out here for a while then either?" Joshua slammed his car door and went around helping his girls out.

"No, I was just slogging through one day at a time. I never even brought Gwen out here. I was going to once, but something came up." Seth leaned against the fender. "Oh-oh, looks like we're caught." He turned as a big car rolled up the driveway toward them. A short, balding man about fifty years old hopped out and walked toward them holding out his hand in a friendly gesture.

"Are you the folks that called about looking at the place?" he asked.

"No, our folks used to own this farm. We were just strolling down memory lane." Joshua shook the man's hand.

"What a coincidence," the man replied, as a shiny silver-blue van skimmed up the drive and stopped. "This must be the folks then," he said.

A tall, thin dark-haired man followed by his tall blonde wife both stepped out of opposite sides of the van. The realtor extended his hand again.

"Ray Harris. I trust you are the people I spoke to on the phone?"

"Yes, we called when we saw this place was on the market," the man said.

"This is quite a coincidence." Mr. Harris returned to his explanation of a few minutes before. "These folks here said their family used to own this farm also at one time. Maybe you are acquainted?"

"Rachel! What—? " Seth stepped out of the shadows. "I haven't seen you for most of a year now, and Lance! How ya' doin'!" He pumped his brother-in-law's hand in a warm greeting. "Man, you two are a sight for sore eyes!"

"It's a good thing he isn't more excited." Joshua stepped forward. "He'd probably give you a kiss."

"Joshua!" Rachel squealed in surprise, grabbing him in a huge hug.

"Careful, careful, sis," he cautioned, wincing in pain from his wounds.

"I'm so sorry," she apologized barely restraining herself. "What have you done to yourself, baby brother?" she chided him.

"It's a long story." He brushed off her concern. "I've brought back my wife and baby, and..."

His words got lost at that point, "Wife? Baby?" Rachel exclaimed. "Where?"

Joshua grinned at Mr. Harris, who stared in amazement, "That's the way it is in my family. We men don't count for anything. It's the wives and especially the 'babies' part. This, Mr. Harris, is my sister whom I haven't seen in—over fourteen years? There were ten of us children."

Mr. Harris turned and looked at the house and landscape in awe. "You folks probably know more about this place than I could ever show you," he said. "Do you still want to look?"

"Don't let us intrude," Joshua said. "We were just driving by and wanted to visit with our ghosts of yesterday. We had no idea it was for sale, and we aren't looking to buy. Rachel, this is my wife and daughter, Junko and Mai," he said. "We'll catch up on family news later. Lance?" Joshua extended his hand. "You two go ahead with Mr. Harris. I wanted to show my girls where I grew up. Do you mind, sir?" He asked the agent.

"That's fine with me," Mr. Harris answered. "Do your kids want to get out Mr. McCullough?"

"If you don't mind," Lance said. "If ten kids didn't destroy the place, four more won't either."

"This is our childhood home," Joshua told Junko, as they walked around the outside of the homestead.

"It's too bad it has been allowed to run down." Seth shook his head. "Remember how particular Mom was about her flowers?" He pointed at a jumbled, overgrown bed of flowers, then grinned at Joshua. "The garden was that acre over there."

Joshua repeated Seth's words in Japanese and Junko's eyes grew wide. "One acre?" She stopped to look at another weed-strewn piece of property.

Joshua laughed. "I think it was probably larger than one acre, Seth. It sure seemed like it. Dad's shop looks a bit forlorn also." He stopped to peer into a dusty building as they passed. "He was always so careful to keep it neat and in order."

Seth ambled up to a small faded red outbuilding and opened the creaky door. "There haven't been hens in this hen house for a long time. This path needs young feet to keep it well-worn like it used to be. It's overgrown and almost completely choked by weeds now." Seth took the lead mashing down some of the overgrowth as they walked along a vague path.

Joshua kept up a steady narration to Junko leading out to the barn. He pointed out the area where the orchard had been, where the path up to the back pasture had been, and other places of interest of his childhood.

"And now we come to our favorite entertainment center." Joshua stood outside the old barn. "This used to look huge to us as children, and it's bigger than it looks today. We had so many memories in here." Joshua looked into the now-empty, faded red barn and named the landmarks inside. "Nellie's stall here and Bob's stall was over there." They walked down the alleyway. "Indiana's stall, Bill—the other pony, Sonny," he kept pointing to the different stalls. "We milked cows on the other side of the manger there."

"Yeah," Seth commented, "We often seemed to be on the wrong end of the work." He climbed up the ladder to the haymow far enough to look around. "Still hay in here. Wonder how long it's been here?"

"The loft was bursting with hay in the fall, and through the winter it slowly dwindled. On rainy days," Joshua told Junko, "we used to come out here and put on 'shows,' we called them. We had an old book with radio plays in it. We practiced those plays, and then Dad and Mom and family, and even friends sometimes, would come out and be our audience. We could all play instruments so we even had music. Mostly we just had fun."

"Whoa, chick-a-biddy," Joshua said capturing Mai as she ran down the wide barn alleyway. "You make a good bird in flight." He picked her up and set her on an empty feed barrel. Brushing the wild hair away from her face, he asked his brother, "Why don't we appreciate what we have?"

"Ook, Daddy. What dat?" Mai pointed to something hanging on a peg above her head.

"Well, look at that!" Joshua gave a low whistle. He lifted down old dusty pieces of leather straps connected by a metal bit that hung on a peg above Mai's head.

"Indiana's bridle." Seth examined the dry leather. "After all these years—"

"—When that pony died Dad took the tractor and a hand shovel. We buried Indiana at the top of the hill that overlooks the river," Joshua told Junko. "There will never be another horse like him."

"A whole horse you bury?" Junko's eyes became wide.

Joshua smiled at her. "He was only a pony, but it was a whole pony." He took the bridle, wiping the dust off as they sauntered back to the car, and gently laid it in the trunk, and closed the lid.

Junko smiled as she watched Mai join the other children playing in the yard. Joshua and Seth leaned on the hood of the car telling stories of the bye-gone days, watching as Mr. Harris, Rachel, and Lance came around from the back of the house.

Seth stood as they came toward them. "It's sure not been kept up like when Dad and Mom had it, has it, Sis?"

"No, it hasn't. They were always so particular. One of their golden rules was 'A place for everything and everything in its place,'" Rachel said.

"The bones are still good, though," Mr. Harris said, putting in a good word.

"Well, yes, the bones are still good, but the meat has gotten expensive." Lance frowned at the idea of repairing and renovating.

Mr. Harris looked dejected. "You can make an offer, and we can go from there. If you are interested." He shrugged.

"The old MacDonald had a farm place still has a few good years left in it." Rachel smiled at her brothers.

"I don't like to keep people wondering," Lance said. "We'll talk this over, and get back to you this evening, Lord willing. Thanks for taking your time and answering our questions, Ray," he said with a firm handshake.

"That's my business, Mr. McCullough. Say, did I hear you call this the MacDonald farm?" Ray Harris asked.

"Yes, that's my wife's family's name," Lance said.

Mr. Harris turned to Rachel. "Your dad's name wouldn't happen to be Lewis, would it? Lewis MacDonald?"

"Why, yes. That's my daddy's name," she said.

"His wife's name was Agatha. No, no, that's not right. It did begin with an A of some kind. Perhaps, Ahhh... Ahh, Amanda. Was that it?" He looked triumphant.

"Well, yes that's what their names are," Rachel replied.

"They were the nicest folks," Mr. Harris said. "They were the ones that taught my mamma the gospel and eventually my dad came around too. He had been an alcoholic, and they made the difference for us. My two brothers both went into preaching, and my sisters married fine Christian men. I don't fill the pulpit very often, but I do teach, and my wife, she teaches. When you see them tell them Ray Harris thanks them. It wouldn't have happened without their patient teaching and prayer. Give me a call, Mr. McCullough." He slid into his seat and drove off.

"Here's a couple of chairs." Joshua and Seth dusted the few old lawn chairs they found leaning against the trees. Rachel and Junko sat carefully. "This is pleasant," Joshua said.

"Yes, the breeze makes it tolerable here in the shade." Lance listened as the siblings discussed the house and its history, and the children laughed and played tag in the yard.

"This place needs kids and..." Seth looked around at the two-and-a-half-story house, the old garden space, and the rundown orchard. "A little elbow grease 'ud go a long way."

"At least we know the pattern. It kinda reminds me of the old days. How about you two?" Joshua asked.

"The house needs repair, but the structure is still sound," Lance said.

"We just stopped by for memory's sake," Joshua said getting to his feet. "Seth has been trying to tie up his loose ends. I'm changing occupations—my family and I will be moving to where Dad and Mom are."

"That's great." Rachel's face was a mix of emotions.

"Rachel, you haven't come to terms. I know you haven't. I've been out to where Dad and Mom are—" Seth said.

"—You've been out to see Dad and Mom? That's where you've been? How'd you get there...and why?"

"I don't know how or why. When Gwen left me a note that she was leaving... I just went crazy...but, the oddest thing happened. Do you know where Mom and Dad are?" he asked.

"No, but they left an address with someone," she said.

"I didn't have it. But...I was so far gone. Only thing I remember—I'm sitting on a curb leaning against something cold and metal, and an older guy, in a suit, is speaking to me. I passed out and the next thing I know the same guy joggles me awake, helps me out of the car, gets my feet pointed up a driveway, and he leaves. I didn't know where I was. It's pitch dark out, but I stumble to the backyard. I sit down listening to someone playing the piano. After a bit, Jo starts talking to me. I thought both of us had died, but I didn't know whether we were in heaven or hell. But he had food and knew what he was doing. You know how Joshua is; he'll keep ya on the straight and narrow, or make ya wish you were. I don't know who that guy was that carried me all that way, but I've turned that corner. Put the past behind me. It's been ten years, Rachel. Dad and Mom have been grieving over us..."

"I've been ashamed of how I stomped out of their lives. I can't forget my behavior," Rachel said, as she and Lance stood also.

"You know what it is?" Seth asked.

"Lance says it's pride, and it's wrong. That even if my parents wouldn't forgive me, I should do my part." She looked down at the toes of her running shoes.

"First I made things right with God, and then with Dad and Mom. I've been trying to find Gwen—Ben from the car wash told me this morning she was in a car accident. I've looked everywhere. I checked at the hospital. No leads, except some other creep, is looking for her." He frowned. "If she'll give me another chance, with my family praying for me, I'll make it this time." He ran his fingers through his hair.

"He's right, sis. Mom and Dad would welcome you back, but... We need to be getting back to the motel," Joshua said changing the subject. "Mai needs a nap before supper and we may yet leave tonight or early in the morning. I'll give you my number, Rachel. Maybe we can get together sometime. That number will get me anywhere. Seth may have to hire a PI since we need to get back to Dad and Mom's. Laura is supposed to get back in a few days and I want to be there," Joshua said.

"How is Laura doing?" Rachel asked wistfully twisting a strand of her blond hair.

"From all reports, she seems to be doing fine, but Laura is on vacation and we're planning a surprise. You know how surprises go." He gave Rachel a farewell hug and shook Lance's hand. "Give me a call," he said and hurried his family into the car.

CHAPTER—9—

Joshua looked in his rear-view mirror at Seth, "Something told me to back off, leave our number. Let them have some space. We'll put Mai down for a nap and I could use some rest."

"Yeah, I haven't been sleeping well. I'm beat too," Seth said.

AFTER HIS NAP, SETH rolled off the spare bed, stretched, and walked to the stuffed chair by the motel window. "All of my belongings are packed from the apartment and loaded into the rental trailer and the load is secured." He dropped into the chair. "Are you guys ready to go for supper?"

"Mai and Junko are up and everyone's got shoes on. I'd say..." Joshua stopped as his phone rang. "Howdy," he answered. "Sure—directions? Okay, we'll be there in about what? Half an hour? All right. Good 'nough. Bye." He hung up and grinned at the others. "Rachel and supper. Let's go. We'll stop at the mini-mall on the way and pick up some stuff." Joshua waited for everyone to get settled into the vehicle, and then pulled down the street the few blocks to the mall. "We don't want to be too eager, but Mom always said, 'A man's gift maketh room for him...' How about a fresh loaf of this apple fritter bread?" Joshua pointed to the bakery items in the case.

Junko whispered and pointed to an item in the case. "Yes." Joshua picked up the small pitcher of honey butter. "This will be nice too."

"And some chocolates..." Seth picked up a box of hand-dipped chocolates.

"A small bouquet of ruffled pansies. Mom liked pansies." Joshua put the items on the counter to be rung up.

In the car a few minutes later Joshua asked, "Now the question is, can you get to their house?" He pulled back on the street to finish their journey.

"I betcha I can," Seth said. "Go down here four traffic lights. Turn right. Down three traffic lights, turn left. Four blocks, then slow down and count three houses on the right. There you are, the brick veneer on your left..." Seth directed Joshua.

Seth rang the doorbell, then stood aside for Junko, Mai, and Joshua.

"Surprise!" Joshua said when Rachel answered the door. "Well, not much of a surprise...but here we are." He handed her the gifts.

"Oh, wow! Thank you. How thoughtful." She smiled, breathing in the fragrance of the pansies. "So much—you'll have to help me carry them. Lance? He's directing the kids in setting the table...Lance? This bread and butter will go great with the home-canned peaches and spiced pears."

"Yes?" Lance puttered up behind Rachel.

"Lance, take care of these pansies while I take these items and go finish the meal." Rachel handed him the flowers.

"This is a nice house," Joshua said as they sat down in the living room while Rachel put the finishing touches on the meal.

"Thanks," Lance replied. "We've enjoyed it here, but it's time to get out of Dodge, Festus." He laughed. "To have more freedom and more room. I was raised on the edge of a small town. Rachel and I both like the freedom of the country. We want that for our kids too."

"Did you make an offer?" Seth asked.

"We did. It's less than the asking price and we just left it to the Lord," Lance replied with a shrug. "There are two issues we have been discussing since this afternoon." Lance changed the subject.

"Let's hear them." Joshua sat back.

"I would appreciate a prayer before we go any further." Lance paused and bowed his head. After the prayer, he continued, "The issues mostly deal with Seth, Gwen, and Rachel. Seth, I want you to hear me out, buddy. We know where Gwen is. We have talked to her about...what you said. Now, listen, and don't storm out. Gwen has watched you killing yourself for eight years now. She doesn't—she says she can't take anymore. It's killing her too."

The words hit Seth like bullets from a machine gun. He had hoped that the change in his appearance and demeanor would help persuade her to trust him—to give him another chance. Seth's jaw muscles twitched, and the world closed in on him, choking him. He had to get away. He got to his feet. However, time stood still. Things moved in slow motion. He gasped for air as the room spun and blackness enveloped him, and he knew nothing.

He floated above the darkness in slow motion like a disconnected spirit. Someone was rubbing his hands, patting his face, and trying to get his circulation working. Seth spoke in rambling non-thoughts as someone put cool cloths on his face. A pinpoint of light appeared in his darkness while he muttered. The cool cloths continued, and Seth kept muttering. He stopped and listened. "Gwen? Is that you?"

"Sit up, would you? I can't help you where you are," she said in her pleasant, soft voice.

"What?" He twisted away, trying to sit up. Was he dreaming? He couldn't understand what she said. Someone put cool cloths on his face again.

"Hush, and drink this." It sounded like Gwen.

"What is that?" He twisted away. "Naw, I don't want that stuff. It's nasty." It spilled when he pushed it away. He was still lying on the floor, but the circle of light got larger. "Hey, Jo, tell Gwen—wait, I've had enough of those things on my face. I don't want that stuff to drink either." He came out of his ranting and sat up abruptly.

"You tell her yourself, brother." Joshua held a cloth.

"What?" Seth's mind swirled.

"You keep telling me to tell Gwen this, that, or the other thing…You tell her yourself, dude." Joshua twitched his head toward the sofa.

"Where have you been?" Seth turned his head, and his eyes and brain focused on Gwen.

"I might ask you the same question." She sat with her broken leg propped up on a footstool.

"Yeah, but I asked first."

"I've just been waiting for you to come back from never-never land." She smiled. "You gave us a scare, fella."

"I think this has done its duty," Joshua indicated the washcloth, "I'm going to let you two iron things out, and I'm going to go catch up with Rachel and Lance."

"HOW'S IT GOING?" RACHEL handed Joshua a breadstick when he joined them in the kitchen.

"Time will tell," Joshua said.

"At least they're talking. We've been praying for those two for so long," Lance said. "We've been afraid Seth would kill himself with the life he was living. We tried several things…Nothing ever worked."

"It's like Seth said a few nights ago—some things require the participation of all parties," Joshua said. "You can't change someone else. They have to change themselves."

"That's true," Rachel said. "How about yourself? What brought you back, and how did you find Dad and Mom?"

"That's a long story, most of which I can't share." Joshua rubbed his chin in thought. "I can tell you this, it wasn't my purpose or my doing. God opened the door and threw me in."

"EVERYBODY LEAVE?" SETH called after half an hour.

"No, Seth. We're all in here," Rachel called back.

"Joshua—Lance, come give us a hand?"

"You're quite a pair." Lance helped Gwen stand and get her crutches under her.

"You still light-headed, or no?" Joshua gave Seth a hand. "We started with the salad already...waited like one hog for another," Joshua said with a chuckle as they came into the dining room.

"Kids, c'mon." Rachel brought in several covered dishes. "Here, Lance, get Gwen settled. Seth, sit here. We'll just let you two entertain us..."

"This sure smells good, Rachel. Lasagna. Yum. We'll eat our salad last." Seth took Gwen's hand during the prayer. "That's kind of clunky." Seth smiled as Gwen tried to scoop out a portion. "Here, let me help." He gave her a portion then took his.

"Thanks," she said.

"Da nada." He winked.

"This is awkward with this stupid leg like this." Gwen frowned.

"How long will you be in that cast?" Joshua asked.

"Another week. It wasn't a bad break, just a hairline fracture."

"That's good. You'll probably have a boot after the cast comes off. You need to be careful you don't strain it. How did it happen?" Joshua asked.

"I was working my shift at the restaurant when some guy came in asking for Gwen MacDonald and said Seth had been in an accident and was on his way to the hospital. So I clocked out and headed for the hospital. There's that curve down there by Brayton's Hollar. I wasn't going fast…It's a good thing. I came to the curve in the road and didn't have any brakes."

"That's odd," Seth said, shaking his head. "I just worked on those brakes that week when you told me they were hanging up…" He stopped speaking, his words trailing off.

"That's what I told the insurance man. Insurance had it inspected and said the brake lines had been tampered with."

Seth's face paled and he shot a look across the table at Joshua. "The guy looking for…"

"That'd be my guess," Joshua said.

"What are you two talking about?" Lance asked.

"Let me think—I'll tell you later," Joshua said.

"Gwen and I have some news," Seth said with an abrupt change of subject. "Gwen's coming home with us. You know, Joshua, Chuckie was right. Gwen didn't make a choice to be lonely, and I don't have the right to ask it of her."

"Chuckie?" Gwen questioned.

"Yeah, an old friend of mine," Joshua said.

"Gwen doesn't know him as your friend Chuckie. She knows him as Officer Charles Malone." Seth picked up Gwen's hand, examining it with downcast eyes. He swiftly looked into her face. "You know, I love you very much," he whispered.

She smiled, a gentle look in her eyes. "Yes, I know. If I hadn't known that—I wouldn't have been able to hold on for the last eight and a half years."

Joshua had been away, but the story was evident, and he didn't need the book. *Funny, people are the same no matter where they are. His heart ached. Chuck Malone wasn't one to fall in love with just anyone. Joshua knew Seth, and he was sure he knew Gwen.* He sighed.

"I'm going to have to rent a car to get us back to Dad and Mom's though." Seth paused as he ate. "This food is excellent, Rachel. She always was a good cook," he said to Lance. "Well, almost always." He and Joshua laughed. "We won't tell anyone about the half a cup of salt in the cake."

"I had to start somewhere." Rachel had a grieved look on her face. "They just won't let a body live nothin' down." She smiled at her brothers.

Rachel and Lance exchanged a quick look. "Umm," Lance said, "that was the second thing on our list. Rachel has decided she needs to talk to her Dad and Mom."

"If it were one of my children," Rachel said, "I couldn't stand it. There's no reason for me not to make it right. I've hurt Dad and Mom, but I'm the one I've hurt most. Just look, my kids are growing up with only half a family. My husband has never met my parents. What kind of a dope am I?"

"No worse than the rest of us," Joshua said. "It may have been longer before my return if God hadn't opened the door."

Seth leaned back in his chair. "You should see Michael and Lewis. How many years has it been? Same for you as it was for me, right? Man, was I surprised. I can hardly wait till Laura and Anna get home."

"When are you planning to leave?" Lance asked. "We can't be ready tonight."

"How about tomorrow noon or maybe one o'clock?" Joshua said. "We are ready to go. Seth even has his stuff packed and in a trailer. Is there anything else you want us to get out of your apartment, Gwen?"

"I have the things packed I wanted out of the apartment. It will need to be put in the rental trailer. And I have my personal stuff with me here."

"We'll get it out for you...but you keep away from the apartment, Gwen. Matter of fact stay out of sight anywhere," Joshua said.

"I wouldn't be much help anyway—" Gwen's gaze was puzzled.

"I don't want to alarm anyone, but if your brakes *were* tampered with, and we know there was some stranger at the hospital asking for you..." Joshua shrugged. "We can't be too careful. And when we leave here, we'll coordinate the times and meet up down the road at a set time and place."

"Wow, just wow. You think all of this is necessary?" Gwen's eyes were large grey orbs, and her face had blanched.

"Yes, I do. An ounce of prevention..." Joshua squinted at Seth.

"Is worth a pound of cake," Rachel finished for him. "You'd think you have been working in police and crime work, baby brother. You never did tell me about your injuries."

"That's all right, sis. Some things are best left alone." Joshua raised an eyebrow at her.

"Rachel, if we're going to get this together, you and the kids get to packing. Your brothers and I will get to coordinating—where's our maps and whatnot?" Lance turned to the task at hand.

"Guess you're right. I'd better get hopping," Rachel said.

"Good, let's do it." Lance unfolded his Atlas and pulled his pen out of his shirt pocket.

CHAPTER —10—

"So how many more do you have stashed away?" Brother Wilson asked with a half-smile.

"What?" Mr. MacDonald asked in mock surprise.

"We began with Lewis, Laura, Anna, and Michael. That's four."

"Surely." Mr. MacDonald nodded.

"Then, there comes a Seth and Joshua. Two more— that makes six," Brother Wilson continued.

"Yes, four plus two equals six," Mr. MacDonald said.

"Now, Rachel. That's seven. I was just wondering if there were any more, ah..." Brother Wilson searched for words.

"Arrows in the quiver?" Mr. MacDonald said.

"Why, yes, that's the question." Brother Wilson shook his head.

"When we're finished I'll tell you," Mr. MacDonald said, and then turned as Ethel Rudd touched his sleeve.

"You have such a lovely family," she said. "Bernie and I both came from large families. We planned on a large family but sometimes those things aren't up to us. I'm content to labor where the Lord puts me." She sighed.

"There's a blessing in being content," Mr. MacDonald said. "There is a blessing in being where you are planted, and doing your job even if it appears trivial."

"The proverbial cup of water." Ethel's eyes brightened, and she smiled. "So, how long is your family planning on visiting?"

"Rachel and her family won't be able to stay much over the weekend. Lance, her husband, has to get back to his job, but they want to surprise Laura when she gets back. Joshua and Seth and their families are planning to relocate here in the area."

"It will be nice to have them close. We only have one son, and he lives so far away it is a constant source of sorrow for us," Mrs. Rudd said.

"It will be nice to have them close. It wears on a parent when our children are far away. I guess I'll see y'all tomorrow afternoon. Bernie had some things he wanted me to give him an opinion on. So, I'll be dropping in about four o'clock." Mr. MacDonald and Ethel Rudd walked toward the church house door to leave.

"We'll see you then." She and Bernie continued to their car.

"WHAT A CONGREGATION," Lance said. "Everyone seems genuine and committed."

Mr. MacDonald laughed out loud. "If you don't commit here in this life you won't make it to heaven. Mom and I moved here with Anna and Michael, Lewis, his family, and Laura and her family. Mom and I purchased our land and the land the church house sits on. Lewis and his family lived with us in the house they live in now. Laura and Juan bought the house they live in now. They also found an old schoolhouse that was for sale, which they bought and moved onto the church house property. That was our beginning here. There were only ten of us in the beginning; six adults, one young adult, one teenager, and two babies. I believe there were thirty-nine this evening."

"That's amazing," Lance said.

"We aren't committed to numbers. We are committed to seeking the old paths that walk with God. No bells, no whistles, only His will and His way," Mr. MacDonald said.

Mrs. MacDonald and Rachel came to the living room door. "Hey, you two, we're waiting ice cream and dessert for you, and we don't want to drink the ice cream!"

"I guess we'll have to pick this up later." Lance stood and they walked to the deck.

"We're here. Who's leading the prayer?" Mac asked as they joined the group.

"I've got it covered." Lewis opened his Bible to a scripture, and then led a prayer.

"There're enough young people here, Mac, I'm just going to sit still and let them pass out the dessert," Mrs. MacDonald said. "Thank you." She smiled as someone handed her a bowl.

"Thank you." Mr. MacDonald took his bowl and winked at his grandson, Luke. He leaned over and whispered to Amanda and then they leaned back, sitting on the far side of the patio smirking as Lewis the younger explained a project to his brothers that he was engaged in.

"That reminds me of a story I heard last year..." Seth launched into a funny story. Everyone laughed as Seth got to the punch line. Then they dug in and began to enjoy their dessert as it arrived.

Rachel brought her dessert and sat down beside her parents. "I'm not sure how to say this, but what I did was wrong and I'm sorry. Lance has..."

"Rachel." Mac took her hand.

"Yes, sir?"

"I won't tell you it's all right. I won't pretend that you didn't hurt us horribly. I will tell you we love you and are thankful that you've come back. You've paid a price for your sin, and it's time to go forward. You have a godly young man for a husband and lovely children."

"Dad—and Mom, I love you both. I've hurt myself, and I've robbed my family. My kids have been having the time of their lives today. Lance and you, Dad, have hit it off so well, and I have missed you so much, Mom." She smiled at her mother. "I just had a hole in my life. When others would talk about their dads and moms or families, I couldn't join in. When you first left I would meet our family—aunts, uncles, cousins, whoever, and they would ask after y'all and I didn't have an answer. Thankfully, now I do."

"Laura will be so happy to see you. She has suffered much with the loss of her siblings," Amanda said. "We went so long without any word, wondering, praying, hoping. Now within one month, we have received three of you back. God surely works in mysterious ways, and we praise Him."

"Mommy, Mai." Rachel's youngest son brought a new friend.

"What, honey?" Rachel had only half heard her three-year-old son.

"Mai, mommy," he repeated.

"What a little doll," Rachel said, brushing Mai's shiny black hair back into her French braid. "She has such a creamy complexion—How do you do, Mai?" Rachel smiled.

"Berry well, tankoo," Mai responded to her aunt. "Naniel, not mommy." Mai grasped his little hand and made a straight course toward Junko with Nathaniel in tow.

Rachel looked at her parents with an amused twinkle in her blue eyes. "Sorting things out—I need to get back over there." She stopped to give her parents each a hug and a peck. "We are planning a surprise for our mother hen tomorrow, and I can't let the boys get ahead of me..."

"It's been a long time coming, Mac," Mrs. MacDonald said with a wistful sigh.

"There's no great loss without some small gain— I guess that's true."

"How so...in what way are you meaning?" she asked.

"Well, Ahmanda," he drawled, "how many folks—when things didn't go well for us with the children—assumed that it was our fault? That we weren't doing something right?"

"Yes, I beat myself up—I kept asking myself those same questions. Miz Edith said we were too strict, and Miz Earleen said we were too lenient. Someone else accused me in a backhanded way of not loving the children. I know they didn't mean to be unkind, but they were. Job came to mind when he told his friends, '*No doubt ye are the people and wisdom will die with you.*'"

Mac smiled a humorless smile. "Yes, Job came to mind, '*Doth Job still hold fast his integrity?*' Yet, I knew the values we were teaching were the right ones. I can't change what God has set forth, not for love or money as Granny Belle used to say. But I have a deeper ability to suffer and counsel others—I've been through those valleys myself."

"Hey! You two have been whispering in that corner by yourselves far too long," Lewis Junior called to his parents with a laugh at his joke. "Let's have a song and prayer before everyone goes home...."

ANNA WAS SO GLAD TO be home she could have kissed the ground when she came down the ramp at the airport. A stale film coated her tongue, she could taste tired from the trip. The last piece of her journey would be finished soon. Joy filled her heart and she closed her eyes imagining her home. This trip hadn't been any worse than any other trip, but flying tired not just her body but her spirit as well.

"Where is everyone?" Laura looked for the rest of the family as their baggage began to come down the conveyor.

"Lewis had a sudden last-minute job come up that required Michael and the boys to help. That's why Mr. O'Brien brought your SUV for you. The rest will meet us at Lewis and Donna's. Ruth and

Donna have a special lunch ready so you can eat before you go home to rest," Mr. MacDonald said.

Laura frowned, disappointment and agitation showing in her face and manner. "But they always come to meet us, and Michael said he had a surprise for me, and ..." She was almost in tears.

"Mi Amore—" Juan soothed his wife who was uncharacteristically upset, "do not put yourself out. You know they would be here if they could."

"Anna and I have brought back so many parcels we almost had to buy an airplane to transport them." Laura laughed, her good humor returning as they stowed their belongings into the vehicles.

Anna napped for the short time it took to drive from Hermon to Beetle River, then on to Lewis'sfarm and woke slowly as they turned up the drive. "I am so glad to be home. I don't know why I leave this place." She stretched after she stepped out of the van and inhaled a deep breath, gazing around at her brothers' house, the large barn, and the peaceful scenery. "Michael wrote that there was some excitement, and he would explain when we got home." Anna picked up her bag and turned toward the large house.

"Most of the excitement happened while I was away also," Mr. MacDonald said.

"We were excited to hear about your eyesight returning, Mom," Laura said.

"Yes, but I still need help. Mac, help me find that thing here before we go in." Mrs. MacDonald began rummaging in the back seat.

"Y'all go on in we'll be along shortly." Mr. MacDonald waved for the rest of his family to go on into the house.

When Laura and Juan got to the yard gate, Anna turned to wait for her mom and dad.

"Come on, you two. Didn't you find that thing you were looking for?" Anna's eyes narrowed. "What are you two doing? How funny," she said. "You must not have found that *thing*."

"Surprise!" chorused from inside the house when Juan opened the door for Laura.

"Oh...Oh!" Laura gasped for breath.

"Mi Amore, you must be more careful, especially in your condition," Juan half carried her to the sofa. "A glass of water, por favor... Gracias," he whispered to Donna as he handed Laura the glass.

"Michael," Laura scolded her brother when she could speak, "you didn't warn me!"

"I was sworn to secrecy, and I didn't know Rachel and family would be here."

Rachel pulled up a chair beside her. "Laura Elizabeth," she took her sister's hand. "It's been too long..."

"And you didn't share your news either," Michael said.

"What news?"

"The word 'condition' in this neck of the woods generally denotes..." Michael's final words were drowned in the following laughter.

"That is not exactly how we had intended to make our announcement." Laura frowned at her brother and husband when the noise finally quieted down.

"But—you announced it first." Juan smiled at her.

"Make yourselves homely," Lewis said. "Dad, will you do the honors? Then we can eat, and do some serious catching up."

"I have a verse right here." Mr. MacDonald opened his Bible and read Psalm thirty verse five, *'For His anger is but for a moment; His favor for a lifetime; Weeping may tarry for the night, But joy cometh in the morning.'* Let's pray."

After the amen echoed around the table, Mr. MacDonald held up a hand. "Just a moment, before we dig in. Lewis?" He turned to his oldest son. "Lewis has something he wants to say."

"I'm not good for long announcements." Lewis said, "I guess Laura and Juan, Donna and I began this whole grandchild thing, and it looks as if our portion will end together... That's my announce-ment, so let's eat." Lewis began to pass the food.

Joshua looked across the table at his oldest sister. "Congratula-tions are in order, Sis. This must have been quite a vacation?"

"Family duties in Juan's hemisphere are an experience. When did y'all make it back?" Laura unfolded her napkin and took a sip of tea.

"It's been about four weeks for me. I think it was right after you left. We've been anxious for you to get home."

"I'm glad the journey is over. Anna and I had lots of fun..."

"But you can only have so much fun," Anna said with a chuckle, taking a helping of green beans and bacon before handing it on. She looked over at Michael. "I picked up some of those items you want-ed."

"Your wife's name is Gwen?" Laura asked with a smile at the young woman with her leg in a cast.

"Yes," Seth said.

"I hope everyone is treating you well?" Laura looked across at Gwen. "You've been here not quite a week? And Junko? You've not been here much longer either?"

"Yes. Almost a week." Gwen finished buttering her dinner roll. "These rolls are so good. They remind me of my Alice's." She closed her eyes savoring the flavor.

"Alice? Was that your Aunt?" Seth asked.

"No—a friend and confidant," Gwen said.

"Junko joined me just before we went back to Forrest City for a visit. Then we all made the journey back at the same time," Joshua said.

"That's how Seth and Rachel came back?" Laura guessed.

"No, but that's another story for another day." Joshua finished his steak and potatoes.

"When do Edwardo, Juanita, and Raul come in?" Michael asked.

"Tomorrow late," Juan said. "They were supposed to come in yesterday, but we had several things come up. What happened with the car? You said there was an accident?"

"Yeah, well, those visitors you had at the store a few weeks before you left?" Michael paused and looked down the table at Juan.

"Si, yes, they didn't—" Juan's eyes grew large.

"They did. After they came back, I had decided it would be best to close the store for a few days. I was on my way home, when..."

"I hadn't heard. Are you all right?" Laura's fork clattered onto her plate. "You didn't get hurt?"

"Rolled the car, went to the emergency room. Had a bang on my head but they patched me up. Doctor says I have to be careful still, but nothing major. I can tell you I'm glad y'all have made it home." Michael stuck the rest of his dinner roll in his mouth.

"YOUR FAMILY IS ALMOST—OVERWHELMING." Gwen and Seth strolled along the path under the fruit trees to a small alcove surrounded by flowers at Mac and Amanda's hideaway.

"I'm sorry, babe. I guess I never thought about it before." Seth pursed his lips and frowned.

"It isn't bad, but...coming from just Aunt Zoe and myself, then just you and me for most of the past nine years. Suddenly I find I'm sitting at a lunch table with twenty-three people, all of whom are my close family relatives. I'm just...overwhelmed." Gwen sat on a stone bench with an arched canopy of vines and flowers.

"I guess it's a good thing we aren't all here." He sat beside her.

"Not all here?" She pulled away and stared at him. "Oh, right. You have a brother and sister that aren't here."

"Yes, and James...of course," he said, and sighed.

"This place is heavenly. " Gwen looked around at the arbor covered with blooming roses. To the left was a little fountain of water that splashed onto mossy rocks into a miniature pool of water where tiny silver and gold fish darted in the shade of the overhanging trees.

"This is our lovers' bench." Mrs. MacDonald startled them with a sudden appearance. "Would you like some iced tea?" She laughed as she handed them glasses of cold tea. "I didn't intend to make you jump. It's just hot out here, and I figured I would find you two 'lovers' at this particular spot."

"Thank you, ma'am." Seth took his glass.

Gwen took a sip. "This tea is excellent."

"Thank you." Mrs. MacDonald said. "I'll let you two get back to your conversation. I just thought some refreshment might hit a spot or two. Don't forget to bring your glasses in when you come."

Gwen and Seth watched as Mrs. MacDonald disappeared.

"She seems very thoughtful," Gwen said fanning herself.

"Just don't get her angry." Seth smirked. "I saw her angry once, and she was full of thought, but..." He laughed at the memory. "I was thankful I wasn't the poor man she was angry at."

"I would say if you only saw her angry once in your life, that's a good record. I've been angry with you much more than once in our nine years, love," she said. "Your Dad and Mom... something's different about them."

"They take marriage and family seriously. I just pray, Gwen, that you will give us a chance." He ran his fingers lightly up and down her arm, his eyes serious.

"Time will tell." She looked out at the scenery. "The perfume from those flowers is just right...This spot would be even more heavenly in the moonlight."

"'Scuse me, Uncle Seth and Aunt Gwen," a little voice piped up, "but Mamma and Aunt Laura thought y'all would like to come see some pictures." Seven-year-old Rebecca spoke quite close.

"Whoa, baby! What you doin' scarin' your Uncle Seth out a ten years of growth?" Seth exclaimed.

Rebecca giggled. "Oh, Uncle Seth, I didn't scare you out a ten years growth!"

Seth stood and patted his niece on the head. "Well, it sure 'nuff felt like it. If I don't grow anymore it'll be all your fault, sugarplum. Come on, darlin', duty calls." He winked and offered Gwen a hand.

CHAPTER—11—

"You know, Seth gave it a name." Mr. MacDonald and Lance relaxed in the lawn chairs under Lewis and Donna's shade trees Sunday at the potluck. "He called it a lazy man's salvation—a salvation that doesn't require commitment." Lewis Senior fanned the air with his napkin. "But that's not what Jesus taught or brought. Can you pick out the folks here that are family?"

Lance looked at the group of people. Smoke spilled from the grill as people were laughing and eating. The older children were getting up a volleyball game, and some men were working on a game of horseshoes. "Some people look more like others, but they act like family."

Mr. MacDonald smiled. "They are family. You see, when we moved here we taught the truth. No gimmicks, no buffet-style gospel, just the straight gospel—with love. As family, we get together often, pray for each other and try to support one another. This is our life. It is who we are. The bickering and fighting among saints is caused by a lack of love."

"The old pride of life?" Lance asked.

Lance's daughter Debra ran toward the two men. "Daddy, come play volleyball with us. I want someone who can play good—on my side," she wheedled.

"Just a second, honey. I'm afraid we won't get to finish this conversation on this visit, but it has been a real treat." Lance excused himself.

"Come on, Daddy, please hurry!" The young girl begged.

GWEN HAD EASILY SORTED people into their proper spheres as life settled into a pattern. It was like a dance where everyone knew where they were supposed to be, and when they were supposed to be there. Neither the men nor the women were pushy or domineering. The men were each the head of their respective families. The women were quiet...not shy, not wallflowers, just quiet-spoken and capable.

The atmosphere in Donna's large outdoor *summer* kitchen on this late July day was hot and steamy. There was a light breeze that carried the pungent smell of herbs, spices, and tomatoes everywhere pervading every nook and cranny. If she closed her eyes, Gwen could imagine herself on vacation in Italy or perhaps along the sea coast of Greece. She felt safe and accepted here among the laughter and conversation. The summer kitchen itself was large enough to hold the eight women and the two young girls working together and all of the vegetables and a passel of young children that occasionally wandered through.

"Do you need a break?" Ruth came over to where Gwen was running the food processor. "Go sit by the fan for a bit. I'll take over."

"Thanks, it is hot," Gwen said giving up her spot and moving over to sit in front of a fan, watching as Ruth took over where she had been.

"How is your leg doing?" a small blonde woman asked timidly sitting beside her.

"Much better. I go back to the doctor tomorrow then I should get this boot off." Gwen recognized the shy woman as someone she had met at church. She searched her memory for what information she had overheard. "How about yourself...You were ill a few weeks ago?"

"I've been getting stronger, but I still get tired easily." They were silent for a time, neither one being much at talking.

Gretchen spoke again. "This is fun. Working together like this. I'm glad Miz MacDonald invited me today."

"Everyone seems to get along well." Gwen found the difference between Gretchen and herself to be stark. They were an odd pair. She guessed that their age was nearly the same, yet the similarity ended there. Gretchen was like a timid flower that needed coaxing to bloom. Both had suffered much from husbands who had suffered from addiction. But where the suffering had seemed to grind Gretchen down and wear her away, Gwen had learned patience and resilience.

"I'm not used to a large family, and I'm still trying to figure things out," Gwen said.

"I have two sisters and a brother, but we aren't close," Gretchen said. "Within the last two months, I have grown close to the people from church. They are like the family I never had, and I've learned so much about the Bible, Jesus, and salvation. My husband, William, and I have been given a new life."

"Are you ready to go home now, kiddo?" Mrs. MacDonald came over to Gretchen.

"Yes, all I have to do is round up my young 'uns. Nice to talk to you. I'll put you in my prayers," Gretchen said to Gwen. She stooped to gather up her belongings then stood to leave. "Thank you to everyone for your patience. I've never preserved anything before, and I have enjoyed learning. William will enjoy the fruit of our labor."

"Here." Donna and Ruth packed up samples of tomato sauce and ketchup.

"Thank you all so much. Billy—Billy you and Lolly bring the baby and come on now." Gretchen stepped out the door as the children came running.

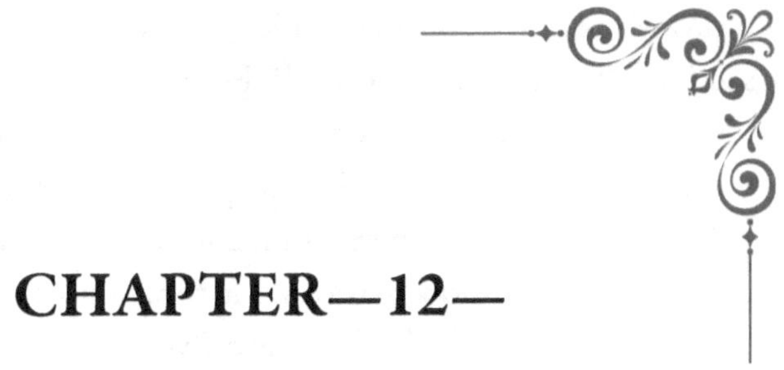

CHAPTER—12—

Ruth poked at the microwave buttons and waited for her cinnamon roll to heat up. "Well, I think the last month we put up enough tomato sauce, ketchup, soup, ragu...everything tomato for an army. I won't miss the hot weather of July. One more week and it is back to the old grind, my friend. Are you up to the task?"

"It gets harder for me to leave, but praise God, this is my last year." Michael pulled two cinnamon rolls off the pan and plunked them on his plate. "The call of the locusts and the coming of the fall weather...I miss that."

"It's too easy to get set in your ways. This gives you opportunities to see things."

"Yeah, all sorts of things." He stuck his plate in the microwave as she took hers to the table.

"Aye, Michael, you have to think of opportunities," she teased. "So, what are you going to do when you've finished?"

"Well." He spoke seriously as he brought his plate over and sat down at the table in the breakfast nook at Mac and Amanda's hideaway. "I think I'll start my own business."

"You do?" Ruth blinked in surprise. "What kind of business?"

"I think I'll come back and open a pool hall."

"Aye, Michael!" Ruth rolled her eyes at him and then took a sip of her tea.

"Maybe not that business." He grinned at her. "Ruth—" He tore a section off of his cinnamon roll. His voice took a thoughtful turn. "A few weeks ago my brothers were commenting on something."

"Why am I not surprised?" She picked at her roll with her fork.

"They do tend to comment on a lot of things, but, well, Ruth..." He was stumped at how to go on. He took a sip of tea.

"Michael Hosea, I don't believe I've ever seen you at a loss for words." Ruth continued pulling her roll apart carefully.

"Well, their comments kinda made me wonder. There are several things I have thought about doing when I finish school. For work I mean. But I can't think of my future life without thinking of marriage." Michael began toying with his napkin.

"I didn't know you were interested in anyone." Ruth frowned as she tried to recall a name.

"Well, I am." He frowned at her response and lack of attention.

"Oh? Who is this young woman?"

"That's what I was getting to. It's kinda-sorta you, Ruth." He was still irked that she was not paying attention.

Ruth stopped pulling her cinnamon roll apart and put her fork down. She was silent, slowly wiping her fingers on her napkin. Cradling her cup in her hands she asked, "Why?"

"Why?" he repeated startled. "Why? There are many reasons. I could look forever and never find anyone as perfect as you...and I can't imagine my life without you."

"What about...Donna?"

He looked puzzled. "What about Donna?"

"Yes...or Laura?"

Michael raised an eyebrow at her as if she was confused. "What do you mean?"

"I can't imagine my life without you either, but I can't imagine my life without your folks, or without Lewis, Donna, Laura, and Juan. You are people I love..."

"But not people you would marry," he said.

"Exactly."

"So, what you are saying is you aren't wanting to marry me?" He ran his finger over the handle of his cup.

"Michael...you are my dearest friend, and friendship is a good start. If you had asked me a year ago, I would have said yes...but sometimes the obvious course is not the correct one. I'm still praying that God will show me the direction for my life. At this point, it doesn't seem that marriage is in my future. At least not for now." The haunted look returned to her eyes.

"So, my lady," he lapsed into their familiar terms, "that's what has been bothering you."

She stared silently at the table for a few minutes then looked up at him, agony mirrored in her eyes. "Yes," she whispered.

"I'm so sorry," he said.

"I know, Sir Lancelot—that is why you are my dearest friend."

"So, the answer is no." He looked out the window as if looking for answers that were not there.

With her cup partway to her lips, Ruth stopped.

"Aye, Michael." He spoke for her.

"Michael, I do love you...but there is love—and then there is love. Life has a way of changing, sometimes slowly and sometimes quickly. But someone will come into your life that will be important. It will be neither by day nor night—" she said.

"Neither walking nor riding, neither dressed nor undressed. I've read that story also, Ruth." Michael sat back in his chair and exhaled. "There are a lot of important people that come and go in our lives, Ruth. One thing I know is I will always love you and I will wait until you feel the time is right."

"Oh, Michael." She picked up her cup and looked at him sadly.

"GWEN?" MRS. MACDONALD called.

"Yes, ma'am," Gwen said putting down her newspaper. She looked over at her mother-in-law.

"Could you take Mac out some iced tea? He's been outside almost all afternoon working in the orchard and..."

"I sure can. I've been sitting too long. Just point me in the right direction." Gwen smiled at Mrs. MacDonald.

"Here's the cup and the thermos." Mrs. MacDonald handed the items to Gwen. "I'll help you out the door, and you just follow the path up around and it will take you to the orchard. I'm working on a project and Mac should have been in some time ago."

"That door always gives me a moment of pause even though Seth has explained the theory behind it." Gwen waited as Mrs. MacDonald placed her hand on the woodwork, and what had looked like a large window slid open. Stepping into the late summer afternoon sun, she followed the pea gravel path. Soon the summer would yield to autumn, a time of year Gwen loved. At home Ralph, her gardener, would be preparing her estate for fall. The smell of the leaves and gardens and fields, the roadside vendors, all the fall memories made her homesick. It had been few and far between, but she had been able at least once a year to slip away for a few days to visit her home. Seth had never questioned where she went, and she never revealed any more than that she was going home for a visit. Strange she had never thought of her husband as a man of mystery, but his family and all this was a side she never imagined. He was still unaware of her secret.

"Mr. MacDonald?" Gwen looked around, bewildered at not seeing her father-in-law.

"I'm up here." He said peering out from between branches of a fruit tree.

"Mother sent you some iced tea. I'm supposed to scold you for not coming in for a rest," Gwen said.

"Consider me scolded then," Mr. MacDonald said. "And thank you." He backed down the ladder and hung his basket of ties on a ladder rung. After walking to a nearby bench he sat in the shade of a plum tree and took the jug of tea. "Your leg seems to have healed?"

"Good as new," Gwen said. "I'm glad to have that boot off. What are you doing out here?"

"These trees will need some pruning when they go dormant and...Say, I've got a cup here. Would you like to use this glass for tea?"

"Sure. It's kind of hot out here..."

"And you know what they say, don't you?" Mr. MacDonald asked with a twinkle in his eyes.

"I will when you tell me," Gwen said with a laugh.

"Never drink unless you're alone, or with someone."

"I'd never heard that one before."

She shook her head as he handed her the glass of tea. She listened to her father-in-law explain that he used the colored strips to signal branches that would need pruning, or in some cases insect damage that needed to be addressed, or other things. Her mind wandered slightly as he talked. He reminded her of her head gardener, Mr. Ralph. Mr. Ralph had treated her as an equal in his explanations, showing her the different flowers and sometimes even different procedures to transplant or reproduce them. Even when she was a child, Mr. Ralph would patiently take her on tours around her aunt's property. The reminder of home was like the opening of a wound. Would her Great Aunt Zoe have approved of Seth? She had not married within what was considered her own league nor thought through her decision to marry Seth. It wasn't his ups and downs, but she couldn't put a name to the real problem with Seth. *Oh, Aunt Zoe, I miss you so much*...Aunt Zoe had surprised Gwen on her appraisal of people more than once, and her opinions were always spot-on correct. *Auntie, I know you would've liked Seth and his family. I know you would've.* And Aunt Zoe had insisted on more than one occasion that *it's char-*

acter and the ability to do the right thing for the right reason that counts.

"...so you see we have twenty fruit trees in here, and it's important to keep after them or they'll get away from you."

Gwen's mind came back as Mr. MacDonald came to an end of his explanation.

"Wow, that's a lot of work... Why go to all this trouble to keep your lives simple?" she asked. Thoughts of all kinds fluttered in her mind. The first thing you noticed about this older man was his intense blue eyes that burned with life. He was proper, but not stuffy. A large-boned man with large, strong hands, yet even with the littlest children he was tender and gentle like a mother. She could see where Seth got his love of children.

"We don't make a living here—we live here. It's important to remember where our 'daily bread' comes from. We gain insight from living on the land. There are enough troubled times in the world around us. We don't isolate ourselves from the world, but we try to prepare for whatever may come our way. Proverbs twenty-two verse three tells us *'A prudent man seeth the evil, and hideth himself; but the simple pass on and suffer for it.'* A person will work one way or the other. This is the way we choose. Which would you rather be?"

"But," she cleared her throat and wrinkled her brow, "some things I have done and never questioned the right or wrong of it. There are decisions I have to make. I can't be half-hearted, nor pretend that I'm something I'm not."

"You're right on that, but may I put it into simpler terms?" he said.

"I could use that." Her face puckered into a frown.

"It comes down between the commitment of putting off the old man of sin and taking up the challenge of holy, godly living. The Lord's church has always had to guard against the unconverted amongst them who would turn believers into something less. Something lukewarm," Mr. MacDonald said.

"I had not thought of it like that before," she mused. "I've been struggling." Gwen sat down beside him.

"I can see that," he said.

"Being part of a large family has given me pause." She frowned.

"Has someone been unkind? Is there another reason, apart from the size?" He asked.

"No. No one has been unkind. If I had known I was choosing a family...this one would have been first on my list," Gwen said.

"Is my son not treating you properly?" The older man's brow wrinkled.

"Oh, no, sir. Seth is every inch a gentleman. I could not ask for a more patient, gentle suitor. Maybe that's the problem. You see, he's so patient and loving and that's the side of him I was drawn to first. His love of children makes me want to forget my questions. It would be so easy just to say I accept everything. To fall back into the old relationship." She blushed.

"My dear child, do not think because I'm an old man that I have forgotten the passion of youth, the strong desires between a man and wife," he said. "This orchard looks good on the outside, but it wouldn't look good without care. I search through the trees and branches for anything that's needing attention. If there's something, I flag it. You and Seth made a commitment to each other, and a commitment to God based on what you saw on the outside. You met at church, which is a good start, but— how could you go for almost nine years and not know about his family? How could he go nine years and not know of your circumstances? But at this stage that is not relevant. It comes down to you and Seth and God. You've made the commitment and you need to figure out how to finish this together. This isn't a throw-away issue. How do we get beyond the outside of someone and honestly make it work?"

"I see what you mean." Gwen's brow was still furrowed. "Hmm, lots of things to think on."

"I hope this helps. We will pray...and thank you for the ice tea and the break," he said putting the empty cup on the jug.

"Thank you. I have a lot to pray over too."

"I WANT BOTH OF THESE two precious people to be happy, but is there a good answer?" Mrs. MacDonald asked the next day.

"Gwen said she would pray about it, but sometimes life moves slowly," Mr. MacDonald said. "I feel a special need to pray for Seth and Gwen, and Ruth and Anna as well. I sense a restless spirit in all three of the young women. I would say I'm concerned."

"I believe Michael asked Ruth to marry him. I know she loves him, but...?" She said.

"We need to pray. It's in the Lord's hands. That's all we can do," He said.

CHAPTER—13—

"No, Gwen, I don't understand." Seth scowled. He was not patient at this moment. "I don't understand why you feel as if you're too close to me. I don't seem to be able to get close enough to you." Seth was usually laid back and easygoing. In their nearly nine years together, Gwen had never seen him irritable like this. He had grown different in some way during this last summer, and the blue eyes that always saw the humorous side of things blazed with passion at the moment, not humor.

"Well, I've bought a ticket and I'm leaving tomorrow." She gritted her teeth and her eyes flashed like a childish little girl.

"I don't understand, babe, why?" He took a deep breath to calm the wild beat of his heart.

"I'm a city girl," she said, raising her chin. "I like living in town. Being out here has been peaceful and nice. I love you," she continued more gently. "I even love—all of your family. But I miss the hustle and bustle of the city. I miss being able to...well, I just miss city life." Not able to look into his face, she turned away.

They were again in the arbor. The lush green leaves and the abundant blooming flowers of summer were turning into pre-autumn. Nature roasted in the oven-heat of late July early August. It would soon turn into languid, warm days sliding into cool nights. The flowers sent out their last frantic blossoms as if they could sense this was their last hurrah for the year. Within a few more weeks they would succumb to the advancing cooler weather. Although the water in the fountain still trickled and the fish still played in the shade of the trees they, too, would soon be gone.

Seth was silent, not wanting things to end this way. "I'm sorry I went back to Forrest City," he said bitterly. "If I had not gone back I could have dreamed that it might have been different. This way there is no dream, it's just—the end." He looked toward the setting sun. "I won't see you off tomorrow. I'm not made of stone or wood. I love you too much to watch you go." He turned to her suddenly, encircling her with his strong arms he pulled her toward him, forcing her to look into his face and eyes. "No," he repeated, "I'm not made of stone or wood. I won't kiss you goodbye either. Your lips no longer belong to me. Go back to your city since it means so much."

Gwen was breathless from the power of his nearness as well as from the ferocity of his words, the compelling fragrance of his cologne— all would remain in her memory forever. She could not have replied even if she had the words, for as his last words were spoken, he was gone.

She sat down on the stone bench stunned. Was this really what she wanted, she asked herself. The tears were there but would not come. She felt as if her heart had been ripped out and stomped on, as if she had a raw and bleeding wound. Her Seth that she had suffered for all these years, the man she had put up with all this time, his foibles, his weaknesses, his ups, and downs—he had just left her. She had never seen him so strong, so powerful, and yes, so beautiful. She had never needed him so acutely in her life. Yet he had just left her, and for what? His family? His new life? His God? What had she expected? Had she expected him to become her lame follower and trot by her side in obedience? She had no answer.

So she sat. Was it a minute, an hour, or a day? She did not know. Someone was speaking to her. She looked up to focus on those kindly blue eyes and his voice.

"Daughter? Gwen, can I help?" Mr. MacDonald asked.

"Yes," she said, her voice hollow and dead. "I need a ride to the airport tomorrow."

"Daughter," he said, "I don't know what has happened, but running away is not the answer. You are in no condition to be traveling." He took her cold fingers in his large warm hands. Her face was pale and ghastly as if all the blood had drained out of it.

"Papa, will I have to find someone else to take me then?" she said in a pathetic voice.

"No, no, but please reconsider? You'll break my heart if you leave."

"He left me." Her dazed eyes refused to focus.

"Surely you misunderstood..."

"No, he left me," she insisted.

"If you desire to leave, we will not hold you here against your will." Mac sighed.

"Thank you, Papa." her voice was stunned and lifeless.

"YOU TWO ARE VERY DEAR," Gwen said the next morning as she kissed Mr. and Mrs. MacDonald goodbye at the airport. "I couldn't have chosen better in-laws. I'm sorry it didn't work out."

They watched with heavy hearts as she walked away from them. They waited until the plane taxied down the runway and lifted into the clear blue sky.

"I gave her our number and address. I told her to please keep in touch, and if she ever needed anything, we're still her family," Mr. MacDonald said.

"This can't be the end, Mac. It's not at all what we prayed for, and those two love each other too much. They belong together." Tears glistened in Mrs. MacDonald's eyes.

"You and I know that," he said. "Every one of our family can see that—just—those two can't. And it's more one of them than the other. We have other concerns at home that we need to tend to. We will have to leave Gwen in the hands of the Almighty where she belongs."

So it was mother and son sitting on the arbor bench in the early afternoon sunshine. They needed no words and she prayed in her heart, *Oh my God, somehow, merciful heavenly Father, please make this come out right.* And she cried for them.

GWEN'S FLIGHT WAS UNEVENTFUL. There were few passengers on the flight to Chicago. There was a young man and an older woman, possibly his grandmother, two businessmen, another older woman traveling by herself, a middle-aged couple, several other nondescript passengers sitting toward the back, besides Gwen and her seatmate.

"My name is Gwen MacDonald," she introduced herself as she found her seat and settled into it. "What is your name?"

"Melissa Tavish. I'm on my way back home," the young girl said.

"Have you been traveling a long way?"

"From California."

"That's a long way for you to be traveling all by yourself."

"My father and mother say I'm very mature for a ten-year-old. Besides, the stewardesses watch out for me," she said.

"I can see you're mature. Were you visiting an aunt or family member?" Gwen asked.

"I was visiting my mom. She's an important business woman, and I got to spend an entire week with her," the little girl boasted. "She lives in California, but my Dad and I live in Chicago."

"Do you get to see her often then?"

"About three times a year. Some day we will go on vacation together," Melissa said in a matter-of-fact voice.

"Don't you miss your mom?" Gwen tried to understand this young girl's perspective.

"I did at first," Melissa said candidly. "I was only five, and I didn't understand that Mom wanted her own life. I used to cry myself to sleep."

"That was tough," Gwen said.

"It was, but Dad said we can't force people to do things. Even though when you marry someone you make a promise to them and to God, and that Mom broke her promise to us."

"Didn't that make you angry at her?"

"Daddy and I had to pull together and help each other. We pray for Mommy, and we still love her even though breaking promises is bad, and what she did was wrong."

Gwen frowned, "Isn't that somewhat—judgmental?"

"I don't... I don't know what judgmental is. I only know it's the truth," Melissa said, her blue-gray eyes wide and innocent.

Gwen sat back as the stewardess brought snacks. "Thank you," she said, thankful for the interruption and a chance to change the subject. "This part of the flight isn't very long. You'll be home soon." She smiled at her companion. They both sat comfortably in their seats finishing their bagel and cheese.

Not long after they had finished, the pilot began circling, preparing for the descent.

"Do you need anything from the overhead?" Gwen asked Melissa as they prepared to leave the plane.

"Yes, that pack right there." Melissa pointed.

"Here you go." Gwen pulled Melissa's backpack down as well as her own carry-on.

As they reached their destination, Melissa ran and embraced a stocky man of medium height waiting for her. "Daddy, this is Gwen MacDonald. She sat beside me on the flight."

Gwen nodded and acknowledged the introduction. "You have a very sweet girl there, Mr. Tavish."

"I believe so. Thank you for keeping an eye out for Melissa," he added. "I'm concerned when she travels by herself. God watches over her often through the kindness of strangers like you."

Melissa's father was a good-looking man in his late thirties. He looked comfortable in his dress clothes as if they were his work clothes. His attitude was friendly, yet there was sadness and wariness in his eyes.

"It wasn't a problem at all—And nice to meet you," she said in an offhanded manner.

Mr. Tavish bent to pick up Melissa's backpack. He looked preoccupied with moving on with his life as he smiled down at Melissa.

As he stood up, Gwen caught his puzzled gaze, and she felt even more uncomfortable. She was a petite five foot two inches in height. Slender and girlish for her age, people often mistook her for being younger than she was. This morning she must look a mess since she had barely run a comb through her short cinnamon-colored hair. Nor in her frantic haste to reach the airport did she apply her make-up or even take time to match her skirt and blouse. Even though they were name brands they felt like someone else's clothes. All this combined to make her look disjointed with her pale, haunted face and the large blue-gray eyes especially pathetic.

"Are you staying in Chicago, or do you have a layover here?" Mr. Tavish asked.

"No, I am flying further east, and yes, I do have a horrendous layover," Gwen said.

"I have a few minutes and—" He paused. "So many people have shown kindness to me by watching out for Melissa, I would like to repay it just a little. How about a cup of coffee and maybe a sandwich? It will help pass a small portion of your time," he said.

Gwen hesitated. "It is a four-hour layover—but I wouldn't want to impose."

"No strings here. I don't normally do this, but there's a coffee shop down here on the right." Mr. Tavish pointed down the hall.

"WE'LL TAKE TWO COFFEES," Mr. Tavish ordered as the waitress paused at their table, "and one banana split. Wouldn't you care for something to eat?" he asked Gwen.

She shook her head. "No, no really I'm fine."

After the waitress left to get their order, Mr. Tavish looked at Gwen. "Quite frankly, you don't look fine. I don't mean to be rude, but you look as if you could use a friend."

She mentally chewed on his statement. Generally, Gwen would never dream of confiding in a stranger, but... "I'm not sure what I'm doing or even what I want," she said. "Melissa shared with me that you and your wife have had problems..." Gwen went on hurriedly as Mr. Tavish's face clouded, "Oh, no, don't be angry with Melissa. She didn't go into details. Just that her mom lives in California and you two live here, and it doesn't take great intelligence to figure it out. My husband and I are having...problems. He left me...and I left him...now we've left each other." She shrugged.

"So who doesn't love whom anymore?" Mr. Tavish asked with a touch of sarcasm. He poured cream into his coffee and stirred in two teaspoons of sugar.

Gwen chewed on her lower lip considering the question. "That's the sixty-four dollar question. We both love each other beyond belief. I love Seth so much I would die for him."

"But you won't live for him?" Roland Tavish continued to stir his coffee.

"Oh, I don't know what it is!" she blurted. "In three weeks we will have been married for nine years. For most of those years, I've suffered through his ups and downs. He's never been unfaithful with another woman, but his other woman has been alcohol. Anyway, he had a family problem that I was unaware of when we married, and it kept dragging him down."

"A family problem?" Roland asked. "I suppose he came from a broken home with an alcoholic father."

"No, no, nothing like that. He has a lovely family. The problem is with Seth himself." Gwen's brow wrinkled as she tried to name the problem. "His family is…" she paused, remembering her father and mother-in-law, and Seth's sisters and brothers each in turn, "it's large, and warm, and loving, and especially Christian."

"So," he puzzled, "how did he have a family problem?"

"Seth wanted to do his own thing—apart from God—which also meant apart from them. I met him when there was only his one sister and himself. I didn't know all of these other people existed."

The waitress brought a refill, then Roland questioned, "How did you get where you are now?"

"Can you follow a twisty tale?" She screwed up her face trying to think where to begin.

"I can try," he said.

"Two months ago I left Seth a note at our apartment. I was tired of his ups and downs. I couldn't stand watching him kill himself when he drank. When he found the note, he went on a drinking binge. Now things become confusing. A few days later when he comes back to half-alive, someone has driven him across the country several states away from our home to the Midwest where his family lives now. At the same time, on my end of the world, some guy came into the restaurant where I was working and told me Seth had been in an accident and was on his way to the hospital. I was speeding toward the hospital when I missed a curve and hit a tree. I was in the hospital overnight with a hairline fracture on my leg. Seth's sister came and picked me up the next day, and I stayed with her for a few weeks. Meanwhile, Seth, who hadn't been in an accident, was at his oldest sister's house. He was gone for a couple of weeks getting dried out and back on his feet. He made peace with his family and with God. He came back after me, and we decided to give it one more try. So, we went back to live with his family on a trial basis."

"He wasn't in an accident after all? But you were?"

"Yes, that's correct." She frowned.

"If you love him, and his family isn't the problem, what is the problem? Why are you here and he's there?" He sat back toying with his spoon.

"He needs his family?" She said.

"But you're part of that family, aren't you?"

Gwen was silent for a moment. "I guess you're right."

"Then why are you here and he's there?" he asked again.

"You don't understand."

"No, I don't. That's why I'm asking."

"His family is different."

"Different? I thought you said they were a warm and loving Christian family."

"They are all of those things. It's the Christian part that I'm having trouble with..."

"Ah," he said, his eyes narrowing, "now we are getting somewhere."

"Well, I'm a Christian," she answered, blushing. "That isn't the problem. The problem is their degree of commitment and mine aren't quite the same."

"What part of the commitment are you having trouble with?" Roland asked.

"They live and work together." Her brow creased with thought. "Serving God and one another seems to be their life."

"There is something wrong with that?" He raised his eyebrows. "Sounds like a good place to live and raise a family."

"The men run the families, and the women—" She stopped not knowing how to describe the women.

"The women what?" He pursed his mouth into a frown.

"They are second..." Her words trailed off.

"Second what? Fiddle?" He guessed.

"In command, I guess." Gwen blinked and frowned.

"The company I work for has a CEO, a head that makes the decisions, yet that person doesn't make decisions without input. Are the men tyrants? Are the women abused... unhappy?" he asked.

"No on all counts. They work together as a team supporting each other." She frowned and spoke crossly. "They believe in honesty, integrity, and there is this godly living thing, and everything together, I don't know. They're different." She stopped speaking, annoyed.

"It sounds like a difference we could all be better with," he said softly, almost to himself. "What have you got invested in this marriage, anyway?"

"Almost nine years of my life." She spoke quickly, in a belligerent tone.

"Okay, some time. What else?"

Gwen blinked at the question. "What?"

"What have you invested?"

"My heart?" she questioned.

"Okay, let's try this. I'll ask you some simple questions. What's his favorite color?"

"Blue," Gwen replied quickly.

"What's his favorite food?"

"Probably Italian. He loves lasagna." She answered slower with thought.

Roland asked, "What is his favorite outfit he likes you to wear?"

She looked down at her hands before answering. "I don't know."

"His favorite candy?" The raised eyebrows were back.

"I don't know that either." She still looked down.

"What doesn't he like you to wear?"

"Sweat pants and tube tops." She grinned.

"How often do you wear them?"

"Tube tops aren't in style..."

"How often?"

"Sweatpants? Far too often." Her eyes were downcast as she toyed with her coffee cup.

"What is his favorite restaurant?"

"The one I work at." She looked up and smiled at him.

"Okay, one final question." He smiled back. "How does he like you to wear your hair?"

"Long and soft." She whispered again, not meeting his gaze.

"You have put up with him for how many years?" Roland did not speak sarcastically, but he could have. "You have invested what in this marriage?" He said softly.

Gwen continued to stir her coffee and ponder. "I have been so busy with my martyr thing. I never looked at it like this before. I guess maybe I'm some of the problem too. But I still have to answer the commitment question... and that's the real problem, isn't it?" She looked up at him. "Talking to someone who isn't involved—well, I appreciate you taking the time," she said.

"Mrs. MacDonald." He cocked his head sideways and returned her gaze. "Seriously, if I can help others avoid the heartache I've endured... You see, decisions are what life is made of. Good decisions versus bad decisions. Marriage is a commitment, an agreement between God, a man, and a woman. It's a bedrock foundation upon which society is built, and something worth fighting for, worth working at. You could turn around." His gaze was piercing.

"Yes, I could," she whispered.

"But you aren't going to, are you?"

"No," she replied.

"Don't wait too long. Come along, Melissa, we need to be getting on home." He spoke to his daughter then turned back to Gwen. "Don't wait too long."

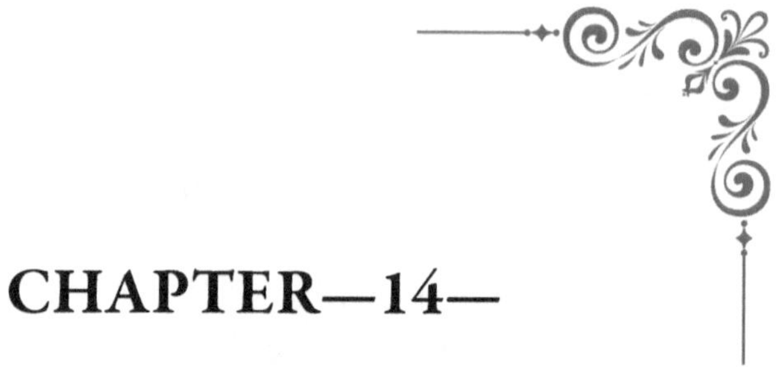

CHAPTER—14—

Gwen sat soaking in the early morning sunshine as it streamed through the large bay window in her bedroom. Her hand trembled slightly as she sipped her tea. The morning paper lay on her lap as she tried to come to terms with being back at her estate. Gerald, her aunt's butler, had met her early evening flight the day before. It had been a long trip even though it was not a late flight. She hadn't slept well for days since she had decided to come back home. She was exhausted from the strain of how to tell Seth. She knew it was going to be traumatic, but she didn't know how excruciating. Her mind kept replaying how he looked in the last moments before he disappeared.

There was a light tap on the door before Alice, her maid and confidante, came in with a tray. "Your breakfast, Miss," she said as she efficiently placed the poached eggs, crisp bacon, and hot buttered English muffins off the tray and onto the small table.

"Thank you, Alice." Her words were businesslike. "Have you received word about a full-time chef yet?"

"Yes, they will be sending someone out today. However, it will take some time to switch and rearrange the kitchen. We've gotten out of a routine since there's only been the three of us left here."

"I appreciate your filling in until then. Mr. Howl, Aunt Zoë's advisor is scheduled to visit at two o'clock this afternoon."

"Yes, Miss." There was little emotion in the maid's manner, even though they had been close in past years.

"I have asked him to call to fill me in on the affairs of the estate."

"Shall I send out for pastries and such for tea?" Alice asked.

"That would be wonderful." Gwen closed her eyes and smiled. "Oo, Annie's delicious pastries. Is she still doing business?" Gwen remembered fondly the wiry Italian woman who passionately loved cooking, baking, and children.

"She is, and she still has those wonderful cream puffs, éclairs, and heavenly things. She has begun to pass her business on to a niece and a granddaughter."

"I don't have any plans for this evening at this time," Gwen said with a heavy sigh. "So something simple for supper would be fine. Soup and a sandwich or a salad. I'm not very hungry, Alice dear." She tenderly grasped the older woman's hand. The distance between them faded.

"I'm so glad that you have returned, Miss Gwen." Alice gently caressed the soft, young hand holding hers. "So many years have passed. I hope you know I'm still your dear Alice and you will always be my precious Gwen. Since Madam's passing, this house has been waiting for your return. Will you be staying long, Miss, if I might ask?"

"You may ask, Alice, but at this time I have no concrete plans." Gwen frowned then smiled at her maid. "It will be alright. I've missed you, and Gerald and Ralph..."

"We are all glad to see you home, Miss. I'll be back for the tray in a little bit." Alice also added softly, "We have been so lonely without you."

Gwen finished her breakfast and sat swirling the remnants of her teacup. Her conversation with Roland Tavish still chased through her mind. *Was she wrong, was she right? Was it because she enjoyed the martyr role she played? "Poor Gwen," her friends would say, "her husband's gone again." Did it make her feel good to be the 'strong one?'* She was his pillar of strength, and now he didn't need her in that role any longer. She gazed into her cup as the words of a fortune-teller came back from the past.

"Come one, come all to Madam La Rue's tent of fortune! She will reveal all. Is there someone in your future?" It was a charity fair, and her teacher, Miss Grober, was playing the part dressed as an old woman fortune teller. Her aunt and she went into the tent to have their fortunes told. What a routine! She used neither cards nor the crystal ball but read Gwen's fortune from her teacup. "Your life will be hard and easy." She foretold. "Do not make hasty decisions. Choices that seem easy often lead to a hard path, but the choices that go with the less-traveled road will lead to the better life."

Strange that her advice was sound, but many times that's the case with good advice. Did it apply to this situation? The choice to marry Seth had been so simple, yet it had led to a hard path. This decision felt so hard. But now, taking up the cross of commitment looked like the path of the less-traveled road and it looked very hard. *If I stay here at my estate, life would be so... easy...or would it? She wondered.*

The late-summer morning was warm, but with a hint of something coming in the air. The heavier skirt and a light sweater felt good as she stepped outside. Her eyes searched the landscape hungrily as if it were the face of an old friend. Just where was the old caretaker? Her boots crunched with each brisk step she took. Gerald had said she would find Ralph, the caretaker, out here. Ah, there he was working over a flowerbed.

"It's so good to be back, Ralph. How long it has been!" Gwen observed that the caretaker's previously salt and pepper hair was now entirely white, but the same wrinkled face still smiled at her. "You know," she continued, "I'm going to insist that you hire helpers."

"Funny ting, Miss Gwen," he replied to her comment, "I'm not the spring chicken no more." He shook his head with vigor. "And was tinking of maybe I could use a little help. Dis mornin' I 'ave someone come by lookin' for work. He says he is in between chobs an' he says he can start any time. I look over his references, dey look purty goot. I goin' to call dis afternoon. Maybe he start tomorrow, Missy."

Gwen smiled fondly at the old caretaker who stood with his nondescript black felt hat in his hands kneading it into a new shape. "Don't hesitate, Ralph. I would suggest at least two more helpers."

"In da summer I 'ave a lawn care service mow, but I still do da flowers an' garden. Miss Alice, she likes to 'ave fresh vegetables and flowers. I could use someone to help with ole Juniper and Starr. You goin' to want ta ride today, Missy?"

"Tomorrow, Ralph. I want to get settled in first," she said. It was good to hear the old familiar name that he had always used for her.

"Dat goot, Missy. Ole Ralph will polish up da tack and brush up dem horses. Dey'll be ready for you in da mornin'. Come wid me. I show you my new flowers…" He still had a comical way of ducking his head as he spoke and keeping up a steady stream of conversation as he led the tour of the outside of the house as well as the gardens and the stables. "My artritus flare-up in da cool wedder. Dis new fella would sure be fine if he works out," he said at the finish of the tour, still waving his hands in animated conversation.

"That will be good, Ralph. I'll see you in the morning." Gwen looked at her watch as she turned toward the house.

"Alice? I have enough time for a shower before lunch, don't I?" Gwen asked as she entered the house.

"Yes, Miss, and I'll lay out your outfit for the afternoon. Do you want your meal served in your room or the private dining room?"

"I hate to ask it of you, but I would like a bit of a short rest before catching up on some correspondence…"

"No problem, Miss. Get your shower, and I'll have your lunch brought up. You want to be rested when your company comes at two this afternoon. Mr. Howl is always punctual."

GWEN SAT BEHIND THE heavy oak desk in the library perusing several documents when Gerald, the butler, knocked at the doors.

"Mr. Robert Howl Senior to see you, Miss," he announced.

"Show him in, please," she said. She put down her pen and came out from behind the desk to greet her visitor. "Oh, Uncle Robert!" she exclaimed as the older man entered the library. "You look older than I remember, but it makes you look so handsome and wise," she added, hugging him.

"Let me look at you, little Gwen," the older man replied, holding her out at arm's length appraisingly. "If I were only fifty years younger. You just get more gorgeous as you grow up," he said. "So, what brings you back to our little hamlet?"

"I need to sort things out and make some decisions. I've been wrestling with problems, and I needed some time by myself." Uncle Robert, as she had always known him, had certainly grown older, but he was still handsome with the type of face and manner that often drew others to him in confidence—a helpful trait for a lawyer.

"My son and his wife have invited a few close friends for this evening. If you have no other plans, we would love to have you join us."

"Oh, no, sir, I would not want to impose. Especially on such short notice." Her eyes grew wide in panic.

He laughed as he shook off her excuse. "It is short notice for you, but it isn't an imposition. You know how these things go. We always have more than enough food and room. Besides my grandson, Bobby, is back from Europe. He has been complaining of boredom and no stimulation. I would like to shake him up a bit, and you are the item to do the trick."

"You do remember I'm married?" she said.

"No strings attached. I just want to show him that we have pretty women here also." He spoke with a conspiratorial tone.

"Uncle Robert, I've only been back not even twenty-four hours...I don't know what's in my closet, and I don't think I can get my hair done on such short notice. I'm sure the women of this area would take exception to me being a model for them." She listed several excuses.

"Oh, pshaw! Let me call Agnes. I'll have her set another plate then we can get on with our business here." He pulled a phone out of his pocket.

"I need to speak to Alice while you are making your call. Excuse me." Gwen hurried to the door. She shut the heavy door firmly behind her as Alice rolled the cart down the hall. "Alice, Uncle Robert insists I come for dinner." She hissed in a whisper. "I just can't go!" She was in a panic. "I have nothing to wear, and look at my hair! And..."

"Take a deep breath—put on a good face. Alice will take care of everything. Just leave it to me." Alice winked, nodded, and raised her eyebrows as Gwen opened the door and they walked into the library.

"Would you care for some tea?" Gwen began to pour the tea. How good to have Alice to take care of things. *I've missed Alice so much.*

"Well, it's set. Dinner is at eight. You will know most of the people who are invited. Most are middle age or older. Except for Bob of course and yourself. Now, let's get down to the business you called about." Mr. Howl opened his briefcase and pulled out papers.

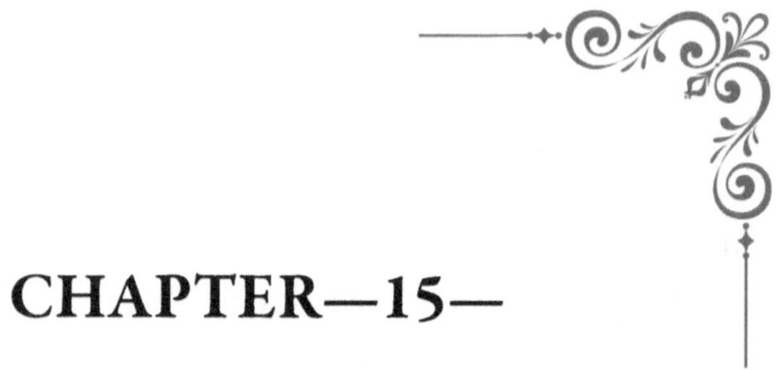

CHAPTER—15—

"I have called Louie DuVall. He's a close friend of mine, a fantastic hairdresser, and he will be arriving in an hour. As to your clothing, I have maintained your wardrobe." Alice walked to the closet and after a short time, she brought back three garments. A red sequined sheath dress, a shiny bronze dress, and a shimmery silver-blue gown. "Since Mistress taught you to purchase clothing and accessories that would wear well, I occasionally had them sent to the cleaners so that they would be ready for just such a time as this. Although they are all three adequate, I would suggest..."

"Oh, Alice, this blue frock is exquisite." Gwen sighed as she caressed the soft material and watched it shimmer in the light. "I don't remember ever buying such a dress. It must have been in another lifetime..." *It would be so easy...* she did not dare finish the thought. As Alice went to her shoe closet, Gwen unwrapped the picture of Seth and herself taken a week ago and placed it carefully on her dressing table. Alice placed her matching high heel shoes under the blue dress then went to check her bath.

"It's ready, Miss. I'm sorry you don't have time for a long leisurely bath, but you did get a nap and still have a bit of time while Louie gets set up. Don't rush, relax at least a bit."

Stepping from her bath, she vigorously dried off and surveyed her neatly stored silk lingerie. Another deep sigh escaped her, *How long? It's been too long!* She pulled the luxurious slip gently over her head and let it slide into place.

"Too thin, Miss. You haven't been eating right," Alice said as she hurried into the ample bathroom. "You've gotten too thin. I don't care if it is the style, you look as if a strong wind would blow you away. Here, I brought your robe. Mr. DuVall is at the front door." Alice held the robe for Gwen to slip into. Wrapped in her comfortable robe Gwen sat at her vanity.

Gerald the butler tapped lightly.

"Enter."

"This way, if you please, Mr. DuVall." Gerald opened the door bringing in several cases containing hairdressing items followed by a small thin man with a little mustache. Alice had already pulled a chest in place for Louie DuVal to set some of his accessories on.

"Onlee for Alice would I do such a thing!" The hairdresser exclaimed and waved a hairbrush for emphasis. "I do not this thing without protest. My Alice she 'as a way—I do this for her." His words stopped and he blinked rapidly as he looked at Gwen's hair. "Oi! Madam! Who were you angry with when you 'av your 'air done? I see never such a style in my bad dreams." He touched her hair in amazement. "And such pretty 'air too. It's shame to ruin such pretty 'air. Leave it to Louie, I work the miracle." Under his breath, he added to himself. "We need the miracle."

An hour later, Gwen gasped, wide-eyed in surprise. "Oh, Louie, you are magnificent! What a gorgeous hairstyle. I don't even know that person in the mirror. And in only an hour, yes, it is at least a small miracle." She took note that he had washed, blow-dried, and with the aid of a fall as well as a silver-blue scarf, had made her short choppy hair look elegant.

"I told you, Louie would work the miracle." His chest expanded and he stood on his toes, adding two inches to his height. "And so pretty." He gave her a final approving look. "If you just take care of your 'air. Do not that to it again." He shook his finger at her as if she were an erring child.

"Yes, sir." She smiled at him.

"Oi, madam, you should smile always. You 'av such a pretty smile. It is no wonder Alice, she love you." He began to pick up his tools and pack them into their carriers.

"Alice is very special," Gwen said, smiling at Alice. "I have missed my friend and confidant more than I ever knew."

"I DON'T WANT TO GO." Her words were muffled as her head disappeared and Alice helped her slip the toga-style dress over her head, taking care not to alter the new hairstyle. "I feel coerced into the whole thing." She frowned in annoyance.

Alice clasped the right then the left shoulder fasteners into place, and let the silvery-blue material fall in soft folds from the silver fasteners at each shoulder to just above her slender ankles. A matching silver belt, silvery-blue heels, and a light blue mohair sweater completed the perfect outfit. The elegant clothing flattered Gwen's beautiful blue-gray eyes and reddish-brown hair.

"Well, you can't hide forever, and at least you will be among friends. You need a bit of makeup—to add some color. You've gotten so pale," Alice said as she applied some foundation and a dab of rouge. "And here's the final touch, some lipstick, and the necklace and matching earrings."

"But, if Uncle Robert is my friend, he would have given me more time to be prepared. My hair was a total mess—as Louie so tacitly expressed, and what if I hadn't had such a faithful caretaker as you, Alice? I wouldn't think a friend would do such a thing." Gwen's face wore an angry, puzzled look.

"All's well that ends well, besides, you are stunning, lamb." Alice handed Gwen the beautiful blue sapphire earrings and matching necklace.

As Gwen gazed at her reflection in the mirror, tears began to roll down her cheeks. "Oh, Alice, what have I done, and what am I to do?"

"What's the matter?" Alice held Gwen's face in one hand and blotted the tears with the other as she cautioned. "Careful, now, don't ruin your face."

Gwen retrieved the photo from her dresser and showed it to her friend. "The sapphires are the exact color of his eyes, Alice. I can't explain why I'm here and he is there. Furthermore, I love him so much it hurts, and I miss him like I would miss my heart." She placed her hands over her heart.

Alice surveyed the handsome face in the photograph. "He has an honest face, and yes, the bluest sapphire eyes...but it's time for your car, Miss." Alice urged while cleaning away the tear stains. "When you return we will finish our conversation."

"You are right—It was the color that reminded me of him." Gwen blew her nose and took a deep breath. "What is that about putting a good face on things?"

"A light dusting of powder, and you'll look good as new." Alice brushed powder across Gwen's face to cover the tear stains. "Right as rain, dear." She smiled.

There was a light tap at the door. "Miss, your car is waiting," Gerald informed her.

"Very well, Gerald. I'm coming." Gwen picked up her small handbag. One final look in the mirror before she composed her face. She pulled her shoulders up straight and walked confidently to the door.

Gwen sat back in the roomy limousine and attempted to relax. She had been absent from this lifestyle for so long. She prayed the Lord would give her the backbone she needed to face the lions. Even your friends in this world could be vicious. Thoughts swirled through her mind on the drive to Mr. Howl's estate. Did Uncle

Robert have hopes and ulterior motives for insisting she come this evening? She didn't remember his grandson, Bobby—or rather Robert Howl III, to be more precise. But what a fait accompli if he could pair his grandson with Gwendolyn Aurora De Winters, daughter and wealthy heiress of the late Beauregard F. De Winters IV. Gwen sighed. At least as Alice had said, she would be among friends.

NOT MUCH HAD CHANGED on the outside of the Howl estate as the chauffeur pulled around the drive. He waited as the doorman opened her door. Gwen took a deep breath then mounted the steps in a regal manner and waited in the front hall to be announced by Purcell, the Howls' butler. She watched as Mrs. Howl approached, extending her cat-like claws in greeting, her countenance all aglow.

"Good evening." Agnes Howl grasped Gwen's hands. "We are so glad you could come. When Father told us you were home again, it just would not do to let someone else be the first to welcome you back into society." The middle-aged woman's eyes narrowed slightly. "You look just..." She paused taking a long look at her subject. "...absolutely stunning. I don't know what he was thinking. He said the flight had been long, and maybe you were a little tired."

"Agnes, dear—" She brushed a kiss across her hostess' cheek. "—it is so good to see you." *Well, Gwen thought, you old cat. Time has not been kind to you.* She took note that the flaming red hair was still well-coiffed, nails were manicured, tailored clothes were in the latest style, makeup applied perfectly— none of which could hide the numerous lines beginning to crease her mask. *You,* she thought, *are not aging well...*

"Come in and let me introduce you to the other guests." Agnes took her elbow, guiding her into the sitting room. "You already know Mark and Gloria Wallace, Bill and Betty Sague, as well as Joe and

Carla Benton. Do you all remember Miss Zoë Lind's niece, Gwendolyn? It's Mrs. Gwendolyn MacDonald now isn't it?" she asked. "This is Lawrence and Rila Worth," she continued. "They have been in our area only a few years, but Larry is doing some marvelous things in the business world. And of course, this is our son, Robert. You may remember Bobby from when you were younger."

"Purcell has announced that dinner is ready." Robert Howl II joined the group. "Come along, dear." He offered his arm to Agnes and led the company into the dining room.

"I certainly remember your Aunt Zoe," Mr. Benton said as Gwen was seated next to him. "She was a hard-headed businesswoman. One thing I can say about Miss Zoe Lind, however, she was a person who'd go the extra mile to help folks. She helped Bill and Mark, as well as myself, get our start. You know, we went to the bankers and presented our ideas. No, they wouldn't help. Too risky, they said. Then we were sitting in Artie's Restaurant, a pretty dejected bunch you can believe. Artie comes over to our table and he says, 'You know Miss Lind comes in every week or so to see how I'm doing.' 'Yeah?' we said, wondering what that had to do with us. 'Well,' Artie said, 'she helped me get my start here when no one else would. I could put in a word for you next time I see her.' Your Aunt Zoe was quite a lady."

"She was. I still can't believe she's gone," Gwen said with a sad smile.

"Gwendolyn?" Robert Howl III addressed her.

"You may call me Gwen." She stifled a yawn.

"If you'll call me Bob. All of my close friends call me Bob."

"I think I'll settle for Robert then, but with all the Roberts how do you keep everyone straight?" He was a good-looking fellow, average height, dark, almost- black hair, sad brown eyes—and annoying.

"That's why you should call me Bob. Anyway, I don't recall ever meeting you before. Have you ever been to Europe or England? Where have you been hiding?"

"I have been to both—not recently, however—and I haven't been hiding anywhere."

"I was just telling Grandfather a few days ago that this is the dullest place on earth. No one stimulating at all, but now—"

"—Robert," Gwen whispered behind her dinner napkin, "is that woman glaring at you? Or is she glaring at me? Every time you speak to me she has a definite scowl on her face."

"You know, Rila does have a strange look to her doesn't she?" he whispered back. "In all the time I've known her I've never noticed that, but she looks a little different tonight. Maybe she doesn't like the salad. I think it's just the lighting. What do you think?"

"It may be the roast duck, or the salmon pate' didn't agree with her. The soup was delicious, so that couldn't have been it..." Gwen said.

"Mrs. MacDonald, is it?" Mr. Benton sought her attention.

"Yes, it is."

"I don't know of anyone by the name MacDonald around here.... Do you plan on being in this area for long?"

"My plans are indefinite at this point, Mr. Benton."

"I was definitely going to leave for Europe, but now my plans are indefinite as well," Bobby said, eyeing Gwen. "I have found something much more interesting."

"No thank you," Gwen refused the wine. "I don't drink alcoholic beverages."

"It's time to retire from the table anyway. Would you mind if I came to call on you tomorrow?" Bobby asked.

"I don't know what I have planned for tomorrow. My calendar and schedule are still in limbo," she said. "but afternoons still have visitation hours around here, right?"

"Yes they do...What?" Bob turned to respond to Mrs. Worth. "Shh, don't talk so loud, Rila. What? Well, it really isn't any of your business." He frowned at her. "I think you've had too much wine. Perhaps Mrs. MacDonald was just afraid you'd drunk all of it, Rila, so she didn't take any. That was a joke for heaven's sake... No, she said she doesn't drink alcohol... How should I know? Probably doesn't like it, I would say. No, she's not underage." He tried to extricate himself. "Well, Dad wants to... say it's time for me to...with the other men, you know. Good night, Rila, and..." He turned congenially to Gwen. "I'll see you tomorrow." He made his escape.

Gwen decided she had put on a good face long enough. She turned to her hostess. "Agnes, thank you for inviting me this evening, but as this is my first full day back. I do hope you won't think ill of me to leave so early?"

"I am so glad to see you back. I'm sure we will have many more opportunities for social exchange." Agnes played the part of a gracious hostess. "Is your husband coming to the area also? I don't believe I've ever heard the name MacDonald from this area. Is he from overseas?"

Rila began laughing a loud shrill laugh. "No, I've heard of him. Isn't he the world-famous 'old MacDonald' that had a farm?"

"You have him confused with someone else." Gwen practiced her withering look at the speaker. "Our plans are rather nebulous. I'm sure I'll be having company soon. Good night, all." She turned to make her exit.

"That's okay, it's time for all good babies to be in bed anyway." Rila snickered.

"My aunt had an answer for everything." Gwen turned looking down at the loud, uncouth woman. "Right now a scripture from the Bible that she often used comes to my mind. Proverbs I believe it was..."

"Bible?" Sneered the drunken woman. "That isn't one of my latest reading materials."

"The tongue of the wise uttereth knowledge aright; But the mouth of fools poureth out folly. Good night, all." Gwen turned and regally swept out the door.

CHAPTER—16—

The next morning Gwen stepped outside into the languid late August air just as the sun began to peek over the horizon. The leaves were still firmly attached to the trees, not even hinting at what lay in store for the future landscape within the next few weeks. The beautiful October season would come and the turning of the leaves would be seen in every nook and cranny of the landscape. The last sweet smell of summer would soon turn to the pungent crisp autumn aroma. Gwen breathed deeply to fill her lungs with the bittersweet morning air. She entered the cobblestone alleyway of the horse barn and came to her gelding's stall. The old caretaker was busy with a brush in hand.

"Here, let me do that, Mr. Ralph." She deftly removed the brush from his grasp.

"Missy, I was just gittin started. I forgot what an early riser you were. There's no reason for you to do that." He objected strenuously as she whisked the tool out of his hands.

"Mr. Ralph, you know how Aunt Zoë always insisted I learn to take care of my horse. Besides, I enjoy the barn and animal smells. It's so good to be back." She began to brush firmly the horse's already smooth coat. "Please get the tack while I finish."

Ralph brought the saddle, blanket, and bridle just as Gwen was leading Juniper King out of the stall. In no time at all, she found herself riding along the bridle path at an easy pace. She reached a spot overlooking the river and drew up watching the sunlight on the dark green leaves as well as the warm air rising from Juniper's body. She stroked his neck, softly talking to him. He seemed to enjoy the outing as much as she did.

"You know, old boy, there is only one thing wrong with this moment," she said wistfully. "I wish that Seth were with me. Don't get me wrong, you're good company and I've missed our rides, but I miss him. If he were here, this moment would be perfect." She sighed then turned her horse, and they loped down the trail.

After the invigorating ride, the shower felt good. She let the warm water slide over her unaccustomed stiff muscles then vigorously towel-dried, hoping to avoid some of the saddle soreness. This was Gwen's time of the morning as she sat eating her breakfast, reading the paper, the sun dancing through the windows. There was a tap on the door as Alice came bearing a large box from the florist, and a smaller one as well.

"What?" Gwen's eyes showed her surprise.

"You'll have to open the box, Missy, and read the card." Alice handed her the florist box.

"Oh, Alice, they are just gorgeous!" Gwen exclaimed as the perfume from the dozen long-stemmed red roses filled the room. "It says 'From your most ardent admirer, Robert Howl III.' Alice, I can't accept these. What will I do?"

"I wish someone would send me such beautiful flowers and chocolates." Alice sighed. "But leave it to me if you are sure that you don't want them."

"I would love to have the flowers and chocolates, but not with the ties it would encourage. You do see that, of course, don't you?" Gwen asked.

"Yes, I do, lamb. And you're right...It just seems like it would be nice if your ties were here. Not somewhere else." Alice's voice quivered.

"Robert Howl III knows I'm married. What kind of a tie would that be?"

"Leave these to me." Her voice became firm. "You're completely right! That rat," she added under her breath. "And, oh, by the by, the new chef is in the kitchen and appears to be quite capable. Do you have any plans for today that I can take to him?"

"Not right now, Alice. I'm going out for a short while this morning...before lunch that is. We will need to be prepared for callers this afternoon. Perhaps he could prepare something for then. Have him send up the menus so I can look them over...and we'll have to organize our calendar."

"ROBERT HOWL THE III," Gerald announced as he showed Bobby to the sitting room.

"May I be seated?" Bobby asked.

"Unless you plan on standing that would be wise," Gwen said. "I'm impressed that you have at least retained some of the old social graces."

"So, how has your day gone? Did you save this evening for me?"

"I'm busy this evening," she said in a cool voice.

"So fast? I thought I was a fast worker. Who has me beat?" he asked.

"You are not my social secretary. That is none of your business." She practiced her raised eyebrow face.

"Ouch!" he replied. "How about tomorrow lunch?"

She looked at him in mild awe. "You are very tenacious. You must be a good lawyer. Would you care for some tea?" She poured him a cup anyway.

"Some say I'm a decent lawyer, and yes, I am very tenacious. You haven't answered my question. How about tomorrow lunch?" He helped himself to a petite four.

"You wouldn't by any chance know what was wrong with Mrs. Worth last night, would you?" she asked.

"I'm sure it was the salad that didn't agree with her. She had the green around the gills look, I think...Don't you? These are excellent, by the way." He closed his eyes savoring the tasty treat. "Remarkable. You don't usually find petite fours this exquisite here in the states."

Gwen's eyes narrowed. "She was certainly unpleasant. No, I'm sorry. I'm busy tomorrow lunch also."

"Well, you can't blame a guy for trying. When is your other half going to show up? Anybody that would let a good-looking woman like you get too far from him can't be too smart." He eyed her serenely.

"Maybe he just trusts me, as I trust him." Gwen frowned.

"Now that's a thought." He rose.

"Didn't you come for tea?" She was startled that he was preparing to leave.

"No." He picked up his hat. "I can get tea anywhere. I'll just check again later."

"Check later? About what?" Gwen asked.

"About lunch sometime. I'll see you later then." He turned and walked himself to the front door.

"WELL, I NEVER!" ALICE fumed after the few other guests had made their appearance and gone. "The nerve of that man!" She picked up the brush and began to style Gwen's hair.

"Calm down now." Gwen closed her eyes, thoughtfully considering the events of the afternoon, then opened them again. "Do you know anything about him?"

"Not really," Alice answered. "But I will ask around and see what I can find out."

"I would appreciate it. My compliments to the new cook. That tea tray was fabulous! I'll be down to meet him later and go over the menus for the coming week. I'll check into getting you some more help. I'll need to have a few guests in. That was probably Uncle Howl's ulterior motive... My schedule is beginning to fill up, I'm afraid. I'd hoped for a time to be alone—a time of quiet."

"You never did tell me about your—problem." Alice frowned as she worked over the hairstyle. "But perhaps you don't care to share," she added tactfully.

"I have a snapshot in my purse, an early photo," Gwen explained. "But this larger picture from my suitcase—" She pointed at the picture on her dresser. "—That is a more recent photograph of us as a couple. It was taken just a few weeks ago."

"He is quite good-looking." Alice appraised the likeness before her. "What happened? Did someone else come between you? Was he a fortune hunter?"

"Seth doesn't even know I have money," Gwen said. "He wouldn't care anyway. You would like him, I think." She mused for a moment. "He's a good six foot plus, and, as you say, very good to look at, but..." She hesitated. "He's very chivalrous, and I love him very much. When I told him I was leaving, he wouldn't even kiss me goodbye. He said that since I was leaving him my lips didn't belong to him." Tears slid down her cheeks.

"My pet." Alice frowned. "I thought you said you loved him. I thought you said..." She stopped in confusion. "For what reason would you leave him?"

"Oh, Alice, where to begin? I needed space to think, to pray, to maybe come to an understanding. When I married him, I just liked what I saw. I liked the way he was good not just to me, but to his sister, to children, to older folks. He was always kind and courteous to everyone. Our ninth anniversary is coming up in a few weeks. We've had so many ups and downs. Only this summer did I find the reason as to why he is the way he is. He has the most fabulous family I have ever met."

Alice sat down, scrutinizing every detail of the picture. "But this doesn't make sense. I must be older than I thought—I'm not putting things together."

"Since I have no family, I didn't think it strange that when I first met him there was only himself and his recently married sister as a family. I never asked about his father, mother, or anything. He said his family was gone, so I just assumed—I don't know what I assumed. Until this summer he fought alcohol addiction constantly. He'd be sober for a time, maybe months, then out of the blue, the sheriff would show up bringing him home after finding him sleeping in the park, or in the street, or wherever he found him." Gwen's mind slipped back. *The light but insistent, rap-rap-rap at the apartment door. "Ma'am? Ma'am? Mrs. MacDonald?...Officer Charles Malone here..." Rushing to the door, that late night, she threw the door open. A tall, lanky police officer was propping Seth up as he clung to the officer. She had never met Officer Malone before, but it would be the first of many encounters in the next nine summers. "Found him sleeping in the gazebo in the park...No charges, but I have to issue a warning..."*

She continued speaking, "This summer I had decided I couldn't stand to watch him killing himself that way. I left him a note that I was leaving."

"Oh, Miss, that had to be a hard decision—but a note?"

"It was a hard decision. A very, very hard decision."

"Where does the family come in?"

"He disappeared after reading the note. It turns out he was drunk, and an old family friend drove him across the country to reunite him with his family. He does have a father, a mother, and several siblings. A large, religious family, and I'm struggling with that."

"Are they some type of cult? But, no, you said they are a fabulous family, not repulsive. So, what is it you are afraid of?"

"I'm afraid of commitment, I'm afraid I can't do it. I'm afraid of being out of control. I'm afraid I don't know who I am, and I am afraid I will get lost," Gwen said.

"Those are a lot of *afraids*. Let's just work on one afraid at a time? Sit still now while I finish your hair, and let Alice think things over for a time. When is your supper engagement at the Bentons?"

CARLA BENTON GREETED Gwen. "I'm so glad you could make it on such short notice, dear. You have already met our guests this evening, Bill and Betty Sague, at the Howls'. This is our daughter, Maryann—and Joe's mother, Sophia Benton, who lives with us. Nothing big, you know. But we are all friends...and we're friendly," she said with an honest, endearing smile.

"Do you like to travel?" MaryAnn asked Gwen, who was seated between the elder Mrs. Benton and the daughter, MaryAnn, on Gwen's right. "Grandmother has been almost everywhere. If you ever need an opinion of any place, here or abroad, just ask her."

"That's good to know." Gwen smiled. It was encouraging to meet someone like Maryann, an unpretentious young woman who seemed to have her head in the real world.

"Yes, from Alaska to Australia, America to Russia. Big countries and little, Grandma's been all over. Tell Mrs. MacDonald about the hunting trip you and Granddad went on up in Alaska, Grandma."

"Oh, honey, she doesn't want to hear about that old trip!" Mrs. Benton, a pleasant-faced older woman, brushed her granddaughter's request aside.

"On the contrary...I would love to hear your stories." Gwen was at once put at ease by her two companions.

"Joe Senior and I enjoyed fishing," Sophia Benton began the story. "We had an invite to go to Alaska to fish for rainbow trout. There were four of us camping in an old cabin when the biggest brown bear

I have ever seen burst through the flimsy door to raid our cabin—in the middle of the night—Four people were scrambling to get out of that cabin as well as a bear wrapped in a sheet. It seemed a shame to shoot the foolish bear. Joe grabbed the big old shotgun and let off a loud blast. He didn't intend to hurt the silly bear and he didn't, although it did frighten the animal. Last we saw of him, he was loping off into the woods dragging a large white sheet." She interrupted her story, turning to Carla. "You will have to tell Anajoli this is the best soup he's prepared all month, Carla. It is splendid!" Mrs. Benton finished the story about the Alaska fishing trip that turned into a bear escape.

"Tell her the one of getting caught by the tide that time," Maryann was ready with another story.

Mrs. Benton allowed the filet of salmon to be placed in front of her, then she said, "Just one more, Maryann, our guests will be bored to tears otherwise. Joe and I were off the coast at a small inlet. When we went out to fish, the tide was out. We were there for quite some time when Joe went back up the shore to fetch something we'd left with our main supplies. He wasn't gone long, but it was long enough that by the time he returned the tide was quickly coming in. I had realized something else. The boots I was wearing were mired in the mud, and I couldn't get out. Joe had to literally pull me out of my boots. By that time we had to swim for safety... We were sopping wet, and I had no boots when we made it back to shore."

"Mrs. Benton, you should write a book!" Gwen said wiping her tears as she laughed heartily. "Is there any advice you would give an unadventurous person?"

"Well, we had a friend who spoke fluent Chinese and he invited us to go with him to China. We were all set to go, our bags packed, tickets bought—everything, but our friend had to back out of the trip. I told Joe I'm afraid. What would happen if...well, you know I don't speak any Chinese and I could die and all sorts of what if's.

But Joe said we may never get this chance again. He said, 'I'm going Sophi, and if something happens along the way, I'll just wake up in heaven instead.' It was a trip of a lifetime and the chance never came again."

"Oh, my, Mrs. Benton..." Gwen stopped at those words. "I have never heard such wonderful stories. You definitely should write a book."

"Oh, she has lots more stories," MaryAnn said. "I've been recording them and compiling them into a book."

Mr. Benton pushed back from the table. "That's enough stories for the time being. I suggest we retire with our coffee to the parlor if you don't mind."

"We are so glad you came," Betty Sague exclaimed as they relaxed in the parlor. "You just seem to add a sort of sparkle tonight."

"Attractive young ladies have a way to do that...add a little something extra to the gatherings, that is." Carla Benton smiled at Gwen.

"Well, I'm still trying to get acclimated, but I have enjoyed the evening tonight. Thank you for inviting me, and I've enjoyed your stories, Maryann, and Mrs. Benton..."

"Sophi is fine, dear." She patted Gwen's hand. "And we certainly have enjoyed your company."

CHAPTER—17—

"I like coffee in the morning before I take my ride—Mike is it?" The morning interview with the new chef was progressing well. "I like my morning coffee dark and strong with cream and sugar. I've been very pleased with your meals and menu plans so far. I've made some notes, suggestions as it were, and authorized you to hire help for special occasions. Do you have any questions or comments?"

"No, ma'am, not at this time. Other than I'm pleased to find a kitchen garden in production, and a small greenhouse for extending the garden. I will need to hire a few extra serving people who may also become more full-time help between Miss Alice and me."

"Yes, Alice will need extra help. It's well that you've thought of this. Here are your menus with my notes. I will be filling in the special meals as my calendar changes so you know in advance. My Aunt Zoe had several business dealings which I've left in the hands of my lawyer for the last several years. I will try to keep most of the meals on the smaller side."

"I have a certain specialty store in town that I use and will rely on Alice for references for local stores and farms beyond what we can get from our garden here. For a time I worked on a cruise ship, so handling larger gatherings shouldn't be difficult, but I do appreciate notice. By the way, your coffee is ready if you're so inclined before your ride this morning?"

"Fair exchange." Gwen handed Mike, her new cook, the schedules and menus for the week as he brought her prebreakfast portion of coffee.

"What do you think of our new cook, Miss?" Alice asked as Gwen sipped her coffee.

"I like that he knows his stuff, and he's thinking ahead."

"I thought so. His resume and recommendations are impeccable. I wasn't sure at first sight. He won me over in spite of the ponytail and those weird glasses. Not only does he do a wonderful job, but he's also very personable and quiet," Alice said.

"And he makes a superb cup of coffee. I'm off for my morning ride now." Gwen drained her cup and replaced it in the saucer. "I'll see you when I get back, and we'll go over schedules."

"THANK YOU, RALPH. DID you get your help hired yet?" Gwen asked as Ralph led Juniper King out of the stable.

"I did. An' a good worker he's been. 'e 'elp me real good. Dis mornin' I 'ave him in the kitchen garden now, but he's good in the stables too. I tink maybe when you finish your ride I want you to look at a new horse, and can meet the new man. You'll see," Ralph said.

"The main thing is he's doing his job and you're pleased with him. My ride won't be as long this morning. I'll meet your horse and your new hire when I get back." Gwen swung Juniper around toward the bridle path that led to the lake.

It was one of the shortest riding paths on the property, but Gwen loved this path. She stopped to watch a doe and her fawn grazing in a meadow, and then quietly turned and rode off down the path toward the lake. This was her private world of peace. There was a small beach with a beach house and a picnic table set back along the shoreline close to the path. To the left of the beach house, there was a dock for small boats. Juniper King loped along the beach then they swung around back up toward the path beside the picnic house. Gwen turned to look back at the peaceful lake before heading back to the house.

"Oh, King, I wish I weren't torn in two pieces here. I miss him so, but..." She breathed deeply of the forest smells. At that moment, a ragged image flashed through the trees not far from where she was, and a huge tree began to topple in her direction. Gwen grabbed Juniper King's mane and hunkered down low as he bolted down the path toward home. It was an even shorter journey home due to the speed at which the horse flew. The horse, once frightened, would not be reined in. Leaning low along King's neck, Gwen's only hope was to hold on like a burr, hoping that Juniper King would slow down as he came to the stable. She could see the ground like a blur as they burst out of the trees, but the horse didn't waver to slow down.

The sudden pounding of hooves came behind her and a voice called out, "Whoa, whoa. Slow down, boy."

Gwen could feel the lessening of King's stride little by little, as the other rider drew alongside her. At last, the rider was close enough to reach over and grasp the bridle reins, bringing King to a walk then to a stop.

Much to Gwen's chagrin when she tried to dismount, her legs were like dishrags and she fell into the arms of her would-be rescuer. In her state of delirium, her first thought was that it was Seth, and without inhibition, she clung to him. Even as her mind cleared and her situation came into focus, she still hoped she would look up into the sapphire blue eyes of her husband. Disappointment jolted through her as she peered up into hazel eyes and a latch of dark brown hair covered by a backward baseball cap.

"I'm sorry. I thought... I didn't mean—" She stammered, unable to think straight. She struggled to stand on her wobbly legs.

"That's alright, Miss." He touched where the brim of his cap should be. "Think nothing of it. I've had a recurring dream of a beautiful young woman falling into my arms. Now I can move on to the next recurring dream—Miss." He smiled and continued to support her until she could stand.

The caretaker, Ralph, came whizzing along on his grounds cart. "Missy, Missy, are you okay? You gave this old man a horrible pain. Are you alright?" He said struggling out of the cart.

"Thank you," Gwen said as she regained control of her legs and stood on her own. "Yes, thanks to this Good Samaritan, I'm doing better."

"Come sit down, Missy," Ralph said. "This is the new hired man I spoke of. Dis is Matt, Matthew Hastings. I dinna know, Matt, you's a trick rider too. Dat's not on your papers," The groundskeeper said with a chortle. "Bring dem horses back to da stable. Missy'll ride back with me." He and Matt helped Gwen into the grounds keeper's cart.

"We were bringing the red gelding out a the stable 'cause I was looking for you purty quick—not dat quick but we heard da horse acoming. I thought uh- oh someting not right he's comin too fast."

"It was certainly timely for me. How did you get a bridle..." Gwen stopped speaking as the hired man, Matt, led the two horses across the back yard and up the circle drive close to where Gwen and Ralph sat conversing in the cart.

"No, der wasn't no bridle, just the lead shank. Say, what you tink a dat horse?" Ralph called out to Matt.

"Not bad. He's got plenty of action, good conformation, and pretty quiet," Matt said with a grin. "What set your horse off, Miss? He was trembling when I first started back."

The memory hit Gwen, and it felt like all the blood drained from her face. "A tree...and I don't know—a tree down by the lake...We, I had turned back from the lake, I saw—" Gwen tried to put thoughts together. What should she say in front of this new man? She could tell Ralph, but what about Matt? And would even Ralph under-stand? "I don't know what, but I saw something and this tree fell at us, and King took off like lightning. I'm glad he stuck to the path all the way home. Alice— I need Alice." Gwen began to tremble as the severity of what happened came upon her.

Matt tied the horses to the back of the cart, scooped up Gwen and carried her to the front door, and rang the bell. "Miss De Win-ters would like her maid, Alice." He placed Gwen in the capable arms of Gerald, then walked back to Ralph and the horses.

Alice came scurrying to the foyer. "Upstairs, quickly. To her rooms, Gerald."

"Yes, ma'am." The big butler carried her as if she were still a child.

"We'll put her on the couch in front of the fireplace. You go have Mike—the cook— bring up a tray. Some hot tea and her breakfast."

"Yes, ma'am." Gerald laid Gwen on the couch and turned back to the door.

"Alice, oh, Alice, I saw... I saw..." Gwen was trembling.

"What is it, lamb? You saw what?"

"At the end of the path...just before the tree fell—"

"Tree fell? What tree fell?" Alice said as she knelt beside the couch. "Start again, pet."

"I was on my ride. I went down to the lake around the beach and paused on the path above the beach house and picnic tables. It was so quiet, and I was looking out over the peaceful scene. Just as I turned, I saw a blurred movement, and a tree fell toward King and me."

Alice put a finger to her lips, as there was a light tap on the door, and the cook called out, "Breakfast."

"Put it right here." Alice pulled the end table a little closer. "Thank you, Mike. I'll call or bring the tray down when I come."

"Very well, ma'am. Will this be everything then?"

"Yes, I believe it is," Alice said after looking over the items. She waited until he left the room then asked, "Are you sure you saw something? What could it have been?" She poured a cup of tea and handed it to Gwen.

"I don't know what—or who it could have been." Gwen blew on her tea. "It happened so fast, but I know I saw it." She sat quietly as she drank her tea, not speaking, only thinking.

"I'll have Ralph and Gerald go out and look at the area," Alice said at last. "Eat up your breakfast. We'll take care of it."

"Get some pictures, please?"

"Yes, that's a good idea. I'll be back in a bit."

By the time she finished her tea, Gwen was calm enough to eat her scrambled eggs, bacon, and muffin. Alice came in quietly and laid out her clothing for the morning.

"Your clothes are ready. Ralph, Gerald, and Mr. Hastings took the cart down to investigate." Alice picked up the tray.

"Hastings. That's an odd name. I've heard of someone else with that name." Gwen wrinkled up her face in thought. "It doesn't go with the first name of Matt though. When at first I met him, I thought he was Seth, but he sure doesn't look like Seth."

"It was providential he was where he was. Ralph told me they were bringing out that new horse to look him over and have him ready for you to inspect. When you came streaking by on King he didn't even hesitate, just threw the lead shank over Red's neck and swung on bareback like he'd ridden that horse a hundred times in that condition."

"Let me know how Ralph, Gerald, and Hastings get along and what they find," Gwen said.

"I will, Miss." Alice shook her head as she left the room with the tray.

"ALICE—HOW EMBARRASSING," Gwen said the next morning.

"Gerald, Ralph, and I think you should have an escort after the tree episode," Alice said firmly.

"I don't feel right about taking Ralph's new hired man away from him for even a short time every day. And Ralph wanted Red, the new horse, for me, so Juniper King has a bit of a breather. He's getting older, you know."

"We don't care if you're embarrassed or not. We're concerned about being safe rather than sorry." Alice's dark eyes flashed insistently.

"Since you put it that way, I understand. The other morning Hastings was teasing me," Gwen said. "But it wasn't the best situation. When King stopped running, I was so shaken that I literally melted off the horse and fell into Hastings's arms. My legs were like water and shaking. Hastings felt solid like Seth, and when I realized he wasn't Seth I tried to apologize. Hastings said, 'It's alright, Miss, I have a recurring dream of a beautiful woman falling into my arms and now I can move on to my next recurring dream.'"

"That's cheeky—And funny." Alice stopped and stared at Gwen. "We'll keep an eye on him anyway. Ralph likes him though. Says he's a willing worker, very talented, and a good sense of humor." Alice turned, busying herself to hide the smile on her face.

CHAPTER—18—

Gwen looked at the flowers and chocolates and shook her head. "I do like both of those gifts, I just wish…" she stopped with a heavy sigh.

"I'll take care of them. I wish for your sake as well." Alice picked up the gifts to dispose of them.

"It's uncanny how he seems to know when I don't have a lunch engagement. So far he's come to visit whenever I'm home. I've got a plan for this afternoon. Maybe I'll trick him this time. Have you found out anything more about him?"

"He's just back from Europe, as his father told you. He was jilted by a young English debutante, and since then he has been something of a loose-living sort of guy. As to how he knows when you are here or not—" Alice shrugged. "—I don't know."

It was a lovely morning. Gwen went out just before lunch, walked through her favorite diner, and out the back door into a hired car. The driver let her out at her kitchen door then drove back to town. It might have been a good trick but it did not succeed.

"Robert Howl the third," Gerald announced at 2:00 that afternoon as he showed the visitor into the sitting room.

"Hello, Robert." Gwen frowned at him.

"Hello, Miss De Winter. How about supper this evening?" he asked. "I know the perfect little hideaway."

"It happens to be Mrs. MacDonald. What are you afraid of? Commitment or...? You know you're safe, pursuing a married woman, right?"

"Oh, no, my Gwendolyn..."

"I'm not your Gwendolyn, and I have plans." She continued to frown at him.

"Maybe I am just wishing." He sighed and frowned back at her. "I would be a perfect gentleman."

"Why do you insist on sending flowers and chocolates even though you know I refuse to keep them? And what do you need a perfect hideaway for if you are pledged to be a perfect gentleman?"

"Well," he paused, "I can't honestly answer any of those questions. You look as if you need flowers, chocolate is good for your health, and the restaurant is Italian with the best cuisine anywhere—perfect hideaway or not."

"I've got plans for the evening," she insisted.

"Who is he?"

"A dinner engagement with friends, not a friend."

"Lunch tomorrow?" he proposed.

"Busy tomorrow also."

"All right my final offer." He picked up a tea cake. "Lunch the following day?"

"I have shopping to do that day. I guess I could meet you at...where?" she questioned taking a sip of her tea.

There was a tap on the door as Gerald announced, "Mr. Nicholas Martinez, Miss."

"Oh, good. Robert, have you met my friend, Nick Martinez?" Gwen asked.

"No, I don't believe I've had the pleasure." Robert Howl III said with a snobby tone. His ridiculous pose left him with the appearance of trying to look down his nose at someone who stood above him.

"Robert, this is Nick Martinez, my friend. He's a man of the cloth..." Gwen said.

"Pretty poor cloth," Robert said.

"Robert!" Gwen's eyes went wide in shock.

"That's okay, Mrs. MacDonald. This suit is pretty cheap, but like I tell my son, it isn't what you put on that makes you who you are." Nick Martinez grinned. "Robert here doesn't know that I have to minister to more than one person. Some of my people are poor and some are like you, Mrs. MacDonald—Gwen. And the good ones like Gwen don't care about a person's clothes."

"That says something about both Gwen and the poor," Robert said.

"Yes, it does," Nick said raising his eyebrows at the thought. "I'd never considered it like that before, but that's right. Oddly enough, it says a lot about human nature."

"I need to be heading on." Robert stood to leave. "Good to have met you, Mr. Martinez. You can always tell the merits of a person by their reactions to criticism." Robert grasped the preacher by the hand in a firm handshake.

"Thank you, I think..." Nick said with a puzzled look on his face.

"Coffee?" Gwen said after Robert had left. She poured a cup and handed it to her visitor. "There are several scones, shortbread, and pastries. I would prefer if you made your own choices." She offered him the tongs. "I'm glad you came back, and please don't let Robert's comments keep you away."

"Mrs. MacDonald..."

"Gwen is fine if you don't mind that I call you Nick?"

"We should get along well." He made his choice from the tray. "The scriptures tell us to remember humility, and I'm not easily put off. You don't always choose who you meet along the way of life but you can choose how you react." He bit into a scone and scanned the room. "These pictures on the wall—are these family?"

"Yes." Gwen rose and joined her guest. "Yes, this is my Aunt Zoe, some of her friends and acquaintances. These are my parents, Doctor and Mrs. De Winters..."

"Some impressive friends and acquaintances I would say—and here?" Nick asked.

"Aunt Zoe had studied and worked as a nurse. She was doing mission work in India when my parents died in a car accident. This picture is her as she returned—as soon as word reached her."

"That is even more impressive."

"It isn't a good photograph...I'm not sure why it's included in this grouping of pictures." Gwen scrunched up her brow, looking closely at the picture, noting several people in the snapshot.

"Why didn't your family just relax, take it easy? They didn't need to...work. They could have just floated along like most ultra-rich people."

"It has to do with the scripture *to whom much is given, much is expected*. I don't even know where that is, but my aunt believed and quoted it..."

"Ah, yes, *Luke 12:48 'For unto whomsoever much is given, of him shall be much required: and to whom men have committed much, of him they will ask the more.'* I'm not sure how that fits exactly, but it is worthy of looking into." Nick appeared thoughtful.

"My Aunt Zoe was a stickler for humility. No matter who a person was, she had the uncanny knack for reading people."

"That is a knack. She had another knack as well."

"What's that?"

"I never met your aunt. She's been gone how many years now?" Nick asked.

"I didn't think you had met her. She's been gone ten years now." Gwen looked quietly out the window.

"Some people put on a pretty good show. Like Robert hinted at, some people look good on the outside. I've been working here for about five years now and some of my people knew your aunt. They still speak of her with deep admiration and respect. It reminds me of something I read once. Two men were fighting off some peasants. One man was a freeman from Connecticut and one man—I think he was a king in disguise. The pair were vastly outnumbered, yet the kingly man threw back his head, and laughing, he charged right into the battle. This caused the Connecticut man to wonder in himself if there really is something different about a king...”

“Interesting,” Gwen said thoughtfully. “So, what are you saying?”

“I'm saying that a title isn't anything except an empty title if the character isn't there. People of royalty are what they are sometimes because of training, but sometimes also because somewhere in their ancestry they had an ancestor who was more.”

“More?” Gwen asked.

“Yes, more. And your aunt was more. She was humble even though she had immense physical wealth. She didn't act snobbish with others. People have told me she was kind, gentle, generous, and more.”

“She was all of those things. I read a book titled *Little Princess* when I was young, and there were some timeless truths in the book that stayed with me. Many of those truths were taught to me by my family—not just Aunt Zoe.”

“Have you and your husband made amends yet?”

“When Seth married me, he married someone he thought was like the girl next door. I've never told him differently, and I lived and worked like the girl next door. I don't know how he'd handle coming here—I don't think he'd fit in.” Gwen and Nick walked back to the sofa and chairs.

“Why's that?”

“He's a down-to-earth person getting his life straight. He doesn't put on airs, and he'll tell you what he thinks. Sometimes just a bit...” Gwen hesitated, searching for the right word.

"Straight-forward? Abrupt?" Nick said.

"Yes, abrupt, or some people call it tactless. In this society, I get along well because of our family name. I don't have to beat around the bush or take a back seat. But even I don't say certain things. One thing I love about Seth is if you ask him a question, he'll give you an answer, whether you like it or not," Gwen said with a snicker.

"I'd love to meet your Seth. He sounds like someone I could like being around."

"I've decided to put together some way to take care of my estate here and move to where Seth and I will be close to his family. I've been praying over our differences."

"What kind of differences?"

"He's one of the younger children of ten ...not the youngest, but his parents have been raising children for quite some time and they haven't changed their beliefs to fit current fashion."

"That is a double-edged sword."

"Yes, and it's something I'm struggling with. There are some types of clothing and habits I've adapted that have become acceptable that maybe shouldn't be acceptable."

"Maria and I go back to our mothers' country for visits and I can tell you there is a stark difference between what's acceptable here in this country and what isn't acceptable there. What we see happening here is frightening. There is such a thing as having too many things on the outside but being destitute or bankrupt on the inside."

"Ha, that was in your sermon Sunday. '*And he gave them their request; but sent leanness into their soul.*'"

"*Psalm 106:15*—that is gratifying, someone not just listening but remembering." A wide grin spread across Nick's face. "Well, I'd better be going. I've got things to do."

"I'm glad you stopped by. You've got little people at home, yes?" Gwen asked. "Let me have Alice box up some of these goodies for you to take..."

"Oh, ho, you better be careful there. My girls will send me back every day if you send them treats." He laughed.

Gwen smiled. "You'll have to bring them along someday. This house has needed little people's feet for a long time."

GWEN WOKE SLOWLY FROM the nightmare in which she was standing in a long, dark hallway. She could sense danger and felt the panic rising within her, but in the dream, there was nothing except darkness. As she lay there listening there was a sound so slight that maybe it was her own breathing. Or was it someone else's breathing? Usually, it was a relief to wake up from her nightmare, but tonight it was almost the same—waking or sleeping. Was it the dream or had there been a noise that had woken her? She lay listening, her heart pounding in her ears.

She had decided it was a figment of her imagination when she heard a slight scrabbling sound coming from the balcony windows. This time of the year, the balcony windows were all firmly latched. She had checked these windows before she turned out the light. She held her breath. It might be the wind, but...was that a shadow? Angrily throwing back the covers, and slipping into a dressing gown, her bare feet stepped silently on the floor.

She crossed her room and passed through the hall to the door of her maid's room. Tapping softly, she hissed, "Alice, are you awake?"

Alice answered her knock quickly. "What is it?"

"I am sure someone was on my balcony. I wanted a backup before I confronted them," she whispered.

"I'm right behind you, dear." The maid pressed a button that alerted the butler. "Gerald will be here in a few moments also," Alice whispered as she wrapped herself in her dressing gown. The pair silently retraced Gwen's steps. Gerald joined them just as they reached the windows, and Gwen unlocked them and flung them open. There was nothing but the wind blowing the leaves against the lattice on the balcony.

"Oh!" Gwen exhaled loudly. "I was sure I heard someone!"

"I'll take a look around. No use for you two ladies getting cold," Gerald insisted firmly as he ushered them inside and stepped back onto the balcony.

"I am so sorry, Alice. I was having one of my nightmares, and when I woke up I must have heard the wind in those leaves. I was sure that I saw a shadow. I overreacted," Gwen apologized profusely.

"That is quite all right, Missy, that is what we are here for," Alice said. "Why don't I go get you a warm glass of milk from the kitchen?"

"There now, don't go worrying," Gerald said reassuringly. After stepping back into the room and closing and locking the door firmly behind him, he pulled the light curtains together. "There isn't anything for you to worry about. I've shut out any draft that might find its way in. Miss Alice, you start a little fire in the fireplace here. I will go down and get the warm milk. Tomorrow, I propose, putting heavier curtains on these windows. No wonder our girl had a bad dream with the draft these chilly nights. You get things warmed up, and I'll be back directly."

Alice straightened up after starting the fire. "There's the fire, and thank you for the milk, Gerald." She handed it to Gwen. "Drink up your milk then get back to bed. I'll be right here." When Gwen had drunk the milk, Alice pulled the covers up and tucked them in. "Good night, now," she said as she walked to the door.

"What was it you found?" Alice asked Gerald at the top of the stairs before returning to her room.

"In this light?" Gerald answered with a furrowed brow. "It did appear as if there was a smudge of mud by the window—I'll have to check further in the morning. We'll have to be on guard," Gerald said with a frown.

"THIS HAS BEEN AN ALMOST perfect day, Alice. I've done some visiting this afternoon, had time for light reading and relaxing. I've even entertained a few friends for the evening, but... I can't put my mind at ease about last night."

"Why is that?" Alice finished brushing Gwen's hair and turned down the bed covers for the evening. "You know Gerald said for you not to worry."

"I haven't had one of my nightmares for a few years now, and the more I think about last night, I don't believe it was my imagination...and there was a footprint in the flower bed," she said.

"Gerald and I didn't want you to worry," Alice said after a pause. "We didn't want to deceive you, but this will make it easier in a way. The French doors are locked, we've put up the heavier curtains, and from now on, I sleep in here on the sofa. No," Alice raised her hand and spoke firmly as she saw Gwen about to protest. "No, it will be no good. If you don't consent I will sleep in the hall, propped up against your door."

"YOU KNOW, SIR, I WAS very young. I don't remember anything about my parents' deaths. I was just wondering...You see, Aunt Zoë would never discuss it, or allow anyone else to discuss it around me." Gwen sat across the desk from Robert Howl, Sr.

"It was an accident on a drizzly, overcast—a gray, autumn afternoon. The roads were wet and just a little slick. The brakes failed as they were on their way home that late afternoon. They came to a curve and couldn't slow down." Uncle Robert frowned and pulled on his lower lip. "A terrible accident. Your aunt Zoë was away at the time, but she came straight home, of course."

"What a blessing Auntie was," Gwen commented mostly to herself. "I have missed her." The large leather chair Gwen sat in appeared to swallow her up. "I don't know what to do. A few months ago I was at work in a restaurant." She stopped at the surprised look on the older man's face. "Well, my husband didn't know me by my aunt's name, which he might have recognized. My legal name is Winters, and he never asked about my past. I never told him who my family is...and I wanted to remain busy like a normal person."

"I see," Mr. Howl spoke as he made a notation on a slip of paper. He put his fingertips together and waited for her to continue.

"So, I was at work when some fellow came in and told me my husband had been in an accident and was on his way to the hospital. I left work immediately, but on the way—" She exhaled slowly. "On the way to the hospital my brakes failed, and I missed the curve. I had several bumps and bruises and a broken leg. My husband was away at the time, so his sister came and took me home."

Mr. Howl sat up, leaned forward, and put his hands on his desk. His dark eyes almost bored a hole into hers as he demanded, "This man, what did he look like?"

"It happened so quickly...All I could think of was Seth needing me, possibly dying. I panicked." She tried to recall a face and identity. "Dark hair, dark eyes." She grimaced.

"Was he tall? Did he wear glasses? Was there anything! Anything at all that you might be able to recognize him by?" the lawyer pressed.

"No, he was about average height," she continued trying to remember. "There was something that I didn't like about him, but nothing I could identify him by," she said. "But Seth hadn't been in an accident." Gwen sat quietly for a moment trying to be discreet. "I had decided to leave Seth, my husband, due to... He had a drinking problem, and it was killing him and I couldn't stand watching him die day by day. At this point, a family friend intervened and Seth was getting the help he needed to get on his feet. He and his brother tracked me to the hospital where I'd been treated after my accident.

One of the nurses at the hospital mentioned someone else—a greasy-haired man had been asking about me. The nurse said she didn't tell that man anything."

"So, are you saying there may be a connection?" He sat back in his comfortable swivel chair, put his fingertips together, and frowned at this information.

"The insurance company said my brakes were tampered with. My aunt was killed in an accident also. She was wearing a coat that was similar to mine, and in her rain hat it would have been an easy mistake to make."

Robert Howl gazed at Gwen, a thoughtful look on his face. "Why are you making these speculations? You have a reason beyond what you have given?"

"I have been back two weeks. Someone has been following me. Last week a tree fell over, missing my horse and me by mere inches, and the night before last, someone attempted to gain entry into my bedroom from the balcony."

"It's not mere fancy?" he asked.

"I could resent that question, but.... No, it is not a woman's hysterical misgivings. There is no proof as to being followed. Maybe the footstep behind me that doesn't quite stop in time, or the image in the shop window that disappears too quickly. Little things." She shrugged. "There are pictures of the tree being tampered with before it fell. I have Alice, as well as Gerald who saw the footprint on the balcony and in the flower bed from the other night. What sort of proof do you need?"

"Hmm," he pondered with a frown. "I could hire a private detective—a bodyguard. What do you want to do?" He began writing on a sheet of notepaper.

"A bodyguard would work for a short while," she mused. "But for how long? And if these things are connected, this person has been around for a long time. Someone with a grudge that doesn't want to—die. If someone is out there we have to come up with a way to end this."

"Right. Give me a few hours to get things in place, to make some arrangements..."

"I have a lunch engagement with your grandson. I can come back here in a few hours. What would you suggest?"

"I would suggest a chaperone." The older man smiled then added, "Have Bobby bring you back here about three this afternoon."

"THEIR FOOD IS EXCELLENT." Robert perused the menu and offered Gwen advice. "Is there anything you prefer?"

"Surprise me." She folded up her menu, not caring what she ate. Robert ordered the meal, and Gwen thought about Seth. Robert and Seth were about the same age, but Seth was taller and much thinner. Robert's hair was almost black whereas Seth's was a red gold. Robert's eyes were brown, but Seth's eyes were blue. Would this always be her life? Comparing anyone she met with Seth? "I don't drink wine," she told him suddenly. "You know I don't drink wine."

"I thought that perhaps..." He stopped as she shook her head no. "What would you like?" He sighed as he signaled the waiter.

"Just iced tea with sugar and lemon will be fine."

"Why not lemonade?" he joked.

"Because I prefer tea...with sugar and lemon."

"Do you mind if I have something else?"

"Suit yourself," she answered with a cool shrug.

"We'll change our order to iced tea," he said when the waiter approached.

The weather was mild, and they were able to enjoy their meal on the terrace. There was a bite in the morning air, but by noon it was too warm for a jacket.

"I need to slip into the powder room. I'll be back shortly," Gwen said.

"HELLO, BOBBY." DAVE Aberdeen scooted his chair over from another table. "What are you doing here, and who's the gorgeous gal with you?"

"No one interested in you." Bobby Howl cut his acquaintance short. "She's my grandfather's client and married."

"When has that ever stopped Robert Howl, III... or Dave Aberdeen for that matter. We're both pretty flexible—"

"Maybe, but this woman doesn't drink, smoke, or party. Not your sort of gal, Davy old boy."

"Not your sort either. So what's the scoop? Plenty of money? What?"

"Well—" Bobby warmed up a bit to the subject. "She's kind of intriguing—unpredictable. She's got loads of money, but...She's not like most women our age. She's quiet, intelligent—her husband must be crazy to let a jewel like her loose. She's worth her weight in gold...even without her fortune."

"I've got enough crazy women in my life. I think they're all unpredictable...Oh, oh, here's Chelsea. Talk about unpredictable, I'll catch you later."

"Yeah...later." Bobby turned as his phone rang. "Hello?" He ended his phone conversation as Gwen came back from the ladies' room.

"SO, WHERE WERE WE BEFORE being interrupted?" he asked.

"I like sugar and lemon in my tea." She stirred her glass of iced tea. "Tell me about yourself, Robert. Are you a lawyer also?"

"Yes, and no. I make a living following the family business, but art is my passion."

"Do you paint or collect?"

"Both...maybe that is why I find you so captivating. The way the sunlight highlights your hair. The way autumn colors bring out the warm tints in your complexion and make the blue-gray of your eyes so compelling." He gazed into her eyes.

She frowned at him. "Robert the Third... I understood you to say you would be a perfect gentleman."

"Do you mean I'm not being a perfect gentleman?" he wore an innocent, boyish expression.

Gwen laughed. When the waiter materialized at her elbow with a tray of food, she jumped.

"Pardon, madam," he apologized as he steadied the tray and set the plates down.

"What's the matter, Gwen?" Robert frowned. "You glance around nervously, not looking at anything. Does it have to do with the fact that my father told me to escort you back to the offices after our meal, and to not let you out of my sight?"

"When was that?" she questioned with a raised eyebrow.

"I was talking to him when you returned to the table."

"Oh...I see."

"It's hard to carry on a conversation, by one's self, and you never did answer my question."

"I don't know," Gwen said. "I've known several people who could carry on a conversation by themselves. I'm sorry, though, yes it probably does have to do with those instructions," she sighed. "Robert?" she wrinkled her brow and looked at him through narrowed eyes.

"Yes?" He partially listened as he attacked his salad.

"Would you kiss me?" she asked.

"Well, now," putting down the fork he put his hand over hers, "Anything to accommodate a lady." He smiled.

Pulling her hand away, she picked up her tea. "Knowing full well I'm another man's wife, you would still kiss me?" She took a sip of tea.

"I have to gather flowers where I may." He shrugged.

"You can't really believe that." She sat back, picking at her food.

"What is that?" His expression turned dark. Picking up his fork, again he assaulted his salad.

"Gathering the flowers—playing the field." She frowned.

"Why not? What difference does it make?"

"You don't believe that any more than I do." She studied his face.

"Why wouldn't I?" After taking a drink of his tea, he sat back.

"What are you looking for? I think you're scared of making a mistake. The idea of not getting what you're chasing is fascinating—No commitment, no mistake."

Robert spoke angrily. "I'm beginning to agree. You're alluring because you're just out of reach. About the time I think I'm getting to first base, someone moves the base. If you are looking for a perfect gentleman what are you doing here?"

"Someone else asked me a similar question several weeks ago, and I continue to ask myself the same thing."

"For what reason did you agree to come to lunch with me?" He continued to scowl.

"I don't know exactly why. I think it's because you've got a good heart. I think it's because you need something to believe in."

He opened his mouth to speak, but closed it. His face relaxed from a scowl into thought as he began his main course. "I can't believe you just said that to me."

"Well, I did, and I don't know where that came from. Now that I've said it...It's true isn't it?" Gwen's eyes became shrewd. "A woman hurt you badly and there are plenty of that kind of women out there. There are some good females out there as well. You need to look in the right place. Probably not at the horse...or dog racing track...We'll need to have this boxed up. I can't eat this lasagna."

"What? Why not?" He stared at her plate.

"It's—I just can't."

"Sure, but—Waiter, we need a box here." He signaled then turned back to Gwen.

"Thank you." She finished her salad and sipped her tea while waiting for the box.

"I haven't had anyone tell me that. Not since my grandmother passed away. I've missed her. You're too young to remind me of my grandmother, but you are the most confusing woman I know."

There was no comparison between Robert and Seth, Gwen decided as they left the restaurant. She was quiet during the ride back to the office. Riding along the peaceful highway that showcased the beautiful scenery gave her a short time to reflect on the last few weeks and wonder about the answer to her other problems. She came out of her reverie as they pulled up in front of her lawyer's office. Robert the III had slipped back into his easy-going lame persona during their ride. After coming around to her side of the Lincoln he opened the door and helped her out. "And right on time, Mrs. Mac-Donald," he said with a sarcastic twist as he stepped to the front door and held it open.

He waved at the secretary as they crossed the outer room, opened the door to his grandfather's office with a flourish as if presenting a prize. He spoke as they entered his grandfather's spacious office. "Here we are, sir—according to directions—safe and sound."

CHAPTER—19—

"Mrs. MacDonald," Robert Howl introduced, "I would like you to meet Mr. Franklin O. Green. Franklin, this is your new employer, Mrs. Gwendolyn MacDonald. Would you, uh, like to have, uh..." he broke off suddenly as the detective rose and stalked around Gwen, talking out loud as if she were a piece of merchandise being inspected.

"That hairstyle is atrocious—You need a large hat." Mr. Green smirked, entertained by his joke. "That silk scarf looks good though, and those pumps go well." He agreed with himself. "Nice sensible shoes. I like that jacket." He reached out and fingered the texture of the coat. "Good quality. Wrong color lipstick. Hmm, not bad all things considered." He finished his appraisal by taking out a large handkerchief and wiping his face.

"Mrs. MacDonald...Gwen. I'm sorry, would you like a seat?" Robert Howl apologized. "This detective came with a high recommendation."

Gwen sat feeling a bit of shock as she looked over the man in front of her. It was not just because he was cross-eyed, or that he walked with a gimp. Gwen could handle disabilities; she could also handle different nationalities, so that wasn't a problem. The look on both Robert Sr. and Robert's grandson's faces told Gwen that they felt the same way. For some reason, Bobby—Robert III —appeared to bristle up in a challenge by this guy. As if one of them was an intruder. What a ludicrous thought! Besides the bushy black hair that apparently a comb could not conquer and the aforementioned characteristics, the detective was rude and annoying. In short, there was nothing that any self-respecting woman would even be attracted to, Gwen thought with a shudder.

"I guess I'll take the case," the man decided as if he had a choice in the matter. "So, are you ready to go, Miss, uh Mrs. McDougal?"

"It's MacDonald. Mrs. MacDonald. I'm not sure, Mister Green, if you are the man for this job." Robert Sr. scrutinized Franklin O. Green as if he were a new species. "I know you were highly recommended, but you have to understand Mrs. MacDonald will not put up with just anyone. She meets and is in a different society than what you are accustomed to. You will have to..."

"Oh, hoity-toity. I see how it is. Well, not to worry." The man brushed off the old lawyer's objections. "Come now, Mrs. MacDonald, we'll have everything right as rain in no time. Come, come, let's be going now." The detective handed Gwen a shoulder-length blonde wig and a pair of sunglasses and urged her out of the room. "There's a car waiting." Franklin Greene grabbed Gwen's elbow and escorted her out a back door, shutting it abruptly as Robert III stood.

"Well," Robert said after his curt departure, "this game isn't over yet."

"I don't know, Bobby," the older lawyer said softly, "I think this is a mistake."

"WHY DO YOU WEAR YOUR hair cut so?" asked Franklin Green. "You'd look much more attractive with it longer," he enunciated in perfect English with a clipped accent.

"Why do you think you can talk to me in such a fashion?" Gwen's response was cool. "As if I even care what you—a stranger—think?" *How incredible*, she thought. *This man is offensive, pushy, and abrasive, not to mention that he appears to be the most dis-*

jointed person I have ever met. "Mr. Greene, I may be young, but I'm not stupid, nor will I be cowed by your behavior. We will have a difficult relationship at best under these circumstances."

"I see." His eyes narrowed as he spoke. "It's always good to have a backbone. I admire people who can speak for themselves."

Neither one spoke during the half-hour trip home, and they arrived without any further ado at Gwen's estate.

Gwen and the stranger entered the foyer. "Alice, this is Franklin O. Greene. He's a private detective who will be staying with us for a few weeks. We will have coffee in the parlor in twenty minutes. And are there any pastries?"

"I'll check, miss," the maid replied crisply. If she was surprised by her mistress' new appearance or her escort she did not show it in any way.

"Mr. Greene..."

"You can call me Frank," he replied offhandedly. "Most folks just call me Frank." He gazed around.

"I prefer Mr. Greene." Gwen lifted an eyebrow. "I'll show you to your room. You will send for your luggage?"

"I don't carry my luggage all over with me when I'm working, ma'am. Yes, I'll send for it."

"Just follow me then. You can at least wash your face and refresh yourself before our repast. The parlor is this room here on the right." She motioned as she walked past it toward the stairs. They climbed the wide stairs to the third floor, and she opened the door just catty-cornered across the hall from hers. "I will expect our interview to commence in twenty minutes. Can you find your way back to the parlor?" she asked.

"I'm sure I can. And I still say you are most attractive with the longer hair—blond isn't even too bad, but you're definitely fabulous as a redhead. Twenty minutes, then." He clumped past her and into his quarters.

Gwen closed her eyes as anger rose in her. She was caught off guard, and that infuriated her more than the comment. Was he laughing at her? Was there something in his face—perhaps it was his mocking attitude? Maybe it was his familiar manner, especially for one who was working for her. He never looked directly at her, so how did he know how she would look best? She frowned.

Catching her reflection in the mirror as she entered her room—the longer hair did look attractive. "Arg," she grabbed the wig and threw it across the room onto her vanity. "Humph," she added for emphasis as she brushed her lengthening hair. It was growing slowly since she had returned. Mr. Tavish's conversation—and the comments of the hairdresser—needled a spot in her conscience.

Twenty minutes later, Mr. Greene opened the door for Alice and clumped into the parlor after her. Clumped was the only way to describe the way he walked.

Alice brought the tray of coffee and an assortment of tarts as well as scones into the parlor. Setting it down on the table she asked, "Is there anything else, ma'am?"

"That should be sufficient, Alice. Thank you."

"Yes, ma'am," Alice spoke formally and left the room.

Mr. Green quizzed, "She is your servant? How long has she been in your employ?"

Gwen raised her eyebrows coolly.

"Let's get something straight." Frank Greene leaned forward and frowned roughly in her direction. "I am not your servant. I am here to help you because you have a problem. If I am to help, I must have your co-operation."

"Alice has been with my family since I was two years old. She came to work for my parents at that time," Gwen said with a sigh. "Our caretaker, Ralph, has been here longer than I have. Other than Gerald, the butler, they are the only two I retained after my aunt's death. The chef is new, and Ralph has hired some new men to help with the lawns and gardens. The new people came with references, which you can review." *He's right, if we are to get this cleared up, I'll have to put my irritation aside.*

Gwen poured the coffee automatically asking, "Would you like cream or sugar?"

"No, I take mine straight." His manner became less rough. "Your parents died twenty years ago when you were...?"

"Eight," she said.

"Your aunt died ten years ago when you were eighteen?" he asked.

"Yes," she answered.

"You were married?"

"I am married," she said.

He raised his eyebrows in surprise. "I understood you live here alone with only your hired help."

"I have been back here only a short time," she said without explanation.

"So when is your husband due to arrive?"

"He isn't." She didn't look him in the eye.

"Most people get married to be together, but maybe it isn't the same for the rich and famous?" His face twisted into a frown.

"I'm not rich and famous." The tension returned between them.

"You're in the book of Who's Who. That makes you famous, and you are certainly rich by most standards." He scowled.

"So my family is wealthy, and my family is listed in the book, not me." She glared back.

"Your husband is the issue here." He ran his hand through his hair. "Is he expected to show up or not, and have you parted on friendly terms, or might he be the...ah...problem?"

"He is not expected to show up. I don't know on what terms we parted, and he is not the problem." She emphasized each statement.

"Where's he from, and what's his background?" Detective Greene relentlessly drained every drop of information from her. "You were living in North Carolina, but his family— and at this time your husband—are living in the Midwest?"

"That's right," Gwen said.

"You were working at a restaurant in North Carolina when you got the message that he was in the hospital?" Franklin Greene gave Gwen a sideways look. "Honestly, I can't believe you lived a life like a normal person for nine years. Why in this world would you do that with this type of life waiting for you?"

"No matter what you can or can't believe, that's the way it was." There was a knock on the door.

"Ma'am, I've come for the tray," Alice said softly and entered to remove the tray.

"Inform the chef to add Mr. Greene for supper, and please prepare a guest room," Gwen said with a frown.

Alice did not question her mistress, nor show surprise. "Which room would you like prepared, ma'am?"

"The Blue Room. And have Gerald bring Mr. Greene's luggage up when it arrives, please."

Alice raised her eyebrows slightly but said nothing.

Gwen looked at Alice and smiled. "It's alright, Bunny." She used a childhood nickname.

The older woman's eyes warmed, and she returned the smile. "Yes, Miss Gwen."

"OH, ALICE, I HAVE TO say Mr. Greene is not quite as annoying as I first believed. Sometimes he's worse!" Gwen said later in the week, "He complains because he has to rise early, and he complains because he doesn't like horses. Yesterday he complained because I insisted that he dress the part when we went to the Petersons." She sighed. "I don't think there is any hope for this... disjointed man, but the least he could do is attempt to improve." She quietly contemplated the latest development while Alice massaged Gwen's neck and shoulders. "Have you found out any more about Robert the Third?" Gwen asked.

"Well, lamb, you were right. There are all sorts of rumors about Robert. He sounds like a scoundrel at least. Yes, there were rumors about him and that woman, Mrs. Rita Worth. She's a case. He was in Europe for quite a few years. Matter of fact, most of his education was overseas. The story is that he was engaged to marry a very beautiful young girl but shortly before the wedding—well, you know the story. Someone with more money sweeps the beautiful young woman off her feet, and leaves the other poor bloke with a broken heart, or leaves him looking like an idiot."

"Or at least feeling like one," Gwen said. "Anything else? Debts? How does he spend his time and money? Friends? Does he have any good qualities?"

"Well, he does like the horse and dog races. He has some friends, but they aren't any more reputable than he is. Some of them are rather shady characters." She wrinkled her brow. "When is your friend Leila supposed to arrive?"

"She should be here anytime now." Gwen glanced at the clock. "Have you prepared her room and informed the chef? I'm sure it will be good for Leila to come for a visit. It hasn't been long since she lost her husband, and it will distract her mind for a time."

"It will be good for you as well, Miss. I'll go check how things are progressing. The new help has been a blessing. You rest for a while. I'll be back."

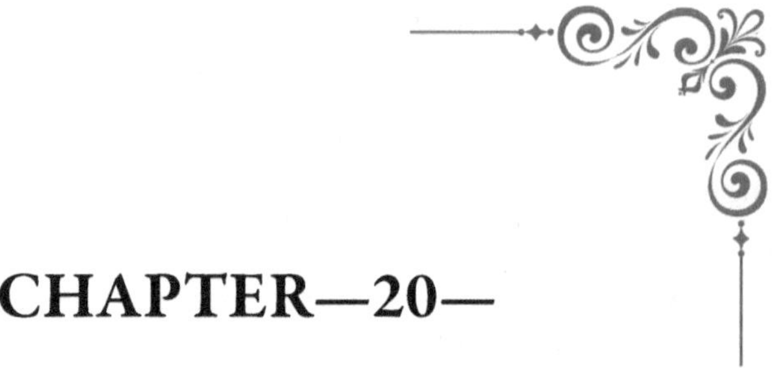

CHAPTER—20—

Gwen was throwing her saddle on Roman Red the next morning when she heard the familiar clomping coming across the driveway.

"Thank you, Mr. Hastings," she said. The newly hired man brought out a gentle old horse Ralph had found for Mr. Greene to ride. "I appreciate you saddling Mr. Greene's horse for him. Not that I couldn't..."

"Ms. MacDonald," Mr. Hastings said, "If you didn't insist on tacking your own mount..."

"I know. You don't feel right about me doing your job. That's fine. My Aunt Zoe insisted I learn to care for my own animal." Gwen stroked Red's neck and jaw. "You're a good boy, aren't you?" she whispered to her horse.

Mr. Greene stood waiting as Gwen and Hastings led the horses to the stable door. "I'm almost getting accustomed to your morning ride. Say, your friend Leila doesn't ride, does she?"

"No, Leila had a bad experience with a horse when she was a teenager. She can ride, but isn't real keen on it."

"I'm not keen on it either. I like to have both feet on the ground..."

"Mr. Hastings used to ride with me until you came, of course," Gwen said.

"That wouldn't hardly do now would it, ma'am?" Mr. Greene challenged with a dark look.

"I don't suppose it would, but he never complained." Gwen grinned at Mr. Greene. "I suppose we need to be getting on with our ride. I have several errands to do before lunch, and we have dinner out this evening. Mr. Hastings?"

"Yes, Ms. MacDonald?" He held her horse and gave her a hand up.

"Thank you." She shifted in the saddle, waiting as Mr. Greene positioned his horse by the mounting block and mounted clumsily. "Are you ready then, Franklin? We are going on the shorter path down by the beach this morning. Mr. Hastings, you can tell Ralph we won't be gone long."

"Will do, ma'am." He touched his cap as they rode away.

"Matt Hastings is a strange young man, don't you think?" Mr. Greene asked.

"What makes you say that?"

"He should be married with a family at his age, but he's just a drifter. A very smart drifter, and he should be a chick magnet."

"A what?" Gwen blinked in surprise.

"A chick magnet. A good-looking man who has to beat the girls off with a stick."

"I guess I'd never thought about it..." Gwen's face wrinkled up as she thought over this new term.

"Of course, you wouldn't. Now, an outcast like myself would. I see it all the time. A good-looking guy like Mr. Hastings there can't walk down the street without attracting attention."

"The outside of a person isn't always a good judge of the inside, Franklin." Gwen stopped her horse at the edge of the meadow.

"No, it isn't." He sighed. "Sometimes a scoundrel can have a fair face. You just never know."

"Oh, look," Gwen whispered and pointed to a doe with twin fawns. "I only saw one fawn the last time I was here...and the outside of a pot doesn't tell you a thing about the inside stew." She nudged her horse into motion down the path toward the beach.

"Do you like to fish?" she asked as they rode along the water. Then she turned up the incline to the forest.

"I did at one time, about twenty years ago."

"We should have the boat brought down and have a small picnic down at the beach." She pulled her horse to a stop to give him rest after the upward climb. *How spooky, that glassy-eyed look in Franklin's eyes, and has his mind slipped into the past?*

"My Aunt Zoe used to have a year-end picnic. We just barely have time. I'll see what Alice thinks." Gwen talked more to herself since Franklin Greene's attention was somewhere else.

"Yes, I enjoyed fishing at one time. Zoe Lind, she was quite a lady..." he said as they drew close to the drive by the stables.

"You knew my aunt?" Gwen said in surprise.

"*Of* your aunt. I knew *of* your aunt." His eyes became guarded.

"Ah, Ralph," she said as her caretaker materialized out of the stable door. "I must fly to get ready for breakfast. If you—or Hastings—could put Red away for me, I'd be grateful." Gwen slid off and handed the reins to Ralph.

"I sure will, Missy. And I've hired another helper besides Hastings. I'll have him take Mr. Greene's horse. You go on now."

"We'd best hurry. Leila will be wondering where you are." Gwen laughed as she hurried back to the house.

"I DON'T KNOW WHAT TO think, Alice. I find it amusing how everywhere Mr. Greene is, Leila shows up. She seems to be infatuated with him. If she wasn't afraid of horses, I know she'd be out there when we go riding."

"I find him confusing. There is something odd about him, and I don't trust him," Alice said as she brushed Gwen's hair. "He can move quietly—when he wants to. It's odd."

"At least Franklin and I have come to a sort of truce. What do you think of having a late summer picnic like Aunt Zoe used to have?"

"I can ask Mike, the cook. So far I've had no complaints whatsoever with his work, nor his meals. Although...as I think on it, Mr. Greene has developed a habit of drinking coffee with Mike in the kitchen at strange hours. Sometimes morning—but not always any specific time. So, a large or small picnic?" Alice got back to the subject at hand.

"Smaller. I don't have many close friends like Aunt Zoe had..."

"That should be doable. Oh, look how much your hair has grown. Louie DuVall would be so pleased." Alice pinned a neat upswept hairstyle then, placed the brush on the dressing table. "Let's get down to breakfast."

"DID YOU SLEEP WELL, Leila?" Gwen swept into the small dining room. "And I see you've made it down as well, Franklin."

"I did sleep well. I haven't slept that well in at least a year," Leila said.

"And since I didn't have to powder my nose and change my clothes I found my way to the coffee pot before you did." Franklin brandished his coffee cup as proof.

"Well, there you have it," Gwen said as she picked up her plate and investigated the buffet table and its offerings. "I won't mention that I hit the coffee pot *before* I went riding, Franklin." She smiled as she brought her plate back to the table. One of the new maids poured her coffee after she sat down.

"Touché, Franklin. Gwen got you that time." Leila smiled at him.

"I guess she did," he said in good humor. "What's your routine today, Ms. MacDonald?"

"Leila and I have some errands in town this morning. We need to pick up some items for Mike from his culinary specialty store. Home for lunch, and dinner at the Bensons this evening." The conversation flowed around her as she ate. She watched as Leila asked Franklin a question and listened when he went into a complicated answer. What a blessing Leila was for herself and Mr. Greene. *I have been allowed my freedom to come and go and to carry out a semblance of a routine. Too bad it didn't help Franklin improve in his basic faults, but he's a bit more congenial.* She sighed. *I doubt I'll ever grow accustomed to his clumping, the fact that he never looks directly at me, or that his hair always seems to have a will of its own.* Gwen took a bite of her scrambled eggs. *And his unpredictable rudeness can be quite jarring.*

"What time will you ladies be ready to go?" Franklin said as he drained his coffee cup.

"I just need a sweater. How about you?" Gwen asked.

"About ten minutes should do me," Leila said.

"Good, I'll meet you two at the car then." He clumped out of the dining room.

"AFTER LUNCH, I BELIEVE I'll take a short rest, Leila. I've been looking over some legalese documents, and they give me a headache. And some of the decisions I'm being asked to make…" Gwen sat quietly for a few moments. "I'll need some quiet before Mr. Howl's visit this afternoon. On a better note, we'll be having the boats brought up and our autumn picnic will take place next week."

"That's exciting. Your cook, Mr. Mike, is the best. He's funny—and where did you find that Mr. Hastings? They're like the funniest pair I know," Leila said.

"I told you," Mr. Greene spoke up from the depths of the auto's cushions as Gerald drove them back from the morning outing. "A chick magnet."

"A chick magnet?" Leila questioned. "I don't think either Mike or Hastings would qualify as a chick magnet. I do appreciate a good sense of humor, but I prefer men with a scholarly bent, like yourself, Franklin. No, they're ordinary guys and the one has a small but wicked scar...Well, I'll need a bit of a rest, too, after lunch," Leila said as they were pulling into the home driveway.

"Gerald, don't forget the few items we brought back for Mike. He was really keen on wanting some special herbs, so make sure you get these to him right away. And, Leila, here are your packages." Gwen handed several bags to Leila and picked out her own parcels. She turned as Mr. Greene clumped up behind her.

"Let me take those herbs to Mike. I suggested he try some of these with his mutton for lunch," he said.

"Sure, Franklin, here they are." She held them out for him. "I appreciate that—I didn't know you were into cooking?"

"Well, I've studied it a bit. I've been cooking for myself for quite a few years now." He took the basket with the pungent herbs.

How can someone so easily distracted work as a PI? The glassy-eyed stare he gets...and his mind is occupied somewhere else. Gwen shuddered.

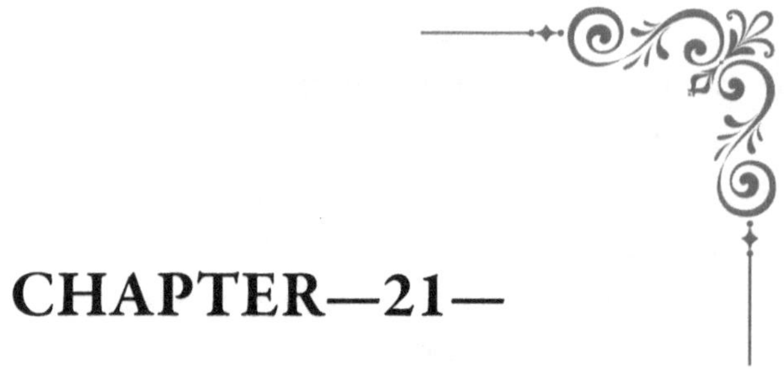

CHAPTER—21—

Gwen pulled her pale, dusty blue chiffon dress over her head and touched up her make-up. It was time to take up her spot in the parlor where she would entertain her guests. The color of blue accented her eyes, hair, and complexion. She sighed and paused a moment, picked up and held the picture of Seth and her together. A tear slid down her cheek and fell on the glass covering the photograph. She sighed again and replaced the picture. *This will never do,* she thought as she dabbed away the tearstains. She caught sight of her image— a stranger she didn't recognize— staring back at her from her mirror. She appraised this stranger with detached interest. From her shoulder-length cinnamon-colored hair swept up into a loose, simple, French twist, to her chic chiffon dress, and her pastel blue pumps, she was well dressed but not overdressed. Mr. Tavish's question came to her, *Of your clothing, what's your husband's favorite outfit he likes?* Yes, Seth would like this outfit, but more importantly, *God would approve also.* She looked around for where *that* voice had come from. She looked at the image again. Yes, God would approve. She looked pleasant but not on display. Time to go down and be ready.

"Thank you, Alice, for taking care of the flowers and candy. I never have figured out how he knows when I'm here in the afternoon, but Robert and his Grandfather should both be here..." Gwen's words were cut short by the butler, Gerald's, light tap and announcement.

"Ma'am—Robert Howl Senior and Robert Howl the Third to see you."

"Show them in, Gerald. That means you need to bring the rest of the refreshments, Alice." She smiled.

"Hello, Gwen." The elder Mr. Howl came into the room. "I hope you're doing well?" He looked around the room as if searching for someone. "Where is your, ah, your constant companion?"

"Don't even ask. No matter how I try to shake him that man is ever-present." Robert the Third exploded. "He is the most obnoxious person I've ever met!"

Robert Senior wandered over to the pictures on the wall and stood looking at them while Gwen began to pour tea. The younger man still glowered.

"It's irritating enough to have that Greene fellow to contend with, but today," Robert whispered angrily to Gwen, "Grandfather has decided to tag along."

Handing him his cup, Gwen smiled and poured his grandfather a cup of tea. "Why, Robert the Third, whatever is the matter?" Gwen stifled laughter as she walked over and handed Robert Senior his tea and they exchanged smirks.

"Every time I'm here, I am surrounded by your bodyguard," the younger man growled.

"Well, he is here for a reason, Bobby," Robert Senior said logically. "Maybe he views you as a threat to his charge."

"Enter." Gwen answered a light tap on the door and Mr. Greene himself clumped in.

"Well, speak of the devil." Robert III spoke loudly with a dark look at the newcomer.

"It has to be good." Mr. Greene grinned his lopsided grin at his adversary.

Robert did not respond in kind.

"Sit down, Franklin." Gwen smiled sweetly. "Have some tea and shortbread. Here, let me help you." She watched Robert out of the corner of her eye then winked at Mr. Greene. *Was that wicked of me?* Gwen wondered, *Robert is already glaring at Franklin.* She turned her full attention to Mr. Greene. He flashed his lopsided grin in response to her wink as she handed him his plate. *Good grief, she had to agree with Robert about this man. One minute he was so aggravating, just as Robert had said, then five minutes later he could turn around and be quite endearing. Although she decided he was never endearing to Robert.* "Where is Leila?" she questioned.

"Now, that is a fifty-four million-dollar question, but she is sure to show up soon." Again Franklin spoke with a lopsided grin.

There was another light tap on the door as Alice entered. "I've come to pick up the dishes, ma'am. Do you need more hot water? Is there anything else you would care for?" And she added more pastries.

"Hello?" Leila's head popped in the open door. Leila's long, dark brunette hair was held back with a green and red flower clip that matched her pale green summer dress and pale green ballet slipper flats.

"Oh, Leila, don't you look lovely! I was just wondering where you were." Gwen's smile lit up her face. She patted the sofa space beside herself. "Come in and sit down. Would you like some tea, shortbread, or anything?" She was fond of her friend. "Perhaps, Alice, we do need more hot water?" Gwen said, "and some fresh dishes? You should be receiving invitations for our autumn picnic. It's supposed to be very small compared to Aunt Zoe's usual affaire, but I thought it would be a nice touch..."

"Madam—" Gerald spoke from the doorway. "—A delivery man just brought these." He brought in a bouquet containing red and white miniature roses, pansies, and baby's breath.

Gwen's eyes went wide, her heartbeat quickened, and she handed Leila her cup as her hand trembled. "Card? Gerald? Is there a card? Is there a message, Gerald?" She looked for the card.

"No, madam. Just the flowers, madam."

"Oh, Gwen!" Leila breathed as she set down the cup. "Those are so absolutely beautiful. They look like velvet, and their aroma fills the entire room," she exclaimed as she knelt beside Gwen and gently touched the deep velvet petals. "How lucky you are, girl. Could they be from..." she whispered to her friend as their heads bent together.

"I don't know." Gwen's face had gone from pale white to flushed and was now back to a semi-blanched color. "I don't know, Leila. Gerald, please take care of these—these beautiful flowers," she said handing them to Gerald.

"As you wish, Miss," Gerald said.

THE OLD LAWYER'S EYES became shrewd. The other two men did not look exceptionally happy. He understood Robert, but Mr. Greene? What would he look so foreboding, so angry, about? Perhaps it was time to check a little deeper into this Franklin O. Greene, the old lawyer mused. He had been shocked when the department had sent out this character. He did not look the part of a top-notch private investigator.

"So, how's the investigation coming along, Franklin?" Robert Howl Senior asked casually after a sip of tea.

"As well as can be expected," the man answered, his face unclouding. "We should be wrapping it up in a week or two."

Suddenly Mr. Greene became the focal point as all eyes riveted on him. Each person had his or her reason. Gwen's eyes were full of hope, Leila's were full of wonder, but as with a changing kaleidoscope, now it was the older man and his grandson who were a study. Robert III just was not very happy no matter what was happening.

"Is that so?" replied the old lawyer. His eyes narrowed. "Have you found the answer? Is there more to this as my young friend has deduced?" There was something that nagged in the back of his mind.

"I can't say more than that." Mr. Greene brushed the question aside. "But everything is on track."

"We'll certainly be looking forward to your findings then. Mrs. MacDonald, I'll talk to you at our next appointment. I think Bobby and I will need to make a few more calls this today, so we'll wish you all a good afternoon."

CHAPTER—22—

"Are you ready to go? Alice is looking for my wrap. It's too cool for this chiffon material without something for my shoulders," Gwen said looking in the mirror. "You look nice, as usual, Leila..."

"This is such a beautiful picture." Leila gazed at the picture on Gwen's dressing table. "Do you think maybe the flowers were from him?"

"It's our anniversary coming up, and pansies were our flowers. They just have to be from him, but how?" Gwen stopped to smell the flower arrangement sitting on an end table. "I miss him so much."

"I've been struggling since Lloyd passed away. I don't know how you can stand this self-imposed isolation."

"I can't always leave this beautiful estate, Gerald, Alice, and Ralph sitting and waiting. I must get loose ends tied up here. And I have to make decisions, real decisions."

Alice bustled into the room. "I found two shawls, Miss. I didn't know which one you would like best."

"They're almost identical. So soft and just the right touch of warmth," Gwen said as she fingered the shimmery crocheted yarn. "I think I'll use this one and, Leila, why don't you take the other one?"

"Gerald has the evening off. Mr. Hastings will be driving your party to the Bensons, Miss."

"Gerald has the evening off?" Gwen's eyes widened.

"Yes, he's visiting a family member in the hospital…no, miss, nothing for you to be concerned about. Go and enjoy yourself." Alice patted her on the arm. "I heard Mr. Greene going down to the foyer a few minutes ago. You best get going or he'll be huffing and puffing." She opened the chamber door and waited for the two women to exit the room.

"You young ladies look nice tonight," Franklin said as they stood watching the car pull around to the front steps. The chauffeur came up the stairs and escorted Gwen down to the limo. Franklin offered an arm to Leila, who smiled up at him as he escorted her to the waiting vehicle.

Franklin shut the door after Leila had seated herself, then he slid into the front passenger seat. "Of all your friends, Mrs. MacDonald, I find the Bensons to be my favorite," he said.

"They are real friends, Mr. Franklin. The others are business acquaintances and not close. Aunt Zoe was helpful to the Bensons when no one else would help them get a start."

"I'd gathered that. Not just them either…Your aunt has helped quite a few people."

"Yes, she is greatly missed and not just by me." Gwen sighed as her thoughts wandered through events of the last few weeks. "She told me on more than one occasion, God had given her the blessings she had, and she wanted to use those blessings to help others." A picture of her aunt flitted through Gwen's mind. Her perfectly coiffed blond hair, her clothing perfectly tailored, but her gentle unlined face relaxed, open and honest, always observing the world and people around her.

"Always do the right thing, Gwendolyn, always do the right thing," Aunt Zoe said.

"—But Auntie, how will I know what's the right thing?" Gwen had asked as fear suddenly struck her heart.

"Don't overthink it, my dear. You'll know what's right."

"At least she wasn't overbearing and self-important like so many upper-crust bourgeoisies…" Franklin blurted.

"My aunt was not bourgeois. I thought you didn't know my aunt anyway." A shadow passed over her features. Her eyes narrowed and she stared at the back of Franklin's head.

"Only rumors, only rumors." He turned his head to look back at her. "Her friends say, for all of her money and influence, she never made them feel like she was above them."

"Aunt Zoe could trace her heritage back to the kings of Sweden. It's in her book—"

"Oooh!" Leila exclaimed. "That means you're royalty."

"I can't hardly think that's true." Gwen smiled. "I don't feel like I'm royalty, and wouldn't I feel different? If I was?"

"I don't think feelings have anything to do with it, girl." Leila laughed. "Why, I've read all sorts of romantic novels where the princess…" Leila stopped at a loud guffaw from the front passenger seat.

"I think you're right, Leila, feelings don't have anything to do with it," Franklin said. "But I don't put any stock in those crazy romance novels. In real life, people are the same no matter what. Some just have fancier outsides than others."

"It's the character, actually, that makes people different," Gwen said. "Aunt Zoe used to say that having money gave people the opportunity to be really good, or really evil. It gave them choices, but it didn't make them into what they chose."

"Ah, here at last." Franklin watched as they pulled around to the front of the large, spacious house. "Choices certainly do show the world who we are, and choices have consequences," he said. Opening his door after the car was parked, he moved to help Leila out of the back as Hastings helped Gwen and escorted her to the door.

"Thank you, Mr. Hastings. We'll probably be an hour and a half until I need the car, but the Bensons usually provide a place and a light meal for the drivers on these occasions around the back of the main house," Gwen said with a smile. As she looked up into his face she noticed the scar Leila had told her about. It was about one to two inches long to the right of a dimple on his chin. There was something familiar in the shape of his face, and there was something about...*No*, she thought, *Seth doesn't have a scar like that at all.*

"Thank you, Ma'am, I'll probably just stay with the car, but I'll keep it in mind." Hastings touched the brim of his driver's cap and turned toward the car as the great door opened on the house.

"Mrs. MacDonald, and friends," the Bensons' butler announced and stood aside, and the great hall swallowed them up.

Promptly ninety minutes later, it was a rewinding of their arrival, as the chauffeur met the party at the house door. Hastings offered his arm and Gwen slipped her arm into the crook of his elbow as he escorted her back to the vehicle, holding the limo door as she swiveled back into her side. Franklin Greene escorted Leila down the steps.

Gwen inhaled slowly, taking a deep breath. What was that haunting perfume? A very light aroma, not strong, but it triggered a memory. She frowned slightly before speaking. "I am ready for sleepy bye. How about you, Leila?"

"Oh, yes. That was a scrumptious meal, and I enjoyed the company, but yes, I'm ready for my beauty sleep. How about you, Franklin, did you enjoy your evening?"

"Thank you for asking, and I did."

"Mrs. Sophie is so fun, and I like the daughter," Leila said.

"All around good people." Franklin's gaze seemed preoccupied as he turned toward the front.

"In the morning we'll be getting our boats back. Ralph and the guys have been cleaning and setting up for the picnic. Picnic day is approaching quickly." Gwen snuggled back in her shawl.

"Thank you, ma'am, for sending a plate of food out," Hastings spoke into the mirror.

"You're quite welcome, but it was Mrs. Bensons' idea. She's very thoughtful like that," Gwen said. "Did you get a nap, Hastings?"

"Too many people around," he said.

"What?" There was a chorus from Gwen and Franklin Greene.

"People coming and going. Never saw so many non-essential servants. And then there was some dude that got mixed up. Thought he needed to fix our tire, but…"

"Well, I never!" Gwen blinked in surprise.

"Fix our tire?" Franklin's eyes narrowed. "What do you mean?"

"It was maybe twenty minutes after I'd parked there in back of the house. I'd just settled back when I heard someone at the rear of the car." The chauffeur signaled and changed lanes as he drove. There was light traffic around him, and he watched for their turnoff.

"So, what then?" Franklin Greene asked.

"I got out and asked the guy what he was doing. He said he'd been called to change a flat tire. I asked him if he saw a flat tire, and which tire was he supposed to change. He was so confused he didn't know anything. Didn't even know who he worked for."

"That's fishy," Franklin muttered. "Did you get his name? Any information at all?"

"No, he was in a real hurry to get out of there," Hastings said.

"You didn't follow him?" Leila asked. Her eyes were as large as saucers.

"No, ma'am, I stayed with the car…"

"Wise choice, Hastings. Wise choice," Franklin said, pulling at his lower lip in thought.

CHAPTER—23—

"What's on the agenda for today?" Franklin Greene helped himself to the sausage, eggs, and biscuits at breakfast two days later.

"We've got some clean-up and repair on the boat ramp and lake house in preparation for the picnic. We are renting canoes for the boat races," Gwen said with a frown. "I don't know a lot about the boats, but..."

"I could look that over for you, Mrs. MacDonald. I have some knowledge in that area," Franklin volunteered.

"I would appreciate that." *Why can I never figure this cantankerous disjointed anomaly of unpleasantness out? He does have a wide sphere of experience, but there isn't ever any rhyme or reason why or when he'll be agreeable or what would trigger an agreeable response.* "Mike has all of the food and menu worked out and ordered. There are only a few specialty items to pick up. Just odds and ends. Robert Howl Senior will be here in an hour...He'll probably stay for lunch..."

"Snoopy old lawyer," Franklin grumbled. "Have you tried these biscuits, Ms. Leila?"

"I have, and the local honey is tremendous with them. We used to make a hole in the side and squeeze honey butter into the biscuit. Scrumptious in fresh biscuits."

"You came from humble beginnings?" Franklin asked in surprise.

"Most people would call it humble, I guess." Leila finished her bite of biscuit and smiled.

Alice brought in more hot coffee. "Would anyone like a refill?" She offered as she filled the empty cups.

"Have you told Mike we'll have an extra place for lunch?" Gwen asked Alice as she continued through the small dining room.

"Yes, pet, he's been told," Alice said. "And Ralph has a couple of carts waiting outside ready for the work at the shelter house...and some decorations when you three finish breakfast."

"I think I'll run up and get a flannel shirt and be ready. What about you two?" Gwen pushed back from the table. "We can meet at the front door in ten minutes."

Gwen felt like running up the stairs and making a quick snatch of her flannel shirt then dashing back downstairs, but she felt the weight of being brought up with the admonition of *don't run in the house, walk like a lady, and make a grand entrance*, but especially *remember who you are*. She walked quietly upstairs to her rooms. she stopped at the door to her room. What was that smell? It reminded her of something similar to the one in her car last night. That was funny. She picked up her shirt, hesitating as she passed her flowers, still poised on the end table. Taking a deep breath of their fragrance, which had only become more vigorous as they aged, a heavy sigh escaped her. "Only a few more days, and I'll be done here..." she whispered.

"I've got my jacket." Leila stood just outside Gwen's door. "Are you ready to go?"

"Yes, I'm on my way." Gwen hurried to the door. "We need to keep moving to get things ready. There's enough chill in the air, we're pushing this picnic. I think Aunt Zoe usually had her picnics earlier," Gwen told Leila. They came into the foyer to meet up with Franklin. "Oh, hello." She stopped as Hastings came in the door. "You're up and busy...What's this?"

"I have been given charge by Mr. Ralph of these carts and their contents." Hastings opened the front door and waved at the carts sitting in front of the house. "Mr. Greene, if you will captain this cart." The young man pointed at the second cart in line. As Mr. Greene stumped around to the driver's side, Mr. Hastings helped Leila into the passenger's side then guided Gwen into his cart.

"You worked that pretty slick, Mr. Hastings," Gwen said as she settled into his buggy. He jumped into the driver's side, heading off down the path. "Robert should take lessons from you," she said with a chuckle.

"Ha! I've left people like Robert in the dust years ago," Hastings said with a sideways grin. "Besides, what choice was there?" He let the question hang.

"I can see how that would work. Have you got decorations figured out?"

"Since it's an autumn picnic, we're going to have a New England beach theme and the decorations match the theme. Mike and Alice have worked out the menu—Clam chowder and French onion for soups, lobster rolls, fried scallops, fried..."

"And desserts—I see how it goes...It sounds like Mike and Alice have that down. And do you and Gerald have the entertainment chosen?" Gwen asked with a smile.

"Alice and Gerald had to work on entertainment. They have boat races, a horseshoe toss, and a scavenger hunt, and a string band coming for entertainment," Hastings said. "Everything is cleaned. All we're doing is setting up for where the food and grill will be. Alice is sending some of the maids to arrange tables in the shelter area."

"I need to be back at the house in an hour, so we'll need to be working fast." Gwen frowned.

"What we need you to do is look over the area and make sure it meets with your ideas, Ms. MacDonald, and we'll have you back to the house." Hastings parked up by the shelter house. After hopping out, he unloaded some of the equipment and decorations out of his cart. "Ho, there Mr. Greene," he called. "Grab some of that stuff out of your cart and just put it over on the far side of the shelter house."

"Will do, then I need to head down to the boats to check them over. Are they in yet?"

"They are arriving as we speak, sir." Hastings waved in the direction of a large truck backing up to the docks.

"Missy—" Mr. Ralph appeared from the side of the shelter house. "—Let me show you the layout for this evening. This here's what we've got. Horseshoes over here..." He took Gwen's arm and began the tour.

"THIS LOOKS LIKE WHAT I'm thinking of," Gwen said as she continued through the paperwork her lawyer, Mr. Howl, had brought her. "I can't promise I'll be here often, and I can't leave everything just hanging. Gerald, Alice, and Ralph are in charge, but they are going to retire. I'll need a committee and someone in charge to manage a tourist schedule here."

"I understand, Miss Gwen. Even though I do wish you'd reconsider. Too many of the younger generation are moving away—leaving the area, but they don't know what for."

"We may all come home again someday, Uncle Robert. Life is uncertain."

"What are your plans then? Have you made arrangements to reconcile with your husband or..."

"I've been waiting to finalize things here, and find out what Mr. Greene has come up with." Gwen took a sip of her coffee and weighed her words. "I've decided to dismiss him. I feel—a sense of distrust."

"He came with high recommendations, but I can't imagine why. I was shocked." Robert Howl shook his head. "I don't understand. The guy's more like a lunatic."

"And I can't leave with this hanging over my head. I feel more strongly than ever that my gut instinct is right. There is something wrong here." Gwen sighed. "In some ways, it would be so easy to just stay here. I've missed the freedom that having financial security brings."

"Learning to live on a budget is good. Living like a real person is good. Many wealthy people who want their kids to grow up and be responsible and to take over a family business teach their children how to do those things," Mr. Howl said. "What about your children? Do you plan on having children?"

"Would you like some more coffee?" Gwen filled Mr. Howl's cup. "Yes, we did plan on children." Gwen topped off her cup of coffee. "We had a baby boy. He was born with health problems. He was two weeks old when Seth noticed he wasn't breathing right. We took him to the emergency room—I begged the person at the desk, but little Eddie kept growing colder. He died in my arms as we waited."

"I'm sorry. I didn't know."

"Of course, you didn't know. I haven't even told Alice. And I don't wear a sign. I wouldn't expect you to know." Gwen dabbed at her eyes while she mentally put the hurt and pain back into its box in her heart. "I'll sign these papers and you'll be able to finish this. Are you ready for the picnic tonight…You will stay for lunch also?"

"Certainly, on both accounts," Mr. Howl said. "Even Bobby is planning on being there this evening."

GWEN LOOKED AT HER reflection in the mirror. "I'm hopeful that I'm dressed right for the evening. What do you think, Leila? Not too bundled up, but we will be closer to the water."

"You look gorgeous, and I think you'll be fine. Just make sure you have a jacket in case you get chilly. I have mine," Leila said and held up a matching corduroy jacket.

"You two young women look ready for the evening," Alice said as she helped oversee the beginning activities. "We'll have the scavenger hunt first, then the boat races. That should get the appetites ready for the meal and..."

"Thank you." Gwen looked at her list of clues for the scavenger hunt and waited to find out who her teammates would be. She watched as Ralph pulled names out of the hat for team A, then team B. She was on team C.

"Oh, how fun," Maryann Benson said as she and Sophia Benson joined her. "We're on your team and...Carl Hague."

"I don't believe I know Mr. Hague well," Sophia said.

"That's what makes these events fun," Gwen said. "Let's get coordinated here and see what we can do."

"NO, I DON'T DO CANOE races." Gwen frowned at Hastings. "You'll need to find someone who can paddle a canoe."

"That's all right." Hastings helped Gwen into the small craft. "I can paddle for the two of us. I turned down a scholarship for...Here, put on this lifejacket, sit down and sit still."

"A scholarship for canoeing? That's impressive. I don't know many colleges that give scholarships for that," Gwen said.

"The goal here is to paddle to the small island." Gerald pointed to it. "Tag the person out there and grab a scarf. The first one to bring their scarf back here wins the race. On your mark, get ready, set, go." Gerald fired the starter pistol and the twelve canoes were off.

By the time they reached the halfway mark, there were four front canoes. Franklin and Maryann Benson, Carl Hague and Leila, Robert Howl and Sophia Benson, and Hastings and Gwen.

"You'll need to come in slightly from the backside of the lake," Gwen said. "There's a logjam on the upper side." Gwen had closed her eyes at the beginning of the race, but with the smooth motion of the boat sliding through the peaceful water, she had relaxed. Opening her eyes, she noticed Hastings could indeed paddle the canoe for both of them.

Without comment, Hastings followed her prompting, and their craft slid around the tip of the island. Robert and Sophia became entangled in the logjam, and the other two front canoes were scattered between Robert and Sophia's canoe and Hastings and Gwen.

"There's the person, and there's the scarf," Gwen said as they both spied the fluttering object at the same moment. Hastings maneuvered in. He threw his tag to the person, caught the scarf with his paddle, and tried to flip it over to Gwen, but only half of the scarf came loose.

"Just take what we've got. We've checked in first..." Gwen said. They began to slide back toward the shore.

Being the first one to the island was a benefit only on the way out. The canoes now struggling toward the island continued to get in the way of those who had been there and were on their way back, creating problems. Hastings maneuvered around one canoe only to be blindsided by another and spilled into the lake.

Gwen's fear of water took hold of her as she dunked under the surface. She came up gasping and choking for air. Bobbing up and down aggravated her situation, and she began fighting her rescuer.

"Stop fighting me, babe," someone said in her ear and everything went blank.

"I DON'T' KNOW HOW YOU got her in that canoe," Alice scolded Hastings. "She's deathly afraid of the water."

"I told her to sit down and sit still. I'd paddle for both of us," Hastings said as he wrapped a blanket around Gwen and carried her up beside the firepit. "She had a lifejacket on..."

"He's right, Alice. I did have a lifejacket on—where's Seth?" Gwen began looking at her guests, searching for Seth's face.

"I need to go help Mike." Hastings rose abruptly and walked to the shelter house.

"You're going to be fine, pet," Alice said with a frown. "Seth isn't here."

"But he was speaking to me when I was in the water," Gwen said.

"No, the only person with you was Hastings," Alice said. "Relax. Helen, one of the new hires, is bringing you some dry clothes and it's time to eat. Then we'll retire to the house to listen to the jazz band."

The jazz band Alice had hired to play for the last two hours had drawn everyone back to the house as the final touch. As the band began to pack up, the guests began to bid farewell. "Thank you all for coming," Gwen said so many times she lost count.

With a lighter heart and a sigh of relief as the front door shut behind the last guest, Leila exclaimed, "I feel like kicking off my shoes, but other than your dunking, everything went well."

"I would like to compliment you two women," Franklin said. "You both did an excellent job of hostessing this evening. I find most of your friends to be quite interesting, Mrs. MacDonald, and Leila, that one gentleman seemed very attentive to you. Didn't you think so?" he asked, turning to Gwen.

"There are not many things Franklin and I agree on," Gwen replied smiling at Leila, "but I think that is one thing we do agree about."

Leila blushed slightly. "Frank," she wheedled, "Why don't we retire to the music room and you play the piano for us."

"Surely," he agreed. "Perhaps we could have some coffee brought in. I almost feel my second wind coming on. What do you ladies think?"

One reason he was so aggravating was everything looked wrong about him. He clumped, guffawed, and snorted at inopportune moments. How could this disjointed man do anything that called for coordination? He possessed the quality of everything being at odds. If Franklin Greene wasn't annoying he was nothing. Why had the police department so highly recommended him? He didn't fit that mold. Play the piano? He didn't look that part either. Gwen sighed. *Well, what did it matter with her? She was going to cancel his work for her tomorrow anyway...*

"If you don't mind, Franklin, I'll check to see how Mike is coming with the kitchen work and ask Alice if she would like to join us," Gwen said.

"No, I don't mind," Franklin replied, "You could ask the girls and Mike—Hastings, Ralph, and Gerald, too, for all I care. Just a little coffee is all I ask. I've played for worse audiences than that. And worse pay too."

A chill went up Gwen's spine. Even in jest, his words carried the hint of a threat. More than once she had the malevolent impression he didn't like her or her kind.

GWEN COULD HEAR THE piano keys talking as she left the music room and turned toward the kitchen. She stopped abruptly as the sounds of a scuffle came from the kitchen. Peaking carefully around the doorjamb before entering, she was relieved to see that it was only the kitchen help scurrying to get things packed away.

"What a relief," she said as she entered the kitchen. "With all the noise, I thought there was a battle going on in here. Franklin is playing the piano, and we're winding down before heading up to bed...Kind of kicking our shoes off for a breather. We were hoping there was some coffee left, and maybe some hors d'oeuvres?"

"Yeah, we'll bring some in shortly," a new hire said. "We're just cleaning up."

"Where's Mike?" Gwen asked, looking for her cook. "And where's Alice?"

"I'm right here." Alice appeared in the kitchen door Gwen had just vacated. "What do you need?"

"We were going to relax a bit while Franklin plays the piano. If you and the new girls would like to join us for some leftovers and coffee in the music room, you're invited."

"The girls might appreciate a cup of coffee, but they will have to rise early to tidy up. I'll bring a pot of coffee and be along right behind you, Missy," Alice said.

Gwen slipped into the music room unnoticed and sat almost out of sight. Alice followed her closely, bringing in a large pot of coffee. The newly hired maids brought in some cups, cream, and sugar and joined the group. One of the newly hired men brought in the leftover cannoli, but said the cook had declined the invitation for coffee, saying that morning came early.

Alice sat on the sofa beside Gwen and listened as Mr. Greene impressed the group of listeners. "I am surprised," Gwen spoke softly to Alice, "I wouldn't have thought our Mr. Green could play his way out of the proverbial paper bag. Look at how he draws his listeners into what he's playing."

"I'm concerned." Alice smiled as if they were discussing something pleasant and sipped her coffee. "...since these two house guests arrived. It seems one or both of them are always present."

"I think I've had enough of Franklin Greene, but I don't know what to do next," Gwen said.

"Mr. Greene is odd. He doesn't always clump noisily, and there are several oddities about his personal habits," Alice said.

"I find it difficult to adjust to his mood swings..."

"Gwen—" Leila sat, balancing on the arm of the couch. "—Why don't you sing a song with me?"

"It's been a long time. What song do you have in mind?" She rose with a smile and set her cup on the end table.

"I don't know. Whatever Frank wants to play, I guess." Leila shrugged.

"As long as it isn't anything difficult. We'll talk later," Gwen whispered to Alice.

"Say, I'm going to go get some more sandwiches and raid the kitchen," one of the girls offered. "If that's all right with you?" she asked.

"That will be fine, Helen," Alice agreed, absently watching as Leila and Gwen began to sing an old Irish ballad. Mr. Greene played several selections, mostly songs from movies. Leila and Gwen sang "As Time Goes By." After that Mr. Greene launched into "I'll Be Loving You."

"Leila, you sing that one, would you?" Gwen whispered. "I just can't."

"If you'd rather not, we won't even go there." Leila touched Franklin on the shoulder and shook her head at him.

"You two don't know that one?" Franklin said, slyly arching his eyebrows.

Gwen decided at that precise moment she did not like this man. He was mocking her. She knew that he was toying with her in some fashion and for some reason. How he knew that song would be unbearable for her she didn't know, but he did know it. The threat was real and the danger was pressing on her from all sides. The last few weeks had brought her closer to decisions and brought back painful memories.

She walked to the glass doors that led to the upper flower garden. After opening them, she walked out into the night, still perfumed by the late-blooming autumn flowers. Looking up at the constellations in the deep black sky, she wondered where Seth was at this moment. She missed him so much. They had made many decisions together in the last nine years. Now it hurt not to be able to ask his opinions, to talk to him about some of these decisions, and have him there when she needed him.

And she did need him. She felt so alone, so vulnerable, and so lonely. The beautiful pansies, roses, and baby's breath flowers from the other day, and now their song had brought back too many memories...feelings she preferred to leave buried. It was chilly out tonight and she shivered. Was it just from the cool weather or was there something else? The doors behind her opened quietly. Gwen was disappointed to hear the clump of Franklin Greene behind her.

"It is too cold to be out here without a jacket," he said roughly as he held out a wrap. "Not to mention your dunking a while ago...not good."

"Thank you," she said perfunctorily. Why hadn't he taken the hint and left her alone? He stood leaning against the low railing that marked the boundary around the patio.

"It's a beautiful evening out," he spoke more kindly than previously. "There's the dipper," he pointed out. "Did you know that Polaris has not always been the North Star?"

"It is beautiful out. No, I was not aware of that fact." She spoke icily.

"So, you're wondering where he is, what he's doing? Perhaps even who he's with?" He was cruel again. "Mr. Seth Matthew MacDonald," he began, "Age thirty-one, six foot two, one hundred ninety pounds, soaking wet, that is. Number eight out of ten children—from a poor family. Loser of losers, married to Gwendolyn Aurora Winters, a wealthy heiress. How did you get hooked up with that loser, anyway?" he mocked her.

She turned on him vehemently. "You don't know Seth. You don't know his family. I don't know how you know what you think you know, but nothing you've said is anything for that matter. The rest of you men look like cheap imitations compared to Seth. He isn't a loser. Yes, I'm wondering where he is, what he's doing, but not who he's with," she said in a flat tone of voice.

"For your information," Franklin spoke confidently, "there is a very attractive auburn-haired young unmarried woman that lives with him and his parents. Maybe you shouldn't be so sure of yourself." His eyes narrowed.

"His younger sister and brother also live with them," Gwen said, her eyes flashing with anger. "I think you and I are not compatible, Mr. Franklin O. Greene. Perhaps the police department needs to send someone more qualified for this job." She knew she was out of control and that angered her. Aunt Zoë had drilled into her that it was important to control her emotions, and her thoughts as well as her reactions. Gwen turned away from her persecutor. She was about to storm up to her room when he grasped her arm firmly yet gently.

"Don't go yet," he commanded. "You won't get away from me that easily."

"What do you mean?" Her eyes narrowed. Was he trying to intimidate her again? "I will not be bullied by you or anyone else." Gwen yanked her arm away from him.

He laughed at her suddenly. "You remind me of my daughter. I wouldn't try to bully you, missy. I just like to see your eyes when you are angry. It's too bad your husband won't ever know how you feel."

There it was again. That was a threat? "Who are you and what do you think you are doing?" she demanded. "I told you I would not be bullied." Her eyes flashed and her lips were set in a firm straight line. "Do you think you can get away with this intimidation?"

"And just who is going to stop me?" he said with a chuckle and a slight twist to his mouth.

The lights winked out in the music room. Gwen realized that she was indeed alone with this stranger. The glass doors opened and a man's voice questioned, "You ready to go, man?"

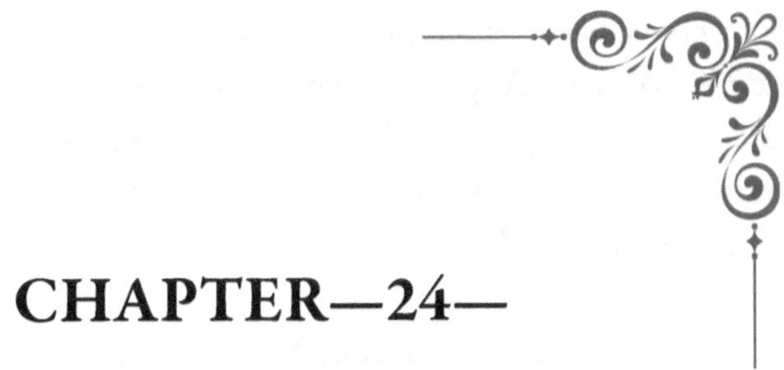

CHAPTER—24—

"We blew it, Bobby. She's gone, and no one knows where, my boy." Robert Howl Senior leaned back in his office chair. "I've watched the tragedies in Gwen's life— Zoë Lind was a close friend of mine, so were Dr. de Winters and his wife, and I'm beginning to think maybe I'm too old for this." He looked up at the ceiling contemplating retirement. "The police said they didn't find anything suspicious, but now what? Gwen's gone, Franklin O. Greene is gone, Matthew Hastings and one other recently hired man have disappeared as well as Alice, Gwen's maid. And the new cook, Mike, is in the hospital."

"Even with all of our backup of the backup, we still lost her," Robert said. "And what happened to the cook?"

"He was hit on the head as he was bringing food in from the picnic last night." The older man sighed as his secretary keyed her microphone.

"Yes, send the officer in. I'm waiting," he spoke into the intercom. Turning to his grandson he said with a sigh, "Yes, I'm thinking of retirement."

The door opened and a young uniformed officer entered. "Mr. Howl and Mr. Howl?"

The two lawyers rose and shook hands with the officer. "Any word, sir? How did this happen? I'm confused." The elder lawyer spoke for both of them.

"Frank has been employed at the police department for a good number of years. Approximately twenty-six years. He's a good worker and, until now, quite reliable. His wife and daughter were killed in a traffic accident almost twenty-four years ago. He was on the original case when Mr. and Mrs. de Winters died in the traffic accident," the officer said.

"So, what about Miss Lind, Was he on that case also?" Robert III questioned.

"Only in a secondary role. This could be why there was not much found and no foul play reported. The trail is cold, but he could have been involved with these bizarre happenings," the officer replied.

"Do you have any idea why? Is there a motive?" asked the older lawyer.

"No, but no one was looking for a motive, so... It was shortly after his wife and daughter died that certain oddities in his behavior emerged."

"Did it have to do with their deaths?" Mr. Howl mused. "How is the cook doing? He took a nasty blow to the head."

"It's hard to say about Franklin's behavior. The cook will be alright, just needs to rest and take it easy. We've tried to contact his family, but can't trace him anywhere. Not him or that other fellow that helped the caretaker."

"Matthew Hastings? Has Hastings been found or has he disappeared? What about the group that came to help out for the picnic? Where did they come from?" Mr. Howl asked.

"HAVE TO WAIT, AUNTIE?" she replied in her sleep.

"I think she's coming around," someone whispered.

"We're almost there," another voice said.

Fog swirled through Gwen's mind, and she puzzled over questions. *Where am I?* echoed in her bewildered mind. Disconnected pieces replayed in a disjointed puzzle. The picnic—its games. The company—the music, conversation—the food—different impressions. Radio music blared on in the vehicle. The music was interrupted by an announcer speaking then someone snapped it off.

"Turn that off, you fool! That would be a dead giveaway!" a voice growled.

"This silence is weird. I have to have some kinda sound, music, something," the voice whispered.

"Don't blow it now. We've just begun," the deeper voice admonished. "We're here."

Gwen could feel the vehicle slow and turn, then slowly continue up a very rough driveway or road. The driver zigzagged continuously, but there were still many times it felt as if they dropped into a hole and had to drive up out of it. She attempted to reposition her body and stretch her cramped arms and legs, but nothing wanted to respond. As if her head was not part of the rest of her body. They came to a stop. Two doors opened and slammed shut. They were not being silent now. The two back doors folded open and the cot she was cocooned in was rolled towards the back.

"Be careful," a voice instructed. "You need to be careful," it demanded again.

"What the devil..." the second voice began with a squawk.

"Watch it! And do as I say!" the first man said, angrily pushing the other fellow away. "I'll just carry her myself. You don't have any sense at all, do you?" Whoever was talking must have bent over then Gwen was lifted carefully just before she again passed out.

GWEN FELT THE SUN WARMING her face as it streamed into the room, telling of the passing of an unknown quantity of time. She lay quietly, her eyes closed, trying to recall where she was and what had happened. She rolled over and opened one eye just enough to see her surroundings. She closed her eye when she realized it was an unfamiliar room. Her eyes burst open suddenly as she came awake with a jolt, remembering vividly the events of the previous evening.

Throwing back the covers, she sat up scrutinizing her surroundings. Although the surroundings were not unpleasant, they were unfamiliar. The mattress she had been enveloped in was soft and luxurious, covered with the white eyelet sheets, a soft blanket, and a thick comforter. The sun flooded through the large French windows swathed in curtains of burgundy and white. The overall impression was a rustic setting that was sumptuously comfortable and in which the quality of the furnishings outweighed the quantity.

A soft rug at her feet as well as house slippers just her size waited as if she had walked out of them as she retired. She slid her feet into the shoes and stood, feeling slightly woozy. Gwen took a few steps toward the French windows. Using the bedside table for support, she made her way slowly to one of the two chairs positioned in front of the windows. Leaning on the arm of the chair, she scooched around, sat gingerly in the high-backed comfortable chair, and looked out at the world beyond her room. The view was breathtaking.

The leaves were changing colors, and this two-story cabin stood in the sea of a forest. There were no signs of smoke from neighbors' chimneys or of a road or civilization anywhere. The few outbuildings around the house were not well kept. Gwen stood and tried to open the window latch, but she could not open it or find a lock. She gazed through the glass panes at the small balcony just outside her room.

Turning her attention back to the room, she noticed a cozy fire that crackled on the grate in the fireplace. There was a Victorian dressing table on the right side of the room next to the French windows, and a large wardrobe next to a door in the wall. The fireplace was flanked by a door on each side.

Still in shock, Gwen scanned the scenery outside her window, then placing her head in her hands, she sat for a few minutes hoping the world would stop spinning. She had a slight headache, a dull throbbing.

The rattle at the door on the right side of the fireplace startled her. She looked at the door with trepidation.

"Alice!" she cried as her maid appeared carrying a tray. "What ...?"

"Oh, Missy." Alice set down the tray on the small table between the chairs by the windows. "I don't know anything, only that I'm here to help take care of you. At least they didn't separate us. I'd rather be here with you and not know anything, than back home knowing everything except where you are." She hugged Gwen and stroked her hair.

"I don't understand what's going on—why are we here?" Gwen returned the hug.

"There must have been something in the coffee last night. I woke up here this morning. I've brought you some breakfast. Eat your breakfast and I'll tell you my news."

"News? Already you have news?" Gwen lifted the lid off the tray and gasped. "Mercy, you'll have to help me eat this. There isn't any way I could eat all of this, especially in my frame of mind. There's an extra plate. If I move this toasted bagel over here and portion some of the scrambled eggs onto the bagel plate..." Gwen finished by putting the piping hot eggs and sausage onto the bagel plate, pouring a cup of coffee, and sliding it over to Alice.

"Thank you," Alice said as she sat in the second chair. "I haven't felt like eating until I've seen that you're doing all right. You'll never guess the news."

"I guess I won't." Gwen spread cream cheese on her bagel and took a dainty bite.

"I woke up early like I usually do. I was disoriented not knowing how I got here or why. So I explored through my room, and after exploring it I began investigating around the rest of the house. My room wasn't locked—only your door was. I went downstairs, and as odd as it seems, Hastings was fumbling around in the kitchen."

"Hastings?" Gwen's eyes grew wide and she stopped eating her eggs. "What do you mean he was fumbling around in the kitchen?"

"This is my guess, whoever was in charge of the kidnapping—well, Hastings was in the wrong place at the wrong time. Instead of Mike the cook, they grabbed Hastings by mistake."

"I—I just don't know. This is unbelievable. What's the point in this?"

"I don't know either, but I sure hope Hastings has more talent than just taking care of horses." Alice took a sip of her coffee. "Eat up, lamb, we don't know what this day may bring. We'll need to prepare for the day. I hope there are clean clothes. I woke up in the same clothes I had on last evening...and I see you are in the same predicament."

"Yes, I haven't been able to check the room out, only what I can see. I've had a dull ache in my head and I'm somewhat wobbly on my feet. There's a beautiful view, but my windows are either locked or stuck shut."

"His breakfast was good," Alice said as she placed her knife and fork on her plate. "Hopefully he has more in his repertoire than one meal. You sit while I look around and see what we've got here."

"There isn't a lot of furnishings, but the room is pleasant," Gwen said. "I suppose one of those doors is a closet, and I hope that behind one of the doors is a bathroom."

Alice opened the first door. "Indeed it is a closet, and it even has a few skirts and blouses. But they have been here for quite some time." She shook out a tweed skirt then hung it back and picked out a white blouse, looking them over. "Probably just right for this time of year. They look warm." After closing the closet door, Alice moved on to the door on the left side of the fireplace. "Ask and it shall be given—it's a very nice bathroom." She threw the door open so Gwen could see inside. "If you want to lean on me, I'll help you into the bathroom." Alice helped Gwen to her feet.

"I believe I'll be all right now. I've been up a bit and had some breakfast. I don't know what was in that coffee, but it was effective." Gwen went slowly toward the bathroom. "I don't know if I'm in wonderland or the Twilight Zone. There hasn't been a cookie that said 'eat me,' but none of this makes sense."

"I'll continue to look around while you're in the bathroom. Take your time. I'll see what else is out here and maybe..." Alice stopped speaking as there was a knock on the door to the room. "Take your time, I'll answer it."

Gwen closed the bathroom door but could hear muffled conversation of Alice and some man's voice then the door to the room shut.

"There's a box of your clothes here, lamb. If you want to prepare a bath, I'll get some clothing laid out." Alice spoke through the bathroom door.

GWEN CAME OUT OF THE bathroom just as Alice finished making the bed and cleaning up from their meal.

"What a relief to bathe and put on clean clothes, Alice. Did they bring some clean clothes for you as well?"

"Hastings brought your trunk up and said he had left a trunk for me in my room. I think after we get you settled I'll go get a bath and change too. After all this stress you need to rest and build up your strength."

"How do I prepare for the day when I don't know what's going on? When the day is a mystery?" Gwen heaved a sigh. She sat at the dressing table and began to examine the orderly drawers.

"We'll manage somehow," Alice said with a furrowed brow. "I'll brush your hair before I leave." She pulled a brush and comb off the top of the box of clothes.

"Oh, look." Gwen held up a book from one of the drawers. "Look what I found. Just as if the Gideons had been here—a Bible in one of the drawers. For the short time I spent with Seth's family this summer, I developed an appreciation for their prayer life. They go before the Lord in prayer—for everything. I'm not there yet but maybe we could have a prayer?" Gwen looked down as the Bible fell open at the bookmark.

"Alice! Listen." Gwen began to read. "*Psalm forty-six, God is our refuge and strength, a very present help in trouble. Therefore will not we fear, though the earth be removed, and though the mountains be carried into the midst of the sea; verse 3: Though the waters thereof roar and be troubled, though the mountains shake with the swelling thereof...10 Be still, and know that I am God: I will be exalted among the heathen, I will be exalted in the earth. 11 The LORD of hosts is with us; the God of Jacob is our refuge. Selah.*" She closed her eyes for a minute then opening them she spoke with conviction. "I don't know what's going on, but I needed that."

"Too often we wait until we're in dire circumstances to turn to the Lord. We shouldn't wait for troublesome, stressful things to happen, but we do." Alice laid the brush down. The thin barrier between Alice and Gwen evaporated. "What a pretty bookmark." Alice ran a finger over the picture of a bouquet of pansies. "And it goes well with our situation."

"The passage and the pansy...remember the flowers last week? The pansy was our flower, Seth and I, that is. I don't know where those flowers came from, but it was our anniversary. And now it's as if the passage and the flower have been sent a second time to comfort me."

"Let's have a prayer, then I'll take this tray back downstairs. While you rest I'll clean up and be back within an hour," Alice said. They bowed their heads.

CHAPTER—25—

As they finished their prayer, there was a tap and a rattling at the door, announcing a visitor. Gwen quickly replaced her new-found treasure before the door swung open.

"I see that you two are getting on. I hope that you have found everything you need. Even if it may not all be to your liking."

Although the form and appearance had changed somewhat, there was no disguising the voice of Mr. Franklin O. Greene.

He laughed at the look on their faces and smirked as he asked, "So, just what are you two fine ladies gaping at? What happened to your manners? Surely someone taught you it is impolite to stare."

"Has no one ever told you it is impolite as well as illegal and several other things to kidnap people?" Gwen said angrily with more courage than she felt.

"Oh, so the little bird still has courage enough to chirp," he said. "I like courage. It's a good quality. Take that tray back to the kitchen," he said looking at Alice.

"Don't worry. I'll be all right," Gwen said before Alice could protest.

Her face drawn up in tight disapproval, Alice picked up the tray and started for the door.

"Straight to the kitchen." He moved aside and held the door open. "And no side journeys." His manner was jovial as if he was enjoying the moment.

"Humph!" Alice said, her dark eyes flashing at him as she passed.

He shut the door firmly behind Alice and turned to Gwen. "You know, when I entered your household I was supposed to find a way to do you in, as they say."

"So, what are you waiting for?" Gwen asked with a bitter tone.

Mr. Greene pulled his wallet out of his back pocket and slipped an old photo out. He crossed to the window, handed the picture to Gwen, and stood sideways to her as he gazed out over the endless tops of the trees.

Gwen scanned the picture of a pretty, dark-haired young woman and a dainty little girl sitting in a large swing under a large green tree on a summer day. It was a poignant scene as the pretty woman smiled at the camera and the little girl played with a long, dark strand of the woman's hair.

Since Gwen had stood when Franklin had entered, she now sat on the dressing table bench studying the picture. Then she quietly observed the other occupant of the room. She puzzled over the fact that he was no longer the disjointed fellow with the thatch of unruly black mane. His hair was close-cropped and graying at the temples. He no longer clumped when he walked, and he could look directly at her. He was trimmer than what his previous attire made him look like, but his eyes were the same light brown as well as the lopsided grin when he was amused. She did not know this man in either form, so the purpose of the former disguise was a mystery to her.

After allowing her time to peruse the picture, he drew up the chair, and seating himself, looked at her intently. "That's my wife and daughter."

"How precious. You must be very proud of them." She knew there was more to this.

"They were killed twenty-four years ago. There was a certain doctor with a certain hospital that was too busy with a dinner affair and didn't see fit to come in when he was called. It wasn't an emergency to him," he said with bitterness.

"That's so sad." Gwen looked back at the picture. "I know how painful it is to lose loved ones, not just once but twice. The picture is so touching. But that doesn't answer why you want to do me harm—or at least that you did want to do me harm—nor why you haven't finished what you set out to do."

He blinked as her words startled him, and he looked at her closely. "The doctor who couldn't be bothered was the honorable Doctor Beauregard L. de Winters," he responded in a low voice, watching her expression.

Something had warned her before he revealed this last fact, and she did not flinch. It was as if God placed an answer in her mouth. "That seems a cowardly accusation from someone who prides himself on being fair and accurate." She looked him steadily in the eye.

A blaze of anger flared across his face, but he retained his self-control. "What do you mean a cowardly accusation?"

"If the shoe were on the other foot and some stranger accused you of such things to your daughter, would you not feel indignant? I mean, first of all, I can neither agree with you nor defend my dead father. Also, he is not here and can neither explain nor defend himself. So, of course, you can just blast away and not accomplish anything except to perpetuate your feelings of revenge." Gwen handed the picture back to him.

The anger was replaced by a shrewd, thoughtful look. He paused and stared out the window. "Had she lived, my Lydia would be the same age as you. When I came to your estate I believed I knew what you and your highfalutin' family were like. Rich and spoiled, enjoying the careless life of ease, not caring for anyone besides yourself, that's what I believed I would find."

"So, what happened?" she asked.

He shrugged. "Things aren't always what we think. You are young, and whether you want to admit it or not, vulnerable. Alice loves you, and you in turn love her. Gerald is devoted to you, and

Ralph, you know he loves you too. I saw how you love and care for them. I was so shocked when you cleaned out that horse stall and groomed your own horse the other day. It was a good thing my teeth are part of my face or they'd have fallen right out of my mouth. Rich? Yes, you are, but sitting in on some of your dinner parties opened my eyes as to the other side of the coin. There's a responsibility that goes with all the rest. You know, if my daughter were alive, I would like for her to have all the pretty things you have. All the luxuries I could give her, and I can't fault some other bloke for providing those things for his little girl either. So it entered my mind that since it was your father that deprived me of my little girl, I would take you as a replacement. You don't have a father, and I don't have a daughter. That seems to be a fair exchange."

"But what about my other life? The one I belong in? You can't pick people up and move them like chess pieces," Gwen said. She furrowed her brow, trying to wrap her mind around his words. *I can't be hearing correctly. He has to be crazy.*

"You'll have a new life here. I brought Alice—for you. J.R. grabbed the wrong fellow instead of Mike, your cook—but breakfast was a good start. Eventually even a new husband. Voila, a new life." His words carried a note of self-satisfaction as if he had thought of everything.

"Incredulous." Gwen's eyes grew wide. "I cannot comprehend how you think you can pull this off. Did you check your forehead one day and it said 'God' on it, or just what?"

"You'll get used to it here. If you were cooperative, you could even have as much freedom as you would like. The new husband wasn't part of the original idea, but—This is quite a beautiful place, quiet and serene, no neighbors for miles and miles. It used to be my mother's brother's land. Livi and I had dreams of repairing and turning it into a lovely home. We had so little time. We did a lot of the work ourselves. Lydia was born here," he said. "But it's gone now."

He stood abruptly, his arms folded. His demeanor darkened. "You can think it over, although you don't have any choice. It might sound better as you consider the alternative."

Gwen blinked in shock as the door shut swiftly behind him. Oh, Lord, this can't be happening. She retrieved the Bible and clutching it, she traced the gold letters with a finger. It was the King James Version, just a plain black cover with gold lettering. Opening it to the front she read in neat handwriting: "Given to Lydia Joanna Greene, May 5, on the occasion of her fifth birthday: From her loving father and mother Franklin and Olivia Greene." The date was May fifth, twenty-three years earlier. What a coincidence she and Lydia Greene were the same age. May fifth was Gwen's birth date also. Lydia would be twenty-eight if she were alive today. There was a picture of the pretty young Mrs. Greene and a much younger Franklin. They were quite a handsome pair. Gwen sighed. It was as if she were allowed a look behind the façade of Mr. Greene. *Who is he besides frustrating and confusing?* Gwen leafed through the pages. There were many underlined passages scattered throughout the text which showed it had been used not merely something for show.

In the very back, there was a small pocket envelope in which a small key nestled. *That's curious,* Gwen thought with a frown as she examined the pocket and its contents. *If I weren't so tired—I have thought that someday I would spend more time and read through the Bible.* She replaced the small key in the envelope. Her eyes scanned around the room at the various items. It wasn't an unpleasant room, but under these circumstances... Dragging herself to the bed, she rolled onto the mattress. Still holding the Bible to her heart, she fell asleep.

CHAPTER—26—

"Mike. Mike Chapman," Nurse Marva spoke loudly. "You need to wake up, Mike." She read his name off the chart.

His eyes were lead, and try as he might, they would not open. The voice was unfamiliar, and names floated through his mind. Mike Chapman wasn't one he remembered. Whoever she was talking to must be in the other bed.

"Mr. Chapman," there was a slight movement—she touched his hand. "Wake up, sir. There's someone here to see you."

"Ohayo gozaimasu—" His eyes snapped open, and he stopped speaking.

"Excuse me?" Nurse Marva stepped back, startled.

Words and languages, names and places chased in Joshua's mind. He closed his eyes and tried to understand what and where he was. Nothing made sense. How did he come to be in a hospital?

"That's all right, nurse. I'll take over from here." A slightly familiar voice spoke.

This time the patient's eyes opened more slowly. The face he saw this time wasn't any more known to him than the nurse had been. Words formed in his mind, but he waited until they were alone before he spoke...with caution, this time in English. "What is going on?"

"That's a million-dollar question. I'm breaking protocol coming here like this, but you need to get out of this hospital, and this was the only way it looked like it was going to happen," the man said.

"That name...Chapman? It doesn't sound familiar. I don't know who I am or what I'm doing here. I hate to say this, but I don't know who you are either, for that matter." He swung his feet over the side of the bed and found some slippers.

"This is awkward, but I'm Mark and...What are you doing, man?" his new acquaintance exclaimed in surprise.

"You said I gotta get out of here, so..."

"Yeah, but maybe we ought to take it a bit slow. If you fall flat on your rear, that won't be good. It looks like you should find someplace and just hole up for the next rest of your life..." the man said as he eyed an angry, fresh healing wound on the patient's thigh.

"I think I was going to do that...I can't be sure though, and I don't know what happened. What's on the doctor's report?" The patient sat with furrowed brow waiting for any remembrance.

There was a soft tap on the semi-open door, and the nurse stuck her head in. "More visitors, Mr. Chapman." And she opened the door further.

The first man shrank back, melting into the corner as two men walked in. One was short and walked with a gimp. His salt-and-pepper-colored hair was covered with a soft, nondescript hat. He was dressed like someone who worked outside, and he smelled of the fresh air. The other, a tall thin man, wore a suit and tie and looked like he held a position of importance. The pair were an odd couple.

"Aye, Mr. Mike, it looks like you took the worst of the fight." The shorter of the two men spoke first. "Gerald and I—we were concerned. Mr. Howl was out to question us. He said you was still in the hospital and hadna come to yet."

"I feel like I took the worst of it. I don't remember anything." The patient sat up, tucking the hospital blanket over his wound.

"What's the last thing you remember?" the taller man asked.

"I'm totally in the dark. Start with my first day on the job...whenever that was."

"You don't remember the picnic?"

"No. Nothing."

"You came to work for Missy...Gwen de Winters-MacDonald, three weeks ago. Miss Alice hired you as a chef. Have I gone back far enough yet?"

"Well, Gerald, it's gotta be far enough, we didn't know him before..." the shorter man said. "I'm Ralph and this is Gerald, and we've worked for Missy and her family since we were youngsters. We've been at the de Winters' estate since before even Alice. I'm the outside head groundskeeper and Gerald's the head butler. Most a the rest a the crew was let go when Missy married. That was about nine years ago. Just a few of us old-timers stayed."

"That's so. Ralph and I and Alice—Alice was Missy's close friend and maid who ran the household. Alice came, what? About two years after Missy? We old-timers stayed, but when Missy returned a few weeks ago we had to get more help. You were hired, Mr. Hastings was hired at the same time, and we hired one more outside man and some inside maids."

"The name Gwen and MacDonald ring a bell, but I don't remember anybody named Hastings. My last cooking gig was on a cruise ship...But I don't know what I was doing or why I'd remember a cruise ship." The puzzled, troubled look on the patient's face confirmed his words. "Hmm, Ralph?" He rolled the name into the still swirling recesses of his mind. "Gerald?" He scrutinized the two men intently but without much success in coming to a firm grip on who they were, who he was, or what he was doing. "What happened to put me in here?"

"Missy decided to have a picnic like her Aunt Lind used to have," Ralph said. "Well, a smaller picnic...but we aren't sure what happened after the picnic. The other guy we'd hired, Matt Hastings, was helping me clean up down at the lake. Hastings and you had loaded up the food that was still in the shelter house onto the carts and was taking them back to the house. That's the last I saw of Hastings."

"Up at the Manor, everything had wound down. There was music in the music room but I don't know, I think it was Mr. Greene who was playing. One of the new maids Alice had hired stopped by where I was working in the office and said we were all invited to the music room for coffee and hors d'oeuvres, but I declined. Missy is quite lax about such things...Ms. Lind would not have approved," Gerald said in a tone of disapproval. "I was unaware of anything untoward until...I'd say an hour later when I went to check up on the kitchen work. The kitchen was in disarray, and you were lying on the floor as if someone had hit you from behind. The rest of the house was dark, except—someone must have spiked the coffee. Several people, two new maids, and Missy's friend, Leila, all were knocked out. Sleeping in the music room, they were."

"None of this is making sense to me. I'm not bringing up anything." Mike shook his head. "Nothing."

"After finding you, I called the police and went to check the rest of the house. Missy had hired that Franklin Greene detective to investigate who was stalking her..." Gerald the butler stopped suddenly as the patient put a foot in his hospital slipper. "What are you doing, Mike?"

"I've got to get out of this hospital." He slid his other foot in the other shoe.

"Have you been released?" Ralph took a step toward the patient in case he collapsed.

"I will be," the patient said while rummaging in the closet. "I'm still employed at the Manor, right?"

"I presume so." Gerald watched in shock as the patient grabbed a sack off the bottom of the closet and closed the door.

"I'll be right out. Get the car around here and we'll head back to the Manor House."

"Well, right as rain, sir. Ralph, go down to the desk and tell them we'll be taking Mr. Mike here, with us, and I'll get the car and meet you at the front."

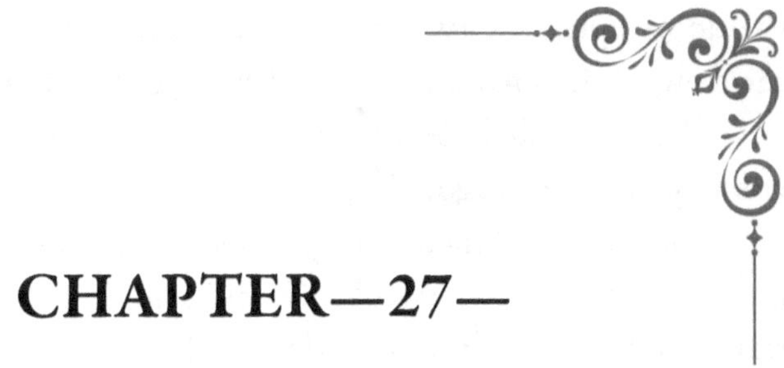

CHAPTER—27—

After the two men scattered to their respective duties, the man in the corner came forward and spoke low through the bathroom door. "Remember, I'm not here, but I'll keep in contact with you. At least we are both on the same page...almost anyway. I'm your contact at the Herberry Specialty shop downtown. Don't forget that. I don't know anything about your identity other than the one you're going by here—Mike Chapman. Make a special run to the shop for something tomorrow. Ask for Mark, and I'll catch you up on what we've got so far. Got it?"

"Yes, I'll be in tomorrow. I guess for now Mike will have to be my name of the hour. Tomorrow," he said, pulling on his pants and old shirt with bloodstains on it.

"Are ya ready?" The voice now was Ralph the groundskeeper. "The nurse, she's comin' behind me. I don think she thinks yous goin' ta leave."

"I didn't come in with anything, did I?" The patient whisked out of the bathroom. Checking in the drawers on the bedside table, he pulled out a wallet and stuck it in his back pocket. "Cover for me, Ralph." Ralph stepped into the hall first, and Mike whipped out in front of him, and they two-stepped as fast as they could go away from the nurse approaching from the other end of the hall.

At the far end of the hall, Mike led Ralph around the corner, and doing double time they made it to the outside doors. After pushing the doors open, the two men walked around the outside corner to the front of the small hospital and slid into the waiting car.

"Dat purty slick. 'Aven't had such a time since I left my home country forty years ago," Ralph said.

"You got out of there pretty quick. It usually takes at least half an hour with all the paperwork," Gerald said, unaware of the hospital staff barreling out of the front door he had just pulled away from.

"Yeah, we got out purty quick fer sure." Ralph turned and grinned at Mike in the back seat. Ralph's eyes twinkled and his weathered brown face crinkled into laugh lines.

"What can I say? Never was good with long goodbyes." Mike winked at Ralph. He took out his wallet and looked through it, still puzzled at his circumstances. *Goodnight, I don't think this could get much worse. I'm positive Mike isn't my name. I don't know who I am or what I'm doing, but I know I'm doing something and it's important. Maybe something will jog my memory when I get back to the Manor.*

BACK AT THE MANOR HOUSE, he let the warm water run down his body, hoping the shower would help him relax. He had tentatively washed his hair and was now wondering if that had been wise. *Maybe I should have waited until tomorrow, he thought. What's done is done.* He turned the water off and towel-dried avoiding his head until last. *I don't know what you're doing for a living, fella, but you need to get out of whatever it is.* He took note of two wounds that were still healing.

It felt good to be cleaned up, but he wasn't sure how much he was capable of doing in his capacity as a hired cook. He slipped into his shoes and found his way to the kitchen office. He pulled some books out of his desk and looked through them. "Come in," he said to a tap on his partially opened door.

"Yes?" He looked up.

"How bad is it?" Gerald stood in the doorway.

"How bad's what? My head could take a new patch, but I've washed all the old blood..."

"There's a first aid kit stashed in here. Ms. Lind was adamant that we have ample kits throughout the house. But I'm talking about your memory. You're running from something, and by the look of the wound on your leg, it's not your first fight." Gerald went over to the shelf behind the desk and reached down a hefty briefcase. "Sit down and let me look at your head." He pulled the hair at the nape of Mike's neck out of the way. "Yeah, looks like it needs a patch, all right." He began applying ointment then the bandage. "Ralph told me how you boys escaped so fast. Said it took him back to when he was a lot younger." Gerald laughed.

"He did good. And you're doing great with this bandage. You must have had several first aid jobs around here," Mike said.

"It's not common knowledge, but I used to work as a fighter. That was before Ms. Lind rescued me. I needed to get out of fighting, and she needed a bodyguard. She rescued Ralph also, but that's his story."

"I'm trying to get in touch with where I've been. The only names that made sense were Gwen and MacDonald, but I don't connect them to anything. No Hastings..."

"Hastings is a common enough name," Gerald said as he finished his first aid job.

"Who am I putting this meal together for this evening?" Mike went out into the kitchen looking through the freezers and refrigerators at his food resources.

"We never prepare for any less than ten. That's a skeleton crew. One of the maids this morning tried to fill in cooking, but I'm sure everyone will be thankful for your return. We do have menus."

"I'll need a trip for supplies." Mike looked over the lists. "As I get organized here, finish telling me what happened after you called the police and ambulance." The cook began pulling together carrots, onions, potatoes, and other vegetables while listening as Gerald began his account.

"It was a mess that I found you in. You'd been hit from behind and knocked out. I threw a cover over you, then I went to investigate the rest of the house. It was a bum devilish mess all around, I can say. I was told Mr. Greene was playing the piano in the music room. Someone had brought in leftover hors d'oeuvres and sandwiches. There was a large pot of coffee. As for people, the three new maids were sleeping soundly in various chairs about the music room and Missy's friend Leila was stretched across the sofa. That is what I saw. What I didn't see was Alice, who would not have abandoned her post whilst people were still up, and I didn't see Missy or Mr. Greene," Gerald said.

"Anything unusual? Did you see anything out of place?" The cook finished chopping the vegetables and put everything into a stockpot.

"On the veranda, I found a shawl and one of Missy's slippers. I assume that's where she was when she was kidnapped." Gerald frowned.

"I've got soup for supper on a slow cook. Show me the music room and describe what and where things were. Maybe after that, I could look around the premises...like starting upstairs in the missing people's rooms? Are all of the maids—and Leila—still here?" Mike asked.

"I believe they are. Leila has been inconsolable. The maids are trying to cope."

"First things first." Mike dried his hands on the towel. "Let's start with the music room."

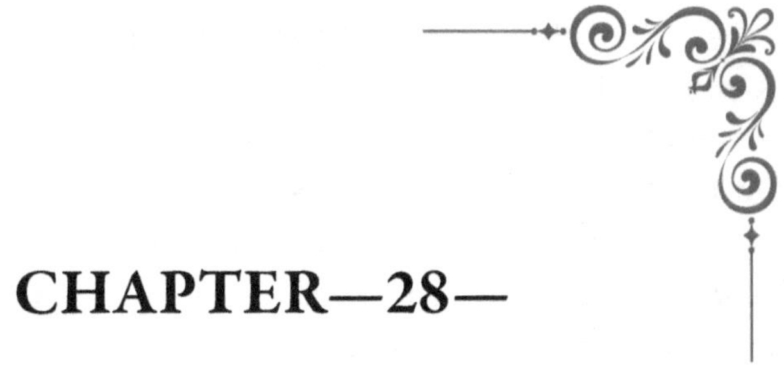

CHAPTER—28—

Gwen's eyes opened slowly and she shivered from the chill in the room. Was that a knock at her door?

"Hello, dearie." Alice bustled in carrying a large old willow twig basket. She set it on the floor by the window. She picked up an afghan from one of the chairs, brought it over, and covered Gwen. Then she gently stroked her hair.

Gwen pulled the cover close and smiled. "Thank you, Alice. Is there any news?" she asked.

"If we were back home there would be. Here I'm just treading water. I did get a bath and clean clothes, but that is the extent of my news. Did Franklin give you any idea what's going on?"

Alice pulled a chair around and sat as there was a tap at the door. A young man with an armload of firewood stalked into the room, stomped across to the fireplace, and sullenly dumped the firewood on the hearth. He then stomped back out and shut the door.

"Well, that was rude. But it was timely." Alice stood and went to put more wood on the fire and tidy up the pile of wood.

"Let's look at what I've brought and we can talk as we work," Alice said. "These are ancient, but I thought these would give us something to occupy our time. For now at least." She motioned toward the basket.

"What are they?" Gwen sat up on the edge of the bed to watch as Alice lifted flat pieces of cloth out of the large woven basket. "How interesting. There are two different samples here. Some are just plain cloth squares with a design printed on them." Gwen held one square, examining it closely.

"Right you are. Then there are these." Alice handed her a second one from the bottom of the basket.

"These are similar, just flat pieces of cloth, except these have beautiful stitches on them so that the pictures on these come to life. These are quite beautiful, but what are they?" Gwen asked as she held up and examined more pieces.

"It's called embroidery," Alice said. "My mother taught me to embroider when I was just small. I can teach you—it will help pass the time."

"These are so beautiful. I have some of Aunt Zoe's needlepoint. That's similar—do you think I could ever do such a neat job?"

"Judging by the way you do almost everything else, yes," Alice said. "These look like the project was going to be sewn together for a quilt, or they could be for some smaller project."

"So you use the hoop to hold the material tight, and there's colored thread—are there directions at all?" Gwen said.

"It's called floss, not thread. Some projects do tell you what colors to use and how many strands of the floss to use. I didn't find any directions like that with this." Alice prepared a fourteen-inch piece of material centering the stamped design on the hoop. She stretched it into place. "Choose some colors you would like to use, and I'll show you how to begin. I've already started one." She held up another square. "I used two strands of blue floss like this..." She separated two strands from the six strands, measured a goodly length, snipped it off the skein of floss, then threaded the small needle.

"I see." Gwen watched the procedure intently. "You bring the needle up through the material—is there more than one kind of stitch here?"

"Yes, this one is a lazy daisy stitch. On these flowers do that stitch..." Alice handed the square to Gwen.

"Only these kinds of flowers have that same stitch?" At first, Gwen was clumsy, but she began on an easy design and improved quickly.

"Now back to the news. As I said this morning, the cook is Mr. Hastings from home," Alice said. "I don't think he knew Mr. Greene before working for you. I think they became acquainted after they came to your estate. I would say there was a glitch somewhere."

"Why is that?" Gwen stopped her stitching.

"Well, I think Franklin meant for the cook to come with us, not Hastings."

"Franklin did say he had intended for someone to nab Mike, but the person grabbed Hastings instead," Gwen said.

"Hastings and Chapman are pleasant to be around— Unlike the man who carried the wood just now. His temperament makes him unpleasant. He is someone we hired last week to help get ready for the party." Alice paused and her lips twisted with a distasteful look. "I'm not sure if there is someone else helping with outside work."

"Is Hastings still friendly? What do you think of him?"

"Hastings's always pleasant but... I think the unpleasant fellow and Franklin are in this together. Hastings was a bit pale and under the weather this morning. I had the impression he is struggling to get a handle on the situation same as we are. And that's all I know." Alice paused with a thoughtful look.

"Well, here's a summary of how the conversation went this morning," Gwen said. "I was shocked but some things are beginning to make sense. For starters, Mr. Greene blames my father for the death of his wife and daughter..."

"Oh no!" A sudden intake of breath and Alice's eyes widened. "What a foul thing to say!"

"Yes, but that's what he said. His wife and daughter were in an accident, and because my father didn't come in immediately, they died."

"Mr. de Winters was always conscientious about his work. He always went the extra mile to help and take care of others. His patients thought the world of him. When your parents died, there was a huge outpouring of sympathy from all sorts of people. People, rich and poor, lined up for blocks at the funeral." Alice's face darkened, and her eyes flashed in anger.

"Franklin said when he first came to work for me he figured he would—I guess I can't say it any other way—he planned on murdering me. He felt justified, I assume, but now he's decided to keep me alive. He's going to pretend I'm his daughter. So here we are in the middle of a large forest. He said there isn't anyone for miles and not to try and get away. I'm not sure how he thinks he can pull this off."

"Nuts. He's nuts. He can't pull it off." Alice shook her head. "He must have bats in his belfry. He seems to be correct on one thing though. We appear to be in the middle of nowhere. He said there were no neighbors for miles?"

"That's what he said. That doesn't make it true. We will just have to keep our eyes and ears open." Gwen frowned. "Last night when we were on the terrace Mr. Greene seemed to have a lot of knowledge about Seth." New thoughts came into her mind. "What he said makes me uncomfortable that he knew so much. He would have had to do some checking on my history when he took the job, but he also said something about I would have a new husband..." She stopped as new fears ran unchecked through her mind. "I'm afraid for Seth. I wish I could warn him in some way."

"You never did finish your account. What did you mean to tell me about Seth?"

"Until this summer, the largest part of our life together Seth would look like a failure. First off his character as a person is...well, he is kind, thoughtful, gentle, and loving. He has never given me a moment to doubt his love for me or his fidelity, and he is always a gentleman. But for all of these years, he struggled heavily with alcohol.

He went back and forth, coming out of a bout with alcohol. He'd be sober for a time then back under. In June this year, I left him a note. I told him I couldn't stand to watch him killing himself bit by bit. I was ready to call it quits. As fate would have it, Seth disappeared at the same time I was in a car accident and laid up with my leg in a cast. I stayed with his sister for the first two weeks. On the third week Seth caught up with me, and he asked for one more chance. We stayed with his family for a few weeks, and I witnessed an incredible transformation."

"But what happened? You left him and came back?"

"I was confused. He had a family—a very large family. I struggled with that. And Seth had changed, and his change needed me to change and..."

"You weren't ready to change?"

"That was part of it. I needed time to decide what was important to me," Gwen said.

"I see," Alice said with hesitation.

"Before Seth had a problem and that made me feel like a *martyr*, but I think that was Satan deceiving me. Like Seth was the problem, but it isn't true. We're all broken people in reality. I've been reading and praying and I never told Seth about me. He doesn't know who I am."

"He doesn't know who you are? That's impossible. How could he not know..." Alice looked at Gwen with doubt.

"I never told him, and he didn't ask." Gwen shrugged. "At one point Mr. Greene described Seth as a drunk, and that was true *before*. But now? The facts don't even begin to give an accurate pic-ture—and now that he's sober, the picture is way different."

Gwen held up the square for embroidery. "It's like the difference between these cloth pieces with only a black and white picture stamped in—kind of flat and lifeless. Mr. Greene said he's 'Seth Matthew MacDonald, eighth child out of ten, age thirty-one, six foot two inches tall, 190 pounds soaking wet.'" Gwen recited the facts as Franklin Greene had. "But that's not Seth."

"Ten children? That is a whole bunch. And you say he's one of the younger ones?"

"Yes, he has a younger brother and a younger sister. For some reason, I assumed there was just him and his older sister—the one I stayed with when I was laid up. He told me about another brother that had died, but that story never made sense."

"How strange. And you never asked about his parents?"

"He told me they were gone."

"And of course with your background, you assumed he meant they were dead?" Alice said.

"Yes, rather short-sighted of me, but that's the long and short of it," Gwen said.

"Just look at how well you are doing!" Alice examined the piece Gwen was working on. "You have a natural talent. Let me show you another stitch for this flower then I'll need to go down and find out when lunch is and how Mr. Hastings is doing at his newfound trade."

Gwen sighed. "I'm still disoriented. I think I'll lie down for another rest as well."

THE DULL HEADACHE GWEN had when she lay down earlier had disappeared by the time she woke an hour later. She tentatively stood and wandered around the room, stopping to place a few more pieces of wood on the fire. She ran her fingers lightly over the rough-hewn stones that made up the fireplace. They were comfortably warm to the touch. She noticed there was one stone that felt a bit loose behind the front rocks. She ran her fingers around the rock, whisking the dust away. She found that not only was it loose, but she could also coax it out of place.

Intrigued at the idea of a hidden treasure, she felt around, exploring the shallow depths, but it was empty except for a piece of paper. Gwen pulled it out and read. "Psalm 23:2 He maketh me to lie down in green pastures: he leadeth me beside the still waters." She replaced the slip of paper and carefully slid the stone back into place. The little key in the back of her Bible nagged at the back of her mind. Going to the other side of the fireplace she checked those stones for anything loose, but all seemed solid.

Back at the dressing table, she sat on the bench to brush her hair. After replacing the brush in its spot, she opened the drawer and removed the Bible. Looking at the small key, she turned it over, examining it closely. Hmm, a small gold key...reminds me of a diary key I used to have. I wonder—

As there was a light tap on her door, she slid the key back into the envelope. "Yes?" She turned toward the door.

Alice opened it and stuck her head into the room. "I've come to tell you it's time to go down for lunch if you're rested and feeling well enough?"

"Let me wash my face and hands." Gwen disappeared into the bathroom but reappeared shortly. "Have you found out anything more?"

"At present, there are five of us here but there may be another person. From the aromas coming from the kitchen, I think Hastings has at least one more good meal left in his repertoire, and I've not come up with an escape plan yet."

"Have you talked to Hastings? Any idea as to what he thinks—where he stands?"

"No, it's much too early for that. He's still looking like he's off-center."

"I don't want to think of him as a kidnapper. Franklin did say they had grabbed Hastings by mistake," Gwen said.

"Well, here we go. Put on a good face and just follow me downstairs."

"I WONDER IF IT MAKES any difference where we sit?" Gwen whispered to Alice as they chose chairs from among the places set for five people at the medium-sized rectangular table.

"I'm sure we'll find out, but here toward the end closest to the kitchen looks good to me. I don't feel right about just sitting down. You sit down and I'll go ask if I can help in the kitchen," Alice said.

"I'd feel better coming with you, but I'll keep our places." Gwen turned her coffee cup over then reached across to Alice's cup.

Hastings appeared at the kitchen door bringing several items for lunch as Alice met him. "Is there anything you want me to bring?" She moved aside to let him pass.

"I've got the soup tureen here. There are several other platters. If you would grab any one of them, they will go on the buffet table over there." Hastings placed the tureen at the head of the table and turned back for another item.

Franklin came in the front door. Wiping his feet on the mat, he hung his coat and hat on the hall tree. "Hello. How's your morning gone so far?" He spoke to Gwen as she looked up.

Before she could answer, there was a distinct noise as a door somewhere in the house opened and a clunking sound was heard in the dining area. She turned at the semi-familiar sound.

"Allow me to introduce my brother, Frederick Greene." Franklin watched her closely.

"How do you do?" For all of her aunt's thorough training, it was all Gwen could do to act normal. This might explain some of the mystery as Franklin's brother clumped up to the table.

"So, this is the pretty bird?" He ignored Gwen's polite greeting and spoke to Franklin. "What's J.R. think?" He looked back at Gwen as if he were appraising a horse or some other animal.

"I don't know what J.R. thinks. Sometimes I'm not sure he thinks at all…" Franklin's words were interrupted as the rude young man who had brought the firewood up to her room came into the dining area.

"So, what do ya think, J.R.?" the man named Frederick asked.

"I don't know. Not my type. I'll have to think about it some more." He squinted at Gwen in a similar fashion as Frederick had.

"I think it's about time to eat, and you both need to sit down and shut up." Franklin scowled at the two men.

Alice sat down between Gwen and the rest of the occupants. "How rude," she hissed to Gwen. "Now we know where he got *his* rudeness from." Alice used her eyes to indicate Franklin.

"I'm not very hungry, Alice. I think I'll just eat this soup and head back upstairs."

"I don't blame you, lamb, that…"

"It's rude to sit and whisper together," Franklin spoke loudly.

"I was just telling Alice I wasn't feeling well, and I think I'll go back to my room." Gwen pushed back from the table.

Franklin nodded. "I suppose you may be excused. It is your first day, and it's been difficult."

CHAPTER—29—

Waking up sluggishly the next morning, Gwen turned over. Supper the evening before had been just as awkward and had not gone much better than lunch. She was not anticipating a breakfast with the group and hoped Alice would bring breakfast up. Just the thought of seeing Frederick or his son, J.R., made her stomach churn.

Today the sun was just coming up, not streaming through the French windows like it had been the day before. She could hear someone chopping wood outside. She found her slippers where she left them and took the few steps to the French doors. Peering through the glass to the outside, she saw no sign of activity, so she wandered over to the dressing table and sat on the bench. She twisted her hair up and pinned it out of the way. Then she made her way to the bathroom and ran her bathwater.

After bathing, she pulled out a clean towel from the closet. Her hand found a knob along the sidewall hidden behind the towels. *How odd...*She quickly slipped into her skirt and blouse then revisited the closet. The knob didn't open easily, but with a firm tug, it swung open. She looked into a tiny nook that held a slender box. She removed the small box and discovered a few pieces of jewelry—a necklace, a matching ring, and a bookmark with a scripture on it: "Psalm 27:5 For in the time of trouble he shall hide me in his pavilion: in the secret of his tabernacle shall he hide me; he shall set me up upon a rock."

"Yes?" She answered a tap on her outer door and quickly replaced the jewelry into the box and returned the box to the small nook. She slid the bookmark into the pocket of her sweater.

"You're up early this morning." Alice carried a breakfast tray in and set it on the table. She set the food off the tray onto the small table between the chairs by the French doors to the patio. "Today's breakfast looks good. I think Mr. Hastings was hiding his talent. He could have been a cook as well as Mr. Mike. There are scrambled eggs with onions, sausage, and cheese, strong hot coffee—just as you like it, and cinnamon rolls..." She said as she pulled the cover off a special container.

Gwen sat down, staring at the tray.

"What's the matter, lamb?" Alice asked.

"I can't—it's just a feeling. There's something about the tray... When I figure it out I'll tell you." Gwen shrugged.

Alice set out two plates. "You're probably pretty hungry after yesterday." She scooped a goodly portion onto the first plate.

"The cinnamon roll and coffee look good." Gwen pulled the bookmark out of her pocket. "Look what I've found. And it's the second one."

"What is it?" Alice put down her fork with the scrambled eggs on it and carefully looked the piece over.

"Just a minute..." Gwen stood and went to the fireplace to retrieve the scripture she had found. "This is the one I found this morning hidden in the bathroom: 'Psalm 27:5 For in the time of trouble he shall hide me in his pavilion: in the secret of his tabernacle shall he hide me; he shall set me up upon a rock.' And this is the one I found yesterday: 'Psalm 23:2 He maketh me to lie down in green pastures: he leadeth me beside the still waters.'" She spread them both in front of Alice.

"Interesting." Alice picked up her cup and studied the two scriptures. "Where's the Bible you found?"

Gwen fetched the Bible from the drawer and handed it to Alice. "Do you think there may be something here?"

"Well," Alice said as she turned through the pages, "Here is this one, and the words 'still waters' are underlined twice. She flipped to Psalm 27. And here 'hide me and set me upon a rock' are underlined twice. It could be this one is pointing toward the one 'upon a rock' and this one is in the bathroom 'by the still waters.' They do appear to be clues, but as to what, and what's the prize?"

"There was some jewelry in the one hiding place, but not expensive jewelry," Gwen said. "There are many underlined passages mostly in Psalms, but I wonder if only those underlined twice have meaning? And this one says upon a rock, not in a rock..." Gwen allowed her eyes to search around the room looking at everything in a new light. "I do wish Seth were here. He was so good with these sort of puzzle things."

Alice made note of where they found the clues and closed them up in the Bible. They were quiet in thought as they finished their breakfast.

"I'll be back after a bit. You should keep your treasure safe." Alice gathered up the dishes and cleaned up after their meal. "I'll take this back down now."

"Our skirmish from yesterday seems to have set me back a bit. I'm going to rest a little. Maybe work on some of those squares afterward." Gwen walked to the bed and lay down.

"You do look a bit pale. I'll cover you up before I leave." Alice picked up the afghan and smoothed it over Gwen.

CHAPTER —30—

"Mr. Chapman, sir..." Leila looked pale and in shock. "I'm glad you're feeling better."

"I'm back home here, but not sure how well I'm feeling." Somewhere in his mind, he moved her down on his suspect list. "What do you know about this Franklin Greene? You didn't know him before?"

"No, Gwen and I were friends from back in school days." Leila twisted her handkerchief into a knot. "Just last year my husband died rather suddenly from a rare disease I'd never heard of before. After Gwen sent me a sympathy card, we've kept in touch. When she returned a few weeks ago, she asked me to come for a visit. Which is why I'm here. That's when I met Mr. Greene. I can't believe that Frank...I mean Mr. Greene would do such a thing." The tears that had formed in her eyes gushed down her cheeks, and she sobbed into her knotted handkerchief.

"You didn't see this coming at all then?" he asked.

"No. I was aware that Gwen and Franklin had their disagreements. They didn't often see eye to eye, but I think Franklin was beginning to see things differently. He and I both came from poor circumstances, but he didn't understand."

"Didn't understand?"

"I've seen snobs up close and neither Gwen nor her family is like that. I visited her back before I was married. I met her Aunt Zoe. There couldn't be a nicer, sweeter, more wonderful person, but Frank had an attitude problem," Leila said. "That night after the picnic I suggested some songs and refreshments, and Frank began to play the piano. Gwen and I used to sing together on occasion when we were in school, and we were singing as Frank played. Then he got snarky and was needling her about a song. She walked outside onto the terrace. The last thing I remember was sitting down on the sofa with my cup of coffee, right after he followed her out the doors."

"All I can remember is bringing in a tray of sandwiches, putting them on the kitchen counter." Mike rubbed a hand over his forehead. "Two things. What was the song?"

"'I'll Be Loving You.' I know Gwen knows that song..." Leila said.

"Next, I'd appreciate it if you'd take the girls, the maids as it were, here in hand. Keep some semblance of order, make sure they get their duties done."

"I can do that, but we should be able to find them?" Leila's eyes implored him to answer.

"I'LL START WITH THE detective's room. Then the other two, Alice and Gwen's rooms. I've got to get my memory back. Working blind like this isn't good. Tomorrow morning I'll need to go into that culinary shop," Mike said to Gerald as they walked up the stairs.

"The police have already been through here but if you think it'll help you with remembering... Mr. Greene was hired to investigate if someone was stalking Gwen. Looks to me like we hired the fox to guard the henhouse." Gerald frowned and opened the bedroom door. "The blue room was his room right here. Alice's room was just back with a door in between. And across the hall from Alice are Missy's rooms." Gerald pointed out the different rooms.

"Thanks." Mike stood in the doorway. *What am I doing here?* He blew a breath out and stepped inside. It was a spacious room that hearkened back to the turn of the century as did the entire mansion.

There was a large fireplace, a table, and chairs in front of the fireplace, a four-poster bed, and a large bay window with elaborate window dressings. The lighting had been renovated. Although the lamps and lighting were reworked, they still retained their original style. *There's enough furniture in this room to furnish a household...*

Everyone leaves something behind even when they think they've picked up everything. He tossed a stray sock into his bag. There were odds and ends, a toothbrush, a comb, a tie tack, a glass, a bag of trash... One man's trash is another man's treasure. He put all of the evidence into a separate bag and labeled it. Next room Alice's.

What a puzzle this person Alice was. Photos in an old album indicated Alice was from a different world or had been a long, long time ago. Alice had not planned on leaving when she did the other night. Ninety-eight percent of her belongings had been left behind. It looked as if someone had rummaged through her belongings and grabbed a few items. *Hmm, does this mean they aren't planning on being gone long? And is that good, or are we working on a time limit? Again he tied up the evidence in its separate bag. On to Gwen's room.*

The other rooms were nothing compared to this side of the house. Gwen herself had not just a bedroom, she had rooms. There was the bedroom and a connected bath, a room with the fireplace, a dressing table, closets, and a semi-private desk in front of a large tower window with upholstered chairs and a side table. This room as well gave the appearance that the occupant hadn't planned on leaving. The bedroom was in order, but the bath had some items spilled as if someone wasn't sure what to take and just randomly grabbed things. Back in the dressing room, several hangers were empty from the closets, and maybe shoes. Back over to the dressing table.

Picking up the picture from the dresser, he sat on the chair closest to the table. Who were these people? The one was Gwen MacDonald he assumed, but the man? For some reason, he knew that he knew that face. Clutching the picture, he had a momentary pain and darkness clouded his vision. He did know that face—And Gwen's face— both ran together. MacDonald...he knew that name. He knew that name...

"Mr. Chapman? Mike?" There was a quiet tap on the door.

"Yes," he said without looking up.

"I was thinking...well, Gerald, the butler..."

"Yes? Wait, now, what's your name?"

"My name's Doris, sir. I saw them leave," the maid said. "There were two vans. I saw them leave...it was almost midnight. There were like two of Mr. Greene, and that one fellow, Chad I think it was, that was hired last. They loaded everyone into those vans."

"How did you see them? I thought everyone was down in the music room."

"I didn't go to the music room. I was tired and didn't feel well. Miss Alice allowed me to go to my room. The vans were both dark-colored, but in the night like that I'm not sure what color."

"Have you spoken to the police?"

"No," Doris said. "They spoke to the others, but I was still upstairs not feeling well."

"LET ME OUT HERE AND you go on and run your errands, Gerald. I have some things I want to pick up here at the Herberry Shop. I'll meet you down the street there a couple of blocks at the bakery," Mike said. He pulled his hat down and opened the car door.

"No rush, I've got several stops to make. I'll see you there. Probably be an hour," Gerald said. He waited until the door shut then drove on.

Mike opened the Herberry Shop door and nodded at the customer just leaving. "Hi," he greeted the tall guy behind the counter. "I'm looking for Mark."

"In the back." The guy motioned with his head.

"Hey, Mark. How's it going?" Mike said.

"I wish I could help you. Is your memory coming back? All I know is you needed a recommendation as a cook. You and someone you called Matthew Hastings. You—we were keeping a watch out on Gwen MacDonald. She's disappeared, and Hastings. But he's on our side."

"I'm still working this blind. So, where did this Franklin Greene come from, and better yet, where's he gone? I have some artifact evidence. Can you get it where it needs to go?" Mike, the cook, handed Mark a sack with the evidence bags. "One of the maids said she saw the vans that kidnapped the victims. She said there were two dark vans, but she didn't know the exact color. There were three males. She didn't have any physical descriptions except two of them looked like Mr. Greene and one was the new hire by the name of Chad."

"What did she mean by that? Two men that looked like Mr. Greene? Humph! Greene himself has been in the area for quite some time, working for the police department and now semi-retired as a private detective," Mark said. "His family emigrated fifty years ago from Lebanon. He's got some very odd history. His mother and father, and he, and his mother's older brother made the trip."

"No other siblings?" Mike asked.

"Not that we can tell."

"Well, I believe I've got some DNA there." Mike pointed at the evidence bags. "When I get that back who knows? Also, keep your eyes peeled in case someone from Mr. Greene comes in. He's into cooking and herbs so... It's a wild chance, but a chance. Here's a list of some herbs I came in for. If you could grab those for me, and here's where you can reach me—at this number." Mike handed Mark a slip of paper.

"I'll get this stuff for you. Be right back," Mark walked out to the front for the products. "Here you go, and my card, just in case." He came back with a bag.

"Thanks. I can't very well go home without my herbs—my excuse for coming. Is there a back way out of here?"

Mike checked his watch as he ambled out of the alley a few minutes later. *Twenty minutes till I'm supposed to meet Gerald. Enough time to collect the order I called into the bakery early this morning. I can sit out of sight at the table and...*

"Thanks, Nina, I'll take a coffee and just sit over here by the window until you have my order ready." Mike took his cup and ambled over to the window table. Sipping his coffee while watching the traffic as it filtered by, he glanced at the clock. Almost ten o'clock, and Gerald ought to be here at any time. The bakery had a significant number of customers coming and going.

Looking back out the window, he spied a young man hustle across the street, glancing over one shoulder, and then looking up and down the street. Mike peered closer at the man. Something about him looked familiar. As the man ducked into the bakery, Mike pulled his hat a bit lower and kept his gaze on his coffee cup. Shifting ever so slightly, he watched the man out of the corner of his eye.

"I'll take a coffee. When will Sheila be back?" the young man asked the woman working the counter.

Mike couldn't hear the reply, but the young man didn't look happy about it.

"I'll be back in a couple of days. Probably in the afternoon," the man said. "Tell her I'll be back to see her." He paid for his coffee and turned to leave.

Oh, good night, Mike saw Gerald pull up and park across the street. The young man stopped and hesitated at the door when he saw the car and Gerald sitting close at hand. *Could it get worse?* Mike held his breath and continued to avert his eyes.

"Order number seven, ready..." Nina at the counter called out.

I guess it can get worse. He still held his breath, but the young man pulled his coat collar up, scrunched his face down into his jacket, and hurried out the door.

"Mike? Your order's ready." Nina looked at the ticket then up at him.

"Sure," he said and exhaled. "Just a minute." He stepped to the door and looked up the street in the direction the young man had disappeared. "I'll be right back." He slid out the door. Mike motioned to Gerald to pull around. "I've got an order. I'll be right back."

Mike hustled down the block searching for the young man. He stopped at the corner and looked up and down. There were several stores where the man might have gone, but he had disappeared. Mike turned around and strolled back to the bakery.

"So," he said at the counter as he paid for his purchase. "Do you know who that young fellow was?"

"Not really," Nina said. "I've seen him on occasion, but he's been in here more often since Sheila Dunde started working here. Matter of fact, he was asking about her today. He said to tell her he'd be back to see her in a couple of days. Is there something wrong? Is he wanted for something?"

"No, he just reminded me of someone that I owe some money. This Sheila Dunde, does she live around here?"

"We don't give out personal info without permission. She's on the schedule for Wednesday. If you leave your name and a number, I can have her call?"

"That's fine, I'll stop back in on Wednesday. I may be wrong about knowing him anyway." Mike handed her the money for the order. He turned as Gerald came in. "Here help me carry this order, Gerald."

"I didn't know if you were back," Gerald said when he opened the trunk and moved a few things aside. "We're almost full here, but let's get this loaded and get home."

MIKE SAT OUTSIDE ON the bench in the kitchen garden. The sun was just peeking over the horizon as he held the picture in his hands of Gwen and her husband. He wondered how to make sense of what was happening. "Come on, Hastings, talk to me, man. What are we supposed to be doing here?" He closed his eyes and bowed his head. *God, I don't know what I'm doing. I don't know—I just don't know...* "*My grace is sufficient for thee: for my strength is made perfect in weakness.*" Well, yes, I know that. He sat up looking around for the speaker.

"How're ya doin?"

Mike jumped at the voice and looked again. "Ralph. I think that whack on the head was more serious than I thought. Usually, when I'm talking to myself I don't expect an answer." Mike laughed.

"Dat's the truth. I's wonderin' if you need some late garden produce? Der's not much left, but Alice she always used what I had..."

"Yes, fresh is always best."

"What da picture ya got," Ralph said, looking at what Mike held in his hands.

"A picture of your Gwen," Mike said. "I'm hoping to jog some memory."

"Yes, I see Missy, but why she 'ave a picture with Hastings?"

"*Hastings?*" Mike looked closer. "Are you sure this is Hastings?"

"Well, now dat I look closer, no, no that's not him," Ralph studied the picture. "When I first looked—but no, it couldn't be him. Hastings, he has dark brown hair and hazel colored eyes. Maybe a brudder wid blond hair and blue eyes." He finished with a laugh. "Purty close, he looked like. I'll get you some of those vegetables. Got a big basket here." Ralph walked off toward the garden.

*I JUST GOT TO MAKE it this time, Jo. I just got to. No, you two need to go. She's in danger...*The words echoed in his mind. *Now if I just knew whose words those are. One voice went with a man, one went with a woman, and who was Jo?* He woke with a sigh. Funny that I remember the cruise ship gig. I remember bits and pieces, but nothing that might explain this. *The only real connection is that picture. I have a hunch that Ralph was right the first time. And that young man. He's familiar, but how?*

"NO, I DON'T KNOW WHERE I'm going." Mike frowned at the local preacher, Nick Martinez. "I'm just wandering in the dark, hopeful that I'm asking the right questions."

Nick smiled at the man sitting across his desk from him. "Well, let me get this straight. The facts as you know them are these, you and someone named Matthew Hastings are here working on something to do with the Gwen de Winters-MacDonald case. Before it was a case. Gwen and her husband Seth MacDonald came from Forrest City? Right?" Nick was quiet for a bit thinking over the information. "Yes, Gwen is a member of our congregation here. As was her great aunt. Let me take this information—I know the preacher there in Forrest City. I'll contact him and see what I can find out. I have had some discussions with Gwen lately since she's been back..."

"I wouldn't ask you to break confidence. I'm just trying to back-track since the attack and get my memory back and shed some light on where her abductors have taken her or them," Mike said with a furrowed brow. "I'll be back in the day after tomorrow, or you can always drive out to the mansion. I'm in the kitchen most of the day there. Just go around to the back entrance."

"Okay. I'll get on this and see what I can find out," Nick said. "This abduction is in the news daily. It seems some news reporter is chasing a tip that she's eloped with some mysterious man. They've seen her in the UK or Paris, or on a cruise. None of these things are credible, but that doesn't stop them from being newsworthy."

"She would be quite a catch, but it doesn't sound at all like the Gwen I've heard about." Mike and Nick stood and shook hands. "If you find out anything, let me know. Remember, the clock is ticking...Time is of the essence."

"We need to have a prayer then before you leave," Nick said.

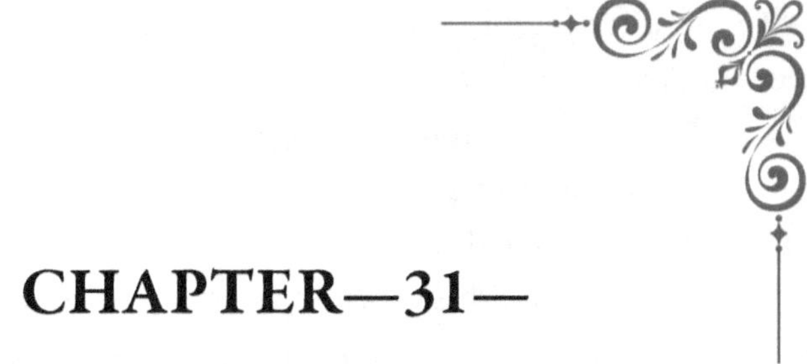

CHAPTER—31—

"**P**salms 23:4 Yea, though I walk through the valley of the shadow of death, I will fear no evil: for thou art with me; thy rod and thy staff they comfort me." Gwen read, running her finger under the verse. Pausing she looked out the window. The whole verse was underlined. *What message does that carry? It's such a beautiful peaceful place here, yet I feel such turmoil and hostility.* Running her finger through the twenty-third Psalm, Gwen noticed in the bottom of the margin a very neat handwritten notation: "See Ecclesiastes 12:12."

Turning the pages in the Bible, she came to Ecclesiastes 12:12. Reading quietly to herself, "And further, by these, my son, be admonished: of making many books *there is* no end, and much study *is* a weariness of the flesh"—she smiled at the idea. Then running a finger under the underlined text "'many books'"... Hmm. Sitting in the chair in front of the French doors, she had her back to most of the room. She turned to look around. Yes, there are quite a few volumes of books scattered around the room, some as decoration, and some on shelves. Gwen sat back around and bowed her head.

Oh, Father God, I desperately need your guiding hand. I don't know what this is saying to me. I don't know what to pray for. I'm confused. I'm so confused. I pray your protection this day on Seth and his family, on Alice, Hastings, and myself. Alice should be coming up soon to tell her... Ah, there was the knock on her door.

"Yes?" she said.

"Time for lunch." Alice breezed in. "And good news, the two wet blankets aren't here." She smiled and sat in the chair across from Gwen. "How's your Bible reading progressing?"

"Let me show you what I have, and you can think on it over lunch." Gwen opened the Bible. "Here, this whole Psalm is underlined...but I noticed this down in the margin." She showed Alice the reference in Ecclesiastes. "And here this is underlined—"

"Many books," Alice muttered. "Hmm, yes, I don't know. There are many books in this room, but we're supposed to look in one spot, I think for many books. Well, let's go down for lunch. We'll look when we come back."

THE SUNSHINE PLAYED peek-a-boo with the tree leaves in the front yard. It was almost pleasant in the dining room, the aromas coming from the kitchen and the warmth from the large fireplace situated in between the living room and dining area. Most of the meal had been placed on the sideboard buffet table with Hastings bringing in the last few items.

"Since Frederick and J.R. won't be here, if you want, you can join us, Hastings?" Franklin said.

"I'll wait and eat like usual," Hastings said. "Don't want to get out of my routine."

"Suit yourself." Franklin smiled at the two ladies in a carefree manner as if a weight were lifted from his shoulders. "Would you like a walk after lunch? Get some fresh air?"

"Just sitting on the porch maybe," Alice said. "Gwen's been feeling ill, and the fresh air might do her some good. We'll take some of our embroideries out and sit for a few minutes. Where did your brother and his son go?" she asked Franklin.

"They went into town—they'll be gone till late afternoon. Can't say that I miss them."

"Next time they go into town, I have a list of things I need from the store," Hastings said. He removed the soup tureen and brought in the peach dessert.

"Make up your list. Probably won't be until the end of the week," Franklin said with a frown. "They're more bar-hoppers than they should be—gonna get them in trouble. I've warned those two and warned them. Make sure you have a warm jacket when you sit outside..."

GWEN PULLED HER SHAWL around and tucked it under her arms. She held out her embroidery hoop with its pictured work and studied it before taking a moment to look out at the scenery. There were two buildings. One looked like it was used as a garage and one for storage.

"The air is fresh and clean here," Alice said as Franklin joined them on the porch.

"Yes, this is where Lydia, my wife, and I had planned on retiring." He sat down and began strumming on his guitar.

"How did you come to be here?" Gwen asked as she continued working on the picture.

"This property was willed to my mother from her older brother, then after she died it came to me." He stopped strumming, looking out with a glassy stare, then resumed after a moment. He spoke in between resting and playing. "She made me promise to take care of my brother. She didn't understand how difficult that would be."

"Why did you have to take care of your brother?" Alice asked.

"When we came to this country, he was a stow-away. My parents were concerned he wouldn't pass the health examination. He doesn't need me to take care of him except he's gotten used to me taking care of things and..." Franklin shrugged and continued to play.

"Oh, I see," Alice said. "He's gotten used to pushing you around, and you just put up with it."

"I guess that's about it. Mother always felt sorry for him, and now that she's gone, he's making up feeling sorry for himself double. That's what happened when he met and married Patty. Not that it would have lasted anyway, but it was during a bar-hopping binge. When she woke up, I don't think she could come to grips with what she'd done. I have to give it to her, she did stay with him until after J.R. was almost five years old."

"I think I need to take Gwen back inside. She looks like she's getting cold," Alice said. She began picking up the squares and embroidery floss and putting them back in the basket. "Did your wife work on this embroidery project? What was she going to do with it once it was finished?"

"I'm sure she had a plan, but she didn't tell me what it was." Franklin continued to look off into the distance.

"No matter. Come, Gwen, let's go in and sit by the fire. Are you having to chop and split the firewood all by yourself, Franklin?" Alice asked.

"So far, yes," he said as he opened the cabin door for the two ladies.

"You would think those other two could be a bit more help, wouldn't you? Thank you," Alice said. She put the basket down between the stairs and the fireplace. "Are you going upstairs?" she asked Gwen.

"I feel like a rest. I do think I'll go upstairs for a while." Gwen laid her square back in the basket.

"I'm going to check on Hastings. He might need some help on the evening meal." Alice scurried off toward the kitchen. Gwen walked quietly up the stairs and closed the door firmly as she slipped into her room.

Something about the last scripture kept running in her mind. Finding the Bible, she looked to Ecclesiastes 12:12 and read it again slowly. "And further, by these, my son, be admonished: of making many books there is no end; and much study is a weariness of the flesh." As she scrutinized the room, one area caught her attention. It was a stone ledge on the wall with several shelves. She went over to the bookshelf and carefully removed all of the books from the bottom shelf. Tentatively pushing the shelf, it seemed pretty solid. Pulling on the ledge, nothing moved. Replacing the books, she looked at the top shelf and repeated the actions.

There was a tap on the door as she began replacing the books. "Come in," she said. She grabbed a dust cloth to give the impression she was dusting. "Oh, Alice, so glad it was you." Gwen sat down looking at the shelf. "I'm just sure it has to be that shelf."

"It could be. Let me look." Alice began running her fingers lightly over the shelves. "Yes, here it is, I think." Her fingers fumbled for a second then the whole bookshelf swung open like a door. "There you go, and here's the prize you're looking for." She handed Gwen a book with a locked clasp.

Gwen involuntarily sucked in a breath as she ran her fingers over the front and back cover. Opening the Bible, she took the key out of the small pocket in the back. "After all of the oddities—the hideaway compartments in this room— I was running out of hiding places for that diary to be in." Gwen slipped the key into the lock. "But I have a feeling this diary has a message for me."

"I came to tidy up a bit before I go back to help with supper." Alice closed the bookshelf then began replacing the books. "We're having barbecue beef for supper. Franklin is out chopping wood—"

Gwen scrambled to slide her Bible and the new book into a drawer at a tap on the door. "Come in?"

"Here's some firewood. This is the kind that warms a person twice." Franklin walked over to the wood box beside the fireplace.

"Good timing. It takes quite a bit of wood to keep this house warm. I'd hate to see it in the winter," Alice said.

Franklin straightened up after throwing a couple of logs on the fire. "You've got a point," he said on his way out the door.

"Hmm, I never." Alice scrunched up her face. "Do you suppose he's having second thoughts here? I'm going back downstairs now that we've found—you know..." she twitched her head at the book-shelf. "I just came up to bring you another blanket."

"Thank you. I am ready for a rest. Maybe after a bit, I'll get some reading in," Gwen said as she lay down and pulled the cover over her.

"THIS IS THE BEST BARBECUE beef I've ever had, Hastings. You and Mike must have learned how to cook at the same school," Franklin Greene said. He pushed himself back from the table.

Hastings brought in the dessert. "Are your brother and nephew supposed to be back tonight? I hope they bring some supplies."

"Yes, they're supposed to be back this evening." Franklin tackled his ice cream.

"I'm too full. I can't eat another bite." Gwen pushed back from the table.

"Thank you, Hastings, but I'm very full as well. Let's go sit by the fire and work on our squares, Gwen. For a little while before bed," Alice said.

Gwen scanned the living room. "This is a pleasant room."

"Did you get any reading done this afternoon?" Alice asked.

"Yes, I did. Quite a bit of reading actually..."

"I hope you ladies don't mind if I join you?" Franklin came in and picked up his guitar.

"No, we don't mind. It's your house." Alice frowned. "Here's an-other new stitch." She bent over the material and showed Gwen a new design.

Franklin began strumming his guitar and humming an old folk tune.

Gwen smiled at Alice, but her thoughts were free to wander where they would as she bent over her embroidery work. *Life is never as certain as we think it is. Last week I was in my own home, a few weeks before that I was with Seth's family, and even a few weeks before that I was in Forest City.* "Life is unpredictable, isn't it?" she whispered to Alice.

"Yes, I agree." Alice turned toward her. "I was thinking life is like what the poet Burns said, 'the best-laid plans of mice and men,'" Alice said with a shrug.

"There is a piece in the Bible that says not to make plans... 'What is your life? It's a vapour, that appears for a little time, and then vanishes away.' My Olivia and Lydia both were great Bible readers and believers. As for myself, I've read through the Bible several times, but there is just something that doesn't jive for me," Franklin said.

"There are a lot of people who say that, Franklin. What doesn't jive for you?" Alice asked.

"I don't know if I can go with one size fits all," he said. Propping his guitar up he began looking at a wooden bird figurine and running his fingers over its smooth surface.

"One size fits all? That's an odd way of putting it. Explain yourself," Alice said.

"There are ten commandments, but sometimes life doesn't fit into a box, and things fall through the cracks," Franklin said.

"I don't know how that can be, but there are laws explaining things to the priests and the elders and judges. They all played a part in the Old Law," Alice said. "It's part of the pattern of life. People can't just make up the rules as they go along—that would be anarchy, and..."

"And like children playing. Remember the time there were those girls at school?" Gwen asked. "Leila and I ended up pitted against a couple of girls who wanted to make the rules at a school we attended. It ended up being ugly, and the girls were expelled because they carried their rules too far."

"God doesn't look at life from down here in the midst of things. He is the wise parent who knows what is best for everyone." Alice bent her head over her embroidery work. "It's like these embroidery projects. Following the patterns given here, the pictures are beautiful," she said.

"Still, things fall through the cracks, and it's hard to put everything into a neat little bundle." Franklin frowned.

"I don't know if life ever fits into a neat bundle, but we are not what life brings to us, we are what we do with the life we have." Alice frowned back. "Some things are right, some things are wrong, and very few things fall through those cracks." Her eyes challenged his, and he looked away.

"I think I'll go get some more wood in. Takes quite a bit of wood for the house." He put down the wood carving and put his guitar back in its spot.

CHAPTER —32—

Gwen sat quietly reading her newfound treasure. As she opened it up, she read the dedication: "Given to Lydia on her seventh birthday"... *Who gives a seven-year-old a diary?* Gwen wondered. *Like a seven-year-old will take care of and write in a diary.* Oddly enough, this young girl named Lydia had written in her diary. Not every day, but much more often than Gwen ever would have.

Gwen looked up as there was a knock on the door. Alice swung the door open for the unpleasant young man as he stomped into the room with an armload of wood. He didn't speak, and his surly, angry attitude seemed worse today than it had been the day before.

She watched as the angry man left the room. "He never does speak. It's like I'm not even here," Gwen said.

"Could be worse." Alice poured Gwen a cup of hot coffee then put the pot down. "He could be heaping unwanted attention your way. Hastings sent up some chocolate fudge muffins. He thought you might enjoy them."

"Thank you, Alice. I was thinking a nice cup of coffee would be welcome, and chocolate fudge? Yum, that's thoughtful. What do you think of Hastings? I always found him kind of confusing." Gwen took one of the muffins and put it on a plate then took a sip of coffee.

"He does a good job cooking, but he doesn't have the flair that Mike had. His first calling was not being a chef. He's a nice young man. I didn't remember him as having such blue eyes though. He reminds me of someone, but I can't quite put my finger on who." Alice wrinkled her brow in thought.

"He didn't have blue eyes, his eyes are hazel. Anyway, I've been reading in this diary. There have been some interesting entries. There seems to be more than one diary, and I'm trying to piece things together."

"Let me clean a bit and you read to me." Alice picked up a dust cloth.

"In some of these entries, Lydia sounds like she's afraid of Franklin—at least she's afraid of someone. For instance, here is one entry. 'I woke this morning thinking it would be a normal day, but I didn't get all of my chores done. Not getting all my chores done put me behind and...' That is the end of the entry and no more until a week later. The next entry is a normal happy day. 'We went fishing. I don't like fishing but Daddy does and Mama and I just sit and read while he dabbles in the lake. What a fun day.' This back and forth goes on almost with a cycle."

"Shh," Alice held a finger to her lips, and Gwen slid the diary underneath the bigger Bible on her lap. There was a knock on the door before it swung open.

"Good morning," Franklin said. "I saw Alice and Freddy come upstairs and thought I might join you in a cup of coffee. But I met Freddy on the way back down."

"You mean J.R? He only stomps into the room with wood and then stomps out," Gwen said.

"Yes, when he was little we called him by his name Freddy. Now he likes the name J.R. Well, I guess his attitude is his problem," Franklin said, as a frown wrinkled his face. "Not much happening here like your life in the mansion." His face still wore its frown. "I suppose this is pretty dull compared to that life."

"I read the Bible, and there are other books here, Mr. Greene. One size may not fit all, but you might be surprised at how much it fits. The Bible tells me in whatsoever state I am therewith to be content," Gwen said.

"Contentment is great gain—I believe that," Franklin said.

"I am surprised at you," Gwen said.

"Why is that? Because I have read the Bible?"

"Would you like a warm-up on your coffee? And a muffin?" Alice said.

"Thank you." He held out his cup then chose a muffin.

"Yes, that, and you're a package of contradictions," Gwen said.

"What contradictions are we talking about?"

"At times you're friendly, even thoughtful. You can be an agreeable companion, being well-read in different topics, if not in-depth at least on a cursory level. You are interested in many things and can be interesting..." she said slowly.

"Where's the contradiction?"

"You can be cruel, curt, narrow-minded, and judgmental." Her countenance appeared as if her mind were somewhere else. "I can understand how your wife and daughter could be afraid of you."

At her last statement, he threw back his head in laughter. "Olivia was never afraid of me—She might have been afraid *for* me, but never afraid *of* me. And as for Lydia, she wasn't afraid either. Lydia was a sweet obedient child and she didn't worry." He picked up one of the embroidery squares and examined it. "I see Alice has found a diversion for the two of you. These are quite pretty. Should make a nice quilt."

"Is that what these were for?" Alice asked.

"I believe so. Olivia liked this sort of thing. I thought that you might like to get out and get a bit of fresh air. I don't have morning horseback riding, but maybe we could have a picnic or something. Perhaps we could widen your horizons. That is, if you promise not to do something stupid." He emphasized the last sentence, scowling at Gwen from under his dark eyebrows.

"You mean like trying to run away, or contact someone?" She made her eyes wide and innocent. "Do you think I could get away then?" She turned her head slightly.

"No," he said, "I'm sure you could not get away, but you could get lost. And since there are wild beasts out there such as bears and mountain lions, I'm concerned with your safety."

"I see." She mulled the information over in her mind. "Thank you. Some fresh air would be nice." After a pause, she asked, "For what purpose is that churlish man here that brings in the firewood?"

"My nephew, Freddy—J.R., has been chosen to be your new husband." Franklin watched over the top of his cup as he pretended to take a sip of coffee.

There were two involuntary gasps. Gwen recovered enough to respond.

"Oh, please," she said in a shocked voice. "That disgusting, childish clown?"

"What do you mean by a disgusting, childish clown?" He scowled at her.

"Look at him," she said. "He's sulking just like an immature, dopey kid. And he's too old to be acting like that. Do you believe he would be material for a deep, lasting relationship?"

"I haven't been around him much in the last few years, and when we were back in civilization, he didn't seem so immature, but.... the more I've been around him the more his flaws show up. Still, I haven't given up on him."

"You've misjudged Seth." She spoke softly, her words hesitant. "He really is ..."

"I've seen your 'Seth' in all of his glory. As the cop was picking him up off the street. He was dirty and he reeked, he didn't know who he was or where he was," Franklin said, angrily cutting her off. "Matter of fact, I almost left you to your fate. I had decided that he would be punishment enough for anyone."

"He did have bad days," she said. "But like most of us, he must control the demons within. He's a favorite among his nieces and nephews, and with people in general." She laughed, remembering how he teased the children. "We had a picture taken just a few weeks ago of the two of us. I'm sure that picture was a much better image than the one you saw."

Mr. Franklin Greene stood and walked to the large window. Standing where he could look out toward the horizon and at the same time watch Gwen out of the corner of his eye. He could see the tears sparkling on her cheeks and in her lashes. *Contradictions,* he thought. *Women were more contradictions than anything else in the world. She should be glad to be rid of that loser. Yes, he had seen the picture she was speaking of, but he had believed it to be a picture from early in their relationship, not a recent one. It did present a much better image than the drunken vomit-smeared creature he had witnessed being picked up off the street by the cop. He was surprised as he considered this new information.*

There was a tint of red to her light brown hair, and her wide, blue-gray eyes were nothing like that of his Lydia's. However, there was an air of vulnerability that reminded him painfully of his deceased daughter. There was also that courage in the face of all odds. It had sometimes made him laugh secretly as it had gotten Lydia into more than one scrape. It was hard to realize even after all these years that his beloved wife and daughter were not coming home. He still missed them achingly.

He glanced more directly at her. "Your hair is growing. Alice does a very nice job with it."

"Yes, Seth always liked it long. I don't know why I cut it. Probably to be spiteful," she said. "Funny how I always made some excuse."

"You need to forget about him," Mr. Greene said more sharply than he had intended.

"You might as well tell my heart to forget to beat or the sun to forget to rise. You might as well try to control the weather. We have been married for nine years. We have had good times and not-so-good times, but he is my heart. I love him."

The look in those wide, blue-gray eyes made him shiver. "Well, go ahead, pine away for him if you insist, but it's useless. You are no longer a married woman, and nothing you say can bring the dead to life." With a frown, he stormed to the door and pushed his way out.

IT WAS A LONG, DARK hallway. There might have been a light at the end, but Gwen couldn't make one out. Always in this bad dream, there was the feeling of danger, panic, and fear. Would this nightmare never end? She woke up with a shiver. They had been here a week at least. Since her conversation with Franklin, some things had changed for the better. She was allowed a bit more freedom here and there. She had even tried to look at the young man, J.R., in a more kindly light, but he never looked any better.

Gwen shivered in the night. She got up and put more wood on the fire. Sitting on the sofa, she waited until the small pieces of wood caught fire then she put several larger pieces on and walked to the windows. Wrapped up in her warm robe and the afghan, she pulled one of the chairs over to the window and sat in the shadow of the curtain to watch the eerie night outside. The moonlight made everything look like a photographic negative. Everything was illuminated and bright. The trees on the landscape were like silhouettes as well as the barn, the shed, fence posts, even the cat slinking across the barnyard. The moonlight streamed in the window, casting dark shadows inside just as it did outside. Gwen sat watching and waiting. She did not know for what, for the passage of time meant nothing to her. She had tried to keep a calendar of sorts, but it felt surreal. Was no one trying to find them? Maybe they should try to escape. Was it lethargy, or Franklin's warning? Why hadn't they tried to escape? Maybe God was telling her to be content? Whatever it was, she felt God's promise that "all things work for good to them that love the Lord" was for her, even in this situation.

She didn't believe Franklin. If Seth was dead, she would know it, feel it in some way. No, she did not believe he was dead. And she began to pray for God to cover them both, and bring them back together safely. When it came down to what was important, things like this helped define important.

Gwen watched the peaceful night shadows as they lay in the moonlight. The shadows looked stationary. They should look stationary, but that shadow moved. First, it was a part of one tree, then it became part of another tree.

Gwen had named the dog that roamed freely during the day Pooch. On several of her excursions, she had attempted to befriend him, but he didn't seem to like that name. Was the dog free or restrained at night? Was he the shadow? No, there was Pooch and there was the shadow. Pooch greeted the shadow in a friendly manner.

Would the shadow hurt or help her? She could hope that it would help her. Whoever it was seemed to belong here as they disappeared around the house. Gwen yawned. It was chilly here by the windows and she was shivering. *The nightmare is passed, and it is time to go back to bed.* After she placed a few more logs on the fire, she crawled sleepily back into her covers and pulled them up around her chin.

CHAPTER—33—

"Wake up, lamb," Alice placed the tray on the table and gently prodded the soundly sleeping Gwen. "My, but aren't you sleeping late this morning?"

"Oh, my! I should say!" Gwen rolled over and stretched in the warm sunlight streaming in the window. "I had one of my nightmares last night and went back to bed late, or early. I don't know which." Alice held her slippers for her. "Thank you." She laughed. "So, what's the news?" She noticed that Alice was about to burst.

"Last night when I went to bed, everything was the same old thing. This morning the cook and I are the only ones on track. The surly young man wasn't around for breakfast that I could see."

"I don't know what's what. ...because I couldn't sleep last night, I was watching out my window for a while. I saw a shadow slipping through the trees and around the house. I wonder?" Gwen pondered the latest developments.

"I sometimes wish I were young again." Alice sighed heavily and picked up the brush for Gwen's hair. "These last years have gone too fast."

"Sit down, Bunny." Gwen grabbed the brush out of Alice's hand. "Remember how I used to comb your hair when I was young? I would pretend I was a hairdresser? Let me brush your hair for once. You always wear it in the same old way, but it is still such a beautiful black," she said. "I envy you. Just look how long and thick it is. I used to buy a hair magazine on styles..." Gwen chattered away as she combed, fluffed, and finally braided Alice's thick black tresses.

"Women in my family didn't cut their hair. For some reason, they associated long hair with beauty. Like in the Bible, it was their crown of glory," Alice said.

Gwen dropped her comb in surprise. "Why, Alice." She stooped to pick up the comb. "I didn't know you weren't born in America. What country are you from?"

"I went to school to learn to speak without an accent," Alice said. "I heard I would get a better paying job."

Gwen stopped talking, and Alice and Gwen turned when they heard a light tap and the door opened.

Mr. Greene bent to pick up a napkin that had dropped from the tray, and when he straightened up, he was looking into the dark eyes of a stranger.

"See there, Bunny, you just needed a new hairstyle. Don't you agree, Franklin?" Gwen teased, slyly noticing that Mr. Greene was speechless, and that didn't happen often.

"Oh, my." Alice blushed deeply. "You must change it back—" and she reached up to pull the pins out.

"No, you mustn't." Mr. Greene stopped her. "You've been hiding too long as it is," he said. "You aren't old, nor are you unattractive. Why, what was that hairdresser's name? The one who would 'absolutely die' for hees Aleece?" he mimicked Louie Du Val to the letter. The words and manner made both of the women laugh. "Why have you never married?" he asked. "You know one mistake in life should not sentence you to a lifetime of loneliness."

A picture flashed through Gwen's mind of a young, dark-haired woman and a little girl sitting in a swing on a summer's day. "What does he mean, Bunny?" Gwen knelt and looked up into her companion's face. Age was a relative thing. When she was eight years old, eighteen-year-olds seemed so sophisticated. Twenty-eight-year-olds were almost ancient. Yet looking into Alice's face, now Gwen realized that what Franklin said was true. For the first time, she became conscious of Alice as a person. Dark eyes, some would call them black, well defined by the dark brows and rimmed with long lashes, black hair that Gwen had always admired, a creamy complexion with a hint of blush still evident on the cheeks. Why had she been so blind to just how pretty Alice was? Maybe it was the hairstyle, but whatever it was, it had been effective. "Have you been so awful lonely, Alice?" She reached up and gently caressed her face.

"Oh, my dear, dear child," Alice said as tears slipped down her cheeks. Cradling Gwen's head in her lap, she stroked her hair. After a short time, Franklin handed Gwen the napkin he had retrieved, and she straightened up to dab at Alice's face.

"Well, Alice, aren't you going to answer Missy's questions?" he said.

"It wasn't a mistake. Bruce and I were married. I don't know what you know or how you know it, but our child was not..." She faltered. "She was legitimate and wanted and loved. Bruce believed that his family would accept us, the baby, and me, but he was killed before any arrangements could be finalized. I had only a little money, and I didn't know what to do. Being a young widow, I did what I believed was the best thing for my beloved daughter." Alice sighed.

"I became acquainted with a young, wealthy couple at that time. They had just lost their baby, and couldn't have more children. The woman was recuperating as they were traveling. We— the young woman and I— became close friends. It eased her grief to visit and play with my baby. A few weeks after they left to continue their trip, her husband contacted me. He offered to adopt my baby and give her a good home as well as love and security. It broke my heart but the money Bruce had left us was almost gone. I knew I would have to find some way to make a living, and what could I offer my baby?

"I did what I thought would be best. I took what money I had, and I found the best school that would teach me to be the best housekeeper and prepared to follow my child to America. My friends had promised me—I would have a place with them. So, I studied hard, I worked hard, and I learned everything I could. It was two, long, hard, painful years, and all I could think of was the day when I would be with my child again. My friends and I exchanged letters and pictures and kept in touch. They were very loving and good people, no matter what you or anyone else may say, Mr. Greene. Money doesn't make a person good or bad. There are just as many people without money that are nasty and unpleasant." Her dark eyes flashed.

"Yes," he said with a frown. "I've come to the same conclusion. You two are required at the dinner table in an hour." With a final look at the pair, he turned and was gone.

FRANKLIN WALKED DOWN the dark hallway. The bitterness roiled up in his throat. How had he spent the last twenty years wrapped up in this tunnel vision of futility? He had blindly hated people he didn't know, blaming them for the loss of the ones he loved so dearly. He knew he was not blameless in this matter, but he felt powerless to change the course of the way things were going. The trickle had turned into a flood, and he was caught in the deluge.

Since these folks believe in God—Franklin O. Greene scowled sarcastically as the young woman's words echoed in his memory. '*Did you wake up one morning and God was printed on your forehead or what?' Maybe, I'm not cut out for this running of the world thing.*

"ALICE?" GWEN TURNED her attention from the closed door. "I feel an awful dunce, but I need to ask, were your friends my father and mother, and if so does that mean?" She left the question unasked as she peered up at the other woman.

"Yes, and yes," Alice answered softly. "I have kept their secret all these years. That is the way your Aunt Zoë wanted it. Also, I could see no benefit to disclosing anything."

"Oh, Alice, you have always been precious to me and now you are twice as dear." Gwen smiled and stood. Changing the subject she asked, "What do you think of the dining room ultimatum? Over this last week, I felt like things had changed for the better, but this sounds threatening."

"Yes." Alice frowned. "Threatening for some reason. The way Franklin said what he did sounds like someone or something is behind what he said. I don't like the nephew, but I don't have much contact with him or Franklin's unpleasant brother, Frederick. Franklin is always decent whenever we meet. Hastings and I get along well and we're on friendly terms. However, since this morning something has put a lump in the pudding."

"At one time I believed that Lydia was afraid of Franklin. But let me read these new passages to you." Gwen retrieved a diary from its hiding place and began reading:

Monday, November 21, Today began as a beautiful day, and then, it went downhill from there. He found fault with everything I did. He just made me so angry. Finally, I said some things that I was sorry for, but what is said is said. Mother tries to comfort me as well as be a peacemaker. The downside of that is then he is angry with me, and her as well. My cat has disappeared and I am worried. I am sure he is behind it, yet I can't prove it. I am sure he is twisted in his mind as well as in his body. I wish we could be free from him. –L-

"That doesn't sound like she's afraid of Franklin ...but here are some other entries:"

Tuesday, November 22, More of the same. I think I'll just stay in my room most of the day. I don't like his son either. He's just like him.

He's a bully. Always has to cheat or if he doesn't win he calls names and accuses others of cheating. My cat is still missing. –L-

Thursday, November 28, Mother and I will be leaving for a week. I am so glad. It has become unbearable here. I know my cat is dead. That awful boy told me he knew 'he' had drowned it. He was gloating when he told me. I told him to go away and shut up, that I didn't like either of them. –L-

Friday, November 30, We are packed and ready to go. Mother told me to be really nice to Freddy. To tell him I was sorry, and that we will see them in a few days. To tell him we would bring him back something nice from the city. I think Mother is afraid of something. I am afraid too. –L –

"These entries are just before they died, and it looks to me as if there is someone else they are both afraid of, and it isn't Franklin, as I had believed," Gwen said.

"That gives me the willies." Alice shivered. "Make sure you re-place it in the same hiding place that you found it." She nervously looked at the door. "It's time to get ready to go to lunch. I don't like the sound of those last entries—or our lunch assignment either."

Gwen replaced the diaries, then walked to the French doors and gazed at the overcast sky. "My heart feels like those clouds look. Let's have a word of prayer before we go into the lion's den." She grasped Alice's hand and bowed her head.

"Do you feel better now?" Alice questioned after the prayer and put her arm around Gwen.

"I do feel better now. I would like to call you Mother, but the words are rusty. Maybe someday, but you will always be dear to me, no matter what I call you. I will be glad when this is over." Gwen rest-ed her head on Alice's shoulder.

"It looks as if it might snow," Alice said. Calm enveloped both of them. "I pray that it doesn't. We may be here for some time otherwise. I vaguely recall the impression of an unkempt road on the way in."

"Under the right circumstances, it might not be such a bad place to be snowed in. But not with the present company." Gwen sighed heavily.

"You're right," Franklin's voice was close behind them, "on both counts."

Alice and Gwen both jumped.

"Oh, my!" Gwen exclaimed as they turned. "We didn't hear you. Is it time to go then?"

FRANKLIN'S HEART ACHED. He wished for the peace he saw on their faces. Alice and Gwen had looked so loving, and he recalled another couple that chased tantalizingly across his memory.

"Some time ago I mentioned to you that things are not always as they seem. Well, I want you two to know I am sorry for..." he stopped searching for the right words, "Well, for a lot of things. I don't think I can change things. You know, make them come out right. At one time maybe, but I'm afraid things have progressed too far. I'm not God, and believe me, am I glad. I just wish," he hesitated as he felt his way along. "I wish things were different, and I'm sorry."

"We are ready when you are, Mr. Greene," Alice's dark eyes were like burning coals in her calm face.

He inspected the pair carefully for any flaws in their manner. "In the Bible, I once read about someone, I believe it was a chap named Joab, who found himself outnumbered and he told a fellow soldier, *Let's play the man for the people.* I guess I can identify with that chap. Come what may, let's put as good a face on this thing as we can." So saying he opened the door with a flourish for them to pass into the hall.

THE FOOD AS HASTINGS brought it out from the kitchen smelled delicious. Gwen glanced at the distinctly unpleasant group assembled at the table. The previous disagreeable young man was there as well as Franklin's brother Frederick. He had the same disjointed look and manner, but what was different? Gwen was not able to put a name to what it was. He wasn't the shadow from the moonlight. He couldn't be the person gliding from one shadow to the next, and the dog would not joyfully greet either of these two men. Dogs were a better judge of character. Both Frederick and J. R. had an aura of malice that could be seen and felt.

"Well, brother," Frederick addressed Franklin, "I see you have accomplished at least part of what we set out to do. Have you gotten the two lovebirds together yet?" He spoke with an evil leer that made Gwen shudder inside.

"I'm afraid there's been a glitch in your plans, Fredrick." Franklin pulled uncomfortably at his collar.

"Don't tell me that the young filly has balked at the proposal," Frederick said with a self-satisfied grin.

"Well, she isn't in favor of the idea either, but it's the other end as well," Franklin said.

"What? What do you mean?" Frederick came partway out of his chair. Turning to the churlish young man he demanded. "What is this? This is an opportunity of a lifetime. J.R., what's the matter with you?" Frederick scowled.

"Opportunity of a lifetime?" J.R. spat out. "To be stuck in this hole for the rest of my life? You promised me that I would be rich; that I would have everything I could want. Well, this isn't it. I can't stand this place. There isn't anything happening here, and she isn't at all what I had in mind." He waved his spoon at Gwen. "Man, look at her! I like some dazzle to my woman. Like... you know... Sheila."

"Sheila who?" Frederick growled at his son. "The one with the nose ring and the big lips? Well, we can change some things," he looked down at his coffee then turned to scrutinize Gwen. Frederick said at last, "A wardrobe change, maybe something shorter and a little more... Different makeup, and maybe even a nose ring, although I don't fancy them myself, but if you would like one...." he trailed off.

What am I? Some kind of animal they can just change to suit their whims? Gwen thought. *They're talking like I'm not even here, like what I want isn't of any importance.* Gwen didn't look at either one. She frowned and ate her salad slowly as the pair made plans. Hastings had brought in the salad and now began to serve the soup.

"Something shorter and..." Freddy warmed up to the subject. "We could pick up something next time..."

Carrying the pot of soup, Hastings in one smooth movement poured homemade chicken soup down Freddy's shirt and into his lap. In the ensuing pandemonium, both Freddy and Frederick hopped up and danced around.

"Why you, incompetent..." Frederick shouted. "What in..." the rest of what he was shouting got lost as he hopped up and down.

"Sorry, sorry, I tripped...don't know what happened. Let me go get a towel..." Hastings said, apologizing profusely, and hurried back into the kitchen.

"I am finished here." Gwen stood as she spoke. "And I am ready to go back to my room now. How about you, Alice?"

"Yes, I am too," Alice said, pushing her chair back from the table. "Maybe later we could take a short walk," she said to Franklin as Frederick and J.R. mopped and cleaned up the soup. "It would be stimulating to have a breath of fresh air." She and Gwen walked to the stairs as Frederick and J.R. sat back down.

"You got rid of the first two just to replace them with a new set." J.R. scowled at Gwen and Alice.

"I'll check in later, Alice." Franklin nodded while they walked to the stairs. There was an uncomfortable silence while he waited until Gwen and Alice left the room.

"SO, IS HER HUSBAND taken care of then?" Franklin asked. His mind reeled from J.R.'s words.

"One way or the other." Frederick laughed with a malicious tone and continued to shovel food thoughtlessly into his mouth.

"Just what does that mean?" Franklin's face darkened. He was digesting more than food at this point, but only an observant witness would have noticed. His eyes had taken on a shrewd, watchful demeanor.

"My man set things up so that as the husband was going home his vehicle would malfunction. No more husband." Again the wicked laugh.

"You didn't wait to see the results?" Franklin said. "It may not even have been him."

"Oh, yes. You see he was in town in a store when things were altered. He had to drive home. By now he's history." Frederick leaned back, one arm slung over the chair back.

A thought entered Franklin's mind. "I am finished here as well." He slid his chair back from the table and walked across the living room to the library.

"Yeah," Frederick said to J.R., "a shorter skirt, some flashy earrings, and things, she wouldn't look too bad. You might even want to keep her around a little while." He laughed coarsely at his joke.

"Yeah, right. He'll never stand for it." The younger man gestured toward where Franklin had disappeared. "I tell you, all you have done is give him back the pair you got rid of. The other evening he was playing that guitar and they were diddling with something just like the other two used to do."

"You need to shut up. Stop shooting your mouth off. We'll take care of him all in good time, Freddy my boy. You don't want to spoil things now when we are so close to having something. Even I never dreamed it would be this good," Frederick said.

Indeed, shooting their mouth off seemed to be inherited from father to son. Franklin closed and locked the library door quietly. *Livia, oh my dear, Livia,* he spoke in the darkness to her picture on the desk. *I never wanted to question your death, Olivia, Lydia, even knowing Frederick's evil bend.* Franklin sat down as good and bad memories from the past sifted through his mind. He had never realized just how wicked his brother was. *There are none so blind as those who do not want to see. There's no time to lament over the past. Maybe someday, but not today.* He sighed. Franklin had never tried to thwart Fredrick in anything. *"Oh, my dear Olivia. I am so sorry. I just don't know how I got into this mess. I am so sorry."* He put his head in his hands.

SUPPER WAS A QUIET affair with Fredrick carrying the conversation by himself.

"Tomorrow I need to go into town," Fredrick said to Franklin and Freddy after Gwen and Alice had finished their meal and retired to their rooms.

"It's not wise to have so much activity around here." Franklin frowned at his brother. "What do you need that you must have right now?"

"She needs a different wardrobe. She looks dowdy and old-fashioned compared to the women Freddy is attracted to," Frederick said.

"Won't you two look a little odd shopping for..." Franklin cleared his throat... " ah, women's clothing and such like?" He chided affably.

"We'll just say it's early Christmas shopping for his sister," Fredrick answered, pointing his dessert spoon at J.R.

"Maybe you can pick up some things for the cook while you are at it," Franklin said thoughtfully. "Say, Hastings, you need anything from town?" He addressed the tall man with dark brown hair who was removing the plates.

"I sure do, but some things need to be picked up at a special place. If I write out a list, can you guys get it for me?" Hastings asked.

"Why, I guess we can do that as long as it isn't too difficult to find," Fredrick consented, pleased that his brother was not arguing over his plans. He was sure Franklin had grown fond of the pair just as J.R. had predicted. "Say," he asked as a thought occurred to him, "you don't mind, do you? I mean, she might look pretty flashy with some classy clothes and things, don't you think?"

"Mind? Why should I mind? She's just a rich spoiled brat." Franklin took a drink of his coffee. "Might do her some good to loosen up a bit." He finished his coffee and turned toward the kitchen. "You have your list ready yet, Hastings?" he asked loudly.

Hastings brought the list and handed it to Fredrick and explained how to get to the culinary store he usually purchased items from. "Give the list to the fellow at the counter. Max is his name. He'll pick these things out for you. They're always real helpful."

"Won't they ask questions?" Fredrick was suspicious.

"About what? No different than you Christmas shopping," Hastings said.

"I don't know where you found that guy, but he sure can cook," J.R. commented as Hastings went back into the kitchen. "Kinda funny how he always wears that hat backward and that earring, but he can cook. Did you see that tattoo he's got? He just don't seem like a normal high-class chef. But...." He finished his second helping of dessert.

"Typical Navy guy," Franklin answered offhandedly. "He's worked all over the States, and maybe someplace in Europe. Seems to know a lot of stuff. He was working at the estate before I was." Franklin didn't remind them Hastings had been an outside help, not a cook. "I'm planning on going to bed early tonight. When are you leaving tomorrow?"

"Early enough to make it into town, do our shopping, and be back by, say..." Frederick paused to consider, "ten o'clock tomorrow evening."

"You better not drink and drive these back roads. They can be treacherous in the daylight when you're sober," Franklin said with a scowl.

"Yeah, yeah, you don't have to lecture me." Frederick lit up a cigarette and inhaled deeply. "I can handle these roads and my liquor, brother," he boasted and exhaled just as deeply.

"I must speak to the chef a minute. I guess I'll see you when you two get back tomorrow night. But most likely it will be the morning after."

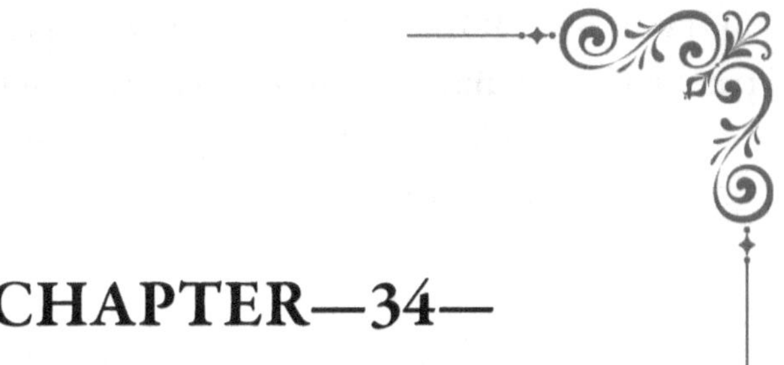

CHAPTER—34—

Nick sat across from Mike in the kitchen office at the mansion. "I'll tell you what I've found so far. It hasn't been easy. My friend, Gary, in Forrest City, was on vacation and just got back. He said earlier this year Gwen had been staying with Seth's sister. Gwen and Seth were having some marital problems but working on them—the last he heard. That's what Gwen told me, that she and her husband were working out some problems."

"So, I still don't know anything." Mike pursed his lips as he fingered his coffee cup. "What's the sister's name, and where does she live?"

"The sister's name is Rachel. She and her husband live in a small town close to Forrest City, and here's her number." Nick handed Mike a slip of paper. "All roads lead to Rome, right? I figured you needed this info since time doesn't stand still."

"You're exactly right. Whoever abducted them didn't take many clothes or supplies. That's not a good sign."

"I'll be praying. If you need anything, or I find out more, I'll be in touch."

Mike watched as Nick walked out to his little Nissan, then he dialed the number he had been given. "I'm sorry, we can't answer the phone," the message on the answering machine began. Mike hung up. *I'll have to try later. Just who do I say I am, and what do I want?...* He wondered how to approach this conversation.

"THIS INFO DOES POINT to another person involved with Franklin Greene. But it is someone who isn't on the record...a ghost or something." Mike thumbed through the report from the evidence bag. "You haven't seen anyone unusual in here then?"

"No, but if I do I'll give you a call..." Mark told him as they sat in the office of The Herberry.

"I need to get down to the bakery. I may be back in an hour. I had a bit of a lead the other day."

"Max and I, we'll be here," Mark said.

Mike walked out the back door into the alley. He pulled the brim of his cap down and, looking both ways, he sauntered out onto the sidewalk. It was only a few blocks over to the bakery. The bell on the door dinged as he walked in.

"Hello," Mike said as Nina came to the counter. "I'd like a coffee."

"No cream or sugar?" Nina said.

"Right. Is Sheila working today?"

"She just came in. Her friend hasn't been here yet...but someone came in asking for you this morning just before lunch." Nina spoke in a soft voice.

"For me? What name did he give?"

"Didn't give any name. A tall, sandy-haired older man with blue eyes. He said you'd know who he was."

"That's funny," Mike said without humor. "Well, I'll sit over at the table for a bit." Grasping his cup, he sauntered to the privacy of the table in the corner and sat in the darkness. Of course, no one here would know of his memory loss. He shook his head. *I know my name's not Mike, but it's the only clue I've got...* Two o'clock. He made note of the time glancing at the large clock on the opposite wall. Unlike the other table by the large double window, this table was situated by a snapshot windowpane. He could see the people on the sidewalk, some shuffling by, some marching, all moving along at their own pace. He settled back in his chair just watching. After half an hour, he approached the girl at the counter. "Can I get a refill, please? And maybe a raspberry flip to go with it?" He noted her name tag said Sheila. "Thank you, Miss. I don't believe I've seen you in here before," he said, making small talk.

"I've been here about a month." She flipped her too-long bangs out of her blue eyes. She snapped her chewing gum as she yanked out a sheet of pastry paper and placed the Danish on it, then wrapped it professionally and placed it in a paper bag.

"I don't get in very often I guess," he said. *Never expected I'd become the next generation,* he thought noting the gold nose ring. *She was someone who'd catch a younger man's eye in these days maybe. Too much eyeshadow and lipstick for me, but I'm not looking...*

"Just a job in between. My boyfriend and I will be moving on in a week or so." She rang up his pastry.

"Heading south for the winter maybe?" He handed her the money.

"We haven't decided yet. Maybe heading to Europe for our honeymoon."

"Thanks." He picked up his Danish and coffee refill. "All the best then," he said with a nod and sauntered back to his table. He had told Gerald he didn't know how long he would be in town, and it looked like he might be here for quite some time. He had found a fill-in chef from a local cooking college for this evening, leaving detailed written instructions with Leila. He looked up as the bell on the door tinkled. *What luck.* He nodded as Nick stepped inside.

Nick nodded but continued to the counter. "Coffee with cream and sugar. How's Sheila today?" Nick said with a grin.

"I'm doing well, Preacher. How's the preaching business?" She flipped her hair out of her eyes.

"Not bad. I'm always busy." He grabbed his coffee and sidled back to sit across from Mike. "How's your business going?"

"Not near as brisk as yours. You know Sheila there?"

"Yeah, people either love you or hate you. She needed some help. Poor kid, only been here a few weeks. Needed help finding an apartment and getting a toe-hold. That's usually when people love you the most."

"Do you know her boyfriend then?"

"No. Must be someone new. She didn't come with one anyway," Nick said. "I need to be heading off. I just stopped by for a coffee. I have an appointment in forty-five minutes."

"I'm just waiting. Hopeful the good Lord will give me a nudge, I guess," Mike said with a smile. "I never did get ahold of that Rachel gal. Their answering machine must be pretty full."

"Maybe they're on vacation?" Nick said.

"Yeah, that's my luck..."

"Now, everything happens for a reason," Nick said standing up. "Take care—and you take care too, Sheila. I'm praying for you," he called out with a friendly wave toward the counter.

There was a muffled answer. As he walked to the door it opened, and the bell on the door jingled. He nodded as Sheila's young man entered and Nick continued out the door. Mike hunkered back into his seat in the dark corner and became interested in his pastry and coffee as he strained to hear the conversation at the counter.

"How much longer is your shift?" the young man asked.

"I have three hours and a little clean-up time. How long will you be in town?" Sheila said.

"I've got some shopping...Three hours? We could go out and do supper and hit some bars. That work for you?"

"Guess so. Supper and a few drinks? Sounds good." Sheila flipped her hair out of her eyes.

"Yeah, I need to pick up some stuff. You know of a place called the Herberry? I need some stuff from there."

"That's just down the street to the corner and two stores to the right. Will you be back to pick me up?"

"I'll be back a little before six. I'll have to drop another person off downtown after shopping, but that's it."

The young man bent toward the girl, but she put up a hand. Shaking her head she mouthed the word *later*. Another customer came in as the young man left. Mike watched him disappear then grabbed his pastry and coffee and headed out the door. *Good time to get out...* He nipped back into the alley and followed it to the back of the Herberry.

"Mark, I need you to slip this bug onto the person of some guy. He's about five feet nine, slender, he's wearing a leather jacket and a blue plaid shirt. He may be here now or sometime before six o'clock."

"Yeah, I'll go check and keep an eye out. You say it could be anytime? I hear the door now."

"I need to get some backup setup and make some arrangements for surveillance. I'll be back later."

CHAPTER—35—

"I have a morning walk planned," Franklin said shortly after breakfast. "It is cold outside, but I know how you enjoy the fresh air."

"What about the other two? Won't it bother them?" Gwen was in a mood.

"No, they are gone for the day. They went to get your new wardrobe," he said.

"That's par for the course." Gwen's eyes narrowed. "Seriously? These men can't force me into marriage to J.R." She spoke bitterly. " I don't know him, let alone love or respect him. Freddy or J.R. whatever you want to call him, he needs to find someone else. Like he said, like Sheila...and what's more, what a farce."

"What do you mean?"

"If someone murdered my wife and child—I don't understand. You rant about how my father killed your wife and daughter, and how I was supposed to replace your Lydia. If you don't mind that it was your brother who killed them in the first place, why I guess you probably won't mind if he does it again." Her brows drew together and her face wore an angry frown.

"Aren't you quick?" His face turned an angry red. "Just what makes you think Fredrick was responsible for their deaths?" His brows drew together in anger.

"Did Lydia keep a diary? I wonder that your wife didn't leave you a note?" Her eyes narrowed. "They were both afraid when they left that day. Freddy told Lydia your brother had killed her cat the day Lydia and he had an argument. And just why was Olivia afraid for you? I can tell you why, but I don't need to, do I?"

"You need to be careful, Missy." His face was dark with anger. "You forget who's in charge here. Maybe we won't go for that walk. Maybe you would look cute in something short and wearing a nose ring."

"I guess I'm easier to push around than your twisted brother and his twisted son." Her eyes flashed in anger.

"Leave my Gwen alone!" Alice pushed her way between the pair. "If you won't help us, the least you can do is not torment us either. I don't believe I have ever met someone who calls himself a man who is so lacking in manly virtue." Alice stood nose-to-nose with Franklin Greene—or would have if she had been a foot taller.

"Oh, don't get in a huff." His color returned to normal. "It's good to have courage. I have a plan…"

"Oh, right! That's incredible. You didn't even know I was here." She scowled at him.

"Get your coats and gloves. We'll go for that walk," he said. "Hastings ought to have a picnic basket ready for us to take."

They walked down the lane that twisted, turned, and was full of ruts. The trees grew close on every side, and there was the pungent smell of autumn in the cold crisp air.

"I think just up here on the right there should be…" Franklin said after he stopped and examined the ground. "Here, the path leads off this way." He led to his right. Shortly they came to a smooth, flat place where the grass was thick but not so long that they couldn't throw a quilt down and set out lunch. Franklin repaired a ring of rocks that held the remains of a campfire, and stacking some kindling in the center of the ring, produced a match and lit a fire.

"It's kind of chilly out here," he commented as the tiny flame turned into a small source of warmth. He lifted a container of Southern fried chicken and set it on a flat rock. "No wonder this thing was so heavy. Here's a Thermos of French onion soup, buttered hot rolls, and another large Thermos." He unlatched the lid and smelled. "Umm, smells like hot chocolate," he said. "I'll leave the dessert in the basket until later. Even after our walk, this food is still hot."

"Don't eat that yet, Franklin." Alice looked down her nose at him as he picked up a piece of chicken and was about to take a bite. "You may lead us in a prayer before we eat."

"Well, I...uh, I," he stammered, his mouth open. "God is good, God is great and we thank thee for this food," he said. "Now can we eat?" He looked like a child who wasn't sure about something but was hoping for the best.

"If that's the best you can do." Alice sighed. "Perhaps you ought to practice more often."

"Maybe next time you or missy ought to lead the prayer," He answered with a frown.

"As a man, you ought to lead, not sluff your responsibility off on Gwen, or me," she said with a squint in his direction. "You'll just have to practice more."

FRANKLIN CHEWED HIS chicken thoughtfully, though his face retained the frown. As he continued to eat, his face reflected moods like clouds drifting across a sky. Alice reminded him of Olivia in so many ways that she was distracting. She could be a bit more aggressive than Olivia, but maybe she had more reason to be...and he didn't remember when he had enjoyed himself so much since.... J.R.'s words echoed in his mind: *I tell you all you have done is give him back the pair you got rid of. The other evening he was playing that guitar and they were diddling with something just like the other two used to do.*

"Oh, look, marshmallows!" He snatched at an excuse to close off any further thoughts along with J.R.'s words from yesterday. "There's a trick to toasting these things just right," he said as he impaled a couple of the sugary treats on the stick. "The fire can't be too hot or too cold." He waited, turning the stick and watching closely before offering the toasted marshmallows to Alice and Gwen.

"These are just right," Alice said as she finished eating. "I'm stuffed."

"We need to be getting back to the cabin. If you two repack this basket, I'll take care of putting out the fire," Franklin said. "We can't stay here much longer. It gets dark in these hills early this time of year, if you hadn't noticed. Hastings and I have been working on the second vehicle. He's a good cook, but he's not Mike. He's good at working on motors and things."

He bent over the fire as Alice put the remains back in the basket.

"Let's go." Franklin picked up the basket, but instead of going back the way they had come, he found a deer track that sashayed off to their left and they went with it.

"I think his mind has slipped?" Alice whispered to Gwen as Franklin took the lead back down the path.

"Yes, or he's just lost—somewhere. Do you know what I mean?"

"Time to be heading for the house, girls," he called jovially over his shoulder as they walked on through gathering shadows. Shortly the cabin came into sight, a few lights beginning to shine in the windows.

"I guess he does know his way around. That was much shorter." Alice frowned.

"You know," Franklin spoke with a sigh, "I love this place. It reminds me of much happier times. However, we are going to have to get out of here before it snows or we will be here all winter. Our second vehicle stopped running or we would leave and be gone. Hastings says it's the plug wires. No matter. We may have to wait until the other two come back. After they go to bed, we'll take that vehicle if we have to..." He spoke casually as if his words were the most natural thing in the world. "Into the house and up to your rooms. Our meal will be simple this evening. So clean up and hurry back down."

"HOW'S IT GOING IN THE kitchen?" Franklin asked as Hastings brought in more coffee.

"Doing well. Everything's cleaned up, and I'll have everything set out there. It'll be a little close by the time we get our stuff and Sam in the van." Hastings wiped his hair out of his eyes.

"Sam?" Franklin wrinkled his brow.

"Yeah, Sam, the dog," Hastings said.

"Dog?" Franklin looked puzzled.

"Yeah, there's been a dog around here ever since we've been here. Just thought he was part of the scenery. I named him Sam. He always comes when I call," Hastings said with a grin.

"Why can't we take the other vehicle and leave now?" Alice asked.

"A new problem has developed. Someone drained the fuel and disabled the engine. There is only one vehicle, and it's the one they have," Franklin said. "I should've seen that coming." He frowned and cleared his throat. "So, pack and be ready to go. We'll bring everything down where we can load it quietly and leave."

"We'll have to leave some things," Gwen said. "There were two vans in the coming and only one in the going."

"Frederick and J.R. are supposed to get back here about ten this evening. We've used supper to clean out any leftovers. Allowing for anything that might come up, we'll plan to leave here at twelve. Can you two handle that?" he said later, after they had finished their supper.

Franklin waited until Hastings disappeared into the kitchen then turned to Gwen. "So, about the room situation. It would simplify things if Alice slept in your room tonight."

"We were already prepared," Alice said. "Gwen has been having nightmares again. She had one the other night in which her friend told her to come home."

Franklin's frown deepened before he spoke again. "Dreams! Stupid dreams! Why would you trust in a dream? How do you know I'm not leading you on a wild goose chase, or just giving you false hope?" he asked slyly. "How do you know that I'm not just as crazy and evil as Frederick and my nephew. I mean, I brought you here, and I planned all this. What do I have to look forward to if I take you two back? Do you think I get a reward?" He pursed his lips and raised his eyebrows.

"You didn't plan all this, did you?" Gwen said. "I don't know a thing, but God does. I do know there are a lot of people praying for me, and I have been praying also. I know there are more things wrought through prayer than this world ever dreamed of."

"I know I'm finished, and I want a good night's sleep." He stood abruptly. Draining his coffee cup, he placed it back on its saucer. "We'll bring down your stuff now. It will all be in one place—handy to switch over to the other van, you know. Be ready. When it's time to leave I'll tap lightly on your door."

CHAPTER—36—

"Gwen—" Alice whispered as she fumbled in the darkness, "It must be time to go."

"I didn't hear the signal." Gwen rubbed the sleep out of her eyes. "The clock reads two o'clock. Must have missed it."

"I heard something. Get your coat and gloves. I'll check the door," Alice whispered again. "The door is unlocked." She turned the handle.

"Where's Franklin?" Gwen stepped into the hallway and her nightmare became her reality. There was no light at the end of this hallway. Not any at all. "Alice?" Her heart pounded against her ribs. As the panic and fright rose to choke the air out of her lungs, her stomach roiled and her legs became cooked spaghetti. Panic continued mounting. "Alice...Where's Franklin?"

"He's not here," an unfamiliar male voice said. "Just follow me."

Gwen swallowed a gulp of air, her courage returning. "What's happened to Mr. Greene? Why's he not here? I don't know you. Why would I follow you?"

"Well..." the voice said.

"Alice—" Gwen said.

"Hey, ouch!" Suddenly there was movement and a muffled sound of a scuffle. "What d'ya mean! Hey!" came from the voice.

Then a resounding thud and the sound of the action. A flashlight from somewhere at the end of the hall and a light beamed out.

A familiar voice called to the first guy, "Did you get them, Max?"

"Get them? Yeah, I sure did. Hey, quit it! I'm on your side! Man, you didn't warn me they were this vicious, sir."

"Vicious? Those two little women? They are so docile, why butter wouldn't melt in their mouths. Say, you two, calm down," Hastings said. "Cease and desist your resistance there. We are here to help." The sounds of a struggle stopped.

"Where are the lights?" Max asked.

"They're malfunctioning," Hastings said.

"Where's Franklin and his brother and nephew?" Alice asked.

"Long story short," Max said. "Frederick and Freddy aren't coming back. The roads are becoming difficult to navigate, and Frederick spent too long bar-hopping to drive out here... We were following them. Their van swerved off the road into a ravine, and that's when we found Mr. Greene scouting around on foot—trying to check on them."

"Yo, dude," Hastings said bringing a kerosene lamp. "Are y'all ready to go? Mr. Greene says to put some speed on it so we can get out of here."

"Oh! Oh, Gwen!" Alice gasped as she clutched at the younger woman.

"Hey, take the lamp." Hastings thrust the lamp at Max. "I'll take the little woman." He lifted Gwen holding her gently. "I guess she was just overcome with emotion. Alice, you just follow me. Then we'll be on our way."

The cold air and the snow falling on her face revived Gwen enough for her to realize it was not a dream. She tentatively touched the dear face she thought she might never see again. It was enough for the moment to just be held.

"Whoa, babe, it'll be all right." He smiled down at Gwen. "If we make it off this mountain, that is."

"How did I not recognize you until..." Gwen said in confusion. "There were times I had premonitions, but your eyes weren't blue and your hair isn't dark brown, and what about that scar?" She said, peering at his jaw.

"Contacts can change eye color—except I lost them in the fracas of getting here, and then there is such a thing as a wig. And no, I don't have a scar. Jo, I mean Joshua does though, and we can switch out on occasion. Remember the *twin* designation?"

"What are you two babbling about?" Alice asked.

"Alice, I would like you to meet Seth MacDonald, disguised as Matthew Hastings," Gwen said. "And where is Joshua? Was he with you all the time?"

"Joshua?" Seth called as they came out to the van. "Jo, where are you?"

"Who are you hollering at?" Mike slammed the back doors on the van and stuck his head around the side.

"You, Jo. Gwen was asking about where you are," Seth said.

"So, I'm the Jo in my memory...Get in, we can compare notes on the way down."

"And this, Alice, is my brother-in-law, Joshua MacDonald, disguised as Mike Chapman," Gwen said. "I don't care where I go now," she murmured as she reached up and touched Seth's face. "I have been so worried about you. They tried to tell me you were dead. I just prayed and prayed. Then they tried to force me to marry..." She rambled until she stopped with a shudder.

"It's all right, babe." He gently stroked her hair away from her face. "It's all right." He held her close a moment before they slid into the van. "Jo, how did you find us? The last I saw of you, J.R. had whacked you on the head, just before someone knocked me out."

"I woke up the next day in the hospital. I've had bits and pieces coming back to me, but for the most part, I've been searching blind, not remembering who I was or what I was doing. The only key was Gwen's picture of you two and your names. Mark from the Herberry came into the hospital to tell me he was a link, but he didn't know any more than that."

"I was concerned, but I couldn't do anything. I was where I needed to be. I prayed and let it go," Seth said. "All's well that ends well..."

"You can say that," Max said as he hobbled out the back door. "Those two meek women didn't stomp on your foot and slug you in the eye. How do I explain this black eye and broken foot? I went to pick up two ladies and in gratitude, they began beating me?"

"Save the humor." Franklin rolled down his window. "Everyone get in and let's get going." He waited as they settled into the van.

"Wait, wait." Seth opened the door. "Come on Sam." He waited as the golden retriever jumped into the van. Max got into the driver's seat of the second van.

Franklin pulled out and began down the rough drive toward the road. Turning onto the main road, he gritted his teeth as he maneuvered the switchback roads. "The other van following all right?"

Joshua peered out the back window. "Yeah, they're creeping along slow as we are, but they're coming."

"Say, Jo, when we get home..." Seth said.

"Save it, Seth. When we get home I'm going to kiss the ground. And when I get home for real, I'm never gonna leave again. This cold makes my leg ache like no other, and I've been feeling it come on for some time," Joshua said rubbing his leg gingerly. "No, I don't want to hear it. It was something that had to be done, and if it was mine in trouble, you'd have been with me too. And when Mother speaks we listen," he said, closing the subject.

"What's he talking about?" Gwen whispered.

"I was about to tell him how much I appreciated his help, sticking with me, watching over you, risking his life. He just said not to mention it. Although it was Ruth who said you were in great danger, and she was afraid for you, not Mother."

"My suggestion is that those of you who believe in a Supreme Be-ing..." Franklin spoke up as they sat at the edge of a ravine after slid-ing uncontrolled toward the side of the road. "If you want to get off this mountain in one piece, pretend you are the sailors with Jonah."

"What is he talking about?" Alice asked.

"Pray," two voices answered at once.

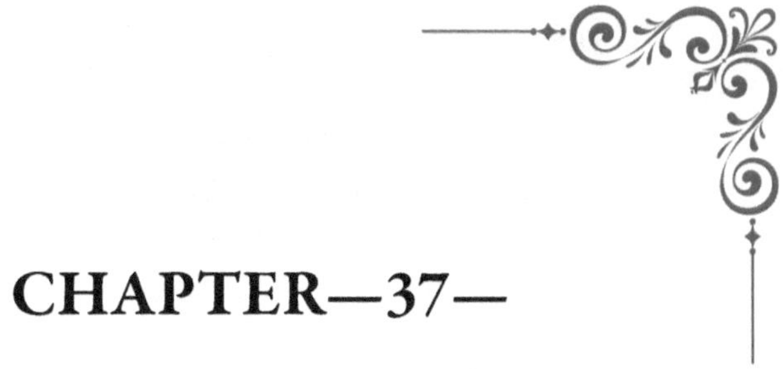

CHAPTER—37—

Gwen stretched lazily as memory returned gradually. She rolled over, but Seth's side of the bed was empty. She grabbed her warm, fleecy wrap, shoved her feet into her slippers, and wandered out into the room with the fireplace.

"Good morning," she said. Shivering slightly, she wrapped her robe tighter around her body. "What are you doing?"

"I'm getting some fire started here, right?" Seth turned as the fire continued to grow and blazed up. "Electricity was off, but Gerald and Ralph have a generator and they're getting it working."

"Oh, look how Currier and Ives it appears outside!" Gwen stood at the window looking out over the landscape. "I'm glad to be off that mountain safe and even more glad to be home." She hugged Seth as he joined her at the window. "I would like to believe I will never take life for granted again. Everything is so quiet and peaceful...You shouldn't have to start the fire. We pay people for that." She raised an eyebrow at Seth.

"Gerald offered, but he's got his hands full trying to get things up and going with this storm. And I'm pretty experienced with fire-places..."

"I'm going to get dressed and go find out where the nuts and bolts of things are. You must have gotten up early," Gwen said.

"If you hadn't noticed, breakfast came early the last few weeks...There haven't been many sleep-in mornings for some of us.

I'm going to go down and see how the generator and backup systems are coming."

"Fair enough. This room has warmed up a bit from the fire, so I'll meet you downstairs in a few," Gwen said.

"WHAT A DIFFERENCE A week makes." Gwen stood beside Leila as they gazed out the huge windows in the afternoon tea room. The snow had disappeared and some semblance of a normal life resumed since their return. "It seems funny. Most of my previous staff is now part of my afternoon tea entertainment," Gwen said. "Alice, Mr. Hastings, Mike the cook..." She continued to stare at the scenery outside the windows. "A week ago I didn't know if I'd ever see this place again. My friends or any of this..."

"I'm so glad you're back. I was afraid we wouldn't ever see you again." Leila turned as Gerald rolled the cart in with the refreshments. "While you were gone, some people still came in the afternoons just because...gossip, you know, and trying to get the latest news."

"I'm not sure how to act now." Seth wandered into the room talking to his brother Joshua. "How much has returned to your memory?" he asked.

"Things are coming back slowly, but it's all been piecemeal, and very little of it makes sense. I was at the pastry shop last week and someone mentioned a tall, sandy-haired, older man with blue eyes had been in asking about me. Funny that he hadn't left a name, but he said I'd know who it was." Joshua rubbed a hand over his forehead.

"I bet that was funny. It could have been any number of people. My guess is Dad," Seth said.

"I've called the number I have for Rachel—our sister," he added, rolling his eyes. "But she hasn't answered nor called back."

"Have either of you called Dad and Mom?" Gwen poured a cup of coffee, handing it to Seth.

"We haven't gotten an answer there either," Seth said.

"It will all come together. We just need to be patient." Alice entered the room followed by Franklin Greene. "Everything has been very confusing since we've been back. Would you care for some coffee, Franklin?" Alice held up a cup.

"Yes, I would." Franklin blew out a breath. "If I were you, I would check on any family you have back home." His gaze bore down on Seth and Joshua. "When Frederick said he'd rigged something, I'm sure he did. Obviously, whoever he was aiming for wasn't the person he got—" He took his cup of coffee. "—But that wouldn't have mattered as long as he thought he had the right person." Franklin looked up as Gerald showed Robert Howl Senior into the room.

"Hello, everyone," Robert said as Gwen handed him a cup of tea. "Thank you." He sat slowly in a chair and made himself comfortable.

Gwen sat on the sofa beside Leila and Alice and sipped her coffee, observing the room. Seth and Joshua rose quickly, went to a private area of the room, and huddled over Joshua's phone. Mr. Howl looked like he had aged ten years. His hair contained more gray and his movements were slower. Everyone looked as if they had fast-forwarded in their lives in some way. Conversation flagged and was light and noncommitted.

"That was some trip down that mountain last week. They must have had trouble getting Frederick and Freddy's car out of that ravine," Mr. Howl said. "It was a good thing you got out when you did. How did this all happen?"

"Life..." Franklin said. "All I heard when I was young was my poor brother this, and my poor brother that. Poor Frederick and how thankful I should be. Frederick grew up feeling sorry for himself. I owed him, the world owed him, and he became angry and resentful. Before her death, my mother made me promise to take care of my brother. Frederick threw that in my face all these years." Franklin sighed heavily. "When Freddy was about five years old, Frederick's wife disappeared. He became more bitter and resentful. I've looked the other way all these years because of the promise to my mother. I tried to help him, but it wasn't the help he wanted. He just wanted to use me. He worked to make me bitter."

Robert Howl looked at Franklin through narrowed eyes. "How could you not know of all the hateful, malicious things he did? How could you not know of all the accidents that he had perpetrated?"

Franklin paused, taking a sip of coffee. "I should have, I suppose. It came together the evening when Freddy made his comment about getting rid of the first two women and replacing them with Alice and Gwen. When Frederick confessed that he had the vehicle rigged so that something would happen to Gwen's husband, and then no more husband—it clicked in my mind."

Leila looked at the cup in her hands. "There is no one so blind as he who will not see." She looked at Gwen, her lips trembling.

"What about the note Olivia left for you, that Lydia mentioned in her diary, Franklin?" Gwen asked.

"I never saw it. Frederick must have destroyed it—or I don't know what—But Frederick and Freddy, their conversation when they thought I wasn't listening about getting rid of me. It just came together."

"I'm glad I found the diary. I wondered at the complicated clues and whatnot. Now I can understand better why—it will be quite a help unraveling this story." Gwen patted Leila's hand.

"I didn't know about the diaries. I did figure that I had to stop him and get you two out of there. It was Hastings," Franklin motioned, "or whatever his name is, that encouraged me. With his presence, I felt like there was at least a way to get out of there. It wasn't me pitted against them, and as Hastings said, ' you don't want to murder those two women, do you?'"

There was a light tap on the sitting-room door, and Gerald entered carrying a huge bouquet of roses.

"Where would you like me to put these, madam?" Gerald asked.

"Are those from…" Gwen wrinkled her brow.

"Madam, here is the card."

"Well, I never!" Gwen laughed as she read the card. "You may set them on the table in the hall."

"Who is it from, girl?" Leila's eyes grew wide. "Do you mind sharing?"

"No, I don't mind sharing," Gwen said with a smile as she handed the card to her friend.

Leila read out loud for everyone: "To my favorite married lady. Your husband is the luckiest guy in the world. P.S. You can tell him that for me. Welcome home. Signed: Your Ardent Admirer, Robert Howl III."

"So you're keeping these?" Alice asked.

"Yes, my 'ardent admirer' knows he is just a friend and that is all he will ever be. Besides, now that I have Seth here with me, everything is all right, and I'm not going to let him far from my sight for a long time," Gwen said.

"Ah, there is Bobby now," Robert Howl Senior said as quick footsteps could be heard coming toward the door. "Where have you been, Grandson?" He looked up as Bobby walked in the door followed by a tall police officer with a black eye.

"I did my good deed for the day. I brought Max here to meet these fine gentlewomen when they weren't in a mean mood. Just to show him how meek they are," Bobby said with a laugh. "I think Max knows everyone here, in a cursory fashion anyway, except perhaps Mrs. Wade. But, just to be sure, this is Seth and Joshua MacDonald," Bobby said as the pair came back to the group. "And Franklin Greene, Alice O'Rourke, Gwen MacDonald, Leila Wade, my grandfather, Robert," he finished the introductions.

"Enter," Gwen said, as Helen, the maid, brought in more cups and more hot water.

"Will you be needing any more coffee?" Helen opened the pot and peered inside. "—I'll be right back with more coffee..."

"Thank you, Miss. Is the new chef going to be able to serve a light repast this afternoon?"

"I believe so, Ma'am. He's working feverishly, but seems to have everything in hand. He is muttering something about keeping everything simple."

"That will be fine. Go get the coffee—" Gwen waited until the door shut. "We can finish the story now. I think all of the interruptions should be over."

"There isn't a whole lot left. Hastings would get a message out somehow if the occasion presented itself." Franklin picked up where he had left off. "When Frederick and his son determined to go to town, it afforded me the opportunity. Of course, it all hinged on getting word to the right people. If any single thing hadn't gone right it would have all fallen apart. I had warned Frederick about drinking and trying to negotiate those mountain roads. But they didn't listen. They did their shopping and stopped at the gourmet store, then they spent the rest of the time carousing and bar hopping. The rest is history. All of his misdeeds caught up with him. Max was tailing them when their car skidded down the mountainside. His backup was close behind. That's when he came across me scouting around on foot, and we continued up the mountain. At the cabin, we quickly loaded our gear and grabbed the women. We could have easily followed down a ravine during the harrowing drive down the treacherous mountain roads."

Alice shuddered at the remembrance. "I won't forget the rest of that story in a hurry. Those two were lost in each other," she motioned toward Gwen and Seth, "I've never seen snow so thick and blinding. There were times when it was just a wall of white. I'm sure it was only by the grace of God even with Franklin's excellent driving that we didn't follow Frederick down the mountainside."

"There were times I thought we were goners myself," Franklin said. "I would attribute it to the grace of the Almighty."

"Frederick and Freddy were unpleasant and I can't say they will be missed, but it seems an awful way for them to die." Gwen gazed at her fingers then looked over at Seth.

"Job four verse eight," Joshua said. "'They that plow iniquity, and sow trouble, reap the same.'"

"Hosea eight verse seven: 'For they sow the wind, and they shall reap the whirlwind,'" Seth said. "I understand how Gwen feels, yet there are always consequences to our actions. Frederick didn't hesitate to sentence others to hideous accidents. Sooner or later we all reap what we sow."

"Speaking of reaping and sowing, Bobby and I need to be going." Robert Senior stood to make his goodbyes. "Is Max riding with you?" he asked.

"Yes, I'll drop him where he needs to go and be right along behind you," Bobby said.

"In a couple of weeks I will be having a farewell party, so keep a spot on your calendar," Gwen said in parting.

"YOU CAN POUR THE LEFTOVER coffee in the small pot, Helen." Gwen let out a sigh of relief now that the company had left. "I was somewhat expecting my friend Nick Martinez to visit, but often he has to visit others from the congregation. Did you find out anything about your family?" Gwen asked Joshua as the new maid, Helen, wheeled the cart out leaving only the small pot of coffee.

"Joshua sent out a message and expects an answer within the afternoon about family in the Midwest," Seth said. "Nick was a help to

Joshua while he was trying to solve this case. He seems to be a pretty centered fellow."

"He is. I met him a few years ago when I flew back for a visit. He hasn't been here a long time. I became acquainted more this time than before. He has a darling family..." Gwen stopped speaking as there was a light tap on the door.

"Miss," Gerald stuck his head in the room, "Mr. Martinez."

"Oh, good. Thank you, Gerald, and Gerald..."

"Yes, Miss, I'll bring back the cart."

"We have some coffee and a spare cup, just some scones and whatnot. Maybe box up some treats for his family," Gwen said. "Nick, I'm so glad you could make it," she said as her guest came into the sitting room.

"I'd have been here sooner, except one of the elderly ladies from church took sick, and I didn't get away from the visit. She has quite a large family."

"Don't take it to heart. It will be all right. Nick, you've met my husband, Seth?" Gwen asked.

"It's good to see you," Seth said, shaking hands with the preacher. "Nick and I have met under different circumstances, but—"

"The voice is familiar, but you don't look..." Nick squinted at Seth.

"Think Hastings with a different twist," Gwen said with a chuckle.

"Oh!" Enlightenment washed over the preacher's face.

"Now that's out of the way, how's everyone else? Your family?" Gwen asked.

"They're doing well." Nick continued to stare at Seth.

"Good. Good, I wanted to invite you to a gala event in a couple of weeks. You and your lovely wife and family." Gwen poured a cup of coffee.

"I want to thank you for the generous funds you gave the congregation. We had our eye on a small building close to where we are, but until now we couldn't afford it. Now we can move from the storefront where we have been meeting into a more stable building." Nick accepted the cup of coffee.

"Enter," Gwen said as there was a light tap on the door.

"Hello, Nick." Joshua ambled into the room. "Good to see you under better circumstances."

"Do wonders never cease? You look different too. How's your head—and memory?" Nick asked.

Joshua sat in a parlor chair. "The memory is still wonky, but it's better. The head has healed. I found out who the sandy-haired man was who was looking for me. I found out why my phone call to the Rachel person was never answered and, of course, I now know why Mike Chapman didn't ring any bell in my memory."

"Well, enlighten me then." Nick chose a pastry and sat back to listen.

"The sandy-haired man was my dad coming to check up on his boys—Seth and me. The reason he didn't come back was that..."

"Wait." Nick held up his hand. "Did you say Seth? This here Seth? And you are brothers?" Nick said, pointing. "How did you pull that off?"

"When Gwen left our home in the Midwest, we had to act fast," Joshua said. " We were told to follow her and make sure she was okay. But we didn't want her to know, of course, so we copped pseudonyms and new identities, dyed his hair dark brown, and got the brown contacts. I had a hairpiece and weird glasses, and we were conveniently looking for work when Alice, Gerald, and Ralph were hiring. I had people contacts, and good references so..."

"I can see your resemblance to each other now, but go ahead," Nick said.

"Okay, now where was I? Back home with my oldest brother, Lewis. He went into the feed store and made his purchase. Something about the price was off, and after he started his pickup he was sitting in his truck looking over his receipt. He turned off the truck and started back into the store when there was a huge explosion. Knocked him into the side of the building and blew out a couple of windows on the store. Dad was here when he got the call about the accident, and he hurried home. Lewis was in critical condition for a while, and Sis—Rachel happens to be our sister— she made a quick trip home."

"Oh, my!" Gwen gasped. Her eyes wide in horror, she almost dropped her cup.

"But he's all right now?" Seth stood, coming to attention.

"Lewis is out of the woods, but he was pretty banged up. Dad was glad to hear from us. He'd read a snippet from the local paper out here about 'a wealthy heiress' being abducted, but didn't know it was about Gwen or that we were involved. What a dilemma that would have been with us in our situation and Lewis in his." Joshua ran a hand through his hair. "I was wondering also about the young girl, Sheila. Have you talked to her?"

"Odd that you asked. I was in Annie's pastry shop the day after the big snowstorm, and Sheila was there. She was upset that J.R. had wanted her to go with him that night after their date, but she had to work the next day and wouldn't go. News hadn't gotten out about the accident with Frederick and Freddy, but long story short, they'd argued because he thought she should just call in sick. She wouldn't do it and leave her job." Nick stopped speaking, just looking at his coffee. "You know—the details aren't known publicly...but the hand of God was in that one for sure."

"We don't usually see the hand of God, but it's there when you look for it. A chance meeting changes lives every day," Joshua said.

"Just look at Lewis. He had gotten out of the truck and was walking back into the store. That saved his life right there."

"I met Sheila when she was down on her luck, lent her some money, and helped her get a start. Since then I've been talking to her about accountability and doing the right thing," Nick said.

"And Seth and Joshua coming out here. Thank God they didn't give up on me. It would have been nice if I'd known they were here." Gwen smiled up at Seth.

"Absence makes the heart grow fonder. You had things you needed to do, decisions to make. I would have preferred to have been helpful, but they had to be your decisions. Like watching kids grow up that need to learn lessons. The hand of God is a better way, but it is sure hard." Seth sat back down in his chair.

"Is that why you spilled the soup?" Gwen's eyes twinkled at him as she hid a chuckle behind her hand.

"I've gotten good at being a klutz. I may be able to market it?" Seth laughed.

"At that moment, if I hadn't been so upset at the turn of things... I think I knew in that incident it was you. There was so much confusion. It didn't register when Alice mentioned your eyes being blue. I didn't interact with you at the cabin, and when you were here, your eyes were hazel," she said.

"I lost one contact when they hit me on the head. Thought I'd best lose the other one." Seth shrugged.

Nick finished his pastry and set his cup on the table. "I need to be going but thought I'd better check-in and make sure everything is going well and say thank you for the gift."

"Alice is getting a box ready for you to take with you. Don't forget I'll be sending the invitation for you and your family. We will all be leaving for the Midwest after the Harvest-Thanksgiving ball," Gwen said.

"We will miss you, but you need to be where it will be best for you and your husband. What will happen to the estate here?" Nick asked.

"I've made arrangements for it to be designated as a historical site. Some local women will take over the upkeep and day-to-day running of the place. They are lining up tours and special events. Alice will be tying things up and following me. She and Gerald and Ralph are in a leadership advisory role, but will continue in semi-retirement. My Aunt Zoe provided them all three with a generous retirement fund."

GWEN WATCHED FROM THE window as Nick carefully placed his box of goodies for his family in the backseat of his small car. Joshua had followed him out, and they stood talking for a few minutes before the preacher slid into his seat and drove off. Gerald and one of the new maids had taken the cart and all of the luncheon items back to the kitchen.

"This is an elegant room. These pictures here on this wall? Are these family pictures?" Seth asked as he stopped wandering around the room.

"Yes, this is my—it sounds strange for me to say— adoptive parents. I haven't told anyone that Alice is my birth mother. I guess I don't think it is something that I feel free to ..." Gwen hesitated.

"Some things are private, and I'm sure you want to let Alice take the lead as to how, who, when, and where to announce your relationship," Seth said.

"That's what I mean. It's been between her and my parents. I've loved them all, and I always will. No matter what."

"I wonder that you ever took to a tall, backward fella like me. Just look at all the important people in your life. Some of these people look like royalty—your aunt is quite the lady here." Seth pointed to a large snapshot.

"Yes, that is a good picture of her and some crown prince. I don't remember who." Gwen smiled at fond memories.

"Huh, this should have given you a clue who you were looking for. At least you should have asked him about this picture..." Seth said.

"What are you talking about?"

"Look at this picture. What do you see—even more important, who?" Seth said.

"I've never liked that picture. It's not a good one of Aunt Zoe. It was right after my parents' death and..."

"I'm telling you to look at the picture. Your aunt is there, but who is this?" Seth pointed at a man standing close but not too close behind Gwen's Aunt Zoe.

Gwen's mouth fell open as she stared at the whole picture. "I've always focused on Aunt Zoe and how poor the picture is. Franklin made several comments that were kind of cryptic, and I asked him if he knew my Aunt. He never denied or confirmed it, either way, just changed the subject and blew it off."

"Yes, I knew your Aunt Zoe." A quiet voice at the door said.

Seth and Gwen spun around as Franklin came up and looked closer at the picture. "I wondered why you never were any wiser. This picture has been here for years."

"Probably because it has been here for years. Many years before I knew you or any of these other proceedings," Gwen said. "And all of the disasters were from your malicious brother, Frederick?"

"I met your aunt in Europe at a party of mutual friends. She was indeed one of the most gracious ladies I've ever met. Other than my Olivia, of course. And yes, it has been Frederick's malevolent fingers that have wreaked havoc in so many lives. I've seen others with handicaps who have done well, but often it's because the parents didn't allow them pity. Knowing how hard it must be, the parents help their kids to get up and get on with life. Mother always taught Frederick to feel sorry for himself, and that was his viewpoint all his life. If he had put his intellect to work for good—well, who knows what might have happened." Franklin shrugged and walked to the door. "I'm glad your oldest brother is doing better. That was a close call."

"It was too close," Seth said. "This year has been a roller coaster of happenings. In a few days, some of my other family will be flying in for our festivities to start the Thanksgiving season. Our brother Michael, as well as Joshua's wife Junko, and our friend Ruth O'Brien."

"Ah, yes, that beautiful redhead." Franklin chortled. "I've heard about her."

"It will be nice to have them here for a visit. We'll fly back on a private plane the day following the party, and Alice will come as soon as she can tie things up here," Gwen said.

CHAPTER—38

Gwen peered into the long mirror. "Do I look alright?"

Seth wrinkled his brow and gave her a long critical look. "If you looked any better, sugar, I don't know how I could stand it. Your slip isn't showing, and everything else looks like it's in the right place too." He reached for her, his intentions evident.

"Seth Matthew MacDonald, you behave yourself!" She barely eluded his embrace. "We have a whole lot of folks arriving in a short time, and a whole lot of people have worked very hard so that you and I will be presentable and ..."

He smiled in his slow, easy manner. "Oh, sweet pea, don't get yourself all in a huff. I tell ya' what. I'll compromise just a bit." Bending down, he brushed a light kiss across her lips. "How's that? And you're all still in one piece, and just as gorgeous as ever. I'll take a rain check on the rest," he said with a smile.

"Honestly!" Gwen rolled her eyes in laughter. "I just don't know what I'm going to do with you!"

"A few days ago you couldn't wait to get him back." Alice entered hurriedly. "I'm not sure what I'm going to do with either of you! Turn around here, both of you." She appraised the pair as they stood obediently under her gaze. "Well, you are both perfect. I have never seen a more handsome couple."

They both had matching dark blue evening attire. His tuxedo accentuated his tall, slender, masculine figure and his wide shoulders. The white shirt and dark blue waistcoat again emphasized his slender physique. Gwen's dark blue gown made her slim figure look chic and glamorous, and complimented her cinnamon-colored hair and wide, blue-gray eyes. Mr. Du Val had created a marvelous braided hairstyle: not overdone, just simple and elegant. A light touch of makeup added color, for her ordeal had left her somewhat pale.

"Yes, you are both perfect." Alice smiled at the pair reassuringly. "I would hug you, except I don't want to mess anything up. Just be yourselves and enjoy the evening."

Seth held out his arm. "Shall we go, darlin'?"

"Ah guess so, sugar," Gwen imitated his drawl. "Come on, Mummy." she held out her other arm for Alice. "I hear Joshua and Michael in the hall—and Ruth, as well as Junko, chattering together."

"Let's go." Alice linked her arm through Gwen's, and like Dorothy and her three companions from the Wizard of Oz, they swept out into the hall.

"I'VE CHECKED THE FLOWERS, the buffet tables, and decorations. Did you check over the menu and food supply, and servers, Joshua?" Alice had to remember to call Seth and Joshua by their given names, but it had become easier in the last week.

"Yes, I've given the newbie chef and his staff strict instructions, and I told them I would keep my eye on them," he said with a smile. "The musicians are already here—Franklin will be helping them and Leila is helping Franklin."

"Nick and his family are our first arrivals. How wonderful, and look at the sweet little girls in those beautiful dresses." Gwen went forward to greet her friend and preacher. "Good evening, Nick...and Lupe and ladies?" She smiled at the three girls dressed in bright-colored satin dresses with lace on every available space. They giggled and stood together shyly holding hands.

"You probably remember, but I'll introduce them. The eldest is Luceia, she is nine, Alyssia is six, and Isabella is three. And what do you say, girls?" Nick prompted.

"Thank you for inviting us, Miss Gwen," they chorused their practiced speech with a slight lisp from the younger two.

"Girls, Miss Helen here has been assigned to take care of you for the evening," Gwen said, introducing her maid. "We will be asking your father to preside over the blessing in about fifteen minutes before we eat. Nick, do the girls want to take a walk around with Helen for that time, or would they like to sit on the stairs and watch as the guests arrive?"

"Girls, what would you like?" Nick waited while they whispered to him. "They want to watch on the stairs."

"Then watch they shall," Gwen said with a smile. "Here are your little charges, Helen. I'd best get back to my duties. I see several others are arriving."

GWEN STOPPED TO SPEAK to Agnes Howl. "I do hope you are enjoying yourself this evening?"

"Indeed, both Robert and I are enjoying the evening. This is the first of the parties for the season, and an affair to remember," Agnes Howl said. "We couldn't have had a better beginning. This orchestra is superb. Where did you find them? I'll have to use them for some of my parties. That is, if they aren't all booked up."

"I'll telephone the number over tomorrow," Gwen said. "Alice can make a note of it for me. I depend on Alice—it's too easy to take for granted those who are near and dear to us."

Agnes frowned at Gwen. "Good help is hard to find."

"So are good friends." Gwen smiled as Leila and a friend maneuvered their way through the crowd. "How is it going, girl?"

"I am so glad you are back." Leila hugged Gwen. "This has been a magnificent affair. The flowers, the food, the music are just dazzling and—" She lowered her voice to a conspiratorial whisper, "—so's that husband of yours. I can't believe he was here all that time...I bet he was the one who sent you those gorgeous flowers way back when," she added. "You better watch that cat, Mrs. Worth, though. She's been making eyes at him." Leila frowned.

They could see Rila Worth hovering like a hummingbird over a choice flower around Seth as he chose another tart and a glass of punch. Joshua and Junko strolled over to the table diverting Rila's attention. Michael joined Joshua and Junko at Seth's side. Rila Worth's face turned to confusion at the addition of the two extra brothers.

"Come on, I just have to go gloat," Gwen whispered to Leila as she turned toward the group. "Mrs. Worth," Gwen said as she swept up beside Seth. "Have you met my husband, Mr. MacDonald? You know, the famous one you were so sure you had heard about in the song, 'Old MacDonald?' Except this is *my* Mr. MacDonald, and he's younger than the Old MacDonald. That one there is my sister-in-law's Mr. MacDonald, and this Mr. MacDonald is another younger one. And—my friend Ruth," she said as Ruth joined the group.

"Nice to have met you, ma'am." Seth nodded slightly in Rila's direction before turning his full attention to his wife. "Darlin', there's somethin' I want to discuss with you. You'll pardon us I'm sure." He grasped Gwen by the elbow and escorted her out of the room.

"Good to have met you, I'm sure." Joshua and Junko made their exit.

"Excuse us also." Michael nodded slightly in Rila's direction as he and Ruth followed the others out of the room.

Robert Howl III sneered as he watched the procedure. "Rila, Rila quite contrary," he said quietly as he sauntered up behind her. "Why don't you stop looking for victims, and just be content at making the one you have unhappy?"

"I don't know what you are alluding to," she hissed at him under her breath. "This is absolutely the dullest evening affair ever," Rila said, though the laughter and conversation flowed all around. "That punch doesn't seem to do much for me—I need something stronger in the worst way and...a cigarette," she added.

Bobby snorted and laughed, finding her situation humorous. "I can't help you with the punch, but there is a smoking room in the house. A few moments ago you looked as if something had caught your attention. Where did those three MacDonald men go? They just disappeared."

Her eyes narrowed. "I don't know what you mean." Her eyes flashed angrily as her mouth still smiled.

"Of course you do," he said. "You should know when you are out-classed. What is that old saying about a silk purse and a sow's ear?"

"You are extremely rude, and I don't know how I ever found you amusing company."

"What I find incredible is that I ever found you interesting," Bobby said. "Good night, and farewell." He smiled and nodded in her direction before walking away.

"YOUR APPEARING ON THE scene when y'all did is appreciated," Seth said as the group left the alcove to rejoin the guests.

"We could see you were about to be eaten alive," Joshua joked. "It seems I always have to rescue you from something, brother."

"Daddy always said everyone has a purpose in life," Seth said with a twinkle in his eyes.

"Ho, Nick, I see you have your family in tow. Are you leaving?" Joshua asked as the preacher and his family walked up.

"Yes, it is getting late and the girls need their sleep. Thank you for the invitation, Gwen. We have all enjoyed this evening. We don't get invitations like this often."

"He's loco." Nick's wife, Lupe, flashed a dazzling smile. "We don't ever get invitations to evenings like this. This has been something the girls will talk of for the rest of their lives. Thank you so much, Mrs. MacDonald."

"You are too kind, Lupe, but we appreciate your words. We appreciate all that you and Nick do. Our maid, Helen, loves children, and I'm sure she enjoyed your girls. They are so well behaved and respectful." Gwen gave Lupe a hug and each little girl a kiss. "God bless you and your family."

Seth handed Gwen his handkerchief as she watched the family exit.

"I'll have a glass of punch, thank you," Gwen said to the maid and handed Seth back his handkerchief. In a moment she turned to the rest of the women with glass in hand. "I'm so glad that you could fly in for our party. I wish Mom, Dad, and the whole bunch could have come, but I'm thankful for you all."

"Thees ees a..." Junko searched for words.

"It's beautiful, just a beautiful mansion," Ruth said. Smiling, she gave Junko a look of encouragement.

"Jes, dat ees what I mean. A beautiful mansion. Thank you, Ruth," she whispered.

"It is good to have people whom I love and trust around me. I will never take that for granted again," Gwen said.

"Sugarplum, speaking of folks you love and trust..." Seth's face wrinkled in confusion. "Whatever do you find to love and trust about that vampire over there?" he said, nodding toward Rila Worth. "There must be something redeeming about her, but I missed it."

Gwen laughed. "I didn't say everyone here was on my best friend list. Matter of fact, she is only here for two reasons. There is such a thing as payback in our social affairs, and then there is another type of payback. She, and her poor unfortunate husband, are here because of you," she said.

"Because of me?" he asked.

Gwen put a soft hand up to his cheek, and they smiled into each other's eyes. "Yes, you see, she made a very rude scene at a dinner party when I first came back, and I wanted her to see what a real man looks like," she whispered.

"Excuse us." Joshua elbowed Seth. "You two love bugs need to remember to contain yourselves." He smirked.

"I've never been more contained in my life, brother," Seth replied, still smiling at his radiant wife.

"I'm ready for the holidays," Michael piped up.

"What does that have to do with anything?" Ruth asked.

"I just thought a change of conversation might help." He grinned at them all.

"I'm glad you're my kid brother." Seth handed him a glass of punch.

"Yeah, why's that?" Michael asked.

"I'm sure I'll think of a reason. Just give me enough time, kiddo."

"Are you all packed and ready to go?" Ruth asked Gwen.

"Seth and I are ready to fly out with you. We will need to come back a time or two to wrap up this case. After we get our own home up and running there are some items I will come back and take with me. Alice and the committee will close up the house for a few months and Alice will follow as soon as we are settled—Oh, hello, Robert," Gwen said as her guest approached.

Bobby joined the group. "This has been a very interesting evening. I can honestly say that I have never seen such gorgeous women all in one family in my memory. Why don't you introduce me so I can at least put names to everyone?"

Gwen's eyes twinkled as she introduced everyone. "You know Seth and Joshua, of course. Well, this is my sister-in-law Junko, Joshua's wife. This is their baby brother, my brother-in-law, Michael, who is escorting our good friend, Miss Ruth O'Brien."

"Oh, so this one isn't taken yet." A light came into his face as he gazed at Ruth.

"Don't get ahead of yourself. To my knowledge, she isn't looking, Robert the Third," Gwen said.

"Well, it never hurts to try," he said smoothly.

"You have to watch this one," Gwen said to Ruth.

"Oh?" Ruth asked.

"He does have that look," Michael said.

"What look is that?" Seth asked.

"The same look that fox had last week."

"Fox? We missed it—" Seth said.

"The one that got shot as it grabbed Arabella the hen out in Mom's henhouse." Michael threw a warning look at the newcomer.

"You may be right." Seth raised an eyebrow with a quiet smile.

"It'll be all right—" Robert turned to Gwen. "—I hear you will be leaving us again shortly. I wish you were staying a bit longer. I know this has been a trying time, but you did put some life in the old place when you came. It will be very ho-hum again when you leave." His words carried a hint of regret.

"That is very generous of you." Gwen was touched. "I'm sure you will find someone else to interest you when I'm gone."

"People who are honestly what they appear are a precious commodity in today's world," he said. "That's why I kept thinking that there was a catch or something more to you than met the eye."

"What meets the eye is plenty for me," Seth said with a dry voice. "The first time I saw Gwen, I had to sit down. She was so gorgeous she took my breath away."

"Ah, you goose, I didn't take your breath away!" Gwen exclaimed, laughing. "We were playing volleyball after church one day, and Tarzan here was jumping for the ball. Although it was an impressive leap, he missed and landed on his back, which knocked the wind out of him."

"I only missed because you were so gorgeous," Seth said as the group laughed.

"I heard through the grapevine that you may be heading for England after this case is all wrapped up?" Joshua asked.

"Well, yes, there is work for our firm in England and Europe. I do enjoy art, and I may be able to indulge my fancy in that field also," Robert said. "I probably won't see everyone again, so goodbye and take care."

Like a blast of withering hot wind, Rila Worth and her husband burst upon the group. Rila was all glitter and tinsel, a climber, always looking for another step up the social ladder, but her husband was a quiet man made of more solid stuff.

"Darling, this has just been too much," she gushed. "I do hope you will be able to attend our small dinner affair in a few weeks."

"We won't be here in a week, if plans continue as they are," Gwen said.

"I was so hoping to extend an invitation to you, and naturally to your husband and his family." Rila smiled coyly at Seth and his brothers.

"We MacDonalds do prefer our farm," Seth said. "It will be so delightful to get home, kick off our boots, and just have ourselves to ourselves, won't it, babe?" he asked Gwen.

"With all those nieces and nephews? I can't wait to get home, but I'm not sure about having time to ourselves. But for you, sweetheart, why I'd follow you anywhere," Gwen said.

"Rila and I are taking our leave for the evening, but I want to express my gratitude for an enjoyable time. It has been a pleasure on my part," Mr. Worth said.

"I'm glad you came and enjoyed the evening. We'll probably meet again on occasion. I'm closing up most of my business dealings here, but we will have some call to return once in a while," Gwen said shaking his hand. "Goodbye for now."

Gwen watched as the couple reached the door. "I don't believe they both came to the same conclusion." She chuckled. "At least judging by Rila's green complexion—which doesn't match her clothing at all."

CHAPTER—39—

"What's wrong, Lamb?" Alice asked. "Are you having last-minute jitters?"

"I love this place. I've loved all that it has meant to me—you, Gerald, Ralph, Aunt Zoe, my parents...It's so much of my life. Even after Seth and I married, this was always waiting for me to come back to if I needed it." Gwen dabbed at the tears silently streaming down her face.

"You aren't losing this beautiful place, merely turning it over to others who will continue to keep it alive and running. You will still be able to visit when you choose. It is a brave and loving thing you are doing."

"Thank you for that, Alice, and yes, I guess I'm having jitters about other things as well. I'm thankful I've already met Seth's family, yet it isn't easy living with someone else." Gwen looked down at her folded hands.

"You seemed to think well of the family when we talked before. Having met Joshua, Seth, Michael, and the girls Junko and Ruth, they are very nice. It will be all right, I'm sure." Alice patted Gwen's hand.

"Yes, and everyone is looking for a different house for Joshua, and now for us to buy our own residence. Joshua, Junko, and their daughter have been living with Laura and her family. I don't know what the future holds for Seth and me. It was such an easy decision

307

when we chose to get married, but now—I'm just slow to come to grips with reality." Gwen stood and walked to the window.

"Hello, Joshua," Alice said as he came to the library door. "Are you and your wife ready to fly out?"

"We are ready. I've been missing my little Mai, now that my memory is returning. I think my replacement will fit in well. I take it your staff will be transitioning to the new situation here as the Ladies Society takes over?" Joshua asked.

"I think most of the crew has decided they want to stay and work," Alice said. "I'd better go check on the meal and table arrangements." She excused herself.

"I think we're packed and ready as well." Gwen turned from staring out the window. "I'm just trying to remember how things look. Trying to impress on my memory so many things."

Joshua walked over and joined her at the window. "You'll be back. Very few of these things are forever situations, and when they are forever situations, they no longer matter as much as we think they will."

"I do plan on being back. The ladies' committee is making plans that will need my input, and there are other things that I'll come back for. And look—" She pointed out the window. "Seth is taking pictures. He's so thoughtful."

"He's a good kid." Joshua watched out the window as his brother walked down the circle drive toward the stables. "I never realized how much I missed him until the night he showed up at Laura's. I never knew how much I missed... Well, that's a different story and a different lifetime."

"I'm afraid, Joshua. What happens when the new wears off and I'm no longer—new? Will everyone still accept me with all of my flaws?" Gwen's eyes were large and fearful.

"Just join the rest of us, flawed, blood-bought people. Dad tells people we're all broken. It isn't until we're broken and trusting in God that God can use us," Joshua said.

Gwen said, "Nick quoted in his lesson the other day as Jesus said to Paul, 'My grace is sufficient for thee: for my power is made perfect in weakness.'"

"'Most gladly therefore will I rather glory in my weaknesses, that the power of Christ may rest upon me.' Second Corinthians, chapter twelve verse nine," Joshua finished. "It's like letting go and letting God take control. I'm going to go check on Junko. She was taking a rest and wanted me to make sure she was up on time." Joshua walked to the door, stopping just before he bumped into his brother. "Hey, Seth, glad you got some pics. Are you ready to go?"

"I have several good pictures, and I'm ready to head out when it's time." Seth stood aside for Joshua to exit.

"Hey, darlin'," Seth said as he came into the library. "Have I got some pictures for you! Didn't want to leave without some reminders."

Gwen looked up into her husband's sapphire blue eyes and smiled. "You smell good. The fresh autumn breeze and outdoorsy perfume." She reached out and pulled him to her in a hug. "I won't ever take for granted these moments. I have longed for a hug ever since I left your Dad and Mom's. I was so wrong to have deceived you for so long, not telling you who I was. And not knowing about you...We were such dumb kids." She relaxed into his embrace, feeling the strength of his arms and her returning strength as well.

"It made no difference. I would have loved you in spite of all this. Dumb I may have been—and I may still be— but I know I love you. We will be stronger together with God. This begins our new adventure." Seth and Gwen gazed out into the early morning sky. "This begins our new tomorrow."

Don't miss out!

Visit the website below and you can sign up to receive emails whenever Donevy Westphal publishes a new book. There's no charge and no obligation.

https://books2read.com/r/B-A-TENK-QTMTB

BOOKS2READ

Connecting independent readers to independent writers.